The Library of Literature

Under the General Editorship of
JOHN HENRY RALEIGH & IAN WATT

Gulliver's Travels

THE LIBRARY OF LITERATURE

TRAVELS

INTO SEVERAL

Remote NATIONS

OF THE

WORLD.

In FOUR PARTS.

By *LEMUEL GULLIVER,*
First a SURGEON, and then a CAP-
TAIN of several SHIPS.

VOL. I.

LONDON:

Printed for BENJ. MOTTE, *at the*
Middle Temple-Gate *in* Fleet-street.
MDCCXXVI.

Gulliver's
Travels

BY

Jonathan Swift

EDITED
WITH AN INTRODUCTION BY
MARTIN PRICE
Yale University

THE **BOBBS-MERRILL** COMPANY, INC.
A SUBSIDIARY OF HOWARD W. SAMS & CO., INC.
Publishers • INDIANAPOLIS • NEW YORK

Jonathan Swift, 1667–1745
Gulliver's Travels was first published in 1726

INTRODUCTION

1. Swift's Life and Career

Jonathan Swift was born in Dublin of English parents on November 30, 1667. In 1689, after studying at Trinity College, Dublin, he entered the household of Sir William Temple as a secretary. Temple, who had been a distinguished statesman, had retired to a rural estate not very far from London. There Swift had access to a fine library and found time to write his first major works. The relationship with Temple was close but not always smooth. It was interrupted several times, notably when Swift took clerical orders and spent more than a year in Northern Ireland as rector of a parish in which the Church of Ireland had little influence. Eventually, Swift returned to Temple's estate, Moor Park, where he remained until Temple's death in 1699. He had, during these years, become master of a great range of learning, which he used playfully and satirically in *A Tale of a Tub* (largely written in the 1690's, published in 1704). That brilliant work had great success; but its satire on the corruptions of the Church was considered impious by some, and there later arose the doubtful rumor that Queen Anne denied Swift a bishopric because the book was offensive to her.

In 1707 Swift was sent by the Church of Ireland to seek financial relief from the Queen; he remained in London for more than a year, writing in behalf of Church interests. During this visit he became accepted as a wit and man of letters and was close to Joseph Addison's literary circle. When Swift returned to London in the fall of 1710, he found the new Tory ministry of Robert Harley, later Earl of Oxford, closer to the principles he could espouse than were the Whigs he had once supported. Those principles included the firm establishment of the Church of England and Ireland and resistance to all Whig efforts to open public office to Dissenters. For most of the four years to follow, Swift became a major spokesman, even propagandist, for the Tories—through periodic essays in *The Examiner* and such influential pamphlets as *The Conduct of the Allies* (1713). When the Tory government was threatened by divisions between Harley and his fellow leader Viscount Bolingbroke, Swift sought to reconcile the ministers; but the ministry collapsed in any case with the death of Queen Anne in 1714.

Swift, who had been appointed Dean of St. Patrick's Cathedral, Dublin, in 1713, returned once more to his clerical offices, which he had undertaken from the first with a strong sense of duty. Although his relegation to Ireland embittered him, he formed a close circle of friends there, including Esther Johnson, whom he had known in Temple's household and had persuaded to come to Ireland, where her income might go farther. She is the Stella to whom Swift addressed the letters now preserved as the *Journal to Stella* and many charming poems on such occasions as her birthday.

Swift was outraged alternately by the Irish passivity under oppression and by the cool effrontery of the Whig ministry of Robert Walpole in furthering that oppression. His battle against Wood's copper halfpence in *The Drapier's Letters* (1724–1725; see Part Three, Chapter Three, Notes 5, 7) made him a national hero. This triumph was shortly followed by the publication of *Gulliver's Travels*.

Swift devoted his later years to clerical tasks and to writing. Of his many pamphlets on church and state affairs, *A Modest Proposal* (1729) is the best known. He continued to add to the large body of poems he had written throughout his lifetime, some lightly playful, some harshly satirical, many devoted (like *Gulliver's Travels*) to shocking men out of harmful illusions. Among his last works were a compendium of the banalities that pass for "polite conversation" and an ironical set of *Directions to Servants*. In his last years, Swift's mind and memory gave way (he had suffered much of his life from labyrinthine vertigo, a disease of the middle ear that disturbed his sense of balance), and he was cared for by others until his death on October 19, 1745.

During the years of his political service in London, Swift had become part of an informal circle of friends that included the chief ministers; such poets as Alexander Pope, John Gay, and Thomas Parnell; and such wits as the court physician and man of learning Dr. John Arbuthnot (the creator of the figure of John Bull). As the Scriblerus Club, they engaged in brilliant literary jokes; the double note of warm personal friendship and keen playful wit marks Swift's deepest attachments to people around him.

II. The Political Circumstances

Swift wrote *Gulliver's Travels* at a time when Robert Walpole, as Prime Minister, ruled England. Walpole achieved this end partly through systematic bribing, partly through hiring third-rate writers to support his cause, and partly through manipulating the boorish German king, George I, whose heart lay in his German home and mistresses. Swift's own acquaintance with courts began under the reign of William III, who came to the throne as a limited monarch in 1689. William was a close, suspicious man, distrustful of political parties and consequently very much their victim. His primary concerns were stabilizing his reign and creating a balance of power that might contain the threat of Louis XIV of France. Although William turned to Swift's patron, Sir William Temple, for advice, he was not persuaded by young Swift, whom Temple sent to court to argue his views. As Swift wrote later of himself, "it was the first incident that helped to cure him of vanity."

Swift's own closest involvement in courts and politics came with his services, in the last years of Queen Anne's reign, to the ministry of Oxford and Bolingbroke. He respected these leaders, themselves men of wit and learning, and he was admired in turn by them, as were the other fine writers of the day. He made common cause with them and endured the pain of seeing their short-lived ministry fall with the Queen's death. Oxford was imprisoned on political charges; Bolingbroke, forced into exile; and Swift himself, doomed to isolation in Ireland. The four years of promise were followed by the growth of Whig power to near-absolutism and the eclipse of an effective opposition party. Even more, King George's indifference to matters of culture made royal patronage a reward for subservience to the Whig interest and an almost infallible guarantee of mediocrity or worse. Satire was the only recourse for a powerless opposition. *Gulliver's Travels* was followed in 1727 by Gay's brilliant image, in *The Beggar's Opera*, of Walpole as a highwayman (Bob Booty was one of his "names") and in 1728 by the first version of Pope's *The Dunciad*, the great satirical tribute to the imminent extinction of culture in England.

Swift's mature life had seen the growth of political parties (and their deceptive slogans) to the point where their possible service to free discussion had given way to virtual monopoly. He had seen the propping of the monarchy by the growth of a national debt, which in theory gave everyone an interest in the stability of the Crown but in practice tended to foster a new moneyed class at the expense of the old landed aristocracy. He had seen a generation of ministers engaged in secret negotiations with their avowed enemy France or discrediting each other with charges and countercharges that were often hypocritical. He had once studied the decline of freedom in Athens and Rome with an eye to the situation in England; whereas he was well aware that the state of affairs in England was not unique, he was also aware that the historical parallels were no source of comfort.

III. The Intellectual Background

Swift was a devoted clergyman in the Church of Ireland, a man with a sense of duty and with deep concern for the future of the Church. He felt that its firm establishment was essential for the moral control of political power, although he had seen men who were virtual hirelings of Walpole made bishops. As a devout Christian, Swift accepted the orthodox view of man's fallen nature; his attitude toward reason is more problematical.

All the evidence we have points to Swift's belief that man's reason was his highest means of conscious self-control. Reason enabled man to see truth impartially, unclouded by passion and in focus as sharply as the more immediate gratifications of his senses. Only through his own reason could man grasp what he needed to know. It was reason itself that told man where reason had to give way to faith in matters reason could not comprehend. "Reason itself is true and just," Swift wrote in a sermon, "but the reason of every particular man is weak and wavering, perpetually swayed and ruined by his interest, his passions, and his vices." The solution for "every particular man" is not to abandon reason but to correct his own "weak and wavering" reason by the clear teachings of Scripture, the agreed moral truths of the wise men of the past, and the consent of the great body of men in all ages. The majority view in England in 1726 might well be fallacious, given the power of fashion and bribery; but the views shared by all nations or all times gave promise of impartiality and soundness. Reason can save man, then, from partiality or stubbornness and also from superstition; it helps him to believe what he must but to resist the false faiths that may dominate for the moment.

In Swift's day, the deists and rationalistic "free-thinkers" insisted upon the ultimate authority of human reason, which they, like Swift, considered "true and just." They believed that reason was uniform in all right-thinking men, and they were inclined to exalt it at the expense of sectarian religious creeds and, indeed, of all religious mysteries. Like the ancient Stoics, they found men's reason confirmed and supported by the rational structure of the universe; and they felt that a detached love of the Whole might guarantee the individual reason of each man and save it from being "weak and wavering." Such men—the third Earl of Shaftesbury was one—were aware of the dangers of passion but believed that individual man might overcome them through self-discipline. As did the Stoics, they trusted the innate sociability of man, his ultimate "goodness."

For an orthodox Christian, such a view was heresy; it revived the Pelagian teachings that Augustine had fought. Moreover, it often fostered hostility to religious doctrine. It rejected a morality based on reward and punishment in an afterlife. And it tended to take a Whiggish political form: a trust in the free self-determination of the people. Swift rejected the optimism of such a view, insisting upon the need for the restraining influence of a political constitution of checks and balances and of a traditional church that preserved the purity of its doctrine. He insisted upon man's need for scriptural authority as a ground for his morality and his need for a vision of Heaven and Hell as a goad and check to his frail human nature. He saw in Whig tendencies the threatened overthrow of the Established Church: if all beliefs were equally tolerated, the fate of the Church would be determined by majority vote. In short, aware as he was of the corrupted nature of the Church and of the constituted state, Swift still felt that they were a necessary restraint upon the private will of men. Pure majority rule, as in the old Greek democracy, often led to a tyranny of demagogues.

Philosophically, Swift trusted reason but hated rationalistic systems. Systems, he felt, were a method of blinding man to facts. They dazzled man with their imposing structures and led him to abandon his common sense. The systematized folly Swift distrusted was to be found in elaborate political theories, dazzling scientific projects, abstruse theological speculation, sweeping programs for social reform. The Third Voyage of *Gulliver's Travels* is full of these (we might add "official" histories, court etiquette, and professional jargon of lawyers or doctors), and they are present in the entire book. Still, if Swift distrusted rationalistic systems, he distrusted no less excessive reliance upon the individual conscience or "inner light" and upon mere brute empiricism (such as the scientific explorations of Lagado), for these might become means of encouraging unthinking self-satisfaction and pride. As we see in Balnibarbi, uncontrolled individualism has a way of becoming unconscious conformity to whatever is fashionable.

Although Swift was a clergyman and often wrote in defense of the Church, his attitudes did not depend solely upon Christian teaching. The traditional wisdom of the past stood beside the clear teachings of Scripture, seldom contradicting them (and to be rejected if it did) but often supplementing them in specific matters. The corruptibility of man was evident from a study of his history as well as from a knowledge of his fallen nature. The fallibility of the private will was as obvious in political competition and sectarian squabbles as in personal acts of sin. The proper nature of man was to be seen in his desire for peace and his moral decency as well as in his beatitude of soul, and in fact the two—morality and grace—were probably inseparable. The secular treatment of man in *Gulliver's Travels*, therefore, does not preclude a Christian meaning (and there are, as the notes indicate, some hints of one), but neither does it demand one. The Christian view of man would accord with and complete the secular view; to state it directly would have been to rely upon authority where reason alone would suffice and, perhaps, to alienate those readers who suspected the partiality of an avowed Christian treatise. Some have stressed the Christian reading of *Gulliver's Travels*, as the section on the Houyhnhnms will indicate; others have rejected such a reading as needlessly limited and forced.

IV. Publication and Reception of *Gulliver's Travels*

"From the highest to the lowest it is universally read, from the cabinet-council to the nursery." So Gay wrote to Swift a few days after *Gulliver's Travels* appeared on October 28, 1726. Gay and Pope observe that few are troubled by "particular reflections"—that is, personal satire upon individuals—and remark that Swift need not have hesitated to name himself as author. ("I would anger the world," he had written earlier, "if I could with safety.") For the book appeared, as the original title page indicates, as the work of one Lemuel Gulliver. As for the manuscript, the publisher received it "he knew not from whence, nor from whom, dropped at his house in the dark, from a hackney-coach."

Swift probably had been at work on the *Travels* since 1720. The last section to be completed was the Third Voyage, and the whole book was revised in the summer of 1725. Swift brought the manuscript to England. However, he had returned to Ireland by the time it was published, and he reported with relish to his English friends, "A Bishop here said that the book was full of improbable lies, and, for his part, he hardly believed a word of it." One wonders whether the "ministerial folks" in England who found *Gulliver's Travels* "a pleasant humorous book" (so Dr. Arbuthnot wrote) were not anxious to avoid seeming nettled. Pope, at any rate, wrote to Swift, "The countenance with which it is received by some statesmen is delightful; I wish I could tell you how every single man looks upon it, to observe which has been my whole diversion this fortnight."

At the start there were few reservations about the book. Only Bolingbroke (Gay reports, but how seriously we cannot be sure) blamed it "as a design of evil consequence to depreciate human nature." But by 1752 we have the fifth Earl of Orrery, who had been close to Swift in his late years, sounding the full note: "Swift has indulged a misanthropy that is intolerable." "In painting Yahoos he becomes one himself." The Fourth Voyage "is a real insult upon mankind." By the end of the eighteenth century, this note was dominant, and critics have returned to the earliest view of the book only in the last few decades. This change in opinion has been brought about by the dispelling of some of the more sensational legends about Swift's life and, even more, by a clearer recognition of the difference between Swift and Gulliver. The misanthropy of the last voyage is Gulliver's. Swift's is of a far more limited kind:

I have ever hated all nations, professions, and communities, and all my love is toward individuals; for instance, I hate the tribe of lawyers, but I love Counsellor Such-a-one and Judge Such-a-one; so with physicians (I will not speak of my own trade), soldiers, English, French, Scotch, and the rest. But principally I hate and detest that animal called man, although I heartily love John, Peter, Thomas, and so forth. . . . I have got materials towards a treatise proving the falsity of that definition *animal rationale;* and to show it should be only *rationis capax* [capable of reason]. Upon this great foundation of misanthropy (though not Timon's manner) the whole building of my Travels is erected . . .

(Letter to Pope, September 29, 1725)

I tell you after all that I do not hate mankind; it is *vous autres* who hate them because you would have them reasonable animals, and are angry for being disappointed. I have always rejected that definition and made another of my own.

(Letter to Pope, November 26, 1725)

In the first passage, Swift insists upon the tendency of institutions to release the worst in men. As soon as personal obligations and sentiments can be replaced by formalities—whether professional, legal, or social—the inherent selfishness and short-sightedness of man are encouraged. When the bond between men becomes an impersonal contract, the letter of the law is all that holds them together, and laws are easily twisted or evaded —or at best given minimal obedience. This is all the more a problem because these institutions have a dignity that makes them resistant to criticism; they provide respectable disguises for meanness and incompetence.

In both passages, Swift implies that it is more sane and charitable to expect of man only what he can perform and to take measures to control moral weakness. The vision of man as a rational animal assumes that he has attained rationality; however, in fact, rationality is always a limit toward which he must move, a standard by which he is judged, rather than a confident possession. "You others" who hate man are those who constantly expect perfection and can never come to terms with the actual. In their high expectations, they fail to provide against corruption and, as in the case of a parent who expects too much of a child, become cruel in the process. Swift abandons neither aspiration nor accurate realism; he insists upon the conditions that must limit all aspiration if it is to be more than a deluded pride in one's exalted vision.

v. Literary Sources and Traditions

Although *Gulliver's Travels* is a highly original work, it draws upon several forms of writing that would have been recognizable to its readers:

1. With the development of commerce and the opening of horizons beyond Europe by voyages of trade and exploration, there arose a great body of travel literature. Such writing, which has its counterpart in antiquity and its modern prototype in the works of Marco Polo, assumed an increasingly "scientific" cast in Swift's day. The Royal Society encouraged mariners to record data of geographical and anthropological interest, in the hope that a sufficient collection might, under study, yield useful hypotheses. Gulliver's cool and careful observations are very much in the style that was encouraged in such reports of travel, and Swift borrows at least one passage directly from a mariner's narrative.

2. Along with actual travel literature arose a large body of "philosophical voyages," or imaginary travels to ideal societies, often highly reasonable and just, located in remote parts of the earth or even on the moon. These works tended to discover men who were simpler and more rational than their European counterparts, and they pointed up the arbitrariness and inadequacy of existing European institutions. Insofar as these works were often optimistic in tone, celebrating man's reason once it was unfettered by the customs and accidents of European history, *Gulliver's Travels* may be said to reverse their tendency and even to satirize them. For Gulliver ends by becoming uncritically adherent to one such society and violently alienated from his own.

3. Behind the "philosophical voyages" lay the old tradition of the "utopia," of which Plato's *Republic* is perhaps the first great example, but which takes its name from the brilliant Renaissance English work by Sir Thomas More. Other writers who worked in this tradition and whose writings Swift read carefully were François Rabelais and Francis Bacon.

4. Finally, many of the themes and illustrations used by Swift in *Gulliver's Travels* are to be found in the moral and political writings, as well as in the sermons, of his day. Such themes are the pettiness and grandeur of man—"the glory, jest, and riddle of the world," as Pope calls him; the problem of tyranny as opposed to the balanced or mixed state; the corruption of institutions; and the cyclical nature of history. The sermons on man's fallen nature often portrayed him as a creature potentially as bestial as Swift's Yahoos, and John Wesley was later to accept the Yahoos as a telling representation of man's sinful nature.

VI. The Character of Gulliver

When Pope addressed Swift in *The Dunciad*, it was by "whatever title please thine ear, / Dean, Drapier, Bickerstaff, or Gulliver!" Swift had written ironically in a series of guises, and each of these fictitious identities or masks was adopted for a specific purpose. None of them is Swift himself, not even the censorious Dean who chides his friends. Some, like Gulliver, are characters whose very lack of understanding is essential to the meaning of the work.

Gulliver is a well-meaning, not very quick man. His technical training has not brought with it any real thoughtfulness, and the book recounts his belated awakening to painful truths. He is uncritical and adaptable; he has a complacent trust in the greatness of man's achievements. When he finally comes to see that man is not a rational animal, he is carried all the way from illusion to misanthropy, and his misanthropy is not to be confused with Swift's. The very presence, in the teeth of Gulliver's horror of his fellow creatures, of so amiable and generous a man as the Portuguese sea captain Pedro de Mendez makes clear that Gulliver's rage can no longer come to terms with reality.

VII. The Fourth Voyage

Most of the controversy about the meaning of *Gulliver's Travels* centers upon the Fourth Voyage. It is there that we have to face all the issues of the book, and our understanding of that section will make sense of all that goes before. The Yahoos have presented a problem in the past, when many readers took them to be Swift's own misanthropic version of mankind. Few today would see them in that way; however, the light in which we do regard them is tied to our view of the Houyhnhnms, and there much argument still exists. The simplest way to state the problem is to set forth the three most common views that critics have taken of the Houyhnhnms:

1. They are an embodiment of the rational life of man. Almost purely rational, they govern their passions completely and limit their needs to what their nature requires. They are free, therefore, of the complications, follies, and viciousness of the other societies in the book; they carry to the furthest extreme the tendencies we can admire in the Brobdingnagians. They act with intuitive certainty; their institutions are minimal and are free of corruption (unlike those of Lilliput, which once resembled those of the Houyhnhnms, as in education). If we are chilled by them, it is because we cannot surrender our worldliness to the dictates of simple virtue. They make us see that we are still, in some measure, Yahoos.

2. They represent a false dream of rationality, such as deists or rationalistic freethinkers advanced in opposition to orthodox Christianity. They are self-sufficient creatures who ignore the claims of a reality beyond the natural; and the simplicity of their lives is a primitivistic daydream of impossible ease in a

benign setting. They have only bland and negative virtues; they lack the warmth and self-sacrificial charity that are the true disposition of the good man. They are complacent and self-satisfied, arrogant in their ignorance, cold and unfeeling in their treatment of Gulliver. Their stratified, quasi-mechanical, closed society is Swift's satire on the illusions of those who worship reason rather than God; it shows the real emptiness of the "advanced" vision of man's natural goodness and perfectibility.

3. They are rational horses, neither ideal men nor a satire upon others' ideals for man. As horses they are simply animal, neither human nor superhuman. Their nature, moreover, is more docile than man's; nonrational horses are more easily tamed than other animals, including some that are considered more noble. It is to be expected that sensible humans (unlike Gulliver) should find their life thin and dull—it is one-dimensional, neither spirited nor spiritual, and we may reject it out of either good or bad motives. But it is consistent in its own way. The Houyhnhnms can absorb what Gulliver tells them, but they are naturally reluctant to deny all their previous experience in order to find in him a new kind of creature (and Gulliver, in his obsequiousness, does not insist upon it). If they treat him with reserve, we must allow for such feelings as we should have if a creature with the least attractive features of a hyena, a rattlesnake, and a vulture should turn out to be rational and talkative and tell us that there were many more at home like him.

VIII. Irony, Comedy, and Satire

There is a constant danger of simplifying Swift's irony. Those, for example, who see the Houyhnhnms as simply admirable or as altogether ludicrous tend to reduce their meaning to one dimension. The rational horses need not be an ideal for man, but neither need they be a caricature of a human ideal. When we read pastoral poetry, we sense that the shepherd's innocent life can free certain human powers and give them a fuller expression than they enjoy in the city or at court. Yet we sense as well that the innocence is not for us, that our natures are not so simple, and that we cannot unlearn what life, for better or worse, has taught us. Swift has gone to great pains to make the Houyhnhnms an embodiment of a life of perfect reason that cannot be lived by man; they are simpler creatures than man, and their simplicity hovers between the "unerring instinct" of social animals and the unclouded "intuitive reason" of disembodied angels. Whether we see that simplicity as subhuman or as supernatural, we must recognize its essential difference from the human condition.

But man has always learned from analogy. Our science fiction today is a steady stream of moral fables in which the nonhuman behavior of other species serves to point up needless human follies and limitations. We must perform an act of abstraction: a creature that is like man may throw light on man without being either a model or a caricature. When Don Quixote sees only giants and Sancho Panza sees only windmills, neither is capable of recognizing analogy. As W. H. Auden has remarked, neither can see that windmills are *like* giants, one because of his madness, the other because of his literal-minded obtuseness. Gulliver suffers from both these faults. Disillusioned with man, he cannot see any saving grace in his own kind; he can see men only as Yahoos. Filled with the illusion that man should be a rational animal, he tries to become a rational horse because this is the only rational animal he has ever encountered. He has tried to make the King of Brobdingnag see that rational power does not correspond to physical appearance, but now he cannot imagine that a rational life can take any form but that of the ideally simple horses. Having recovered from one illusion—that man is a rational animal—he falls into another: that man is completely irrational and that he can make himself over into a rational animal by following literally the model of horses. Gulliver has no gift for abstraction; or at least, his disillusionment is so profound that he has temporarily abandoned abstraction through passion.

This passion is, in large part, a passion of pride. Gulliver cannot tolerate whatever in himself or in his fellow man falls short of the impossible ideal he maintains. He "descends" to treat the generous Pedro de Mendez politely; he shrinks from his wife and children; he seeks the company of stabled horses because they have the same look and smell as the only rational animals he has known; he warns fellow mortals who have pride not to "presume" to appear in his sight. It is a sorry and pathetic mixture of inordinate pride and literal-minded confusion. We see him at the close ranting in his letter to Sympson (see page xxxiv) about mankind's failure to achieve instaneous reform, but we also see the trace of a return to sanity as he recognizes in the Brobdingnagians a more workable model for humans. As Gulliver's passions cool, he may come back to clarity of vision.

But, comically mad as Gulliver is, his views are not to be complacently dismissed. We, as readers, must perform our own act of abstraction. Gulliver's account to his Houyhnhnm master of the corruption of Europe is another instance of his black-and-white vision; as a literal picture of European society, it is neither just nor complete. But Gulliver has become, unconsciously and unknowingly, what Swift has been all along with full and deliberate awareness, a satirist. Gulliver's view of Europe, like all great satire, traces a ridiculous pattern of self-destruction in all man's proudest achievements. It simplifies, it distorts, it brings to the surface the implicit perversion that is comfortably hidden from our sight while we live it out. It insists, like the child in Andersen's fairy tale, that the Emperor has no clothes (as opposed to the "official version" that he must have splendid clothes because he is the Emperor), and it shows us his followers proudly holding the long train that is not there. Satire does not claim to be literally true; it exults in its freedom to reveal what most people refuse to see, and it does that by presenting a new angle of vision from which nothing looks quite as it did. Gulliver is a fool in thinking, with his passionate pride, that he is reporting the literal truth; but Gulliver is Swift's instrument, unconscious but effective, in giving us a splendid satiric image of a world that is only Yahoodom with clothes.

A CHRONOLOGY OF SWIFT'S LIFE

1667 Born in Dublin, November 30.

1682 Entered Trinity College, Dublin.

1686 B.A., Trinity College; remained in residence there.

1689 Became secretary in the household of Sir William Temple, Moor Park, Surrey, England.

1692 M.A., Hart Hall, University of Oxford.

1695 Ordained as priest and took up residence as vicar at Kilroot in northern Ireland.

1696 Returned to Temple's household.

1699 Upon the death of Temple, returned to Dublin as domestic chaplain to Lord Berkeley, Lord Justice of Ireland.

1700 Given parish of Laracor, Ireland, and prebend at St. Patrick's Cathedral, Dublin.

1701 In England with Lord Berkeley. *Contests and Dissensions*, first political tract, published in behalf of Whigs.

1702 D.D., Trinity College, Dublin.

1704 *A Tale of a Tub, The Battle of the Books*, and *The Mechanical Operation of the Spirit* published together, anonymously.

1707 Sent by the Church of Ireland to seek financial aid from Whig ministers of Queen Anne. Resided in London until May, 1709.

1708 *Bickerstaff Papers*.

1709 Left London for Ireland.

1710 Returned to England; renounced Whigs to join Tories; became editor of the Tory journal, *The Examiner*.

1711 *Argument Against Abolishing Christianity* published. *The Conduct of the Allies* and other political pamphlets.

1713 Dean of St. Patrick's Cathedral, Dublin.

1714 After the death of Queen Anne and the fall of the Tory ministry, returned to Ireland to take up duties as Dean.

1720 Probably began *Gulliver's Travels*.

1724 *The Drapier's Letters*.

1726 Visit to England. *Gulliver's Travels* published.

1727 Last visit to England.

1729 *A Modest Proposal.*
1731 *Verses on the Death of Dr. Swift* composed (published 1739).
1735 First collected edition of Swift's works published in Dublin by George Faulkner.
1742 Found of unsound mind; placed under care of guardians.
1745 Died October 19.

BIBLIOGRAPHY

I. Editions of Swift's Works

The two editions of the *Prose Works* most useful to students are those of Temple Scott (London, 1897–1922), with superseded text and canon, but useful annotation; and of Herbert Davis (Oxford, 1939–1959), the best text available, but without annotation. The *Poems* are edited in three volumes (Oxford, 1937; revised, 1958) by Sir Harold Williams, who is also preparing a new edition of the *Correspondence*. Until that appears, the best edition is that of F. Elrington Ball (London, 1910–1914), supplemented by *The Letters of Jonathan Swift to Charles Ford*, edited by D. Nichol Smith (Oxford, 1935) and corrected by George Sherburn's edition of *The Correspondence of Alexander Pope* (Oxford, 1956). There are good editions of individual works, notably *A Tale of a Tub*, edited by A. C. Guthkelch and D. Nichol Smith (Oxford, 1920; revised, 1958); *The Drapier's Letters*, edited by Herbert Davis (Oxford, 1935); and *The Journal to Stella*, edited by Sir Harold Williams (Oxford, 1948). Previous individual editions of *Gulliver's Travels* that have been helpful in preparing this volume are those of Arthur E. Case (New York, 1938), Maynard Mack (all but the Third Voyage in *The Augustans*, Englewood Cliffs, N.J., 1961), and Louis A. Landa (Boston, 1960).

II. Books on Swift, and Especially *Gulliver's Travels*

The latest full biography is that of J. Middleton Murry (*Jonathan Swift, A Critical Biography*. London, 1954), but more reliable is the older two-volume work by Henry Craik (London, 1882; 2nd ed., 1894). Irvin Ehrenpreis, in *The Personality of Jonathan Swift* (London, 1958), has presented some preliminary studies toward his forthcoming biography, *Swift: The Man, His Works, and the Age*, of which the first volume, *Mr. Swift and His Contemporaries* (London, 1962) has appeared.

For recent work on Swift, see Louis A. Landa and James E. Tobin, *Jonathan Swift: A List of Critical Studies Published from 1845 to 1945* (New York, 1945). More recent lists are available in the annual bibliography published in *Philological Quarterly*. Earlier works are listed in the *Cambridge Bibliography of English Literature* and in the bibliography of Ricardo Quintana's *The Mind and Art of Jonathan Swift* (London, 1936; revised, 1953).

The following is a list of the most important recent books that contain extensive discussion of *Gulliver's Travels:*

Bullitt, John M. *Jonathan Swift and the Anatomy of Satire.* Cambridge, Mass., 1953.

Case, Arthur E. *Four Essays on Gulliver's Travels.* Princeton, 1945.

Davis, Herbert. *The Satire of Jonathan Swift.* New York, 1947.

Eddy, William A. *Gulliver's Travels: A Critical Study.* Princeton, 1923.

Ehrenpreis, Irvin. *The Personality of Jonathan Swift.* London, 1958.

Elliott, Robert C. *The Power of Satire: Magic, Ritual, and Art.* Princeton, 1960.

Ewald, William B., Jr. *The Masks of Jonathan Swift.* Cambridge, Mass., 1954.

Leyburn, Ellen D. *Satiric Allegory: Mirror of Man.* New Haven, 1956.

Price, Martin. *Swift's Rhetorical Art.* New Haven, 1953.

Quintana, Ricardo. *The Mind and Art of Jonathan Swift.* New York, 1936; revised, 1953.

———. *Swift: An Introduction.* London, 1955.

Rosenheim, Edward W. *Swift and the Satirist's Art.* Chicago, 1963.

Williams, Harold. *The Text of Gulliver's Travels.* Cambridge, England, 1952.

Williams, Kathleen. *Jonathan Swift and the Age of Compromise.* Lawrence, Kansas, 1958.

III. Articles and Essays

(If the substance of an article has been included in a book listed in II, the article is not mentioned below.)

Barroll, J. Leeds, III. "Gulliver and the Struldbruggs," *PMLA,* LXXIII (1958), 43–50.

Benjamin, Edwin B. "The King of Brobdingnag and Secrets of State," *Journal of the History of Ideas,* XVIII (1957), 572–579.

Clubb, Merrel D. "The Criticism of Gulliver's 'Voyage to the Houyhnhnms,' 1726–1914," in *Stanford Studies in Language and Literature.* Stanford, 1941.

Crane, Ronald S. Review of Martin Kallich (see below), *Philological Quarterly,* XL (1961), 427–430.

———. "The Houyhnhnms, the Yahoos, and the History of Ideas," in *Reason and the Imagination: Studies in the History of Ideas, 1600–1800,* ed. J. A. Mazzeo. New York, 1962, pp. 231–253.

Dircks, Richard J. "Gulliver's Tragic Rationalism," *Criticism,* II (1960), 134–149.

Dyson, A. E. "Swift: The Metamorphosis of Irony," in *Essays and Studies*, New Series, XI (1958), 53–67.

Ehrenpreis, Irvin, "The Meaning of Gulliver's Last Voyage," *Review of English Literature*, III (1962), 18–38.

Elliott, R. C. "Gulliver as Literary Artist," *ELH*, XIX (1952), 49–63.

Fink, Zera S. "Political Theory in *Gulliver's Travels*," *ELH*, XIV (1947), 151–161.

Frye, Roland M. "Swift's Yahoos and the Christian Symbols for Sin," *Journal of the History of Ideas*, XV (1954), 201–217.

Hart, Jeffrey. "The Ideologue as Artist: Some Notes on *Gulliver's Travels*," *Criticism*, II (1960), 125–133.

Horrell, Joe. "What Gulliver Knew," *Sewanee Review*, LI (1943), 476–504.

Kallich, Martin. "Three Ways of Looking at a Horse: Jonathan Swift's 'Voyage to the Houyhnhnms' Again," *Criticism*, II (1960), 107–124.

Kelling, Harold D. "Gulliver's Travels: A Comedy of Humours," *University of Toronto Quarterly*, XXI (1952), 362–375.

Kliger, Samuel. "The Unity of Gulliver's Travels," *Modern Language Quarterly*, VI (1945), 401–415.

Knight, G. Wilson. "Swift and the Symbolism of Irony," in *The Burning Oracle*. London, 1939.

Landa, Louis A. "Jonathan Swift," in *English Institute Essays, 1946*. New York, 1947.

Leavis, F. R. "The Irony of Swift," in *Determinations*, London, 1934; reprinted in *The Common Pursuit*, London, 1953.

McKenzie, Gordon. "Swift: Reason and Some of Its Consequences," *University of California Publications in English*, VIII (1940), 101–129.

Monk, Samuel H. "The Pride of Lemuel Gulliver," *Sewanee Review*, LXIII (1955), 48–71.

Nicolson, Marjorie, and Nora Mohler. "The Scientific Background of Swift's Voyage to Laputa" and "Swift's 'Flying Island' in the Voyage to Laputa," *Annals of Science*, II (1937), 229–334, 405–430; reprinted in *Science and Imagination*, Ithaca, N.Y., 1956.

Orwell, George. "Politics vs. Literature: An Examination of *Gulliver's Travels*," in *Shooting an Elephant and Other Essays*, New York, 1945, as well as in other collections of Orwell's essays.

Peake, Charles. "Swift and the Passions," *Modern Language Review*, LV (1960), 169–180.

Ross, John F. "The Final Comedy of Lemuel Gulliver," in *Studies in the Comic*. Berkeley, 1941.

Sherburn, George. "Errors Concerning the Houyhnhnms," *Modern Philology*, LVI (1958), 92–97.

Stone, Edward. "Swift and the Horses: Misanthropy or Comedy?" *Modern Language Quarterly*, X (1949), 367–376.

Sutherland, John N. "A Reconsideration of Gulliver's Third Voyage," *Studies in Philology*, LIV (1957), 45–52.

Traugott, John. "A Voyage to Nowhere with Thomas More and Jonathan Swift: *Utopia* and *The Voyage to the Houyhnhnms*," *Sewanee Review*, LXIX (1961), 534–565.

Tuveson, Ernest. "Swift and the World-Makers," *Journal of the History of Ideas*, II (1950), 54–74.

———. "Swift: The Dean as Satirist," *University of Toronto Quarterly*, XXII (1953), 368–375.

Wasiolek, Edward. "Relativity in *Gulliver's Travels*," *Philological Quarterly*, XXXVII (1958), 110–116.

Wedel, T. O. "On the Philosophical Background of *Gulliver's Travels*," *Studies in Philology*, XXIII (1926), 434–450.

Winton, Calhoun. "Conversion on the Road to Houyhnhnmland," *Sewanee Review*, LXVIII (1960), 20–33.

A NOTE ON THE TEXT

Travels into Several Remote Nations was first published by Benjamin Motte in two volumes (octavo) on October 28, 1726. The popularity of the book called forth two more editions in the same year and two in 1727. Before Motte published the octavo edition of 1727, he received from Swift's friend Charles Ford a list of corrections. Most of these were used in the fifth printing, which was described as "The Second Edition," and "The Second Edition, Corrected," on the title pages of the two volumes. But apart from small errors, Motte seems to have softened the text in some places and to have dropped passages that might be considered politically dangerous; these were not fully corrected or replaced.

In 1735 George Faulkner, the Dublin bookseller, brought out *Gulliver's Travels* as the third volume of Swift's collected works. Swift sought from Ford a copy of the corrections he had supplied to Motte and probably used them as the basis for further revisions in the text prepared for Faulkner. The most striking addition to the Faulkner text is the Letter to Sympson. One passage (Part Three, Chapter Three, pages 175–177), dealing with Irish resistance to Wood's halfpence, was not printed by either Motte or Faulkner, presumably because of its political explosiveness, and was only printed from Ford's manuscript in 1899. Two passages that appeared in Motte's 1726 text but were dropped from Faulkner's are here restored (Part Four, Chapters Eleven and Twelve, pages 301, 309). Otherwise, the Faulkner text is followed in the main, with corrections taken from Motte or from Ford. (Variants are conveniently presented in Herbert Davis' edition, pages 301–22.)

Punctuation and spelling, including capitalization and use of italics, have been lightened and modernized only where such change conduces to clarity.

One example of a textual problem is to be found in Part Three (Chapter Three, page 173), where Gulliver discusses the power of Laputan telescopes. To the Motte edition of 1726 and 1727 Ford supplies the following additional sentences: "For, although their largest Telescopes do not exceed three Feet, they magnify much more than those of an hundred Yards among us, and at the same time shew the Stars with greater clearness." In the Faulkner text, the end of this is altered to "those of a Hundred with us, and shew the Stars with greater clearness." Sir Harold Williams (*The Text of Gulliver's Travels*, pages 53–55) has suggested that Motte may have omitted a reference to a telescope hundreds of yards long because of its improbability, that Ford may have restored this, and that Swift finally may have reduced the length to more plausible limits in his 1735 revision. But Sir Harold has pointed out that the tubeless telescope used by James Bradley, the Savilian Professor of Astronomy at Oxford, in his observations of Venus in 1722, was 212 feet long. I find it hard to believe that Swift, if he knew of Bradley's telescope, at once could have asserted, in the following sentences, that Laputan astronomical discoveries had far exceeded European and yet reduced the scale of his comparison to a telescope with half the length of Bradley's. I have preferred, therefore, to retain the whole of Ford's addition, on the assumption that it is closer to Swift's meaning.

EDITOR'S PREFACE

Even more than most great books, *Gulliver's Travels* continues to tease (or as Swift would say, "vex") its readers. As soon as general agreement seems to form around one aspect of its meaning, controversy springs up about another. I have not tried, in this edition, to conceal my own point of view, but I have tried not to impose it. My object has been to acquaint the student with issues that have prompted discussion, in the hope of keeping the discussion alive and profitable.

This text is meant to be used with a standard collegiate dictionary, and I have not glossed words that are readily to be found there. (The *Oxford English Dictionary*, in the full or shorter form, is to be preferred because of its special attention to historical usage.) Where confusion might arise from the change that has taken place in the meaning of a word, I have provided a note.

Swift's references to political events of his day are explained where they seem essential to the meaning of the text. A few more are presented in Appendix One. Too much concern with these allusions can serve to limit Swift's meaning excessively and to distract attention from larger issues. Those who wish to pursue them beyond what is given here will find suggestions for further reading.

For aid in the preparation of manuscript I am indebted to two student aides, John Cullinan and Thomas Archbald. For help with collation I must thank my wife. For helpful advice and information I am indebted to Ian Watt, who has acted as general editor. If it is appropriate to dedicate an edition, I would offer this to two future readers of Swift, Maggie and Peter Price.

Martin Price

September 1963

The Publisher to the Reader

The author of these *Travels*, Mr. Lemuel Gulliver, is my ancient and intimate friend; there is likewise some relation between us by the mother's side. About three years ago Mr. Gulliver, growing weary of the concourse of curious people coming to him at his house in Redriff,[1] made a small purchase of land, with a convenient house, near Newark in Nottinghamshire, his native country; where he now lives retired, yet in good esteem among his neighbours.

Although Mr. Gulliver was born in Nottinghamshire, where his father dwelt, yet I have heard him say his family came from Oxfordshire; to confirm which, I have observed in the churchyard at Banbury, in that county, several tombs and monuments of the Gullivers.

Before he quitted Redriff, he left the custody of the following papers in my hands, with the liberty to dispose of them as I should think fit. I have carefully perused them three times: the style is very plain and simple; and the only fault I find is that the author, after the manner of travellers, is a little too circumstantial. There is an air of truth apparent through the whole; and indeed, the author was so distinguished for his veracity that it became a sort of proverb among his neighbours at Redriff, when anyone affirmed a thing, to say it was as true as if Mr. Gulliver had spoke it.

By the advice of several worthy persons to whom, with the author's permission, I communicated these papers, I now venture to send them into the world, hoping they may be at least for some time a better entertainment to our young noblemen than the common scribbles of politics and party.

This volume would have been at least twice as large if I had not made bold to strike out innumerable passages relating to

[1] A corrupted form of Rotherhithe, the south London dock section where Gulliver settled his family after his voyage to Lilliput (Part One, Chapter Eight, p. 70).

the winds and tides, as well as to the variations and bearings in the several voyages; together with the minute descriptions of the management of the ship in storms, in the style of sailors: likewise the account of the longitudes and latitudes; wherein I have reason to apprehend that Mr. Gulliver may be a little dissatisfied: but I was resolved to fit the work as much as possible to the general capacity of readers. However, if my own ignorance in sea-affairs shall have led me to commit some mistakes, I alone am answerable for them: and if any traveller hath a curiosity to see the whole work at large, as it came from the hand of the author, I will be ready to gratify him.

As for any further particulars relating to the author, the reader will receive satisfaction from the first pages of the book.

Richard Sympson.

A Letter from Capt. Gulliver to
His Cousin Sympson[1]

I hope you will be ready to own publicly, whenever you shall
be called to it, that by your great and frequent urgency you
prevailed on me to publish a very loose and uncorrect account
of my travels; with direction to hire some young gentlemen of
either university to put them in order and correct the style, as
my cousin Dampier did by my advice, in his book called *A
Voyage round the World*.[2] But I do not remember I gave you
power to consent that anything should be omitted, and much
less that anything should be inserted: therefore, as to the latter,
I do here renounce everything of that kind; particularly a
paragraph about her Majesty, the late Queen Anne, of most
pious and glorious memory; although I did reverence and esteem her more than any of human species. But you or your
interpolator ought to have considered that, as it was not my
inclination, so was it not decent to praise any animal of our
composition before my master Houyhnhnm: and besides, the
fact was altogether false; for to my knowledge, being in England during some part of her Majesty's reign, she did govern
by a chief minister; nay, even by two successively; the first
whereof was the Lord of Godolphin, and the second the Lord
of Oxford; so that you have made me *say the thing that was
not*. Likewise, in the account of the Academy of Projectors
and several passages of my discourse to my master Houyhnhnm, you have either omitted some material circumstances, or
minced or changed them in such a manner that I do hardly
know mine own work. When I formerly hinted to you some-

[1] This letter first appeared in Faulkner's edition of 1735 and was
probably written close to that date. Since it presumes a knowledge
of the book as a whole, it is better read after the main text than
before it.
[2] The popular book by William Dampier (1652–1715) had appeared in 1697.

thing of this in a letter, you were pleased to answer that you were afraid of giving offence; that people in power were very watchful over the press, and apt not only to interpret, but to punish everything which looked like an *innuendo* (as I think you called it). But pray, how could that which I spoke so many years ago, and at above five thousand leagues distance, in another reign, be applied to any of the Yahoos who now are said to govern the herd, especially at a time when I little thought on or feared the unhappiness of living under them? Have not I the most reason to complain when I see these very Yahoos carried by Houyhnhnms in a vehicle, as if these were brutes and those the rational creatures? And, indeed, to avoid so monstrous and detestable a sight was one principal motive of my retirement hither.

Thus much I thought proper to tell you in relation to your self and to the trust I reposed in you.

I do in the next place complain of my own great want of judgment in being prevailed upon by the intreaties and false reasonings of you and some others, very much against mine own opinion, to suffer my travels to be published. Pray bring to your mind how often I desired you to consider, when you insisted on the motive of public good, that the Yahoos were a species of animals utterly incapable of amendment by precepts or examples, and so it hath proved; for instead of seeing a full stop put to all abuses and corruptions, at least in this little island, as I had reason to expect: behold, after above six months' warning, I cannot learn that my book hath produced one single effect according to mine intentions: I desired you would let me know by a letter when party and faction were extinguished; judges learned and upright; pleaders honest and modest, with some tincture of common sense; and Smithfield [3] blazing with

---

[3] Smithfield, the great London cattle market, had been the scene of the burning of heretics as late as 1612, of murderers even later. Gulliver seems to visualize such a burning of works of false learning as Savonarola was supposed to have ordered in fifteenth-century Florence.

pyramids of law-books; the young nobility's education entirely changed; the physicians banished; the female Yahoos abounding in virtue, honour, truth and good sense; courts and levees of great ministers thoroughly weeded and swept; wit, merit and learning rewarded; all disgracers of the press in prose and verse condemned to eat nothing but their own cotton and quench their thirst with their own ink. These, and a thousand other reformations, I firmly counted upon by your encouragement, as indeed they were plainly deducible from the precepts delivered in my book. And it must be owned that seven months were a sufficient time to correct every vice and folly to which Yahoos are subject, if their natures had been capable of the least disposition to virtue or wisdom; yet so far have you been from answering mine expectation in any of your letters, that on the contrary you are loading our carrier every week with libels, and keys, and reflections, and memoirs, and second parts; wherein I see myself accused of reflecting upon great statesfolk; of degrading human nature (for so they have still the confidence to style it), and of abusing the female sex. I find likewise that the writers of those bundles are not agreed among themselves; for some of them will not allow me to be author of mine own travels, and others make me author of books to which I am wholly a stranger.[4]

I find likewise that your printer hath been so careless as to confound the times and mistake the dates of my several voyages and returns, neither assigning the true year, or the true month, or day of the month; and I hear the original manuscript is all destroyed since the publication of my book. Neither have I any copy left; however, I have sent you some corrections, which you may insert if ever there should be a second edition:

---

[4] In addition to a "complete key" to *Gulliver's Travels* (1726), there was published a spurious third volume (1727), including a "Second Voyage to Brobdingnag" and voyages to Sporunda and Sevarambia. Also in 1727 appeared the *Memoirs of the Court of Lilliput* and, in 1731, *The Travels of Mr. John Gulliver, Son to Capt. Lemuel Gulliver, Translated from the French*.

and yet I cannot stand to[5] them, but shall leave that matter to my judicious and candid readers to adjust it as they please.

I hear some of our sea-Yahoos find fault with my sea-language, as not proper in many parts nor now in use. I cannot help it. In my first voyages, while I was young, I was instructed by the oldest mariners, and learned to speak as they did. But I have since found that the sea-Yahoos are apt, like the land ones, to become new-fangled in their words; which the latter change every year, insomuch as I remember upon each return to mine own country, their old dialect was so altered that I could hardly understand the new. And I observe, when any Yahoo comes from London out of curiosity to visit me at mine own house, we neither of us are able to deliver our conceptions in a manner intelligible to the other.

If the censure of Yahoos could any way affect me, I should have great reason to complain that some of them are so bold as to think my book of travels a mere fiction out of mine own brain; and have gone so far as to drop hints that the Houyhnhnms and Yahoos have no more existence than the inhabitants of Utopia.[6]

Indeed I must confess, that as to the people of Lilliput, Brobdingrag (for so the word should have been spelt, and not erroneously *Brobdingnag*), and Laputa, I have never yet heard of any Yahoo so presumptuous as to dispute their being or the facts I have related concerning them; because the truth immediately strikes every reader with conviction. And is there less probability in my account of the Houyhnhnms or Yahoos when it is manifest as to the latter, there are so many thousands

[5] Vouch for, stand by.

[6] Utopia was Sir Thomas More's name for his "ideal" commonwealth; the name derives from the Greek for "nowhere." More's great ironic work (1516) has much in common with *Gulliver's Travels*, and in particular with the Fourth Voyage. (See Part Three, Chapter Seven, Note 8.) For a discussion of Swift and More, see John Traugott, "A Voyage to Nowhere with Thomas More and Jonathan Swift: *Utopia* and *The Voyage to the Houyhnhnms*," *Sewanee Review*, LXIX (1961), 534–565.

even in this city who only differ from their brother brutes in Houyhnhnmland because they use a sort of a jabber and do not go naked? I wrote for their amendment and not their approbation. The united praise of the whole race would be of less consequence to me than the neighing of those two degenerate Houyhnhnms I keep in my stable; because from these, degenerate as they are, I still improve in some virtues, without any mixture of vice.

Do these miserable animals presume to think that I am so far degenerated as to defend my veracity? Yahoo as I am, it is well known through all Houyhnhnmland that, by the instructions and example of my illustrious master, I was able in the compass of two years (although I confess with the utmost difficulty) to remove that infernal habit of lying, shuffling, deceiving, and equivocating so deeply rooted in the very souls of all my species, especially the Europeans.

I have other complaints to make upon this vexatious occasion; but I forbear troubling myself or you any further. I must freely confess that since my last return some corruptions of my Yahoo nature have revived in me by conversing with a few of your species, and particularly those of mine own family, by an unavoidable necessity; else I should never have attempted so absurd a project as that of reforming the Yahoo race in this kingdom; but I have now done with all such visionary schemes forever.

April 2, 1727.

CONTENTS

LIST OF ILLUSTRATIONS

Part One

A Voyage to Lilliput

The map, which exaggerates the size of Lilliput and Blefuscu (and misnames the capital of Lilliput, properly Mildendo), locates these islands west of the Australian mainland, southeast of Sumatra. Van Diemen's Land was a name applied both to the island of Tasmania (near the southeast coast of Australia) and to the northwest mainland of Australia proper. The map confusingly gives Van Diemen's Land the shape of Tasmania (as in Herman Moll's map of the world of 1719) but places the islands as if Van Diemen's Land were the northwest mainland. Arthur E. Case (*Four Essays on Gulliver's Travels*, page 56) has suggested that all difficulties are resolved if we locate the islands northeast rather than northwest of Tasmania; this puts them well out to sea, where islands belong, and near the thirtieth parallel.

The map shows us two small and roughly equal islands, isolated from the rest of the world. Their closeness is the closeness of enemies who live in each other's shadow, for the climate of the first voyage is one of petty contention and of what Swift called "the spirit of opposition." The Lilliputians, we are told, "see with great exactness, but at no great distance." They have a painfully sharp eye for personal interest (power, prestige, profit) and no breadth or generosity of vision. Of all the mythical societies of *Gulliver's Travels*, Lilliput is the closest to the society of England; and especially political England, for Lilliput is a court-centered world. It has an Emperor who desires power, an Empress who demands punctilious respect, and a group of ministers who advance their careers at the expense of integrity.

The keynote of Lilliput is the corruption of manners and morals. Only after we see the current political practices do we learn, in the sixth chapter, of the original institutions, which once pursued public virtue with the rigorous rationality of Plato's *Republic* or *Laws*. A symptom of corruption is the way in which institutions and even words lose their meanings and can be twisted to serve any selfish official purpose, as in the accusations brought against Gulliver. Finally, Gulliver himself—good-natured, well-meaning, slow to grasp the logic of pettiness—submits uncritically to the corruption of Lilliput (until his own safety is threatened). He reminds us how a great force, like that of the people itself, can be rendered docile and insensible.

Hogs I.

P Mintaon

I Good Fortune

I Naſſow

SUNDA

Sillabar

SUMATRA

Straits of Sunda.

Blefuſcut

Lilliput

Mendendo

Diſcovered AD. 1699.

Dimens Land

Chapter One: The author gives some account of himself and family; his first inducements to travel. He is shipwrecked, and swims for his life, gets safe on shore in the country of Lilliput, is made a prisoner, and carried up the country.

MY father had a small estate in Nottinghamshire; I was the third of five sons. He sent me to Emmanuel College in Cambridge at fourteen years old,[1] where I resided three years, and applied myself close to my studies: but the charge of maintaining me (although I had a very scanty allowance) being too great for a narrow fortune, I was bound apprentice[2] to Mr. James Bates, an eminent surgeon in London, with whom I continued four years; and my father now and then sending me small sums of money, I laid them out in learning navigation and other parts of the mathematics useful to those who intend to travel, as I always believed it would be some time or other my fortune to do. When I left Mr. Bates, I went down to my father; where, by the assistance of him and my uncle John, and some other relations, I got forty pounds and a promise of thirty pounds a year to maintain me at Leyden;[3] there I studied physic two years and seven months, knowing it would be useful in long voyages.

Soon after my return from Leyden, I was recommended, by my good master Mr. Bates, to be surgeon[4] to the *Swallow*, Captain Abraham Pannell commander; with whom I continued three years and a half, making a voyage or two into the Levant[5] and some other parts. When I came back, I resolved to settle in London, to which Mr. Bates, my master, encouraged me, and by him I was recommended to several patients. I took part

[1] Not an uncommon age in Swift's day. Swift himself entered Trinity College, Dublin, at fourteen. Of the two brothers named Gulliver admitted to Pembroke College, Cambridge, in the 1660's, one was fifteen and the other, seventeen.

[2] Bound by contract to serve, usually for seven years, in return for support and instruction in a craft or profession.

[3] The University of Leyden had a famous school of medicine (i.e., "physic"). Thirty pounds would be a fairly liberal annual allowance.

[4] Ship's medical officer.

[5] The Near East.

of a small house in the Old Jury,[6] and being advised to alter my condition, I married Mrs.[7] Mary Burton, second daughter to Mr. Edmond Burton, hosier in Newgate Street,[8] with whom I received four hundred pounds for a portion.[9]

But, my good master Bates dying in two years after and I having few friends, my business began to fail; for my conscience would not suffer me to imitate the bad practice of too many among my brethren. Having therefore consulted with my wife and some of my acquaintance, I determined to go again to sea. I was surgeon successively in two ships, and made several voyages, for six years, to the East and West Indies, by which I got some addition to my fortune. My hours of leisure I spent in reading the best authors ancient and modern, being always provided with a good number of books; and when I was ashore, in observing the manners and dispositions of the people, as well as learning their language, wherein I had a great facility by the strength of my memory.

The last of these voyages not proving very fortunate, I grew weary of the sea, and intended to stay at home with my wife and family. I removed from the Old Jury to Fetter Lane [10] and from thence to Wapping,[11] hoping to get business among the sailors; but it would not turn to account. After three years' expectation that things would mend, I accepted an advantageous offer from Captain William Prichard, master of the *Antelope*, who was making a voyage to the South Sea. We set sail from Bristol May 4th, 1699, and our voyage at first was very prosperous.

It would not be proper, for some reasons, to trouble the reader with the particulars of our adventures in those seas: let

[6] A street, originally Old Jewry, at the east end of the City (the mercantile section of London).

[7] Mistress, a title applied to single as well as married women.

[8] A dealer in stockings and underclothing, in the City.

[9] Dowry.

[10] A street further west, off Fleet Street.

[11] A section across the Thames from Rotherhithe, near the docks.

it suffice to inform him that in our passage from thence to the East Indies we were driven by a violent storm to the north-west of Van Diemen's Land.[12] By an observation, we found ourselves in the latitude of 30 degrees 2 minutes south. Twelve of our crew were dead by immoderate labour and ill food, the rest were in a very weak condition. On the fifth of November, which was the beginning of summer in those parts, the weather being very hazy, the seamen spied a rock, within half a cable's length[13] of the ship; but the wind was so strong that we were driven directly upon it and immediately split. Six of the crew, of whom I was one, having let down the boat into the sea, made a shift to get clear of the ship and the rock. We rowed by my computation about three leagues,[14] till we were able to work no longer, being already spent with labour while we were in the ship. We therefore trusted ourselves to the mercy of the waves, and in about half an hour the boat was overset by a sudden flurry from the north. What became of my companions in the boat, as well as of those who escaped on the rock or were left in the vessel, I cannot tell; but conclude they were all lost. For my own part, I swam as fortune directed me, and was pushed forward by wind and tide. I often let my legs drop and could feel no bottom: but when I was almost gone and able to struggle no longer, I found myself within my depth; and by this time the storm was much abated. The declivity was so small that I walked near a mile before I got to the shore, which I conjectured was about eight o'clock in the evening. I then advanced forward near half a mile but could not discover any sign of houses or inhabitants; at least I was in so weak a condition that I did not observe them. I was extremely tired, and with that, and the heat of the weather, and

[12] The name of the Dutch explorer Anthony Van Diemen (1593–1645) was applied both to Tasmania and to the northwestern part of Australia. See headnote, page 2.
[13] About three hundred feet.
[14] A league was a rough measurement of three miles, on either land or sea.

about half a pint of brandy that I drank as I left the ship, I found myself much inclined to sleep. I lay down on the grass, which was very short and soft, where I slept sounder than ever I remember to have done in my life, and, as I reckoned, above nine hours; for when I awaked, it was just daylight. I attempted to rise but was not able to stir: for as I happened to lie on my back, I found my arms and legs were strongly fastened on each side to the ground; and my hair, which was long and thick, tied down in the same manner. I likewise felt several slender ligatures across my body from my armpits to my thighs. I could only look upwards, the sun began to grow hot, and the light offended my eyes. I heard a confused noise about me, but, in the posture I lay, could see nothing except the sky. In a little time I felt something alive moving on my left leg, which advancing gently forward over my breast, came almost up to my chin; when, bending my eyes downwards as much as I could, I perceived it to be a human creature not six inches high,[15] with a bow and arrow in his hands, and a quiver at his back. In the meantime I felt at least forty more of the same kind (as I conjectured) following the first. I was in the utmost astonishment, and roared so loud that they all ran back in a fright; and some of them, as I was afterwards told, were hurt with the falls they got by leaping from my sides upon the ground. However, they soon returned, and one of them, who ventured so far as to get a full sight of my face, lifting up his hands and eyes by way of admiration,[16] cried out in a shrill but distinct voice, *Hekinah degul:* [17] the others repeated the same words several times, but I then knew not what they meant. I lay all this while, as the reader may believe, in great uneasiness: at length, struggling to get loose, I had the fortune

[15] The scale throughout Lilliput is roughly a twelfth of normal measurements (as in Brobdingnag it is twelve times).

[16] Wonder. ("Admire" and its derivatives are used in this sense, which need not carry approval, throughout the book.)

[17] For comment on the languages of *Gulliver's Travels*, see Appendix One.

to break the strings and wrench out the pegs that fastened my
left arm to the ground; for, by lifting it up to my face, I discovered the methods they had taken to bind me; and, at the
same time, with a violent pull which gave me excessive pain,
I a little loosened the strings that tied down my hair on the
left side, so that I was just able to turn my head about two
inches. But the creatures ran off a second time, before I could
seize them; whereupon there was a great shout in a very shrill
accent, and after it ceased, I heard one of them cry aloud,
Tolgo phonac; when in an instant I felt above an hundred
arrows discharged on my left hand, which pricked me like so
many needles; and besides they shot another flight into the
air, as we do bombs in Europe, whereof many, I suppose, fell
on my body (though I felt them not) and some on my face,
which I immediately covered with my left hand. When this
shower of arrows was over, I fell a-groaning with grief and
pain, and then striving again to get loose, they discharged another volley larger than the first, and some of them attempted
with spears to stick me in the sides; but, by good luck I had on
me a buff jerkin,[18] which they could not pierce. I thought it the
most prudent method to lie still, and my design was to continue so till night, when, my left hand being already loose, I
could easily free myself: and as for the inhabitants, I had reason to believe I might be a match for the greatest armies they
could bring against me, if they were all of the same size with
him that I saw. But fortune disposed otherwise of me. When
the people observed I was quiet, they discharged no more arrows: but by the noise increasing, I knew their numbers were
greater; and about four yards from me, over-against my right
ear, I heard a knocking for above an hour, like people at work;
when, turning my head that way, as well as the pegs and strings
would permit me, I saw a stage erected about a foot and a half
from the ground, capable of holding four of the inhabitants,

[18] Leather jacket.

with two or three ladders to mount it: from whence one of them, who seemed to be a person of quality,[19] made me a long speech, whereof I understood not one syllable. But I should have mentioned, that before the principal person began his oration, he cried out three times, *Langro dehul san* (these words and the former were afterwards repeated and explained to me). Whereupon immediately about fifty of the inhabitants came, and cut the strings that fastened the left side of my head, which gave me the liberty of turning it to the right and of observing the person and gesture of him who was to speak. He appeared to be of a middle age and taller than any of the other three who attended him, whereof one was a page who held up his train and seemed to be somewhat longer than my middle finger; the other two stood one on each side to support him. He acted every part of an orator, and I could observe many periods of threatenings, and others of promises, pity, and kindness. I answered in a few words but in the most submissive manner, lifting up my left hand and both eyes to the sun, as calling him for a witness; and being almost famished with hunger, having not eaten a morsel for some hours before I left the ship, I found the demands of nature so strong upon me that I could not forbear showing my impatience (perhaps against the strict rules of decency) by putting my finger frequently on my mouth, to signify that I wanted food. The *Hurgo* (for so they call a great lord, as I afterwards learnt) understood me very well. He descended from the stage and commanded that several ladders should be applied to my sides, on which above an hundred of the inhabitants mounted and walked towards my mouth, laden with baskets full of meat, which had been provided and sent thither by the King's orders upon the first intelligence he received of me. I observed there was the flesh of several animals, but could not distinguish them by the taste. There were shoulders, legs, and loins shaped like

[19] Person of high social position.

those of mutton, and very well dressed, but smaller than the wings of a lark. I eat [20] them by two or three at a mouthful, and took three loaves at a time, about the bigness of musket bullets. They supplied me as fast as they could, showing a thousand marks of wonder and astonishment at my bulk and appetite. I then made another sign that I wanted drink. They found by my eating that a small quantity would not suffice me, and, being a most ingenious people, they slung up with great dexterity one of their largest hogsheads,[21] then rolled it towards my hand, and beat out the top; I drank it off at a draught, which I might well do, for it hardly held half a pint, and tasted like a small wine of Burgundy, but much more delicious. They brought me a second hogshead, which I drank in the same manner, and made signs for more, but they had none to give me. When I had performed these wonders, they shouted for joy and danced upon my breast, repeating several times as they did at first, *Hekinah degul*. They made me a sign that I should throw down the two hogsheads, but first warned the people below to stand out of the way, crying aloud, *Borach mivola*, and, when they saw the vessels in the air, there was an universal shout of *Hekinah degul*. I confess I was often tempted, while they were passing backwards and forwards on my body, to seize forty or fifty of the first that came in my reach, and dash them against the ground. But the remembrance of what I had felt, which probably might not be the worst they could do, and the promise of honour I made them, for so I interpreted my submissive behaviour, soon drove out those imaginations. Besides, I now considered myself as bound by the laws of hospitality to a people who had treated me with so much expense and magnificence. However, in my thoughts I could not sufficiently wonder at the intrepidity of these diminutive mortals, who durst venture to mount and walk on my body, while one of my hands was at liberty, without trembling at the very sight

[20] Pronounced *et* and meaning *ate*, this form appears throughout the book.
[21] Large casks that held sixty-three gallons of wine.

of so prodigious a creature as I must appear to them. After some time, when they observed that I made no more demands for meat, there appeared before me a person of high rank from his Imperial Majesty. His Excellency, having mounted on the small [22] of my right leg, advanced forwards up to my face, with about a dozen of his retinue. And producing his credentials under the Signet Royal, which he applied close to my eyes, spoke about ten minutes, without any signs of anger but with a kind of determinate resolution; often pointing forwards, which, as I afterwards found, was towards the capital city about half a mile distant, whither it was agreed by his Majesty in council that I must be conveyed. I answered in few words but to no purpose, and made a sign with my hand that was loose, putting it to the other (but over his Excellency's head, for fear of hurting him or his train) and then to my own head and body, to signify that I desired my liberty. It appeared that he understood me well enough, for he shook his head by way of disapprobation, and held his hand in a posture to show that I must be carried as a prisoner. However, he made other signs to let me understand that I should have meat and drink enough and very good treatment. Whereupon I once more thought of attempting to break my bonds, but again, when I felt the smart of their arrows upon my face and hands, which were all in blisters, and many of the darts still sticking in them, and observing likewise that the number of my enemies encreased, I gave tokens to let them know that they might do with me what they pleased. Upon this the *Hurgo* and his train withdrew with much civility and cheerful countenances. Soon after I heard a general shout, with frequent repetitions of the words, *Peplom selan,* and I felt great numbers of the people on my left side relaxing the cords to such a degree that I was able to turn upon my right and to ease myself with making water; which I very plentifully did, to the great astonishment of the people, who conjecturing by my motions what I was going to do,

---

[22] Slender part.

immediately opened to the right and left on that side to avoid the torrent which fell with such noise and violence from me. But before this, they had daubed my face and both my hands with a sort of ointment very pleasant to the smell, which in a few minutes removed all the smart of their arrows. These circumstances, added to the refreshment I had received by their victuals and drink, which were very nourishing, disposed me to sleep. I slept about eight hours, as I was afterwards assured; and it was no wonder, for the physicians, by the Emperor's order, had mingled a sleeping potion in the hogsheads of wine.

It seems that upon the first moment I was discovered sleeping on the ground after my landing, the Emperor had early notice of it by an express,[23] and determined in council that I should be tied in the manner I have related (which was done in the night while I slept), that plenty of meat and drink should be sent me, and a machine prepared to carry me to the capital city.

This resolution perhaps may appear very bold and dangerous, and I am confident would not be imitated by any prince in Europe on the like occasion; however, in my opinion, it was extremely prudent as well as generous. For supposing these people had endeavoured to kill me with their spears and arrows while I was asleep, I should certainly have awaked with the first sense of smart, which might so far have roused my rage and strength as to enable me to break the strings wherewith I was tied; after which, as they were not able to make resistance, so they could expect no mercy.

These people are most excellent mathematicians, and arrived to a great perfection in mechanics by the countenance and encouragement of the Emperor, who is a renowned patron of learning. This prince hath several machines fixed on wheels for the carriage of trees and other great weights. He often builds his largest men of war, whereof some are nine foot long, in the woods where the timber grows, and has them carried on

[23] Fast messenger.

these engines[24] three or four hundred yards to the sea. Five hundred carpenters and engineers were immediately set at work to prepare the greatest engine they had. It was a frame of wood raised three inches from the ground, about seven foot long and four wide, moving upon twenty-two wheels. The shout I heard was upon the arrival of this engine, which it seems set out in four hours after my landing. It was brought parallel to me as I lay. But the principal difficulty was to raise and place me in this vehicle. Eighty poles, each of one foot high, were erected for this purpose, and very strong cords of the bigness of packthread were fastened by hooks to many bandages, which the workmen had girt round my neck, my hands, my body, and my legs. Nine hundred of the strongest men were employed to draw up these cords by many pulleys fastened on the poles, and thus, in less than three hours, I was raised and slung into the engine and there tied fast. All this I was told, for while the whole operation was performing, I lay in a profound sleep, by the force of that soporiferous medicine infused into my liquor. Fifteen hundred of the Emperor's largest horses, each about four inches and a half high, were employed to draw me towards the metropolis, which, as I said, was half a mile distant.

About four hours after we began our journey, I awaked by a very ridiculous accident; for, the carriage being stopped a while to adjust something that was out of order, two or three of the young natives had the curiosity to see how I looked when I was asleep; they climbed up into the engine, and advancing very softly to my face, one of them, an officer in the guards, put the sharp end of his half-pike[25] a good way up into my left nostril, which tickled my nose like a straw and made me sneeze violently: whereupon they stole off unperceived, and it was three weeks before I knew the cause of my awaking so suddenly. We made a long march the remaining

[24] Machines or mechanical devices.
[25] A sharp steel head carried on a short wooden staff.

part of the day, and rested at night with five hundred guards on each side of me, half with torches and half with bows and arrows, ready to shoot me if I should offer to stir. The next morning at sunrise we continued our march, and arrived within two hundred yards of the city gates about noon. The Emperor and all his court came out to meet us, but his great officers would by no means suffer his Majesty to endanger his person by mounting on my body.

At the place where the carriage stopped, there stood an ancient temple, esteemed to be the largest in the whole kingdom, which having been polluted some years before by an unnatural murder, was, according to the zeal of those people, looked on as profane, and therefore had been applied to common use, and all the ornaments and furniture carried away.[26] In this edifice it was determined I should lodge. The great gate fronting to the north was about four foot high and almost two foot wide, through which I could easily creep. On each side of the gate was a small window not above six inches from the ground: into that on the left side the King's smiths conveyed fourscore and eleven chains, like those that hang to a lady's watch in Europe, and almost as large, which were locked to my left leg with six and thirty padlocks. Over against this temple, on the other side of the great highway, at twenty foot distance, there was a turret at least five foot high. Here the Emperor ascended with many principal lords of his court, to have an opportunity of viewing me, as I was told, for I could not see them. It was reckoned that above an hundred thousand inhabitants came out of the town upon the same errand; and in spite of my guards, I believe there could not be fewer than ten thousand, at several times, who mounted upon my body

[26] The temple is probably meant to suggest Westminster Hall, where Charles I of England was tried and condemned to death in 1648. The English were less zealous than the Lilliputians, and the Hall has continued to be used in spite of the "martyrdom" of Charles (as Swift and others—particularly Tories and Jacobites—considered it).

by the help of ladders. But a proclamation was soon issued to forbid it upon pain of death. When the workmen found it was impossible for me to break loose, they cut all the strings that bound me; whereupon I rose up with as melancholy a disposition as ever I had in my life. But the noise and astonishment of the people at seeing me rise and walk are not to be expressed. The chains that held my left leg were about two yards long and gave me not only the liberty of walking backwards and forwards in a semicircle; but, being fixed within four inches of the gate, allowed me to creep in and lie at my full length in the temple.

Chapter Two: The Emperor of Lilliput, attended by several of the nobility, comes to see the author in his confinement. The Emperor's person and habit described. Learned men appointed to teach the author their language. He gains favour by his mild disposition. His pockets are searched, and his sword and pistols taken from him.

When I found myself on my feet, I looked about me, and must confess I never beheld a more entertaining prospect. The country round appeared like a continued garden, and the inclosed fields, which were generally forty foot square, resembled so many beds of flowers. These fields were intermingled with woods of half a stang,[1] and the tallest trees, as I could judge, appeared to be seven foot high. I viewed the town on my left hand, which looked like the painted scene of a city in a theatre.

I had been for some hours extremely pressed by the necessities of nature; which was no wonder, it being almost two days since I had last disburthened myself. I was under great difficulties between urgency and shame. The best expedient I

[1] A stang was a quarter of an acre.

could think on was to creep into my house, which I accordingly did; and shutting the gate after me, I went as far as the
length of my chain would suffer, and discharged my body of
that uneasy load. But this was the only time I was ever guilty
of so uncleanly an action; for which I cannot but hope the
candid reader will give some allowance, after he hath maturely
and impartially considered my case and the distress I was in.
From this time my constant practice was, as soon as I rose, to
perform that business in open air, at the full extent of my
chain, and due care was taken every morning before company
came that the offensive matter should be carried off in wheel-
barrows by two servants appointed for that purpose. I would
not have dwelt so long upon a circumstance, that perhaps at
first sight may appear not very momentous, if I had not
thought it necessary to justify my character in point of cleanliness to the world; which I am told some of my maligners
have been pleased, upon this and other occasions, to call in
question.

When this adventure was at an end, I came back out of my
house, having occasion for fresh air. The Emperor was already
descended from the tower and advancing on horseback towards me, which had like to have cost him dear; for the beast,
although very well trained, yet wholly unused to such a sight,
which appeared as if a mountain moved before him, reared up
on his hinder feet: but that prince, who is an excellent horse-
man, kept his seat until his attendants ran in and held the bridle,
while his Majesty had time to dismount. When he alighted, he
surveyed me round with great admiration, but kept beyond
the length of my chains. He ordered his cooks and butlers,
who were already prepared, to give me victuals and drink,
which they pushed forward in a sort of vehicles upon wheels
until I could reach them. I took these vehicles and soon emptied them all; twenty of them were filled with meat and ten
with liquor; each of the former afforded me two or three
good mouthfuls, and I emptied the liquor of ten vessels, which
was contained in earthen vials, into one vehicle, drinking it off

at a draught, and so I did with the rest. The Empress and young princes of the blood, of both sexes, attended by many ladies, sat at some distance in their chairs,[2] but upon the accident that happened to the Emperor's horse they alighted and came near his person, which I am now going to describe. He is taller, by almost the breadth of my nail, than any of his court, which alone is enough to strike an awe into the beholders. His features are strong and masculine, with an Austrian lip[3] and arched nose, his complexion olive, his countenance erect, his body and limbs well proportioned, all his motions graceful, and his deportment majestic. He was then past his prime, being twenty-eight years and three-quarters old, of which he had reigned about seven, in great felicity and generally victorious. For the better convenience of beholding him, I lay on my side so that my face was parallel to his, and he stood but three yards off: however, I have had him since many times in my hand, and therefore cannot be deceived in the description. His dress was very plain and simple, the fashion of it between the Asiatic and the European; but he had on his head a light helmet of gold, adorned with jewels, and a plume on the crest. He held his sword drawn in his hand, to defend himself if I should happen to break loose; it was almost three inches long, the hilt and scabbard were gold enriched with diamonds. His voice was shrill, but very clear and articulate, and I could distinctly hear it when I stood up. The ladies and courtiers were all most magnificently clad, so that the spot they stood upon seemed to resemble a petticoat spread on the ground, embroidered with figures of gold and silver. His Imperial Majesty spoke often to me, and I returned answers, but neither of us could understand a syllable. There were several of his priests and lawyers present (as I conjec-

[2] Sedan chairs.
[3] A thick pouting lip like that characteristic of another ruling family, the Austrian Hapsburgs. George I, king of England from 1714 to 1727, came to the throne from Germany at the age of fifty-four. He was ungainly in appearance and manners.

tured by their habits) who were commanded to address themselves to me, and I spoke to them in as many languages as I had the least smattering of, which were High and Low Dutch, Latin, French, Spanish, Italian, and Lingua Franca;[4] but all to no purpose. After about two hours the court retired, and I was left with a strong guard, to prevent the impertinence and probably the malice of the rabble, who were very impatient to crowd about me as near as they durst, and some of them had the impudence to shoot their arrows at me as I sat on the ground by the door of my house, whereof one very narrowly missed my left eye. But the colonel ordered six of the ringleaders to be seized, and thought no punishment so proper as to deliver them bound into my hands, which some of his soldiers accordingly did, pushing them forwards with the buttends of their pikes into my reach; I took them all in my right hand, put five of them into my coat-pocket, and as to the sixth, I made a countenance as if I would eat him alive. The poor man squalled terribly, and the colonel and his officers were in much pain, especially when they saw me take out my penknife: but I soon put them out of fear; for, looking mildly, and immediately cutting the strings he was bound with, I set him gently on the ground, and away he ran; I treated the rest in the same manner, taking them one by one out of my pocket, and I observed both the soldiers and people were highly obliged at this mark of my clemency, which was represented very much to my advantage at court.

Towards night I got with some difficulty into my house, where I lay on the ground, and continued to do so about a fortnight; during which time the Emperor gave orders to have a bed prepared for me. Six hundred beds of the common measure were brought in carriages, and worked up in my house; an hundred and fifty of their beds sewn together made up the breadth and length, and these were four double, which

[4] High Dutch is German; Low Dutch is Dutch; Lingua Franca is the mixture of tongues (like modern Pidgin) used by Mediterranean traders.

however kept me but very indifferently from the hardness of the floor, that was of smooth stone. By the same computation they provided me with sheets, blankets, and coverlets tolerable enough for one who had been so long enured to hardships as I.

As the news of my arrival spread through the kingdom, it brought prodigious numbers of rich, idle, and curious people to see me; so that the villages were almost emptied, and great neglect of tillage and household affairs must have ensued if his Imperial Majesty had not provided by several proclamations and orders of state against this inconveniency. He directed that those who had already beheld me should return home, and not presume to come within fifty yards of my house without licence from court: whereby the secretaries of state got considerable fees.

In the meantime, the Emperor held frequent councils to debate what course should be taken with me; and I was afterwards assured by a particular friend, a person of great quality, who was as much in the secret as any, that the court was under many difficulties concerning me. They apprehended my breaking loose, that my diet would be very expensive, and might cause a famine. Sometimes they determined to starve me, or at least to shoot me in the face and hands with poisoned arrows, which would soon dispatch me: but again they considered that the stench of so large a carcass might produce a plague in the metropolis, and probably spread through the whole kingdom. In the midst of these consultations, several officers of the army went to the door of the great council-chamber; and two of them being admitted, gave an account of my behaviour to the six criminals above-mentioned, which made so favourable an impression in the breast of his Majesty and the whole board in my behalf, that an imperial commission was issued out, obliging all the villages nine hundred yards round the city to deliver in every morning six beeves, forty sheep, and other victuals for my sustenance; together with a proportionable quantity of bread, and wine, and other liquors: for the due payment of which his Majesty gave assignments upon his treasury. For this prince lives chiefly upon his own demesnes,[5] seldom except upon great occasions raising any subsidies upon his subjects, who are bound to attend him in his wars at their own expense. An establishment was also made of six hundred persons to be my domestics, who had board-wages[6] allowed for their maintenance and tents built for them very conveniently on each side of my door. It was likewise ordered, that three hundred tailors should make me a suit of clothes after the fashion of the country: that six of his Majesty's greatest scholars should be employed to instruct me in their language: and, lastly, that the Emperor's horses, and those of the nobility and troops of guards, should be exercised in my sight, to accustom themselves to me. All these orders were duly put in execution, and in about three weeks I made a great progress in learning their language; during which time the Emperor frequently honoured me with his visits, and was pleased to assist my masters in teaching me. We began already to converse together in some sort; and the first words I learnt were to express my desire that he would please to give me my liberty, which I every day repeated on my knees. His answer, as I could apprehend, was that this must be a work of time, not to be thought on without the advice of his council, and that first I must *lumos kelmin pesso desmar lon emposo;* that is, swear a peace with him and his kingdom. However, that I should be used with all kindness; and he advised me to acquire, by my patience and discreet behaviour, the good opinion of himself and his subjects. He desired I would not take it ill if he gave orders to certain proper officers to search me; for probably I might carry about me several weapons, which must needs be dangerous things if they answered the bulk of so prodigious a person. I said his Majesty should be satisfied, for I was ready to strip myself and turn up my pockets before him. This I delivered part in words, and part in signs. He re-

[5] Upon the income of his own properties.
[6] Wages with a sum provided for food.

plied that by the laws of the kingdom I must be searched by two of his officers; that he knew this could not be done without my consent and assistance; that he had so good an opinion of my generosity and justice as to trust their persons in my hands: that whatever they took from me should be returned when I left the country, or paid for at the rate which I would set upon them. I took up the two officers in my hands, put them first into my coat-pockets, and then into every other pocket about me, except my two fobs, and another secret pocket which I had no mind should be searched, wherein I had some little necessaries of no consequence to any but myself. In one of my fobs there was a silver watch, and in the other a small quantity of gold in a purse. These gentlemen, having pen, ink, and paper about them, made an exact inventory of everything they saw; and when they had done, desired I would set them down, that they might deliver it to the Emperor. This inventory I afterwards translated into English, and is word for word as follows:

"*Imprimis*, In the right coat-pocket of the Great Man-Mountain (for so I interpret the words *Quinbus Flestrin*) after the strictest search, we found only one great piece of coarse cloth, large enough to be a foot-cloth for your Majesty's chief room of state. In the left pocket, we saw a huge silver chest, with a cover of the same metal, which we the searchers were not able to lift. We desired it should be opened, and one of us, stepping into it, found himself up to the mid leg in a sort of dust, some part whereof, flying up to our faces, set us both a-sneezing for several times together. In his right waistcoat-pocket, we found a prodigious bundle of white thin substances, folded one over another, about the bigness of three men, tied with a strong cable, and marked with black figures; which we humbly conceive to be writings, every letter almost half as large as the palm of our hands. In the left, there was a sort of engine, from the back of which were extended twenty long poles, resembling the palisados before your Majesty's

court; wherewith we conjecture the Man-Mountain combs his
head, for we did not always trouble him with questions, because we found it a great difficulty to make him understand
us. In the large pocket on the right side of his middle cover
(so I translate the word *ranfu-lo*, by which they meant my
breeches) we saw a hollow pillar of iron, about the length of a
man, fastened to a strong piece of timber, larger than the pillar; and upon one side of the pillar were huge pieces of iron
sticking out, cut into strange figures, which we know not what
to make of. In the left pocket, another engine of the same kind.
In the smaller pocket on the right side, were several round
flat pieces of white and red metal of different bulk; some of
the white, which seemed to be silver, were so large and heavy,
that my comrade and I could hardly lift them. In the left
pocket were two black pillars irregularly shaped: we could
not, without difficulty, reach the top of them as we stood at
the bottom of his pocket. One of them was covered and
seemed all of a piece: but at the upper end of the other there
appeared a white round substance, about twice the bigness of
our heads. Within each of these was inclosed a prodigious plate
of steel; which, by our orders, we obliged him to show us,
because we apprehended they might be dangerous engines.
He took them out of their cases, and told us, that in his own
country his practice was to shave his beard with one of these
and to cut his meat with the other. There were two pockets
which we could not enter: these he called his fobs; they were
two large slits cut into the top of his middle cover, but
squeezed close by the pressure of his belly. Out of the right
fob hung a great silver chain, with a wonderful kind of engine
at the bottom. We directed him to draw out whatever was at
the end of that chain; which appeared to be a globe, half silver
and half of some transparent metal: for on the transparent
side we saw certain strange figures circularly drawn, and
thought we could touch them, until we found our fingers
stopped with that lucid substance. He put this engine to our
ears, which made an incessant noise like that of a watermill.

And we conjecture it is either some unknown animal, or the god that he worships: but we are more inclined to the latter opinion, because he assured us (if we understood him right, for he expressed himself very imperfectly) that he seldom did anything without consulting it. He called it his oracle, and said it pointed out the time for every action of his life. From the left fob he took out a net almost large enough for a fisherman, but contrived to open and shut like a purse, and served him for the same use: we found therein several massy pieces of yellow metal, which, if they be of real gold, must be of immense value.

"Having thus, in obedience to your Majesty's commands, diligently searched all his pockets, we observed a girdle about his waist made of the hide of some prodigious animal; from which, on the left side, hung a sword of the length of five men, and on the right, a bag or pouch divided into two cells, each cell capable of holding three of your Majesty's subjects. In one of these cells were several globes or balls of a most ponderous metal, about the bigness of our heads, and required a strong hand to lift them: the other cell contained a heap of certain black grains, but of no great bulk or weight, for we could hold above fifty of them in the palms of our hands.

"This is an exact inventory of what we found about the body of the Man-Mountain, who used us with great civility and due respect to your Majesty's commission. Signed and sealed on the fourth day of the eighty-ninth moon of your Majesty's auspicious reign,

Clefren Frelock, Marsi Frelock."

When this inventory was read over to the Emperor, he directed me to deliver up the several particulars. He first called for my scimitar, which I took out, scabbard and all. In the meantime he ordered three thousand of his choicest troops (who then attended him) to surround me at a distance, with their bows and arrows just ready to discharge: but I did not observe it, for my eyes were wholly fixed upon his Majesty. He

then desired me to draw my scimitar, which, although it had got
some rust by the seawater, was in most parts exceeding bright.
I did so, and immediately all the troops gave a shout between
terror and surprise; for the sun shone clear, and the reflection
dazzled their eyes as I waved the scimitar to and fro in my
hand. His Majesty, who is a most magnanimous prince, was
less daunted than I could expect; he ordered me to return it
into the scabbard and cast it on the ground as gently as I
could, about six foot from the end of my chain. The next thing
he demanded was one of the hollow iron pillars, by which he
meant my pocket-pistols. I drew it out, and at his desire, as
well as I could, expressed to him the use of it; and charging it
only with powder, which by the closeness of my pouch happened to escape wetting in the sea (an inconvenience that all
prudent mariners take special care to provide against), I first
cautioned the Emperor not to be afraid, and then I let it off in
the air. The astonishment here was much greater than at the
sight of my scimitar. Hundreds fell down as if they had been
struck dead; and even the Emperor, although he stood his
ground, could not recover himself in some time. I delivered
up both my pistols in the same manner as I had done my scimitar, and then my pouch of powder and bullets; begging him
that the former might be kept from fire, for it would kindle
with the smallest spark, and blow up his imperial palace into
the air. I likewise delivered up my watch, which the Emperor
was very curious to see, and commanded two of his tallest
yeomen of the guards to bear it on a pole upon their shoulders,
as draymen in England do a barrel of ale. He was amazed at
the continual noise it made, and the motion of the minute-
hand, which he could easily discern; for their sight is much
more acute than ours: he asked the opinions of his learned
men about him, which were various and remote, as the reader
may well imagine without my repeating; although indeed I
could not very perfectly understand them. I then gave up my
silver and copper money, my purse with nine large pieces of

gold and some smaller ones, my knife and razor, my comb and silver snuff-box, my handkerchief and journal book. My scimitar, pistols, and pouch were conveyed in carriages to his Majesty's stores; but the rest of my goods were returned me.

I had, as I before observed, one private pocket which escaped their search, wherein there was a pair of spectacles (which I sometimes use for the weakness of my eyes), a pocket perspective,[7] and several other little conveniences; which, being of no consequence to the Emperor, I did not think myself bound in honour to discover, and I apprehended they might be lost or spoiled if I ventured them out of my possession.

Chapter Three: The author diverts the Emperor and his nobility of both sexes in a very uncommon manner. The diversions of the court of Lilliput described. The author hath his liberty granted him upon certain conditions.

My gentleness and good behaviour had gained so far on the Emperor and his court, and indeed upon the army and people in general, that I began to conceive hopes of getting my liberty in a short time. I took all possible methods to cultivate this favourable disposition. The natives came by degrees to be less apprehensive of any danger from me. I would sometimes lie down and let five or six of them dance on my hand. And at last the boys and girls would venture to come and play at hide and seek in my hair. I had now made a good progress in understanding and speaking their language. The Emperor had a mind one day to entertain me with several of the country shows, wherein they exceed all nations I have known, both for dexterity and magnificence. I was diverted with none so

[7] Telescope.

much as that of the rope-dancers, performed upon a slender white thread, extended about two foot, and twelve inches from the ground. Upon which I shall desire liberty, with the reader's patience, to enlarge a little.

This diversion is only practised by those persons who are candidates for great employments, and high favour, at court. They are trained in this art from their youth, and are not always of noble birth or liberal education. When a great office is vacant either by death or disgrace (which often happens) five or six of those candidates petition the Emperor to entertain his Majesty and the court with a dance on the rope, and whoever jumps the highest without falling, succeeds in the office.[1] Very often the chief ministers themselves are commanded to show their skill, and to convince the Emperor that they have not lost their faculty. Flimnap, the Treasurer, is allowed to cut a caper on the strait rope, at least an inch higher than any other lord in the whole empire. I have seen him do the summerset several times together upon a trencher fixed on the rope, which is no thicker than a common packthread in England. My friend Reldresal, Principal Secretary for Private Affairs, is, in my opinion, if I am not partial, the second after the Treasurer; the rest of the great officers are much upon a par.

These diversions are often attended with fatal accidents, whereof great numbers are on record. I myself have seen two or three candidates break a limb. But the danger is much greater when the ministers themselves are commanded to show their dexterity; for by contending to excel themselves and their fellows, they strain so far, that there is hardly one of them who hath not received a fall, and some of them two or three. I was assured that a year or two before my arrival, Flimnap would have infallibly broke his neck, if one of the

----

[1] For a fuller discussion of the political allusions, see Appendix Two. Flimnap may be taken as a reference to Sir Robert Walpole, "Prime Minister" (not yet an official title) at the time Swift was writing and a man of great political agility.

King's cushions, that accidentally lay on the ground, had not weakened the force of his fall.[2]

There is likewise another diversion, which is only shown before the Emperor and Empress and first minister upon particular occasions. The Emperor lays on a table three fine silken threads of six inches long. One is blue, the other red, and the third green.[3] These threads are proposed as prizes for those persons whom the Emperor hath a mind to distinguish by a peculiar mark of his favour. The ceremony is performed in his Majesty's great chamber of state, where the candidates are to undergo a trial of dexterity very different from the former, and such as I have not observed the least resemblance of in any other country of the old or the new world. The Emperor holds a stick in his hands, both ends parallel to the horizon, while the candidates, advancing one by one, sometimes leap over the stick, sometimes creep under it backwards and forwards several times, according as the stick is advanced or depressed. Sometimes the Emperor holds one end of the stick and his first minister the other; sometimes the minister has it entirely to himself. Whoever performs his part with most agility, and holds out the longest in leaping and creeping, is rewarded with the blue-coloured silk; the red is given to the next, and the green to the third, which they all wear girt twice round about the middle; and you see few great persons about this court who are not adorned with one of these girdles.

The horses of the army and those of the royal stables, having been daily led before me, were no longer shy, but would come

[2] Probably a reference to the King's mistress, the Duchess of Kendal, who helped restore Walpole to power in 1721 after a period of disfavor.

[3] The ribbons of the Orders of the Garter, the Bath, and the Thistle, honors used by Walpole to reward adherence to his policies. He himself became a Knight of the Bath when that Order was revived at his prompting in 1725, and he was awarded the Garter the next year. This was the first promotion of a commoner to the Garter since 1660 and led to Walpole's popular satirical nickname, "Sir Bluestring."

up to my very feet without starting. The riders would leap them over my hand as I held it on the ground, and one of the Emperor's huntsmen, upon a large courser, took my foot, shoe and all; which was indeed a prodigious leap. I had the good fortune to divert the Emperor one day after a very extraordinary manner. I desired he would order several sticks of two foot high, and the thickness of an ordinary cane, to be brought me; whereupon his Majesty commanded the master of his woods to give directions accordingly, and the next morning six woodmen arrived with as many carriages, drawn by eight horses to each. I took nine of these sticks, and, fixing them firmly in the ground in a quadrangular figure, two foot and a half square, I took four sticks and tied them parallel at each corner, about two foot from the ground; then I fastened my handkerchief to the nine sticks that stood erect and extended it on all sides till it was as tight as the top of a drum; and the four parallel sticks, rising about five inches higher than the handkerchief, served as ledges on each side. When I had finished my work, I desired the Emperor to let a troop of his best horse, twenty-four in number, come and exercise upon this plain. His Majesty approved of the proposal, and I took them up one by one in my hands, ready mounted and armed, with the proper officers to exercise them. As soon as they got into order, they divided into two parties, performed mock skirmishes, discharged blunt arrows, drew their swords, fled and pursued, attacked and retired, and in short discovered the best military discipline I ever beheld. The parallel sticks secured them and their horses from falling over the stage; and the Emperor was so much delighted that he ordered this entertainment to be repeated several days, and once was pleased to be lifted up and give the word of command; and, with great difficulty, persuaded even the Empress herself to let me hold her in her close chair [4] within two yards of the stage, from

_____

[4] Enclosed sedan chair.

whence she was able to take a full view of the whole performance. It was my good fortune that no ill accident happened in
these entertainments; only once a fiery horse that belonged to
one of the captains, pawing with his hoof, struck a hole in my
handkerchief, and his foot slipping, he overthrew his rider and
himself; but I immediately relieved them both, for covering
the hole with one hand, I set down the troop with the other
in the same manner as I took them up. The horse that fell was
strained in the left shoulder, but the rider got no hurt, and I
repaired my handkerchief as well as I could; however, I would
not trust to the strength of it any more in such dangerous enterprises.

About two or three days before I was set at liberty, as I was
entertaining the court with these kinds of feats, there arrived
an express to inform his Majesty that some of his subjects, riding near the place where I was first taken up, had seen a great
black substance lying on the ground, very oddly shaped, extending its edges round as wide as his Majesty's bedchamber,
and rising up in the middle as high as a man; that it was no living creature, as they at first apprehended, for it lay on the
grass without motion, and some of them had walked round it
several times; that by mounting upon each others' shoulders,
they had got to the top, which was flat and even, and stamping
upon it they found it was hollow within; that they humbly
conceived it might be something belonging to the Man-Mountain, and if his Majesty pleased, they would undertake to bring
it with only five horses. I presently knew what they meant,
and was glad at heart to receive this intelligence. It seems upon
my first reaching the shore after our shipwreck, I was in such
confusion that, before I came to the place where I went to
sleep, my hat, which I had fastened with a string to my head
while I was rowing and had stuck on all the time I was swimming, fell off after I came to land; the string, as I conjecture,
breaking by some accident which I never observed, but
thought my hat had been lost at sea. I intreated his Imperial

Majesty to give orders it might be brought to me as soon as possible, describing to him the use and the nature of it: and the next day the waggoners arrived with it, but not in a very good condition; they had bored two holes in the brim within an inch and-a-half of the edge, and fastened two hooks in the holes; these hooks were tied by a long cord to the harness, and thus my hat was dragged along for above half an English mile: but the ground in that country being extremely smooth and level, it received less damage than I expected.

Two days after this adventure the Emperor, having ordered that part of his army which quarters in and about his metropolis to be in a readiness, took a fancy of diverting himself in a very singular manner. He desired I would stand like a Colossus,[5] with my legs as far asunder as I conveniently could. He then commanded his general (who was an old experienced leader and a great patron of mine) to draw up the troops in close order and march them under me, the foot by twenty-four in a breast, and the horse by sixteen, with drums beating, colours flying, and pikes advanced. This body consisted of three thousand foot, and a thousand horse. His Majesty gave orders, upon pain of death, that every soldier in his march should observe the strictest decency with regard to my person; which, however, could not prevent some of the younger officers from turning up their eyes as they passed under me. And, to confess the truth, my breeches were at that time in so ill a condition, that they afforded some opportunities for laughter and admiration.

I had sent so many memorials and petitions for my liberty, that his Majesty at length mentioned the matter, first in the cabinet, and then in a full council; where it was opposed by none, except Skyresh Bolgolam, who was pleased, without any provocation, to be my mortal enemy. But it was carried against

[5] A counterpart of the famous statue of Apollo at Rhodes, which supposedly bestrode the harbor entrance so that ships passed between its legs.

him by the whole board and confirmed by the Emperor. That minister was *Galbet*, or Admiral of the Realm, very much in his master's confidence, and a person well versed in affairs, but of a morose and sour complexion. However, he was at length persuaded to comply; but prevailed that the articles and conditions upon which I should be set free, and to which I must swear, should be drawn up by himself. These articles were brought to me by Skyresh Bolgolam in person, attended by two under-secretaries and several persons of distinction. After they were read, I was demanded to swear to the performance of them; first in the manner of my own country, and afterwards in the method prescribed by their laws; which was to hold my right foot in my left hand, to place the middle finger of my right hand on the crown of my head, and my thumb on the tip of my right ear. But because the reader may perhaps be curious to have some idea of the style and manner of expression peculiar to that people, as well as to know the articles upon which I recovered my liberty, I have made a translation of the whole instrument[6] word for word, as near as I was able, which I here offer to the public.

GOLBASTO MOMAREN EVLAME GURDILO SHEFIN MULLY ULLY GUE, most mighty Emperor of Lilliput, Delight and Terror of the Universe,[7] whose dominions extend five thousand blustrugs (about twelve miles in circumference) to the extremities of the globe; Monarch of all Monarchs, taller than the sons of men; whose feet press down to the center, and whose head strikes against the sun: at whose nod the princes of the earth shake their knees; pleasant as the spring, comfortable as the summer, fruitful as autumn, dreadful as winter. His most sublime Majesty proposeth to the Man-

[6] Document.
[7] A parody of the ceremonious forms of address often recorded in travel books; the style of these, as of the clothing, is "between the Asiatic and the European."

Mountain, lately arrived at our celestial dominions, the following articles, which by a solemn oath he shall be obliged to perform.

First, The Man-Mountain shall not depart from our dominions, without our licence under our great seal.

Secondly, He shall not presume to come into our metropolis, without our express order; at which time the inhabitants shall have two hours warning to keep within their doors.

Thirdly, The said Man-Mountain shall confine his walks to our principal high roads, and not offer to walk or lie down in a meadow or field of corn.[8]

Fourthly, As he walks the said roads, he shall take the utmost care not to trample upon the bodies of any of our loving subjects, their horses, or carriages, nor take any of our said subjects into his hands without their own consent.

Fifthly, If an express require extraordinary dispatch, the Man-Mountain shall be obliged to carry in his pocket the messenger and horse a six days' journey once in every moon, and return the said messenger back (if so required) safe to our Imperial Presence.

Sixthly, He shall be our ally against our enemies in the island of Blefuscu, and do his utmost to destroy their fleet, which is now preparing to invade us.[9]

Seventhly, That the said Man-Mountain shall, at his times of leisure, be aiding and assisting to our workmen in helping to raise certain great stones, towards covering the wall of the principal park and other our royal buildings.

Eighthly, That the said Man-Mountain shall, in two

[8] Grain of any kind.

[9] An allusion to the suspicions of France that remained current in England after the Peace of Utrecht (which ended the War of the Spanish Succession, 1701–1713). English ministers were often accused, sometimes with justice, of being in the pay of France, and France was a base of operations for the Stuart pretender to the throne of England.

moons' time, deliver in an exact survey of the circumference of our dominions by a computation of his own paces round the coast.

Lastly, That upon his solemn oath to observe all the above articles, the said Man-Mountain shall have a daily allowance of meat and drink sufficient for the support of 1728 of our subjects, with free access to our Royal Person, and other marks of our favour. Given at our palace at Belfaborac the twelfth day of the ninety-first moon of our reign.

I swore and subscribed to these articles with great cheerfulness and content, although some of them were not so honourable as I could have wished; which proceeded wholly from the malice of Skyresh Bolgolam, the High Admiral: whereupon my chains were immediately unlocked and I was at full liberty; the Emperor himself in person did me the honour to be by at the whole ceremony. I made my acknowledgments by prostrating myself at his Majesty's feet: but he commanded me to rise; and after many gracious expressions, which, to avoid the censure of vanity, I shall not repeat, he added that he hoped I should prove a useful servant, and well deserve all the favours he had already conferred upon me, or might do for the future.

The reader may please to observe that, in the last article for the recovery of my liberty, the Emperor stipulates to allow me a quantity of meat and drink sufficient for the support of 1728 Lilliputians. Some time after, asking a friend at court how they came to fix on that determinate number, he told me that his Majesty's mathematicians, having taken the height of my body by the help of a quadrant, and finding it to exceed theirs in the proportion of twelve to one, they concluded from the similarity of their bodies, that mine must contain at least 1728 of theirs, and consequently would require as much food as was necessary to support that number of Lilliputians. By which the reader may conceive an idea of the ingenuity of that people, as well as the prudent and exact economy of so great a prince.

Chapter Four: Mildendo, the metropolis of Lilliput, described, together with the Emperor's palace. A conversation between the author and a principal secretary concerning the affairs of that empire. The author's offers to serve the Emperor in his wars.

The first request I made after I had obtained my liberty was that I might have licence to see Mildendo, the metropolis; which the Emperor easily granted me, but with a special charge to do no hurt, either to the inhabitants or their houses. The people had notice by proclamation of my design to visit the town. The wall which encompassed it is two foot and an half high and at least eleven inches broad, so that a coach and horses may be driven very safely round it; and it is flanked with strong towers at ten foot distance. I stepped over the great western gate, and passed very gently, and sideling [1] through the two principal streets, only in my short waistcoat, for fear of damaging the roofs and eaves of the houses with the skirts of my coat. I walked with the utmost circumspection to avoid treading on any stragglers who might remain in the streets, although the orders were very strict that all people should keep in their houses, at their own peril. The garret windows and tops of houses were so crowded with spectators that I thought in all my travels I had not seen a more populous place. The city is an exact square, each side of the wall being five hundred foot long. The two great streets, which run cross and divide it into four quarters, are five foot wide. The lanes and alleys, which I could not enter, but only viewed them as I passed, are from twelve to eighteen inches. The town is capable of holding five hundred thousand souls. The houses are from three to five stories; the shops and markets well provided.

The Emperor's palace is in the center of the city, where the two great streets meet. It is inclosed by a wall of two foot high, and twenty foot distant from the buildings. I had his Majesty's permission to step over this wall; and the space being so wide between that and the palace, I could easily view it on

[1] Sideways.

every side. The outward court is a square of forty foot and includes two other courts: in the inmost are the royal apartments, which I was very desirous to see, but found it extremely difficult; for the great gates, from one square into another, were but eighteen inches high and seven inches wide. Now the buildings of the outer court were at least five foot high, and it was impossible for me to stride over them without infinite damage to the pile, although the walls were strongly built of hewn stone and four inches thick. At the same time the Emperor had a great desire that I should see the magnificence of his palace; but this I was not able to do till three days after, which I spent in cutting down with my knife some of the largest trees in the royal park, about an hundred yards distant from the city. Of these trees I made two stools, each about three foot high, and strong enough to bear my weight. The people having received notice a second time, I went again through the city to the palace, with my two stools in my hands. When I came to the side of the outer court, I stood upon one stool, and took the other in my hand: this I lifted over the roof, and gently set it down on the space between the first and second court, which was eight foot wide. I then stepped over the buildings very conveniently from one stool to the other, and drew up the first after me with a hooked stick. By this contrivance I got into the inmost court; and lying down upon my side, I applied my face to the windows of the middle stories, which were left open on purpose, and discovered the most splendid apartments that can be imagined. There I saw the Empress and the young princes in their several lodgings, with their chief attendants about them. Her Imperial Majesty was pleased to smile very graciously upon me, and gave me out of the window her hand to kiss.

But I shall not anticipate the reader with farther descriptions of this kind, because I reserve them for a greater work which is now almost ready for the press, containing a general description of this empire, from its first erection through a long series of princes, with a particular account of their wars and politics,

laws, learning, and religion; their plants and animals, their peculiar manners and customs, with other matters very curious
and useful; my chief design at present being only to relate such
events and transactions as happened to the public, or to myself,
during a residence of about nine months in that empire.

One morning, about a fortnight after I had obtained my
liberty, Reldresal, Principal Secretary (as they style him) of
Private Affairs, came to my house, attended only by one servant. He ordered his coach to wait at a distance and desired I
would give him an hour's audience; which I readily consented
to, on account of his quality and personal merits, as well as of
the many good offices he had done me during my solicitations
at court. I offered to lie down that he might the more conveniently reach my ear; but he chose rather to let me hold him
in my hand during our conversation. He began with compliments on my liberty, said he might pretend to some merit in
it; but, however, added, that if it had not been for the present
situation of things at court, perhaps I might not have obtained
it so soon. For, said he, as flourishing a condition as we appear
to be in to foreigners, we labour under two mighty evils; a
violent faction at home, and the danger of an invasion by a
most potent enemy from abroad. As to the first, you are to understand, that for above seventy moons past, there have been
two struggling parties in the empire, under the names of
Tramecksan and *Slamecksan*, from the high and low heels on
their shoes, by which they distinguish themselves.[2] It is alleged
indeed, that the high heels are most agreeable to our ancient
constitution: but however this be, his Majesty hath determined
to make use of only low heels in the administration of the government and all offices in the gift of the Crown, as you cannot
but observe; and particularly, that his Majesty's imperial heels

[2] The parties are meant to suggest the Tories (high church) and
the Whigs (low church). George I favored the Whigs; his son,
while Prince of Wales, tried to cultivate both parties, and, because
of his hostility to his father, the Tories hoped for his favor after
his accession to the throne.

are lower at least by a *drurr* than any of his court (*drurr* is a measure about the fourteenth part of an inch). The animosities between these two parties run so high that they will neither eat nor drink nor talk with each other. We compute the *Tramecksan*, or High-Heels, to exceed us in number; but the power is wholly on our side. We apprehend his Imperial Highness, the heir to the crown, to have some tendency towards the High-Heels; at least we can plainly discover one of his heels higher than the other, which gives him a hobble in his gait. Now, in the midst of these intestine disquiets, we are threatened with an invasion from the island of Blefuscu, which is the other great empire of the universe, almost as large and powerful as this of his Majesty. For as to what we have heard you affirm, that there are other kingdoms and states in the world, inhabited by human creatures as large as yourself, our philosophers are in much doubt, and would rather conjecture that you dropped from the moon or one of the stars; because it is certain that an hundred mortals of your bulk would, in a short time, destroy all the fruits and cattle of his Majesty's dominions. Besides, our histories of six thousand moons make no mention of any other regions than the two great empires of Lilliput and Blefuscu. Which two mighty powers have, as I was going to tell you, been engaged in a most obstinate war for six and thirty moons past. It began upon the following occasion. It is allowed on all hands, that the primitive way of breaking eggs before we eat them was upon the larger end: but his present Majesty's grandfather, while he was a boy, going to eat an egg, and breaking it according to the ancient practice, happened to cut one of his fingers. Whereupon the Emperor his father published an edict, commanding all his subjects, upon great penalties, to break the smaller end of their eggs.[3] The people so highly resented this law that our histories

---

[3] What is suggested is the dispute about transubstantiation, i.e., whether the bread and wine of communion literally or only symbolically become the body and blood of Jesus Christ. The particular historical reference is probably to Henry VIII's breaking with

tell us there have been six rebellions raised on that account; wherein one emperor lost his life and another his crown. These civil commotions were constantly fomented by the monarchs of Blefuscu; and when they were quelled, the exiles always fled for refuge to that empire. It is computed that eleven thousand persons have, at several times, suffered death rather than submit to break their eggs at the smaller end. Many hundred large volumes have been published upon this controversy: but the books of the Big-Endians have been long forbidden, and the whole party rendered incapable by law of holding employments.[4] During the course of these troubles, the emperors of Blefuscu did frequently expostulate by their ambassadors, accusing us of making a schism in religion by offending against a fundamental doctrine of our great prophet Lustrog, in the fifty-fourth chapter of the *Brundecral* (which is their Alcoran).[5] This, however, is thought to be a mere strain upon the text: for the words are these: "That all true believers shall break their eggs at the convenient end"; and which is the convenient end, seems, in my humble opinion, to be left to every

---

the Roman Catholic Church and his establishment of the Church of England. The religious conflicts that followed helped to produce such political events as the beheading of Charles I in 1649 and the ousting of the Roman Catholic James II in 1688. Thereafter Parliament, especially with Whig prompting, took measures to ensure a Protestant succession; it settled the throne upon the Hanoverian branch when Queen Anne failed to produce an heir. The accession of George I in 1714 was followed by the first Jacobite uprising (1715-1716), which attempted to restore the Roman Catholic Stuarts to the throne of England.

[4] Punitive measures were taken against Roman Catholics, among others, by the Test Act, which required conformity to the Church of England as a condition of holding office. Catholics were also subjected to double taxation on land and were forbidden to acquire new real estate. At times of stress, they were threatened anew by an unenforced law of 1688 that forbade them to live within a ten-mile radius of London.

[5] Their Koran or Bible. Swift is emphasizing those conflicts over dogma and ritual that have little or no clear basis in Scripture.

man's conscience, or at least in the power of the chief magistrate to determine.[6] Now the Big-Endian exiles have found so much credit in the Emperor of Blefuscu's court, and so much private assistance and encouragement from their party here at home, that a bloody war hath been carried on between the two empires for six and thirty moons with various success; during which time we have lost forty capital ships and a much greater number of smaller vessels, together with thirty thousand of our best seamen and soldiers; and the damage received by the enemy is reckoned to be somewhat greater than ours. However, they have now equipped a numerous fleet and are just preparing to make a descent upon us; and his Imperial Majesty, placing great confidence in your valour and strength, hath commanded me to lay this account of his affairs before you.

I desired the Secretary to present my humble duty to the Emperor, and to let him know that I thought it would not become me, who was a foreigner, to interfere with parties; but I was ready, with the hazard of my life, to defend his person and state against all invaders.

Chapter Five: The author by an extraordinary stratagem prevents an invasion. A high title of honour is conferred upon him. Ambassadors arrive from the Emperor of Blefuscu and sue for peace. The Empress's apartment on fire by an accident. The author instrumental in saving the rest of the palace.

The empire of Blefuscu is an island situated to the northnortheast side of Lilliput, from whence it is parted only by a channel of eight hundred yards wide. I had not yet seen it, and upon this notice of an intended invasion, I avoided appearing

[6] The chief magistrate would here be the ultimate administrative authority in the state—in England, a limited monarchy, Parliament; in Lilliput, the Emperor.

on that side of the coast, for fear of being discovered by some
of the enemy's ships, who had received no intelligence of me,
all intercourse between the two empires having been strictly
forbidden during the war upon pain of death, and an embargo
laid by our Emperor upon all vessels whatsoever. I communicated to his Majesty a project I had formed of seizing the
enemy's whole fleet; which, as our scouts assured us, lay at
anchor in the harbour ready to sail with the first fair wind. I
consulted the most experienced seamen upon the depth of the
channel, which they had often plumbed; who told me that in
the middle at high water it was seventy *glumgluffs* deep, which
is about six foot of European measure, and the rest of it fifty
glumgluffs at most. I walked to the northeast coast over against
Blefuscu; where, lying down behind a hillock, I took out my
small pocket perspective-glass, and viewed the enemy's fleet at
anchor, consisting of about fifty men-of-war and a great number of transports: I then came back to my house and gave
order (for which I had a warrant) for a great quantity of the
strongest cable and bars of iron. The cable was about as thick
as packthread, and the bars of the length and size of a knitting-
needle. I trebled the cable to make it stronger, and for the same
reason I twisted three of the iron bars together, bending the
extremities into a hook. Having thus fixed fifty hooks to as
many cables, I went back to the northeast coast, and putting
off my coat, shoes, and stockings, walked into the sea in my
leathern jerkin, about half an hour before high water. I waded
with what haste I could, and swam in the middle about thirty
yards until I felt ground; I arrived at the fleet in less than half
an hour. The enemy was so frighted when they saw me that
they leaped out of their ships and swam to shore, where there
could not be fewer than thirty thousand souls. I then took
my tackling, and fastening a hook to the hole at the prow of
each, I tied all the cords together at the end. While I was thus
employed, the enemy discharged several thousand arrows,
many of which stuck in my hands and face and, besides the excessive smart, gave me much disturbance in my work. My

greatest apprehension was for my eyes, which I should have infallibly lost if I had not suddenly thought of an expedient. I kept among other little necessaries a pair of spectacles in a private pocket, which, as I observed before, had escaped the Emperor's searchers. These I took out and fastened as strongly as I could upon my nose, and thus armed went on boldly with my work in spite of the enemy's arrows, many of which struck against the glasses of my spectacles, but without any other effect, further than a little to discompose them. I had now fastened all the hooks and, taking the knot in my hand, began to pull; but not a ship would stir, for they were all too fast held by their anchors, so that the boldest part of my enterprise remained. I therefore let go the cord and, leaving the hooks fixed to the ships, I resolutely cut with my knife the cables that fastened the anchors, receiving above two hundred shots in my face and hands; then I took up the knotted end of the cables to which my hooks were tied, and with great ease drew fifty of the enemy's largest men-of-war after me.

The Blefuscudians, who had not the least imagination of what I intended, were at first confounded with astonishment. They had seen me cut the cables, and thought my design was only to let the ships run adrift or fall foul on each other: but when they perceived the whole fleet moving in order, and saw me pulling at the end, they set up such a scream of grief and despair that it is almost impossible to describe or conceive. When I had got out of danger, I stopped a while to pick out the arrows that stuck in my hands and face, and rubbed on some of the same ointment that was given me at my first arrival, as I have formerly mentioned. I then took off my spectacles and, waiting about an hour until the tide was a little fallen, I waded through the middle with my cargo, and arrived safe at the royal port of Lilliput.

The Emperor and his whole court stood on the shore expecting[1] the issue of this great adventure. They saw the ships move

[1] Awaiting.

forward in a large half-moon, but could not discern me, who
was up to my breast in water. When I advanced to the middle
of the channel, they were yet more in pain, because I was
under water to my neck. The Emperor concluded me to be
drowned, and that the enemy's fleet was approaching in a hos-
tile manner: but he was soon eased of his fears, for, the channel growing shallower every step I made, I came in a short
time within hearing, and, holding up the end of the cable by
which the fleet was fastened, I cried in a loud voice, "Long
live the most puissant Emperor of Lilliput!" This great prince
received me at my landing with all possible encomiums, and
created me a *Nardac* upon the spot, which is the highest title
of honour among them.

His Majesty desired I would take some other opportunity of
bringing all the rest of his enemy's ships into his ports. And so
unmeasurable is the ambition of princes, that he seemed to
think of nothing less than reducing the whole empire of Blefuscu into a province and governing it by a viceroy; of destroying the Big-Endian exiles and compelling that people to
break the smaller end of their eggs, by which he would remain
sole monarch of the whole world. But I endeavoured to divert
him from this design by many arguments drawn from the
topics of policy as well as justice: and I plainly protested that
I would never be an instrument of bringing a free and brave
people into slavery. And when the matter was debated in council, the wisest part of the ministry were of my opinion.

This open bold declaration of mine was so opposite to the
schemes and politics of his Imperial Majesty that he could
never forgive me; he mentioned it in a very artful manner at
council, where I was told that some of the wisest appeared, at
least, by their silence, to be of my opinion; but others, who
were my secret enemies, could not forbear some expressions,
which by a side-wind reflected on me. And from this time
began an intrigue between his Majesty and a junta of ministers
maliciously bent against me, which broke out in less than two
months, and had like to have ended in my utter destruction.

Of so little weight are the greatest services to princes when put into the balance with a refusal to gratify their passions.

About three weeks after this exploit, there arrived a solemn embassy from Blefuscu with humble offers of a peace; which was soon concluded upon conditions very advantageous to our Emperor, wherewith I shall not trouble the reader. There were six ambassadors with a train of about five hundred persons, and their entry was very magnificent, suitable to the grandeur of their master and the importance of their business. When their treaty was finished, wherein I did them several good offices by the credit I now had, or at least appeared to have, at court, their Excellencies, who were privately told how much I had been their friend, made me a visit in form. They began with many compliments upon my valour and generosity, invited me to that kingdom in the Emperor their master's name, and desired me to show them some proofs of my prodigious strength, of which they had heard so many wonders; wherein I readily obliged them, but shall not interrupt the reader with the particulars.

When I had for some time entertained their Excellencies to their infinite satisfaction and surprise, I desired they would do me the honour to present my most humble respects to the Emperor their master, the renown of whose virtues had so justly filled the whole world with admiration, and whose royal person I resolved to attend before I returned to my own country: accordingly, the next time I had the honour to see our Emperor, I desired his general licence to wait on the Blefuscudian monarch, which he was pleased to grant me, as I could plainly perceive, in a very cold manner; but could not guess the reason, till I had a whisper from a certain person that Flimnap and Bolgolam had represented my intercourse with those ambassadors as a mark of disaffection, from which I am sure my heart was wholly free. And this was the first time I began to conceive some imperfect idea of courts and ministers.

It is to be observed that these ambassadors spoke to me by an interpreter, the languages of both empires differing as much

from each other as any two in Europe, and each nation prid-
ing itself upon the antiquity, beauty, and energy of their own
tongues, with an avowed contempt for that of their neighbour;
yet our Emperor, standing upon the advantage he had got by
the seizure of their fleet, obliged them to deliver their credentials and make their speech in the Lilliputian tongue. And
it must be confessed, that from the great intercourse of trade
and commerce between both realms, from the continual reception of exiles, which is mutual among them, and from the custom in each empire to send their young nobility and richer
gentry to the other, in order to polish themselves by seeing the
world and understanding men and manners, there are few persons of distinction, or merchants, or seamen, who dwell in the
maritime parts, but what can hold conversation in both
tongues; as I found some weeks after, when I went to pay my
respects to the Emperor of Blefuscu, which in the midst of
great misfortunes through the malice of my enemies, proved
a very happy adventure to me, as I shall relate in its proper
place.

The reader may remember that, when I signed those articles
upon which I recovered my liberty, there were some which I
disliked upon account of their being too servile, neither could
anything but an extreme necessity have forced me to submit.
But being now a *Nardac*, of the highest rank in that empire,
such offices were looked upon as below my dignity, and the
Emperor (to do him justice) never once mentioned them to
me. However, it was not long before I had an opportunity of
doing his Majesty, at least as I then thought, a most signal service. I was alarmed at midnight with the cries of many hundred
people at my door; by which being suddenly awaked, I was
in some kind of terror. I heard the word *burglum* repeated
incessantly: several of the Emperor's court, making their way
through the crowd, intreated me to come immediately to the
palace, where her Imperial Majesty's apartment was on fire, by
the carelessness of a maid of honour, who fell asleep while she
was reading a romance. I got up in an instant; and orders

being given to clear the way before me, and it being likewise a moonshine night, I made a shift to get to the palace without trampling on any of the people. I found they had already applied ladders to the walls of the apartment, and were well provided with buckets, but the water was at some distance. These buckets were about the size of a large thimble, and the poor people supplied me with them as fast as they could; but the flame was so violent that they did little good. I might easily have stifled it with my coat, which I unfortunately left behind me for haste, and came away only in my leathern jerkin. The case seemed wholly desperate and deplorable, and this magnificent palace would have infallibly been burnt down to the ground if, by a presence of mind unusual to me, I had not suddenly thought of an expedient. I had the evening before drank plentifully of a most delicious wine called *glimigrim* (the Blefuscudians call it *flunec*, but ours is esteemed the better sort), which is very diuretic. By the luckiest chance in the world, I had not discharged myself of any part of it. The heat I had contracted by coming very near the flames and by my labouring to quench them, made the wine begin to operate by urine; which I voided in such a quantity, and applied so well to the proper places, that in three minutes the fire was wholly extinguished, and the rest of that noble pile, which had cost so many ages in erecting, preserved from destruction.

It was now daylight, and I returned to my house without waiting to congratulate with the Emperor; because, although I had done a very eminent piece of service, yet I could not tell how his Majesty might resent the manner by which I had performed it: for, by the fundamental laws of the realm, it is capital in any person, of what quality soever, to make water within the precincts of the palace.[2] But I was a little comforted by a message from his Majesty that he would give orders to

[2] Finding so trivial an act worthy of capital punishment is, among other things, an exaggeration of the formal etiquette maintained at Versailles under Louis XIV. For other explanations, see Appendix One.

the Grand Justiciary for passing my pardon in form; which, however, I could not obtain. And I was privately assured that the Empress, conceiving the greatest abhorrence of what I had done, removed to the most distant side of the court, firmly resolved that those buildings should never be repaired for her use; and, in the presence of her chief confidents, could not forbear vowing revenge.

Chapter Six: Of the inhabitants of Lilliput; their learning, laws, and customs. The manner of educating their children. The author's way of living in that country. His vindication of a great lady.

Although I intend to leave the description of this empire to a particular treatise, yet in the meantime I am content to gratify the curious reader with some general ideas. As the common size of the natives is somewhat under six inches, so there is an exact proportion in all other animals as well as plants and trees: for instance, the tallest horses and oxen are between four and five inches in height, the sheep an inch and a half, more or less; their geese about the bigness of a sparrow, and so the several gradations downwards till you come to the smallest, which, to my sight, were almost invisible; but Nature hath adapted the eyes of the Lilliputians to all objects proper for their view: they see with great exactness, but at no great distance. And to show the sharpness of their sight towards objects that are near, I have been much pleased with observing a cook pulling a lark, which was not so large as a common fly; and a young girl threading an invisible needle with invisible silk. Their tallest trees are about seven foot high; I mean some of those in the great royal park, the tops whereof I could but just reach with my fist clenched. The other vegetables are in the same proportion; but this I leave to the reader's imagination.

I shall say but little at present of their learning, which for many ages hath flourished in all its branches among them: but their manner of writing is very peculiar, being neither from the left to the right, like the Europeans; nor from the right to the left, like the Arabians; nor from up to down, like the Chinese; nor from down to up, like the Cascagians; [1] but aslant from one corner of the paper to the other, like ladies in England.

They bury their dead with their heads directly downwards, because they hold an opinion that in eleven thousand moons they are all to rise again, in which period the earth (which they conceive to be flat) will turn upside down; and by this means they shall, at their resurrection, be found ready standing on their feet.[2] The learned among them confess the absurdity of this doctrine, but the practice still continues, in compliance to the vulgar.

There are some laws and customs in this empire very peculiar, and if they were not so directly contrary to those of my own dear country, I should be tempted to say a little in their justification. It is only to be wished that they were as well executed. The first I shall mention relates to informers. All crimes against the state are punished here with the utmost severity; but if the person accused make his innocence plainly to appear upon his trial, the accuser is immediately put to an ignominious death; and out of his goods or lands, the innocent person is quadruply recompensed for the loss of his time, for the danger he underwent, for the hardship of his imprisonment, and for all the charges he hath been at in making his defence. Or, if that fund be deficient, it is largely supplied by the crown. The Emperor doth also confer on him some public mark of his favour, and proclamation is made of his innocence through the whole city.

[1] An imaginary people. This paragraph is a close parody of actual travel literature.

[2] A reference to the old custom of burying bodies with their feet to the East.

They look upon fraud as a greater crime than theft, and
therefore seldom fail to punish it with death; for they allege
that care and vigilance, with a very common understanding,
may preserve a man's goods from thieves, but honesty hath no
fence against superior cunning: and since it is necessary that
there should be a perpetual intercourse of buying and selling
and dealing upon credit, where fraud is permitted and con-
nived at, or hath no law to punish it, the honest dealer is always undone, and the knave gets the advantage. I remember
when I was once interceding with the King for a criminal who
had wronged his master of a great sum of money, which he
had received by order and ran away with; and happening to
tell his Majesty, by way of extenuation, that it was only a
breach of trust; the Emperor thought it monstrous in me to
offer, as a defence, the greatest aggravation of the crime: and
truly I had little to say in return, farther than the common
answer, that different nations had different customs; for, I confess, I was heartily ashamed.

Although we usually call reward and punishment the two
hinges upon which all government turns, yet I could never observe this maxim to be put in practice by any nation except
that of Lilliput. Whoever can there bring sufficient proof that
he hath strictly observed the laws of his country for seventy-
three moons, hath a claim to certain privileges according to his
quality and condition of life, with a proportionable sum of
money out of a fund appropriated for that use: he likewise ac-
quires the title of *Snilpall*, or *Legal*, which is added to his
name, but doth not descend to his posterity. And these people
thought it a prodigious defect of policy among us, when I
told them that our laws were enforced only by penalties without any mention of reward. It is upon this account that the
image of Justice, in their courts of judicature, is formed with
six eyes, two before, as many behind, and on each side one, to
signify circumspection; with a bag of gold open in her right
hand, and a sword sheathed in her left, to show she is more
disposed to reward than to punish.

In choosing persons for all employments, they have more

regard to good morals than to great abilities; for, since government is necessary to mankind, they believe that the common size of human understandings is fitted to some station or other, and that Providence never intended to make the management of public affairs a mystery to be comprehended only by a few persons of sublime genius, of which there seldom are three born in an age: but they suppose truth, justice, temperance, and the like to be in every man's power; the practice of which virtues, assisted by experience and a good intention, would qualify any man for the service of his country, except where a course of study is required. But they thought the want of moral virtues was so far from being supplied by superior endowments of the minds that employments could never be put into such dangerous hands as those of persons so qualified; and at least, that the mistakes committed by ignorance in a virtuous disposition would never be of such fatal consequence to the public weal as the practices of a man whose inclinations led him to be corrupt, and had great abilities to manage, to multiply, and defend his corruptions.

In like manner, the disbelief of a divine Providence renders a man uncapable of holding any public station; for since kings avow themselves to be the deputies of Providence, the Lilliputians think nothing can be more absurd than for a prince to employ such men as disown the authority under which he acts.

In relating these and the following laws, I would only be understood to mean the original institutions, and not the most scandalous corruptions into which these people are fallen by the degenerate nature of man. For as to that infamous practice of acquiring great employments by dancing on the ropes, or badges of favour and distinction by leaping over sticks and creeping under them, the reader is to observe that they were first introduced by the grandfather of the Emperor now reigning, and grew to the present height by the gradual increase of party and faction.[3]

---

[3] As the sale of honors or titles was introduced by James I of England. The corruption and decline of admirable institutions had

Ingratitude is among them a capital crime, as we read it to have been in some other countries; for they reason thus, that whoever makes ill returns to his benefactor must needs be a common enemy to the rest of mankind, from whom he hath received no obligation, and therefore such a man is not fit to live.

Their notions relating to the duties of parents and children differ extremely from ours. For, since the conjunction of male and female is founded upon the great law of nature, in order to propagate and continue the species, the Lilliputians will needs have it that men and women are joined together like other animals by the motives of concupiscence; and that their tenderness towards their young proceeds from the like natural principle: for which reason they will never allow that a child is under any obligation to his father for begetting him or to his mother for bringing him into the world; which, considering the miseries of human life, was neither a benefit in itself nor intended so by his parents, whose thoughts in their love-encounters were otherwise employed. Upon these and the like reasonings, their opinion is that parents are the last of all others to be trusted with the education of their own children: and therefore they have in every town public nurseries,[4] where all parents, except cottagers and labourers, are obliged to send their infants of both sexes to be reared and educated when they come to the age of twenty moons, at which time they are supposed to have some rudiments of docility. These schools are of several kinds, suited to different qualities and to both sexes. They have certain professors well skilled in preparing

---

been the subject of Swift's *A Tale of a Tub* (1704), where the history of the churches is seen as their steady departure from the teachings of the Bible and their partial recovery with the Reformation.

[4] The "nurseries" are schools for "infants" (those not legally adult) of all ages, as succeeding paragraphs make clear. There is a general resemblance to the system of education in Plato's *Republic*.

children for such a condition of life as befits the rank of their parents and their own capacities as well as inclinations. I shall first say something of the male nurseries and then of the female.

The nurseries for males of noble or eminent birth are provided with grave and learned professors and their several deputies. The clothes and food of the children are plain and simple. They are bred up in the principles of honour, justice, courage, modesty, clemency, religion, and love of their country; they are always employed in some business except in the times of eating and sleeping, which are very short, and two hours for diversions, consisting of bodily exercises. They are dressed by men until four years of age, and then are obliged to dress themselves although their quality be ever so great; and the women attendants, who are aged proportionably to ours at fifty, perform only the most menial offices. They are never suffered to converse with servants, but go together in small or greater numbers to take their diversions, and always in the presence of a professor or one of his deputies; whereby they avoid those early bad impressions of folly and vice to which our children are subject. Their parents are suffered to see them only twice a year; the visit is not to last above an hour. They are allowed to kiss the child at meeting and parting; but a professor, who always stands by on those occasions, will not suffer them to whisper or use any fondling expressions, or bring any presents of toys, sweetmeats, and the like.

The pension from each family for the education and entertainment of a child, upon failure of due payment, is levied by the Emperor's officers.

The nurseries for children of ordinary gentlemen, merchants, traders, and handicrafts, are managed proportionably after the same manner; only those designed for trades are put out apprentices at seven years old, whereas those of persons of quality continue in their nurseries till fifteen, which answers to one and twenty with us: but the confinement is gradually lessened for the last three years.

In the female nurseries, the young girls of quality are educated much like the males, only they are dressed by orderly servants of their own sex, but always in the presence of a professor or deputy, until they come to dress themselves, which is at five years old. And if it be found that these nurses ever presume to entertain the girls with frightful or foolish stories, or the common follies practiced by chambermaids among us, they are publicly whipped thrice about the city, imprisoned for a year, and banished for life to the most desolate parts of the country. Thus the young ladies there are as much ashamed of being cowards and fools as the men, and despise all personal ornaments beyond decency and cleanliness: neither did I perceive any difference in their education made by their difference of sex, only that the exercises of the females were not altogether so robust, and that some rules were given them relating to domestic life, and a smaller compass of learning was enjoined them: for their maxim is that among people of quality a wife should be always a reasonable and agreeable companion, because she cannot always be young. When the girls are twelve years old, which among them is the marriageable age, their parents or guardians take them home, with great expressions of gratitude to the professors, and seldom without tears of the young lady and her companions.

In the nurseries of females of the meaner sort,[5] the children are instructed in all kinds of works proper for their sex and their several degrees: those intended for apprentices are dismissed at seven years old, the rest are kept to eleven.

The meaner families who have children at these nurseries are obliged, besides their annual pension, which is as low as possible, to return to the steward of the nursery a small monthly share of their gettings, to be a portion for the child; and therefore all parents are limited in their expenses by the law. For the Lilliputians think nothing can be more unjust than that

[5] Humbler in social station. The class structure of Lilliputian education would have seemed acceptable to most people in Swift's day.

people, in subservience to their own appetites, should bring children into the world and leave the burthen of supporting them on the public. As to persons of quality, they give security to appropriate a certain sum for each child, suitable to their condition; and these funds are always managed with good husbandry and the most exact justice.

The cottagers and labourers keep their children at home, their business being only to till and cultivate the earth, and therefore their education is of little consequence to the public; but the old and diseased among them are supported by hospitals:[6] for begging is a trade unknown in this empire.

And here it may perhaps divert the curious reader to give some account of my domestic,[7] and my manner of living in this country, during a residence of nine months and thirteen days. Having a head mechanically turned, and being likewise forced by necessity, I had made for myself a table and chair convenient enough, out of the largest trees in the royal park. Two hundred sempstresses were employed to make me shirts, and linen for my bed and table, all of the strongest and coarsest kind they could get; which, however, they were forced to quilt together in several folds, for the thickest was some degrees finer than lawn. Their linen is usually three inches wide, and three foot make a piece. The sempstresses took my measure as I lay on the ground, one standing at my neck and another at my midleg, with a strong cord extended that each held by the end, while the third measured the length of the cord with a rule of an inch long. Then they measured my right thumb and desired no more; for by a mathematical computation that twice round the thumb is once round the wrist, and so on to the neck and the waist, and by the help of my old shirt, which I displayed on the ground before them for a pattern, they fitted me exactly. Three hundred tailors were employed in the same manner to make me clothes; but they had another

[6] Public "homes" provided by the state.
[7] Household.

contrivance for taking my measure. I kneeled down, and they raised a ladder from the ground to my neck; upon this ladder one of them mounted and let fall a plumb-line from my collar to the floor, which just answered the length of my coat; but my waist and arms I measured myself. When my clothes were finished, which was done in my house (for the largest of theirs would not have been able to hold them) they looked like the patchwork made by the ladies in England, only that mine were all of a colour.

I had three hundred cooks to dress my victuals, in little convenient huts built about my house, where they and their families lived, and prepared me two dishes apiece. I took up twenty waiters in my hand, and placed them on the table; an hundred more attended below on the ground, some with dishes of meat and some with barrels of wine and other liquors, slung on their shoulders; all which the waiters above drew up as I wanted, in a very ingenious manner by certain cords, as we draw the bucket up a well in Europe. A dish of their meat was a good mouthful, and a barrel of their liquor a reasonable draught. Their mutton yields to ours, but their beef is excellent. I have had a sirloin so large that I have been forced to make three bits of it; but this is rare. My servants were astonished to see me eat it bones and all, as in our country we do the leg of a lark. Their geese and turkeys I usually eat at a mouthful, and I must confess they far exceed ours. Of their smaller fowl I could take up twenty or thirty at the end of my knife.

One day his Imperial Majesty, being informed of my way of living, desired that himself and his royal consort, with the young princes of the blood of both sexes, might have the happiness (as he was pleased to call it) of dining with me. They came accordingly, and I placed them upon chairs of state on my table, just over-against me, with their guards about them. Flimnap, the Lord High Treasurer, attended there likewise, with his white staff,[8] and I observed he often looked on me

[8] The symbol of the Lord Treasurer (the "Prime Minister") in England as well.

with a sour countenance, which I would not seem to regard, but eat more than usual, in honour to my dear country, as well as to fill the court with admiration. I have some private reasons to believe, that this visit from his Majesty gave Flimnap an opportunity of doing me ill offices to his master. That minister had always been my secret enemy, although he outwardly caressed me more than was usual to the moroseness of his nature. He represented to the Emperor the low condition of his treasury; that he was forced to take up money at great discount; that exchequer bills would not circulate under nine per cent below par; that I had cost his Majesty above a million and a half of *sprugs* (their greatest gold coin, about the bigness of a spangle); and upon the whole, that it would be advisable in the Emperor to take the first fair occasion of dismissing me.

I am here obliged to vindicate the reputation of an excellent lady, who was an innocent sufferer upon my account. The Treasurer took a fancy to be jealous of his wife, from the malice of some evil tongues who informed him that her Grace had taken a violent affection for my person, and the court-scandal ran for some time that she once came privately to my lodging. This I solemnly declare to be a most infamous falsehood, without any grounds, farther than that her Grace was pleased to treat me with all innocent marks of freedom and friendship. I own she came often to my house, but always publicly, nor ever without three more in the coach, who were usually her sister and young daughter and some particular acquaintance; but this was common to many other ladies of the court. And I still appeal to my servants round, whether they at any time saw a coach at my door without knowing what persons were in it. On those occasions, when a servant had given me notice, my custom was to go immediately to the door; and, after paying my respects, to take up the coach and two horses very carefully in my hands (for if there were six horses, the postillion always unharnessed four) and place them on a table, where I had fixed a movable rim quite round, of five inches high, to prevent accidents. And I have often had four coaches and horses at once on my table full of company, while

I sat in my chair leaning my face towards them; and when I was engaged with one set, the coachmen would gently drive the others round my table. I have passed many an afternoon very agreeably in these conversations. But I defy the Treasurer, or his two informers (I will name them, and let them make their best of it), Clustril and Drunlo, to prove that any person ever came to me *incognito*, except the Secretary Reldresal, who was sent by express command of his Imperial Majesty, as I have before related. I should not have dwelt so long upon this particular, if it had not been a point wherein the reputation of a great lady is so nearly concerned, to say nothing of my own; although I had the honour to be a *Nardac*, which the Treasurer himself is not; for all the world knows he is only a *Clumglum*, a title inferior by one degree, as that of a marquis is to a duke in England, yet I allow he preceded me in right of his post. These false informations, which I afterwards came to the knowledge of, by an accident not proper to mention, made the Treasurer show his lady for some time an ill countenance, and me a worse. For although he were at last undeceived and reconciled to her, yet I lost all credit with him, and found my interest decline very fast with the Emperor himself, who was indeed too much governed by that favourite.

Chapter Seven: The author, being informed of a design to accuse him of high treason, makes his escape to Blefuscu. His reception there.

Before I proceed to give an account of my leaving this kingdom, it may be proper to inform the reader of a private intrigue which had been for two months forming against me.

I had been hitherto all my life a stranger to courts, for which I was unqualified by the meanness of my condition. I had indeed heard and read enough of the dispositions of great princes and ministers; but never expected to have found such terrible effects of them in so remote a country, governed, as I thought, by very different maxims from those in Europe.

When I was just preparing to pay my attendance on the Emperor of Blefuscu, a considerable person at court (to whom I had been very serviceable at a time when he lay under the highest displeasure of his Imperial Majesty) came to my house very privately at night in a close chair and, without sending his name, desired admittance: the chairmen were dismissed; I put the chair, with his Lordship in it, into my coat-pocket; and giving orders to a trusty servant to say I was indisposed and gone to sleep, I fastened the door of my house, placed the chair on the table, according to my usual custom, and sat down by it. After the common salutations were over, observing his Lordship's countenance full of concern and enquiring into the reason, he desired I would hear him with patience in a matter that highly concerned my honour and my life. His speech was to the following effect, for I took notes of it as soon as he left me.

"You are to know," said he, "that several committees of council have been lately called in the most private manner on your account: and it is but two days since his Majesty came to a full resolution.

"You are very sensible that Skyresh Bolgolam (*Galbet*, or High Admiral) hath been your mortal enemy almost ever since your arrival. His original reasons I know not, but his hatred is much encreased since your great success against Blefuscu, by which his glory, as Admiral, is obscured. This lord, in conjunction with Flimnap the High Treasurer, whose enmity against you is notorious on account of his lady, Limtoc the General, Lalcon the Chamberlain, and Balmuff the Grand Justiciary, have prepared articles of impeachment against you, for treason and other capital crimes."

This preface made me so impatient, being conscious of my own merits and innocence, that I was going to interrupt; when he entreated me to be silent, and thus proceeded.

"Out of gratitude for the favours you have done me, I procured information of the whole proceedings, and a copy of the articles, wherein I venture my head for your service."

Articles of Impeachment [1] against Quinbus Flestrin (the Man-Mountain).

ARTICLE I

Whereas, by a statute made in the reign of his Imperial Majesty *Calin Deffar Plune*, it is enacted, that whoever shall make water within the precincts of the royal palace shall be liable to the pains and penalties of high treason: notwithstanding, the said *Quinbus Flestrin*, in open breach of the said law, under colour of extinguishing the fire kindled in the apartment of his Majesty's most dear imperial consort, did maliciously, traitorously, and devilishly, by discharge of his urine, put out the said fire kindled in the said apartment, lying and being within the precincts of the said royal palace, against the statute in that case provided, etc., against the duty, etc.

ARTICLE II

That the said *Quinbus Flestrin*, having brought the imperial fleet of Blefuscu into the royal port, and being afterwards commanded by his Imperial Majesty to seize all the other ships of the said empire of Blefuscu, and reduce that empire to a province, to be governed by a viceroy from hence, and to destroy and put to death not only all the Big-Endian exiles but likewise all the people of that empire who would not immediately forsake the Big-Endian heresy: he, the said Flestrin, like a false traitor against his most Auspicious, Serene, Imperial Majesty, did petition to be excused from the said service, upon pretence of unwillingness to force the consciences or destroy the liberties and lives of an innocent people.

[1] For the resemblance of these accusations to those brought against Oxford and Bolingbroke, see Appendix One.

ARTICLE III

That whereas certain ambassadors arrived from the court of Blefuscu to sue for peace in his Majesty's court: he the said Flestrin did, like a false traitor, aid, abet, comfort, and divert the said ambassadors, although he knew them to be servants to a prince who was lately an open enemy to his Imperial Majesty and in open war against his said Majesty.

ARTICLE IV

That the said *Quinbus Flestrin*, contrary to the duty of a faithful subject, is now preparing to make a voyage to the court and empire of Blefuscu, for which he hath received only verbal licence from his Imperial Majesty; and under colour of the said licence, doth falsely and traitorously intend to take the said voyage, and thereby to aid, comfort, and abet the Emperor of Blefuscu, so late an enemy and in open war with his Imperial Majesty aforesaid.

"There are some other articles, but these are the most important, of which I have read you an abstract.

"In the several debates upon this impeachment, it must be confessed that his Majesty gave many marks of his great lenity, often urging the services you had done him, and endeavouring to extenuate your crimes. The Treasurer and Admiral insisted that you should be put to the most painful and ignominious death, by setting fire on your house at night, and the General was to attend with twenty thousand men armed with poisoned arrows to shoot you on the face and hands. Some of your servants were to have private orders to strew a poisonous juice on your shirts and sheets, which would soon make you tear your own flesh and die in the utmost torture. The General came into the same opinion, so that for a long time there was a majority against you. But his Majesty resolving, if possible, to spare your life, at last brought off the Chamberlain.

"Upon this incident, Reldresal, Principal Secretary for Private Affairs, who always approved himself your true friend, was commanded by the Emperor to deliver his opinion, which he accordingly did; and therein justified the good thoughts you have of him. He allowed your crimes to be great, but that still there was room for mercy, the most commendable virtue in a prince, and for which his Majesty was so justly celebrated. He said the friendship between you and him was so well known to the world, that perhaps the most honourable board might think him partial: however, in obedience to the command he had received, he would freely offer his sentiments. That if his Majesty, in consideration of your services, and pursuant to his own merciful disposition, would please to spare your life and only give order to put out both your eyes, he humbly conceived that by this expedient justice might in some measure be satisfied, and all the world would applaud the *lenity* of the Emperor, as well as the fair and generous proceedings of those who have the honour to be his counsellors. That the loss of your eyes would be no impediment to your bodily strength, by which you might still be useful to his Majesty. That blindness is an addition to courage, by concealing dangers from us; that the fear you had for your eyes was the greatest difficulty in bringing over the enemy's fleet, and it would be sufficient for you to see by the eyes of the ministers, since the greatest princes do no more.

"This proposal was received with the utmost disapprobation by the whole board. Bolgolam, the Admiral, could not preserve his temper; but rising up in fury, said he wondered how the Secretary durst presume to give his opinion for preserving the life of a traitor: that the services you had performed were, by all true reasons of state, the great aggravation of your crimes; that you, who were able to extinguish the fire by discharge of urine in her Majesty's apartment (which he mentioned with horror), might, at another time, raise an inundation by the same means to drown the whole palace; and the same strength which enabled you to bring over the enemy's fleet might serve, upon the first discontent, to carry it back: that he had good reasons to think you were a Big-Endian in your heart; and as treason begins in the heart before it appears in overt acts, so he accused you as a traitor on that account, and therefore insisted you should be put to death.

"The Treasurer was of the same opinion; he showed to what straits his Majesty's revenue was reduced by the charge of maintaining you, which would soon grow insupportable: that the Secretary's expedient of putting out your eyes was so far from being a remedy against this evil that it would probably increase it, as it is manifest from the common practice of blinding some kind of fowl, after which they fed the faster and grew sooner fat: that his sacred Majesty and the council, who are your judges, were in their own consciences fully convinced of your guilt, which was a sufficient argument to condemn you to death, without the formal proofs required by the strict letter of the law.

"But his Imperial Majesty, fully determined against capital punishment, was graciously pleased to say that since the council thought the loss of your eyes too easy a censure, some other may be inflicted hereafter. And your friend the Secretary humbly desiring to be heard again, in answer to what the Treasurer had objected concerning the great charge his Majesty was at in maintaining you, said that his Excellency, who had the sole disposal of the Emperor's revenue, might easily provide against this evil by gradually lessening your establishment; by which, for want of sufficient food, you would grow weak and faint and lose your appetite, and consequently decay and consume in a few months; neither would the stench of your carcass be then so dangerous when it should become more than half diminished; and immediately upon your death, five or six thousand of his Majesty's subjects might, in two or three days, cut your flesh from your bones, take it away by cartloads, and bury it in distant parts to prevent infection, leaving the skeleton as a monument of admiration to posterity.

"Thus by the great friendship of the Secretary, the whole affair was compromised. It was strictly enjoined that the project of starving you by degrees should be kept a secret, but the sentence of putting out your eyes was entered on the books; none dissenting except Bolgolam the Admiral, who, being a creature of the Empress, was perpetually instigated by her Majesty to insist upon your death, she having borne perpetual malice against you on account of that infamous and illegal method you took to extinguish the fire in her apartment.

"In three days your friend the Secretary will be directed to come to your house and read before you the articles of impeachment; and then to signify the great lenity and favour of his Majesty and council, whereby you are only condemned to the loss of your eyes, which his Majesty doth not question you will gratefully and humbly submit to; and twenty of his Majesty's surgeons will attend in order to see the operation well performed, by discharging very sharp-pointed arrows into the balls of your eyes as you lie on the ground.

"I leave to your prudence what measures you will take; and to avoid suspicion, I must immediately return in as private a manner as I came."

His Lordship did so, and I remained alone, under many doubts and perplexities of mind.

It was a custom introduced by this prince and his ministry (very different, as I have been assured, from the practices of former times) that after the court had decreed any cruel execution, either to gratify the monarch's resentment or the malice of a favourite, the Emperor always made a speech to his whole council, expressing his great lenity and tenderness, as qualities known and confessed by all the world. This speech was immediately published through the kingdom; nor did anything terrify the people so much as those encomiums on his Majesty's mercy; because it was observed that the more these praises were enlarged and insisted on, the more inhuman was the punishment, and the sufferer more innocent. Yet as to myself, I must confess, having never been designed for a courtier either by my birth or education, I was so ill a judge of things that I could not discover the lenity and favour of this sentence, but conceived it (perhaps erroneously) rather to be rigorous than gentle. I sometimes thought of standing my trial, for although I could not deny the facts alleged in the several articles, yet I hoped they would admit of some extenuations. But having in my life perused many state trials, which I ever observed to terminate as the judges thought fit to direct, I durst not rely on so dangerous a decision in so critical a juncture and against such powerful enemies. Once I was strongly bent upon resistance, for, while I had liberty, the whole strength of that empire could hardly subdue me, and I might easily with stones pelt the metropolis to pieces; but I soon rejected that project with horror, by remembering the oath I had made to the Emperor, the favours I received from him, and the high title of *Nardac* he conferred upon me. Neither had I so soon learned the gratitude of courtiers to persuade myself that his Majesty's present severities acquitted me of all past obligations.

At last I fixed upon a resolution for which it is probable I may incur some censure, and not unjustly; for I confess I owe the preserving my eyes, and consequently my liberty, to my own great rashness and want of experience: because if I had then known the nature of princes and ministers, which I have since observed in many other courts, and their methods of treating criminals less obnoxious than myself, I should with great alacrity and readiness have submitted to so easy a punishment. But hurried on by the precipitancy of youth, and having his Imperial Majesty's licence to pay my attendance upon the Emperor of Blefuscu, I took this opportunity, before the three days were elapsed, to send a letter to my friend the Secretary, signifying my resolution of setting out that morning for Blefuscu pursuant to the leave I had got; and without waiting for an answer, I went to that side of the island where our fleet lay. I seized a large man-of-war, tied a cable to the prow, and, lifting up the anchors, I stripped myself, put my clothes (together with my coverlet, which I carried under my arm) into the vessel, and drawing it after me, between wading and swimming arrived at the royal port of Blefuscu, where the people had long expected me; they lent me two guides to direct me to the capital city, which is of the same name. I held them in my hands until I came within two hundred yards of the gate, and desired them to signify my arrival to one of the secretaries, and let him know I there waited his Majesty's commands. I had an answer in about an hour that his Majesty, attended by the royal family and great officers of the court, was coming out to receive me. I advanced a hundred yards. The Emperor and his train alighted from their horses, the Empress and ladies from their coaches, and I did not perceive they were in any fright or concern. I lay on the ground to kiss his Majesty's and the Empress's hand. I told his Majesty that I was come according to my promise, and with the licence of the Emperor my master, to have the honour of seeing so mighty a monarch, and to offer him any service in my power consistent with my duty to my own prince; not mentioning a word of my disgrace, because I had hitherto no regular information of it and might suppose myself wholly ignorant of any such design; neither could I reasonably conceive that the Emperor would discover [2] the secret while I was out of his power: wherein, however, it soon appeared I was deceived.

I shall not trouble the reader with the particular account of my reception at this court, which was suitable to the generosity of so great a prince; nor of the difficulties I was in for want of a house and bed, being forced to lie on the ground, wrapped up in my coverlet.

Chapter Eight: The author, by a lucky accident, finds means to leave Blefuscu, and after some difficulties returns safe to his native country.

Three days after my arrival, walking out of curiosity to the northeast coast of the island, I observed, about half a league off in the sea, somewhat that looked like a boat overturned. I pulled off my shoes and stockings and, wading two or three

[2] Reveal.

hundred yards, I found the object to approach nearer by force of the tide, and then plainly saw it to be a real boat, which I supposed might by some tempest have been driven from a ship; whereupon I returned immediately towards the city, and desired his Imperial Majesty to lend me twenty of the tallest vessels he had left after the loss of his fleet, and three thousand seamen under the command of his Vice-Admiral. This fleet sailed round, while I went back the shortest way to the coast where I first discovered the boat; I found the tide had driven it still nearer. The seamen were all provided with cordage, which I had beforehand twisted to a sufficient strength. When the ships came up, I stripped myself and waded till I came within an hundred yards of the boat, after which I was forced to swim till I got up to it. The seamen threw me the end of the cord, which I fastened to a hole in the fore-part of the boat, and the other end to a man-of-war: but I found all my labour to little purpose; for being out of my depth, I was not able to work. In this necessity, I was forced to swim behind, and push the boat forwards as often as I could with one of my hands; and the tide favouring me, I advanced so far that I could just hold up my chin and feel the ground. I rested two or three minutes and then gave the boat another shove, and so on till the sea was no higher than my armpits; and now the most laborious part being over, I took out my other cables, which were stowed in one of the ships, and, fastening them first to the boat and then to nine of the vessels which attended me, the wind being favourable, the seamen towed and I shoved till we arrived within forty yards of the shore; and waiting till the tide was out, I got dry to the boat, and by the assistance of two thousand men, with ropes and engines, I made a shift to turn it on its bottom and found it was but little damaged.

I shall not trouble the reader with the difficulties I was under by the help of certain paddles, which cost me ten days making, to get my boat to the royal port of Blefuscu, where a mighty concourse of people appeared upon my arrival, full of wonder at the sight of so prodigious a vessel. I told the Emperor that my good fortune had thrown this boat in my way, to carry me to some place from whence I might return into my native country, and begged his Majesty's orders for getting materials to fit it up, together with his licence to depart; which, after some kind expostulations, he was pleased to grant.

I did very much wonder, in all this time, not to have heard of any express relating to me from our Emperor to the court of Blefuscu. But I was afterwards given privately to understand that his Imperial Majesty, never imagining I had the least notice of his designs, believed I was only gone to Blefuscu in performance of my promise, according to the licence he had given me, which was well known at our court, and would return in a few days when that ceremony was ended. But he was at last in pain at my long absence; and after consulting with the Treasurer and the rest of that cabal, a person of quality was dispatched with the copy of the articles against me. This envoy had instructions to represent to the monarch of Blefuscu the great *lenity* of his master, who was content to punish me no further than with the loss of my eyes; that I had fled from justice, and if I did not return in two hours, I should be deprived of my title of *Nardac* and declared a traitor. The envoy further added that, in order to maintain the peace and amity between both empires, his master expected that his brother of Blefuscu would give orders to have me sent back to Lilliput, bound hand and foot, to be punished as a traitor.

The Emperor of Blefuscu, having taken three days to consult, returned an answer consisting of many civilities and excuses. He said that, as for sending me bound, his brother knew it was impossible; that although I had deprived him of his fleet, yet he owed great obligations to me for many good offices I had done him in making the peace. That, however, both their Majesties would soon be made easy; for I had found a prodigious vessel on the shore, able to carry me on the sea, which he had given order to fit up with my own assistance and direction, and he hoped in a few weeks both empires would be freed from so insupportable an incumbrance.

With this answer the envoy returned to Lilliput, and the

monarch of Blefuscu related to me all that had passed, offering me at the same time (but under strictest confidence) his gracious protection if I would continue in his service; wherein although I believed him sincere, yet I resolved never more to put any confidence in princes or ministers where I could possibly avoid it; and therefore, with all due acknowledgments for his favourable intentions, I humbly begged to be excused. I told him, that since fortune, whether good or evil, had thrown a vessel in my way, I was resolved to venture myself in the ocean, rather than be an occasion of difference between two such mighty monarchs. Neither did I find the Emperor at all displeased; and I discovered by a certain accident that he was very glad of my resolution, and so were most of his ministers.

These considerations moved me to hasten my departure somewhat sooner than I intended; to which the court, impatient to have me gone, very readily contributed. Five hundred workmen were employed to make two sails to my boat, according to my directions, by quilting thirteen fold of their strongest linen together. I was at the pains of making ropes and cables by twisting ten, twenty, or thirty of the thickest and strongest of theirs. A great stone that I happened to find after a long search by the seashore served me for an anchor. I had the tallow of three hundred cows for greasing my boat and other uses. I was at incredible pains in cutting down some of the largest timber trees for oars and masts, wherein I was, however, much assisted by his Majesty's ship-carpenters, who helped me in smoothing them after I had done the rough work.

In about a month, when all was prepared, I sent to receive his Majesty's commands and to take my leave. The Emperor and royal family came out of the palace; I lay down on my face to kiss his hand, which he very graciously gave me: so did the Empress and young princes of the blood. His Majesty presented me with fifty purses of two hundred *sprugs* apiece, together with his picture at full length, which I put immediately into one of my gloves to keep it from being hurt. The ceremonies at my departure were too many to trouble the reader with at this time.

I stored the boat with the carcasses of an hundred oxen and three hundred sheep, with bread and drink proportionable, and as much meat ready dressed as four hundred cooks could provide. I took with me six cows and two bulls alive, with as many ewes and rams, intending to carry them into my own country and propagate the breed. And to feed them on board, I had a good bundle of hay and a bag of corn. I would gladly have taken a dozen of the natives, but this was a thing the Emperor would by no means permit; and besides a diligent search into my pockets, his Majesty engaged my honour not to carry away any of his subjects, although with their own consent and desire.

Having thus prepared all things as well as I was able, I set sail on the twenty-fourth day of September, 1701, at six in the morning; and when I had gone about four leagues to the northward, the wind being at southeast, at six in the evening, I descried a small island about half a league to the northwest. I advanced forward and cast anchor on the lee-side of the island, which seemed to be uninhabited. I then took some refreshment and went to my rest. I slept well, and as I conjecture at least six hours, for I found the day broke in two hours after I awaked. It was a clear night. I eat my breakfast before the sun was up; and heaving anchor, the wind being favourable, I steered the same course that I had done the day before, wherein I was directed by my pocket-compass. My intention was to reach, if possible, one of those islands which I had reason to believe lay to the northeast of Van Diemen's Land. I discovered nothing all that day; but upon the next, about three in the afternoon, when I had by my computation made twenty-four leagues from Blefuscu, I descried a sail steering to the southeast; my course was due east. I hailed her but could get no answer; yet I found I gained upon her, for the wind slackened. I made all the sail I could, and in half an hour

she spied me, then hung out her ancient,[1] and discharged a gun.
It is not easy to express the joy I was in upon the unexpected
hope of once more seeing my beloved country and the dear
pledges [2] I had left in it. The ship slackened her sails, and I
came up with her between five and six in the evening, September
26; but my heart leapt within me to see her English colours.
I put my cows and sheep into my coat-pockets, and got on
board with all my little cargo of provisions. The vessel was an
English merchantman, returning from Japan by the North and
South Seas,[3] the captain, Mr. John Biddel of Deptford, a very
civil man and an excellent sailor. We were now in the latitude
of 30 degrees south; there were about fifty men in the ship; and
here I met an old comrade of mine, one Peter Williams, who
gave me a good character to the captain. This gentleman
treated me with kindness, and desired I would let him know
what place I came from last, and whither I was bound; which
I did in few words, but he thought I was raving, and that the
dangers I underwent had disturbed my head; whereupon I
took my black cattle and sheep out of my pocket, which, after
great astonishment, clearly convinced him of my veracity. I
then showed him the gold given me by the Emperor of Blefuscu, together with his Majesty's picture at full length, and
some other rarities of that country. I gave him two purses of
two hundred *sprugs* each, and promised, when we arrived in
England, to make him a present of a cow and a sheep big with
young.

I shall not trouble the reader with a particular account of
this voyage, which was very prosperous for the most part. We
arrived in the Downs [4] on the 13th of April, 1702. I had only

[1] Flag (ensign).
[2] Loved ones.
[3] The Pacific Ocean.
[4] An anchorage near Dover where ships might land passengers
and take on pilots before beginning the difficult navigation of the
Thames estuary.

one misfortune, that the rats on board carried away one of my sheep; I found her bones in a hole, picked clean from the flesh. The rest of my cattle I got safe on shore, and set them a-grazing in a bowling-green at Greenwich, where the fineness of the grass made them feed very heartily, though I had always feared the contrary; neither could I possibly have preserved them in so long a voyage if the captain had not allowed me some of his best biscuit, which, rubbed to powder and mingled with water, was their constant food. The short time I continued in England, I made a considerable profit by showing my cattle to many persons of quality and others: and before I began my second voyage, I sold them for six hundred pounds. Since my last return, I find the breed is considerably increased, especially the sheep; which I hope will prove much to the advantage of the woollen manufacture, by the fineness of the fleeces.

I stayed but two months with my wife and family; for my insatiable desire of seeing foreign countries would suffer me to continue no longer. I left fifteen hundred pounds with my wife, and fixed her in a good house at Redriff.[5] My remaining stock I carried with me, part in money and part in goods, in hopes to improve my fortunes. My eldest uncle John had left me an estate in land near Epping,[6] of about thirty pounds a year; and I had a long lease of the Black Bull [7] in Fetter Lane, which yielded me as much more: so that I was not in any danger of leaving my family upon the parish.[8] My son Johnny, named so after his uncle, was at the grammar school and a towardly [9] child. My daughter Betty (who is now well mar-

[5] Rotherhithe, the dock section of East London, south of the Thames.

[6] About eighteen miles north of London.

[7] Presumably a tavern in a street where Gulliver once lived (Part One, Chapter One, p. 5).

[8] Paupers, and therefore dependent upon what was then the only authority responsible for the poor and indigent, the local parish with its "Overseers of the Poor."

[9] Promising, precocious.

ried and has children) was then at her needlework. I took leave of my wife and boy and girl with tears on both sides, and went on board the *Adventure*, a merchant-ship of three hundred tons, bound for Surat,[10] Captain John Nicholas of Liverpool commander. But my account of this voyage must be referred to the second part of my *Travels*.

The End of the First Part

---

[10] A seaport north of Bombay, then the main center of the East India Company in western India.

Part Two

A Voyage to Brobdingnag

The map places Brobdingnag off the coast of North America somewhat as California was placed in Herman Moll's world map of 1719. (The Gulf of Lower California was believed to extend upward for much of the length of the "peninsula," and Moll seemed uncertain whether Lower California might not be a long island rather than a peninsula.) The dimensions of Brobdingnag are much greater in the text than the map indicates. The map shows it more or less in the location of Alaska—isolated from the mainland by a chain of impassable mountains.

The isolation of Brobdingnag is not shared with an enemy state, as is that of Lilliput and Blefuscu. The giants of Brobdingnag neither act upon nor are influenced by the rest of the world. Their political system is free of dreams of imperial conquest; its problems are solved by internal reforms. In contrast to Lilliput, Brobdingnag has a history of division and corruption that are now corrected. It still holds the possibilities of corruption, but its politics are a means of containing rather than expressing this corruption.

Our first view of the Brobdingnagians shows us the apparent horror of brutal giants, and the behavior of Gulliver's first master supports that impression. But here the pattern of Lilliput is reversed: the gradual disclosure is not of pettiness beneath charm but of decency beneath seeming grossness. The generosity or large-mindedness (magnanimity, in its original sense) of the King and Queen shows the best of Brobdingnag in control of the nation, in contrast to the corrupt court of Lilliput. Here, Gulliver shows what he has learned about politics in Lilliput (his first experience of courts), and he proves himself a would-be Lilliputian minister (with European technology) at the court of Brobdingnag. In his own shortsightedness, in his petty concern for his own prestige, in his desire to show his powers, Gulliver proves himself a more dangerous and terrible figure than the giants.

BROBDINGNAG

Flanflasnic
Lorbrulgrud

Discovered A.D. 1703

NORTH AMERICA

Streights of Annian

C. Blanco

S.t Sebastian   NEW
                  ALBION

C Mendocino

Mount
St Martin

P.to S.r Francis Drake

P Monterey

Chapter One: A great storm described, the long-boat sent to fetch water, the author goes with it to discover the country. He is left on shore, is seized by one of the natives, and carried to a farmer's house. His reception there, with several accidents that happened there. A description of the inhabitants.

HAVING been condemned by nature and fortune to an active and restless life, in two months after my return I again left my native country, and took shipping in the Downs on the 20th day of June, 1702, in the *Adventure,* Capt. John Nicholas, a Cornish man, commander, bound for Surat. We had a very prosperous gale till we arrived at the Cape of Good Hope, where we landed for fresh water, but, discovering a leak we unshipped our goods, and wintered there; for the captain falling sick of an ague, we could not leave the Cape till the end of March. We then set sail and had a good voyage till we passed the Straits of Madagascar; but having got northward of that island, and to about five degrees south latitude, the winds, which in those seas are observed to blow a constant equal gale between the north and west from the beginning of December to the beginning of May, on the 19th of April began to blow with much greater violence, and more westerly than usual, continuing so for twenty days together, during which time we were driven a little to the east of the Molucca Islands and about three degrees northward of the Line,[1] as our captain found by an observation he took the 2nd of May, at which time the wind ceased, and it was a perfect calm, whereat I was not a little rejoiced. But he, being a man well experienced in the navigation of those seas, bid us all prepare against a storm, which accordingly happened the day following: for a southern wind, called the southern monsoon, began to set in.

Finding it was like to overblow, we took in our spritsail, and stood by to hand the foresail; but making foul weather, we looked the guns were all fast, and handed the missen.[2] The ship

[1] Equator.
[2] The mizzen sail. This paragraph, which bristles with nautical jargon, is almost entirely borrowed by Swift from Samuel Sturmy's *Mariner's Magazine* (1669).

lay very broad off, so we thought it better spooning before the sea than trying or hulling. We reefed the foresail and set him, we hauled aft the fore-sheet; the helm was hard aweather. The ship wore bravely. We belayed the fore-downhaul; but the sail was split, and we hauled down the yard, and got the sail into the ship, and unbound all the things clear of it. It was a very fierce storm; the sea broke strange and dangerous. We hauled off upon the lanyard of the whipstaff, and helped the man at helm. We would not get down our topmast, but let all stand, because she scudded before the sea very well, and we knew that the topmast being aloft, the ship was the wholesomer, and made better way through the sea, seeing we had searoom. When the storm was over, we set foresail and mainsail, and brought the ship to. Then we set the missen, main-topsail, and the fore-topsail. Our course was east-northeast, the wind was at southwest. We got the starboard tacks aboard, we cast off our weatherbraces and lifts; we set in the lee braces, and hauled forward by the weather bowlings, and hauled them tight, and belayed them, and hauled over the missen tack to windward, and kept her full and by as near as she would lie.

During this storm, which was followed by a strong wind west-southwest, we were carried by my computation about five hundred leagues to the east, so that the oldest sailor on board could not tell in what part of the world we were. Our provisions held out well, our ship was staunch, and our crew all in good health; but we lay in the utmost distress for water. We thought it best to hold on the same course rather than turn more northerly, which might have brought us to the northwest parts of Great Tartary, and into the frozen sea.[3]

On the 16th day of June, 1703, a boy on the topmast discovered land. On the 17th we came in full view of a great island or continent (for we knew not whether) on the south side, whereof was a small neck of land jutting out into the sea, and a creek too shallow to hold a ship of above one hun-

[3] Siberia and the Arctic Sea.

dred tons. We cast anchor within a league of this creek, and our captain sent a dozen of his men well armed in the long-boat with vessels for water if any could be found. I desired his leave to go with them that I might see the country and make what discoveries I could. When we came to land we saw no river or spring, nor any sign of inhabitants. Our men therefore wandered on the shore to find out some fresh water near the sea, and I walked alone about a mile on the other side, where I observed the country all barren and rocky. I now began to be weary, and seeing nothing to entertain my curiosity, I returned gently down towards the creek; and the sea being full in my view, I saw our men already got into the boat, and rowing for life to the ship. I was going to holloa after them, although it had been to little purpose, when I observed a huge creature walking after them in the sea as fast as he could: he waded not much deeper than his knees and took prodigious strides: but our men had the start of him half a league, and, the sea there-abouts being full of sharp pointed rocks, the monster was not able to overtake the boat. This I was afterwards told, for I durst not stay to see the issue of that adventure, but ran as fast as I could the way I first went; and then climbed up a steep hill which gave me some prospect of the country. I found it fully cultivated; but that which first surprised me was the length of the grass, which in those grounds that seemed to be kept for hay was above twenty foot high.

I fell into a high road, for so I took it to be, although it served to the inhabitants only as a footpath through a field of barley. Here I walked on for some time, but could see little on either side, it being now near harvest, and the corn rising at least forty foot. I was an hour walking to the end of this field, which was fenced in with a hedge of at least one hundred and twenty foot high, and the trees so lofty that I could make no computation of their altitude. There was a stile to pass from this field into the next. It had four steps, and a stone to cross over when you came to the uppermost. It was impossible for me to climb this stile, because every step was six foot high and the upper stone above twenty. I was endeavouring to find some gap in the hedge when I discovered one of the inhabitants in the next field advancing towards the stile, of the same size with him whom I saw in the sea pursuing our boat. He appeared as tall as an ordinary spire-steeple, and took about ten yards at every stride, as near as I could guess. I was struck with the utmost fear and astonishment, and ran to hide myself in the corn, from whence I saw him at the top of the stile, looking back into the next field on the right hand, and heard him call in a voice many degrees louder than a speaking-trumpet; but the noise was so high in the air that at first I certainly thought it was thunder. Whereupon seven monsters like himself came towards him with reaping-hooks in their hands, each hook about the largeness of six scythes. These people were not so well clad as the first, whose servants or labourers they seemed to be. For upon some words he spoke, they went to reap the corn in the field where I lay. I kept from them at as great a distance as I could, but was forced to move with extreme difficulty, for the stalks of the corn were sometimes not above a foot distant, so that I could hardly squeeze my body betwixt them. However, I made a shift to go forward till I came to a part of the field where the corn had been laid by the rain and wind. Here it was impossible for me to advance a step: for the stalks were so interwoven that I could not creep through, and the beards of the fallen ears so strong and pointed that they pierced through my clothes into my flesh. At the same time I heard the reapers not above an hundred yards behind me. Being quite dispirited with toil, and wholly overcome by grief and despair, I lay down between two ridges, and heartily wished I might there end my days. I bemoaned my desolate widow and fatherless children. I lamented my own folly and wilfulness in attempting a second voyage against the advice of all my friends and relations. In this terrible agitation of mind I could not forbear thinking of Lilliput, whose inhabitants looked upon me as the greatest prodigy that ever appeared in the world: where I was able to draw an imperial fleet in my

hand, and perform those other actions which will be recorded
for ever in the chronicles of that empire, while posterity shall
hardly believe them, although attested by millions. I reflected
what a mortification it must prove to me to appear as inconsiderable in this nation as one single Lilliputian would be
among us. But this I conceived was to be the least of my misfortunes: for, as human creatures are observed to be more
savage and cruel in proportion to their bulk, what could I expect but to be a morsel in the mouth of the first among these
enormous barbarians who should happen to seize me? Un-
doubtedly philosophers are in the right when they tell us that
nothing is great or little otherwise than by comparison. It
might have pleased fortune to let the Lilliputians find some
nation where the people were as diminutive with respect to
them as they were to me. And who knows but that even this
prodigious race of mortals might be equally overmatched in
some distant part of the world whereof we have yet no discovery?

Scared and confounded as I was, I could not forbear going
on with these reflections, when one of the reapers, approaching within ten yards of the ridge where I lay, made me apprehend that with the next step I should be squashed to death
under his foot, or cut in two with his reaping hook. And therefore, when he was again about to move, I screamed as loud as
fear could make me. Whereupon the huge creature trod short,
and, looking round about under him for some time, at last
espied me as I lay on the ground. He considered a while with
the caution of one who endeavours to lay hold on a small
dangerous animal in such a manner that it shall not be able
either to scratch or to bite him, as I myself have sometimes
done with a weasel in England. At length he ventured to take
me up behind by the middle between his forefinger and thumb,
and brought me within three yards of his eyes, that he might
behold my shape more perfectly. I guessed his meaning, and
my good fortune gave me so much presence of mind, that I
resolved not to struggle in the least as he held me in the air

above sixty foot from the ground, although he grievously pinched my sides, for fear I should slip through his fingers. All I ventured was to raise my eyes towards the sun and place my hands together in a supplicating posture, and to speak some words in an humble melancholy tone suitable to the condition I then was in. For I apprehended every moment that he would dash me against the ground, as we usually do any little hateful animal which we have a mind to destroy. But my good star would have it that he appeared pleased with my voice and gestures, and began to look upon me as a curiosity, much wondering to hear me pronounce articulate words, although he could not understand them. In the meantime I was not able to forbear groaning and shedding tears and turning my head towards my sides; letting him know, as well as I could, how cruelly I was hurt by the pressure of his thumb and finger. He seemed to apprehend my meaning; for, lifting up the lappet of his coat, he put me gently into it, and immediately ran along with me to his master, who was a substantial farmer and the same person I had first seen in the field.

The farmer, having (as I supposed by their talk) received such an account of me as his servant could give him, took a piece of a small straw about the size of a walking staff, and therewith lifted up the lappets of my coat; which it seems he thought to be some kind of covering that nature had given me. He blew my hairs aside to take a better view of my face. He called his hinds about him and asked them (as I afterwards learned) whether they had ever seen in the fields any little creature that resembled me. He then placed me softly on the ground upon all four, but I got immediately up and walked slowly backwards and forwards, to let those people see I had no intent to run away. They all sat down in a circle about me, the better to observe my motions. I pulled off my hat and made a low bow towards the farmer. I fell on my knees and lifted up my hands and eyes, and spoke several words as loud as I could: I took a purse of gold out of my pocket and humbly presented it to him. He received it on the palm of his hand, then applied it close to his eye, to see what it was, and afterwards turned it several times with the point of a pin (which he took out of his sleeve), but could make nothing of it. Whereupon I made a sign that he should place his hand on the ground. I then took the purse and, opening it, poured all the gold into his palm. There were six Spanish pieces of four pistoles each,[4] beside twenty or thirty smaller coins. I saw him wet the tip of his little finger upon his tongue, and take up one of my largest pieces, and then another, but he seemed to be wholly ignorant what they were. He made me a sign to put them again into my purse, and the purse again into my pocket, which, after offering to him several times, I thought it best to do.

The farmer by this time was convinced I must be a rational creature. He spoke often to me, but the sound of his voice pierced my ears like that of a watermill, yet his words were articulate enough. I answered as loud as I could, in several languages, and he often laid his ear within two yards of me, but all in vain, for we were wholly unintelligible to each other. He then sent his servants to their work, and, taking his handkerchief out of his pocket, he doubled and spread it on his hand, which he placed flat on the ground, with the palm upwards, making me a sign to step into it, as I could easily do, for it was not above a foot in thickness. I thought it my part to obey and, for fear of falling, laid myself at full length upon the handkerchief, with the remainder of which he lapped me up to the head for further security, and in this manner carried me home to his house. There he called his wife and showed me to her; but she screamed and ran back as women in England do at the sight of a toad or a spider. However, when she had a while seen my behaviour, and how well I observed the signs her husband made, she was soon reconciled, and by degrees grew extremely tender of me.

It was about twelve at noon, and a servant brought in din-

[4] Six gold coins large enough to be valued at about sixteen dollars each.

ner. It was only one substantial dish of meat (fit for the plain condition of an husbandman) in a dish of about four and twenty foot diameter. The company were the farmer and his wife, three children, and an old grandmother: when they were sat down, the farmer placed me at some distance from him on the table, which was thirty foot high from the floor. I was in a terrible fright, and kept as far as I could from the edge for fear of falling. The wife minced a bit of meat, then crumbled some bread on a trencher, and placed it before me. I made her a low bow, took out my knife and fork, and fell to eat, which gave them exceeding delight. The mistress sent her maid for a small dram cup, which held about two gallons, and filled it with drink; I took up the vessel with much difficulty in both hands, and in a most respectful manner drank to her ladyship's health, expressing the words as loud as I could in English, which made the company laugh so heartily that I was almost deafened with the noise. This liquor tasted like a small cider, and was not unpleasant. Then the master made me a sign to come to his trencher side; but as I walked on the table, being in great surprise all the time, as the indulgent reader will easily conceive and excuse, I happened to stumble against a crust, and fell flat on my face, but received no hurt. I got up immediately, and observing the good people to be in much concern, I took my hat (which I held under my arm out of good manners) and waving it over my head, made three huzzas to show I had got no mischief by the fall. But advancing forwards towards my master (as I shall henceforth call him) his youngest son who sat next him, an arch boy of about ten years old, took me up by the legs, and held me so high in the air, that I trembled every limb; but his father snatched me from him, and at the same time gave him such a box on the left ear as would have felled an European troop of horse to the earth, ordering him to be taken from the table. But being afraid the boy might owe me a spite,[5] and well remembering how mischievous all

[5] Hold a grudge against me.

children among us naturally are to sparrows, rabbits, young kittens, and puppy dogs, I fell on my knees and, pointing to the boy, made my master understand as well as I could that I desired his son might be pardoned. The father complied, and the lad took his seat again; whereupon I went to him and kissed his hand, which my master took, and made him stroke me gently with it.

In the midst of dinner, my mistress's favourite cat leapt into her lap. I heard a noise behind me like that of a dozen stocking-weavers at work; [6] and turning my head I found it proceeded from the purring of this animal, who seemed to be three times larger than an ox, as I computed by the view of her head and one of her paws, while her mistress was feeding and stroking her. The fierceness of this creature's countenance altogether discomposed me; although I stood at the further end of the table, above fifty foot off, and although my mistress held her fast for fear she might give a spring and seize me in her talons. But it happened there was no danger; for the cat took not the least notice of me when my master placed me within three yards of her. And as I have been always told, and found true by experience in my travels, that flying or discovering fear before a fierce animal is a certain way to make it pursue or attack you, so I resolved in this dangerous juncture to show no manner of concern. I walked with intrepidity five or six times before the very head of the cat, and came within half a yard of her; whereupon she drew herself back, as if she were more afraid of me: I had less apprehension concerning the dogs, whereof three or four came into the room, as it is usual in farmers' houses; one of which was a mastiff equal in bulk to four elephants, and a greyhound somewhat taller than the mastiff, but not so large.

When dinner was almost done, the nurse came in with a child of a year old in her arms, who immediately spied me,

[6] At mechanical frames or looms.

and began a squall that you might have heard from London Bridge to Chelsea,[7] after the usual oratory of infants, to get me for a plaything. The mother out of pure indulgence took me up, and put me towards the child, who presently seized me by the middle and got my head in his mouth, where I roared so loud that the urchin was frighted and let me drop, and I should infallibly have broke my neck if the mother had not held her apron under me. The nurse to quiet her babe made use of a rattle, which was a kind of hollow vessel filled with great stones and fastened by a cable to the child's waist: but all in vain, so that she was forced to apply the last remedy by giving it suck. I must confess no object ever disgusted me so much as the sight of her monstrous breast, which I cannot tell what to compare with so as to give the curious reader an idea of its bulk, shape and colour. It stood prominent six foot and could not be less than sixteen in circumference. The nipple was about half the bigness of my head, and the hue both of that and the dug so varified with spots, pimples, and freckles that nothing could appear more nauseous: for I had a near sight of her, she sitting down the more conveniently to give suck and I standing on the table. This made me reflect upon the fair skins of our English ladies, who appear so beautiful to us only because they are of our own size, and their defects not to be seen but through a magnifying glass, where we find by experiment that the smoothest and whitest skins look rough and coarse and ill-coloured.

I remember when I was at Lilliput the complexions of those diminutive people appeared to me the fairest in the world; and talking upon this subject with a person of learning there, who was an intimate friend of mine, he said that my face appeared much fairer and smoother when he looked on me from the ground than it did upon a nearer view when I took him up in my hand and brought him close, which he confessed was at

[7] A distance of five miles.

first a very shocking sight. He said he could discover great holes in my skin, that the stumps of my beard were ten times stronger than the bristles of a boar, and my complexion made up of several colours altogether disagreeable: although I must beg leave to say for myself that I am as fair as most of my sex and country, and very little sunburnt by all my travels. On the other side, discoursing of the ladies in that emperor's court, he used to tell me one had freckles, another too wide a mouth, a third too large a nose, nothing of which I was able to distinguish. I confess this reflection was obvious enough; which however I could not forbear, lest the reader might think those vast creatures were actually deformed: for I must do them justice to say they are a comely race of people; and particularly the features of my master's countenance, although he were but a farmer, when I beheld him from the height of sixty foot, appeared very well proportioned.

When dinner was done, my master went out to his labourers, and, as I could discover by his voice and gesture, gave his wife a strict charge to take care of me. I was very much tired and disposed to sleep, which my mistress perceiving, she put me on her own bed, and covered me with a clean white handkerchief, but larger and coarser than the mainsail of a man-of-war.

I slept about two hours, and dreamed I was at home with my wife and children, which aggravated my sorrows when I awaked and found myself alone in a vast room, between two and three hundred foot wide and above two hundred high, lying in a bed twenty yards wide. My mistress was gone about her household affairs and had locked me in. The bed was eight yards from the floor. Some natural necessities required me to get down; I durst not presume to call, and if I had, it would have been in vain with such a voice as mine at so great a distance from the room where I lay to the kitchen where the family kept. While I was under these circumstances two rats crept up the curtains, and ran smelling backwards and forwards on the bed. One of them came up almost to my face, whereupon I rose in a fright, and drew out my hanger[8] to defend myself. These horrible animals had the boldness to attack me on both sides, and one of them held his fore-feet at my collar; but I had the good fortune to rip up his belly before he could do me any mischief. He fell down at my feet, and the other, seeing the fate of his comrade, made his escape, but not without one good wound on the back, which I gave him as he fled, and made the blood run trickling from him. After this exploit, I walked gently to and fro on the bed, to recover my breath and loss of spirits. These creatures were of the size of a large mastiff, but infinitely more nimble and fierce, so that if I had taken off my belt before I went to sleep, I must have infallibly been torn to pieces and devoured. I measured the tail of the dead rat, and found it to be two yards long, wanting an inch; but it went against my stomach to drag the carcass off the bed, where it lay still bleeding; I observed it had yet some life, but with a strong slash cross the neck I thoroughly dispatched it.

Soon after my mistress came into the room, who, seeing me all bloody, ran and took me up in her hand. I pointed to the dead rat, smiling and making other signs to show I was not hurt, whereat she was extremely rejoiced, calling the maid to take up the dead rat with a pair of tongs and throw it out of the window. Then she set me on a table, where I showed her my hanger all bloody and, wiping it on the lappet of my coat, returned it to the scabbard. I was pressed to do more than one thing which another could not do for me, and therefore endeavoured to make my mistress understand that I desired to be set down on the floor; which, after she had done, my bashfulness would not suffer me to express myself farther than by pointing to the door and bowing several times. The good woman with much difficulty at last perceived what I would be at and, taking me up again in her hand, walked into the

8 A short sword hanging from his belt.

garden, where she set me down. I went on one side about two hundred yards, and, beckoning to her not to look or to follow me, I hid myself between two leaves of sorrel,[9] and there discharged the necessities of nature.

I hope the gentle reader will excuse me for dwelling on these and the like particulars, which, however insignificant they may appear to grovelling vulgar minds, yet will certainly help a philosopher [10] to enlarge his thoughts and imagination, and apply them to the benefit of public as well as private life, which was my sole design in presenting this and other accounts of my travels to the world; wherein I have been chiefly studious of truth, without affecting any ornaments of learning or of style. But the whole scene of this voyage made so strong an impression on my mind, and is so deeply fixed in my memory, that in committing it to paper I did not omit one material circumstance: however, upon a strict review, I blotted out several passages of less moment which were in my first copy for fear of being censured as tedious and trifling, whereof travellers are often, perhaps not without justice, accused.

Chapter Two: A description of the farmer's daughter. The author carried to a market-town, and then to the metropolis. The particulars of his journey.

My mistress had a daughter of nine years old, a child of forward parts[1] for her age, very dextrous at her needle and skilful in dressing her baby.[2] Her mother and she contrived to fit up

[9] A plant raised in the kitchen-garden for salads or as a cooking herb.
[10] Here, as often, the term probably refers to "natural philosophy," roughly equivalent to what we would call science.
[1] Precocious abilities.
[2] Doll.

the baby's cradle for me against night: the cradle was put into a small drawer of a cabinet, and the drawer placed upon a hanging shelf for fear of the rats. This was my bed all the time I stayed with those people, although made more convenient by degrees, as I began to learn their language and make my wants known. This young girl was so handy that after I had once or twice pulled off my clothes before her, she was able to dress and undress me, although I never gave her that trouble when she would let me do either myself. She made me seven shirts and some other linen, of as fine cloth as could be got, which indeed was coarser than sackcloth; and these she constantly washed for me with her own hands. She was likewise my school-mistress to teach me the language: when I pointed to anything, she told me the name of it in her own tongue, so that in a few days I was able to call for whatever I had a mind to. She was very good-natured, and not above forty foot high, being little for her age. She gave me the name of *Grildrig*, which the family took up, and afterwards the whole kingdom. The word imports what the Latins call *nanunculus*, the Italians *homunceletino*, and the English *mannikin*.[3] To her I chiefly owe my preservation in that country: we never parted while I was there; I called her my *glumdalclitch*, or *little nurse:* and I should be guilty of great ingratitude if I omitted this honourable mention of her care and affection towards me, which I heartily wish it lay in my power to requite as she deserves, instead of being the innocent but unhappy instrument of her disgrace, as I have too much reason to fear.

It now began to be known and talked of in the neighbourhood that my master had found a strange animal in the field, about the bigness of a *splacknuck*, but exactly shaped in every part like a human creature; which it likewise imitated in all its actions; seemed to speak in a little language of its own, had already learned several words of theirs, went erect upon two

---

[3] Gulliver seems to have invented the first two forms, although they derive from Latin *nanus*, dwarf, and *homunculus*, mannikin.

legs, was tame and gentle, would come when it was called, do whatever it was bid, had the finest limbs in the world, and a complexion fairer than a nobleman's daughter of three years old. Another farmer who lived hard by, and was a particular friend of my master, came on a visit on purpose to enquire into the truth of this story. I was immediately produced and placed upon a table, where I walked as I was commanded, drew my hanger, put it up again, made my reverence to my master's guest, asked him in his own language how he did, and told him he was welcome, just as my little nurse had instructed me. This man, who was old and dim-sighted, put on his spectacles to behold me better, at which I could not forbear laughing very heartily, for his eyes appeared like the full moon shining into a chamber at two windows. Our people, who discovered the cause of my mirth, bore me company in laughing, at which the old fellow was fool enough to be angry and out of countenance. He had the character of a great miser, and to my misfortune he well deserved it, by the cursed advice he gave my master to show me as a sight upon a market-day in the next town, which was half an hour's riding, about two and twenty miles from our house. I guessed there was some mischief contriving when I observed my master and his friend whispering long together, sometimes pointing at me; and my fears made me fancy that I overheard and understood some of their words. But the next morning Glumdalclitch my little nurse told me the whole matter, which she had cunningly picked out from her mother. The poor girl laid me on her bosom and fell a-weeping with shame and grief. She apprehended some mischief would happen to me from rude vulgar folks, who might squeeze me to death or break one of my limbs by taking me in their hands. She had also observed how modest I was in my nature, how nicely I regarded my honour, and what an indignity I should conceive it, to be exposed for money as a public spectacle to the meanest of the people. She said her papa and mamma had promised that Grildrig should be hers; but now she found they meant to serve her as they did last year, when they pretended to give her a lamb and yet, as soon as it was fat, sold it to a butcher. For my own part, I may truly affirm that I was less concerned than my nurse. I had a strong hope, which never left me, that I should one day recover my liberty; and, as to the ignominy of being carried about for a monster,[4] I considered myself to be a perfect stranger in the country, and that such a misfortune could never be charged upon me as a reproach if ever I should return to England; since the King of Great Britain himself, in my condition, must have undergone the same distress.

My master, pursuant to the advice of his friend, carried me in a box the next market-day to the neighbouring town, and took along with him his little daughter my nurse upon a pillion behind him. The box was close on every side, with a little door for me to go in and out, and a few gimlet-holes to let in air. The girl had been so careful to put the quilt of her baby's bed into it, for me to lie down on. However, I was terribly shaken and discomposed in this journey, although it were but of half an hour. For the horse went about forty foot at every step, and trotted so high that the agitation was equal to the rising and falling of a ship in a great storm, but much more frequent: our journey was somewhat further than from London to St. Albans.[5] My master alighted at an inn which he used to frequent; and, after consulting a while with the inn-keeper and making some necessary preparations, he hired the *Grultrud*, or *crier*, to give notice through the town of a strange creature to be seen at the Sign of the Green Eagle, not so big as a *splacknuck* (an animal in that country very finely shaped, about six foot long) and in every part of the body resembling an human creature; could speak several words, and perform an hundred diverting tricks.

I was placed upon a table in the largest room of the inn, which might be near three hundred foot square. My little nurse

[4] The commercial exhibition of dwarfs and other abnormal creatures was common in Swift's day, as it has continued to be.

[5] About twenty miles.

stood on a low stool close to the table, to take care of me and direct what I should do. My master, to avoid a crowd, would suffer only thirty people at a time to see me. I walked about on the table as the girl commanded; she asked me questions as far as she knew my understanding of the language reached, and I answered them as loud as I could. I turned about several times to the company, paid my humble respects, said they were welcome, and used some other speeches I had been taught. I took up a thimble filled with liquor, which Glumdalclitch had given me for a cup, and drank their health. I drew out my hanger, and flourished with it after the manner of fencers in England. My nurse gave me part of a straw, which I exercised as a pike, having learned the art in my youth. I was that day shown to twelve sets of company, and as often forced to go over again with the same fopperies, till I was half dead with weariness and vexation. For those who had seen me made such wonderful reports that the people were ready to break down the doors to come in. My master, for his own interest, would not suffer any one to touch me except my nurse; and, to prevent danger, benches were set round the table at such a distance as put me out of everybody's reach. However, an unlucky schoolboy aimed a hazel nut directly at my head, which very narrowly missed me; otherwise, it came with so much violence that it would have infallibly knocked out my brains, for it was almost as large as a small pumpion:[6] but I had the satisfaction to see the young rogue well beaten and turned out of the room.

My master gave public notice that he would show me again the next market-day, and in the meantime he prepared a more convenient vehicle for me; which he had reason enough to do, for I was so tired with my first journey, and with entertaining company eight hours together, that I could hardly stand upon my legs or speak a word. It was at least three days before I recovered my strength; and, that I might have no rest at home, all the neighbouring gentlemen from an hundred miles round, hearing of my fame, came to see me at my master's own house.

[6] Pumpkin.

There could not be fewer than thirty persons with their wives and children (for the country is very populous); and my master demanded the rate of a full room whenever he showed me at home, although it were only to a single family. So that for some time I had but little ease every day of the week (except Wednesday, which is their Sabbath) although I were not carried to the town.

My master, finding how profitable I was like to be, resolved to carry me to the most considerable cities of the kingdom. Having therefore provided himself with all things necessary for a long journey, and settled his affairs at home, he took leave of his wife, and upon the 17th of August, 1703, about two months after my arrival, we set out for the metropolis, situated near the middle of that empire and about three thousand miles distance from our house: my master made his daughter Glumdalclitch ride behind him. She carried me on her lap in a box tied about her waist. The girl had lined it on all sides with the softest cloth she could get, well quilted underneath, furnished it with her baby's bed, provided me with linen and other necessaries, and made everything as convenient as she could. We had no other company but a boy of the house, who rode after us with the luggage.

My master's design was to show me in all the towns by the way, and to step out of the road for fifty or an hundred miles to any village or person of quality's house where he might expect custom. We made easy journeys of not above seven or eight-score miles a day: for Glumdalclitch, on purpose to spare me, complained she was tired with the trotting of the horse. She often took me out of my box at my own desire, to give me air and show me the country, but always held me fast by leading-strings. We passed over five or six rivers many degrees broader and deeper than the Nile or the Ganges; and there was hardly a rivulet so small as the Thames at London Bridge.[7] We were ten weeks in our journeys, and I was shown in eighteen large towns besides many villages and private families.

[7] That is, 750 feet wide.

On the 26th day of October, we arrived at the metropolis, called in their language *Lorbrulgrud,* or *Pride of the Universe.* My master took a lodging in the principal street of the city, not far from the royal palace, and put out bills in the usual form, containing an exact description of my person and parts. He hired a large room between three and four hundred foot wide. He provided a table sixty foot in diameter, upon which I was to act my part, and palisadoed[8] it round three feet from the edge, and as many high, to prevent my falling over. I was shown ten times a day to the wonder and satisfaction of all people. I could now speak the language tolerably well, and perfectly understood every word that was spoken to me. Besides, I had learnt their alphabet, and could make a shift to explain a sentence here and there; for Glumdalclitch had been my instructor while we were at home and at leisure hours during our journey. She carried a little book in her pocket, not much larger than a Sanson's *Atlas;* [9] it was a common treatise for the use of young girls, giving a short account of their religion; out of this she taught me my letters and interpreted the words.

Chapter Three: The author sent for to court. The Queen buys him of his master the farmer, and presents him to the King. He disputes with his Majesty's great scholars. An apartment at court provided for the author. He is in high favour with the Queen. He stands up for the honour of his own country. His quarrels with the Queen's dwarf.

The frequent labours I underwent every day made in a few weeks a very considerable change in my health: the more my master got by me, the more unsatiable he grew. I had quite lost

[8] Fenced.
[9] Sanson's atlas was close to two feet square in page size.

my stomach, and was almost reduced to a skeleton. The farmer observed it and, concluding I soon must die, resolved to make as good a hand of me as he could. While he was thus reasoning and resolving with himself, a *slardal*, or *gentleman usher*, came from court, commanding my master to bring me immediately thither for the diversion of the Queen and her ladies. Some of the latter had already been to see me and reported strange things of my beauty, behaviour, and good sense. Her Majesty and those who attended her were beyond measure delighted with my demeanor. I fell on my knees and begged the honour of kissing her imperial foot; but this gracious princess held out her little finger towards me (after I was set on a table), which I embraced in both my arms, and put the tip of it, with the utmost respect, to my lip. She made me some general questions about my country and my travels, which I answered as distinctly and in as few words as I could. She asked whether I would be content to live at court. I bowed down to the board of the table, and humbly answered that I was my master's slave, but if I were at my own disposal, I should be proud to devote my life to her Majesty's service. She then asked my master whether he were willing to sell me at a good price. He, who apprehended I could not live a month, was ready enough to part with me, and demanded a thousand pieces of gold, which were ordered him on the spot, each piece being about the bigness of eight hundred moidores; but, allowing for the proportion of all things between that country and Europe, and the high price of gold among them, was hardly so great a sum as a thousand guineas would be in England. I then said to the Queen, since I was now her Majesty's most humble creature and vassal, I must beg the favour that Glumdalclitch, who had always tended me with so much care and kindness and understood to do it so well, might be admitted into her service and continue to be my nurse and instructor. Her Majesty agreed to my petition and easily got the farmer's consent, who was glad enough to have his daughter preferred at court: and the poor girl herself was not able to hide her joy: my late master withdrew, bidding me farewell and saying he had left me in a good service; to which I replied not a word, only making him a slight bow.

The Queen observed my coldness and, when the farmer was gone out of the apartment, asked me the reason. I made bold to tell her Majesty that I owed no other obligation to my late master than his not dashing out the brains of a poor harmless creature found by chance in his field; which obligation was amply recompensed by the gain he had made in showing me through half the kingdom, and the price he had now sold me for. That the life I had since led was laborious enough to kill an animal of ten times my strength. That my health was much impaired by the continual drudgery of entertaining the rabble every hour of the day, and that if my master had not thought my life in danger, her Majesty perhaps would not have got so cheap a bargain. But as I was out of all fear of being ill treated under the protection of so great and good an empress, the Ornament of Nature, the Darling of the World, the Delight of her Subjects, the Phoenix of the Creation; so, I hoped my late master's apprehensions would appear to be groundless, for I already found my spirits to revive by the influence of her most august presence.

This was the sum of my speech, delivered with great improprieties and hesitation; the latter part was altogether framed in the style peculiar to that people, whereof I learned some phrases from Glumdalclitch while she was carrying me to court.

The Queen, giving great allowance for my defectiveness in speaking, was however surprised at so much wit and good sense in so diminutive an animal. She took me in her own hand and carried me to the King, who was then retired to his cabinet.[1] His Majesty, a prince of much gravity and austere countenance, not well observing my shape at first view, asked the Queen after a cold manner how long it was since she grew

[1] Small private room.

fond of a *splacknuck;* for such it seems he took me to be as I lay upon my breast in her Majesty's right hand. But this princess, who hath an infinite deal of wit and humour, set me gently on my feet upon the scrutore,[2] and commanded me to give his Majesty an account of myself, which I did in a very few words; and Glumdalclitch, who attended at the cabinet door, and could not endure I should be out of her sight, being admitted, confirmed all that had passed from my arrival at her father's house.

The King, although he be as learned a person as any in his dominions, and had been educated in the study of philosophy, and particularly mathematics, yet when he observed my shape exactly and saw me walk erect, before I began to speak, conceived I might be a piece of clock-work (which is in that country arrived to a very great perfection), contrived by some ingenious artist. But, when he heard my voice and found what I delivered to be regular and rational, he could not conceal his astonishment. He was by no means satisfied with the relation I gave him of the manner I came into his kingdom, but thought it a story concerted between Glumdalclitch and her father, who had taught me a set of words to make me sell at a higher price. Upon this imagination he put several other questions to me and still received rational answers, no otherwise defective than by a foreign accent and an imperfect knowledge in the language, with some rustic phrases which I had learned at the farmer's house and did not suit the polite style of a court.

His Majesty sent for three great scholars who were then in their weekly waiting (according to the custom in that country). These gentlemen, after they had a while examined my shape with much nicety, were of different opinions concerning me. They all agreed that I could not be produced according to the regular laws of nature, because I was not framed with a capacity of preserving my life, either by swiftness, or climbing of trees, or digging holes in the earth. They observed by

[2] Escritoire, writing desk.

my teeth, which they viewed with great exactness, that I was a carnivorous animal; yet, most quadrupeds being an over-match for me, and field mice, with some others, too nimble, they could not imagine how I should be able to support myself, unless I fed upon snails and other insects, which they offered by many learned arguments to evince that I could not possibly do. One of them seemed to think that I might be an embryo, or abortive birth. But this opinion was rejected by the other two, who observed my limbs to be perfect and finished, and that I had lived several years, as it was manifested from my beard, the stumps whereof they plainly discovered through a magnifying-glass. They would not allow me to be a dwarf, be-cause my littleness was beyond all degrees of comparison; for the Queen's favourite dwarf, the smallest ever known in that kingdom, was near thirty foot high. After much debate, they concluded unanimously that I was only *relplum scalcath*, which is, interpreted literally, *lusus naturae;* [3] a determination exactly agreeable to the modern philosophy of Europe, whose professors, disdaining the old evasion of *occult causes*,[4] whereby the followers of Aristotle endeavour in vain to disguise their ignorance, have invented this wonderful solution of all difficul-ties, to the unspeakable advancement of human knowledge.

After this decisive conclusion, I entreated to be heard a word or two. I applied myself to the King and assured his Majesty that I came from a country which abounded with several mil-lions of both sexes and of my own stature; where the animals, trees, and houses were all in proportion, and where by conse-quence I might be as able to defend myself, and to find sustenance, as any of his Majesty's subjects could do here;

[3] Sport of nature.
[4] Cf. Thomas Hobbes in *Leviathan* (1651) IV, Chapter 46: "And in many occasions they put for cause of natural events their own ignorance; but disguised in other words . . . as when they attribute many effects to *occult qualities;* that is, qualities not known to them; and therefore also, as they think, to no man else." See Part Three, Chapter Eight, Note 4.

which I took for a full answer to those gentlemen's arguments. To this they only replied with a smile of contempt, saying that the farmer had instructed me very well in my lesson. The King, who had a much better understanding, dismissing his learned men, sent for the farmer, who by good fortune was not yet gone out of town; having therefore first examined him privately, and then confronted him with me and the young girl, his Majesty began to think that what we told him might possibly be true. He desired the Queen to order that a particular care should be taken of me, and was of opinion that Glumdalclitch should still continue in her office of tending me, because he observed we had a great affection for each other. A convenient apartment was provided for her at court; she had a sort of governess appointed to take care of her education, a maid to dress her, and two other servants for menial offices; but the care of me was wholly appropriated to herself. The Queen commanded her own cabinet-maker to contrive a box that might serve me for a bed-chamber, after the model that Glumdalclitch and I should agree upon. This man was a most ingenious artist and, according to my directions, in three weeks finished for me a wooden chamber of sixteen foot square and twelve high, with sash-windows,[5] a door, and two closets, like a London bed-chamber. The board that made the ceiling was to be lifted up and down by two hinges, to put in a bed ready furnished by her Majesty's upholsterer, which Glumdalclitch took out every day to air, made it with her own hands, and letting it down at night, locked up the roof over me. A nice workman, who was famous for little curiosities, undertook to make me two chairs, with backs and frames of a substance not unlike ivory, and two tables, with a cabinet to put my things in. The room was quilted on all sides as well as the floor and the ceiling, to prevent any accident from the carelessness of those who carried me and to break the force of a jolt when I went in a coach. I desired a lock for my door to prevent rats and mice

[5] These began to replace casements in the late seventeenth century and were still very new and modish, in high London fashion.

from coming in: the smith after several attempts made the smallest that was ever seen among them, for I have known a larger at the gate of a gentleman's house in England. I made a shift to keep the key in a pocket of my own, fearing Glumdalclitch might lose it. The Queen likewise ordered the thinnest silks that could be gotten, to make me clothes, not much thicker than an English blanket, very cumbersome till I was accustomed to them. They were after the fashion of the kingdom, partly resembling the Persian and partly the Chinese, and are a very grave decent habit.

The Queen became so fond of my company that she could not dine without me. I had a table placed upon the same at which her Majesty eat, just at her left elbow, and a chair to sit on. Glumdalclitch stood upon a stool on the floor, near my table, to assist and take care of me. I had an entire set of silver dishes and plates and other necessaries, which, in proportion to those of the Queen, were not much bigger than what I have seen in a London toy-shop for the furniture of a baby-house: these my little nurse kept in her pocket in a silver box, and gave me at meals as I wanted them, always cleaning them herself. No person dined with the Queen but the two princesses royal, the elder sixteen years old and the younger at that time thirteen and a month. Her Majesty used to put a bit of meat upon one of my dishes, out of which I carved for myself; and her diversion was to see me eat in miniature. For the Queen (who had indeed but a weak stomach) took up at one mouthful as much as a dozen English farmers could eat at a meal, which to me was for some time a very nauseous sight. She would craunch the wing of a lark, bones and all, between her teeth, although it were nine times as large as that of a full-grown turkey; and put a bit of bread in her mouth as big as two twelve-penny loaves.[6] She drank out of a golden cup, above a hogshead at a draught.[7] Her knives were twice as long

[6] Very large loaves.
[7] Compare the account of Gulliver's own diet in Lilliput (Part One, Chapter One, pp. 9–10).

as a scythe set straight upon the handle. The spoons, forks, and other instruments were all in the same proportion. I remember when Glumdalclitch carried me out of curiosity to see some of the tables at court, where ten or a dozen of these enormous knives and forks were lifted up together, I thought I had never till then beheld so terrible a sight.

It is the custom that every Wednesday (which, as I have before observed, was their Sabbath) the King and Queen, with the royal issue of both sexes, dine together in the apartment of his Majesty, to whom I was now become a favourite; and at these times my little chair and table were placed at his left hand before one of the salt-cellars. This prince took a pleasure in conversing with me, enquiring into the manners, religion, laws, government, and learning of Europe; wherein I gave him the best account I was able. His apprehension was so clear, and his judgment so exact, that he made very wise reflections and observations upon all I said. But I confess that after I had been a little too copious in talking of my own beloved country, of our trade, and wars by sea and land, of our schisms in religion, and parties in the state, the prejudices of his education prevailed so far that he could not forbear taking me up in his right hand and, stroking me gently with the other, after an hearty fit of laughing, asked me whether I were a Whig or a Tory. Then turning to his first minister, who waited behind him with a white staff, near as tall as the main-mast of the *Royal Sovereign*,[8] he observed how contemptible a thing was human grandeur, which could be mimicked by such diminutive insects as I: "And yet," said he, "I dare engage, those creatures have their titles and distinctions of honour, they contrive little nests and burrows, that they call houses and cities; they make a figure in dress and equipage;[9] they love, they fight, they dispute, they cheat, they betray." And thus he continued on, while my colour came and went several times, with indignation

[8] One of the largest ships in the English navy.
[9] Retinue, following.

to hear our noble country, the mistress of arts and arms, the scourge of France, the arbitress of Europe, the seat of virtue, piety, honour, and truth, the pride and envy of the world, so contemptuously treated.[10]

But, as I was not in a condition to resent injuries, so, upon mature thoughts, I began to doubt whether I were injured or no. For, after having been accustomed several months to the sight and converse of this people, and observed every object upon which I cast my eyes to be of proportionable magnitude, the horror I had first conceived from their bulk and aspect was so far worn off that, if I had then beheld a company of English lords and ladies in their finery and birthday clothes,[11] acting their several parts in the most courtly manner of strutting and bowing and prating, to say the truth, I should have been strongly tempted to laugh as much at them as this king and his grandees did at me. Neither indeed could I forbear smiling at myself, when the Queen used to place me upon her hand towards a looking-glass, by which both our persons appeared before me in full view together; and there could nothing be more ridiculous than the comparison: so that I really began to imagine myself dwindled many degrees below my usual size.

Nothing angered and mortified me so much as the Queen's dwarf, who, being of the lowest stature that was ever in that country (for I verily think he was not full thirty foot high), became so insolent at seeing a creature so much beneath him that he would always affect to swagger and look big as he passed by me in the Queen's antechamber, while I was standing on some table talking with the lords or ladies of the court; and he seldom failed of a smart word or two upon my littleness; against which I could only revenge myself by calling him brother, challenging him to wrestle, and such repartees as are usual in the mouths of court pages. One day at dinner this malicious little cub was so nettled with something I had said

[10] Compare the court rhetoric of Lilliput in the articles (Part One, Chapter Three, pp. 31–33).

[11] Clothes worn for the celebration of the royal birthday.

to him that, raising himself upon the frame of her Majesty's chair, he took me up by the middle as I was sitting down, not thinking any harm, and let me drop into a large silver bowl of cream, and then ran away as fast as he could. I fell over head and ears, and if I had not been a good swimmer, it might have gone very hard with me; for Glumdalclitch in that instant happened to be at the other end of the room, and the Queen was in such a fright that she wanted presence of mind to assist me. But my little nurse ran to my relief, and took me out, after I had swallowed above a quart of cream. I was put to bed; however I received no other damage than the loss of a suit of clothes, which was utterly spoiled. The dwarf was soundly whipped and, as a further punishment, forced to drink up the bowl of cream into which he had thrown me; neither was he ever restored to favour: for, soon after, the Queen bestowed him to a lady of high quality, so that I saw him no more, to my very great satisfaction; for I could not tell to what extremity such a malicious urchin might have carried his resentment.

He had before served me a scurvy trick which set the Queen a-laughing, although at the same time she were heartily vexed, and would have immediately cashiered him if I had not been so generous as to intercede. Her Majesty had taken a marrow-bone upon her plate and, after knocking out the marrow, placed the bone again in the dish erect as it stood before; the dwarf watching his opportunity, while Glumdalclitch was gone to the sideboard, mounted the stool she stood on to take care of me at meals, took me up in both hands, and squeezing my legs together, wedged them into the marrow-bone above my waist, where I stuck for some time and made a very ridiculous figure. I believe it was near a minute before anyone knew what was become of me, for I thought it below me to cry out. But, as princes seldom get their meat hot,[12] my legs

[12] With the enormous growth of elaborate building in eighteenth-century England, it was a standing joke that meat (i.e., food in general) could not be carried the vast distances between kitchen and dining hall without cooling. The ceremoniousness of service

were not scalded, only my stockings and breeches in a sad condition. The dwarf at my entreaty had no other punishment than a sound whipping.

I was frequently rallied by the Queen upon account of my fearfulness, and she used to ask me whether the people of my country were as great cowards as myself. The occasion was this. The kingdom is much pestered with flies in summer, and these odious insects, each of them as big as a Dunstable lark,[13] hardly gave me any rest while I sat at dinner, with their continual humming and buzzing about my ears. They would sometimes alight upon my victuals and leave their loathsome excrement or spawn behind, which to me was very visible, although not to the natives of that country, whose large optics were not so acute as mine in viewing smaller objects. Sometimes they would fix upon my nose or forehead, where they stung me to the quick, smelling very offensively, and I could easily trace that viscous matter which our naturalists tell us enables those creatures to walk with their feet upwards upon a ceiling. I had much ado to defend myself against these detestable animals, and could not forbear starting when they came on my face. It was the common practice of the dwarf to catch a number of these insects in his hand as schoolboys do among us, and let them out suddenly under my nose, on purpose to frighten me and divert the Queen. My remedy was to cut them in pieces with my knife as they flew in the air, wherein my dexterity was much admired.

I remember one morning when Glumdalclitch had set me in my box upon a window, as she usually did in fair days to give me air (for I durst not venture to let the box be hung on a nail out of the window, as we do with cages in England), after I had lifted up one of my sashes and sat down at my table to eat a piece of sweet-cake for my breakfast, above twenty

was also a matter for satire. Pope describes the ostentation of a country house where the dinner guest is "tantalized in state." (*Epistle to Lord Burlington*, 1731).

[13] An exceptionally large lark, served as a table delicacy.

wasps, allured by the smell, came flying into the room, humming louder than the drones of as many bagpipes. Some of them seized my cake and carried it piecemeal away, others flew about my head and face, confounding me with the noise and putting me in the utmost terror of their stings. However I had the courage to rise and draw my hanger, and attack them in the air. I dispatched four of them, but the rest got away, and I presently shut my window. These insects were as large as partridges: I took out their stings, found them an inch and a half long, and as sharp as needles. I carefully preserved them all, and having since shown them with some other curiosities in several parts of Europe, upon my return to England I gave three of them to Gresham College,[14] and kept the fourth for myself.

Chapter Four: The country described. A proposal for correcting modern maps. The King's palace, and some account of the metropolis. The author's way of travelling. The chief temple described.

I now intend to give the reader a short description of this country as far as I travelled in it, which was not above two thousand miles round Lorbrulgrud, the metropolis. For the Queen, whom I always attended, never went further when she accompanied the King in his progresses,[1] and there stayed till his Majesty returned from viewing his frontiers. The whole extent of this prince's dominions reacheth about six thousand miles in length, and from three to five in breadth. From whence I cannot but conclude that our geographers of Europe are in a great error by supposing nothing but sea between Japan and

[14] The first home of the "Royal Society of London for Improving Natural Knowledge," which in 1666 established a museum with a bequest of "a collection of rarities."

[1] Official journeys.

California; for it was ever my opinion that there must be a balance of earth to counterpoise the great continent of Tartary;[2] and therefore they ought to correct their maps and charts by joining this vast tract of land to the northwest parts of America, wherein I shall be ready to lend them my assistance.

The kingdom is a peninsula, terminated to the northeast by a ridge of mountains thirty miles high, which are altogether impassable by reason of the volcanoes upon the tops. Neither do the most learned know what sort of mortals inhabit beyond these mountains, or whether they be inhabited at all. On the three other sides it is bounded by the ocean. There is not one seaport in the whole kingdom, and those parts of the coasts into which the rivers issue are so full of pointed rocks, and the sea generally so rough, that there is no venturing with the smallest of their boats; so that these people are wholly excluded from any commerce with the rest of the world. But the large rivers are full of vessels and abound with excellent fish, for they seldom get any from the sea, because the sea-fish are of the same size with those in Europe and consequently not worth catching; whereby it is manifest that nature in the production of plants and animals of so extraordinary a bulk is wholly confined to this continent, of which I leave the reasons to be determined by philosophers. However, now and then they take a whale that happens to be dashed against the rocks, which the common people feed on heartily. These whales I have known so large that a man could hardly carry one upon his shoulders; and sometimes for curiosity they are brought in hampers to Lorbrulgrud: I saw one of them in a dish at the King's table, which passed for a rarity, but I did not observe he was fond of it; for I think indeed the bigness disgusted him, although I have seen one somewhat larger in Greenland.

The country is well inhabited, for it contains fifty-one cities, near an hundred walled towns, and a great number of villages.

[2] The central land mass of Asia.

To satisfy my curious reader, it may be sufficient to describe Lorbrulgrud. This city stands upon almost two equal parts on each side the river that passes through. It contains above eighty thousand houses, and about six hundred thousand inhabitants. It is in length three *glonglungs* (which make about fifty-four English miles) and two and a half in breadth, as I measured it myself in the royal map made by the King's order, which was laid on the ground on purpose for me, and extended an hundred feet; I paced the diameter and circumference several times barefoot and, computing by the scale, measured it pretty exactly.

The King's palace is no regular edifice, but an heap of buildings about seven miles round: the chief rooms are generally two hundred and forty foot high and broad and long in proportion. A coach was allowed to Glumdalclitch and me, wherein her governess frequently took her out to see the town or go among the shops; and I was always of the party, carried in my box; although the girl at my own desire would often take me out and hold me in her hand that I might more conveniently view the houses and the people as we passed along the streets. I reckoned our coach to be about a square of Westminster Hall,[3] but not altogether so high; however, I cannot be very exact. One day the governess ordered our coachman to stop at several shops, where the beggars, watching their opportunity, crowded to the sides of the coach, and gave me the most horrible spectacles that ever an European eye beheld. There was a woman with a cancer in her breast, swelled to a monstrous size, full of holes, in two or three of which I could have easily crept and covered my whole body. There was a fellow with a wen in his neck, larger than five woolpacks, and another with a couple of wooden legs, each about twenty foot high. But the most hateful sight of all was the lice crawling on their clothes. I could see distinctly the limbs of these ver-

[3] About equal in area to Westminster Hall (approximately 20,000 square feet) but not quite so high (eighty-five to ninety feet). See Part One, Chapter One, Note 23.

min with my naked eye, much better than those of an European louse through a microscope, and their snouts with which they rooted like swine. They were the first I had ever beheld, and I should have been curious enough to dissect one of them, if I had proper instruments (which I unluckily left behind me in the ship), although indeed the sight was so nauseous that it perfectly turned my stomach.

Beside the large box in which I was usually carried, the Queen ordered a smaller one to be made for me, of about twelve foot square and ten high, for the convenience of travelling, because the other was somewhat too large for Glumdalclitch's lap and cumbersome in the coach; it was made by the same artist, whom I directed in the whole contrivance. This travelling closet was an exact square [4] with a window in the middle of three of the squares, and each window was latticed with iron wire on the outside to prevent accidents in long journeys. On the fourth side, which had no window, two strong staples were fixed, through which the person that carried me, when I had a mind to be on horseback, put in a leathern belt and buckled it about his waist. This was always the office of some grave trusty servant in whom I could confide, whether I attended the King and Queen in their progresses, or were disposed to see the gardens, or pay a visit to some great lady or minister of state in the court, when Glumdalclitch happened to be out of order: for I soon began to be known and esteemed among the greatest officers, I suppose more upon account of their Majesties' favour than any merit of my own. In journeys, when I was weary of the coach, a servant on horseback would buckle my box and place it on a cushion before him; and there I had a full prospect of the country on three sides from my three windows. I had in this closet a field-bed and a hammock hung from the ceiling, two chairs and a table neatly screwed to the floor, to prevent being tossed about by the agitation of the horse or the coach. And having been

[4] Cube, since all sides are square.

long used to sea-voyages, those motions, although sometimes very violent, did not much discompose me.

Whenever I had a mind to see the town, it was always in my travelling-closet, which Glumdalclitch held in her lap in a kind of open sedan,[5] after the fashion of the country, borne by four men, and attended by two others in the Queen's livery. The people, who had often heard of me, were very curious to crowd about the sedan, and the girl was complaisant enough to make the bearers stop and to take me in her hand that I might be more conveniently seen.

I was very desirous to see the chief temple, and particularly the tower belonging to it, which is reckoned the highest in the kingdom. Accordingly one day my nurse carried me thither, but I may truly say I came back disappointed; for the height is not above three thousand foot, reckoning from the ground to the highest pinnacle top; which, allowing for the difference between the size of those people and us in Europe, is no great matter for admiration, nor at all equal in proportion (if I rightly remember) to Salisbury steeple.[6] But, not to detract from a nation to which during my life I shall acknowledge myself extremely obliged, it must be allowed that whatever this famous tower wants in height is amply made up in beauty and strength. For the walls are near an hundred foot thick, built of hewn stone, whereof each is about forty foot square, and adorned on all sides with statues of gods and emperors cut in marble larger than the life, placed in their several niches. I measured a little finger which had fallen down from one of these statues and lay unperceived among some rubbish, and found it exactly four foot and an inch in length. Glumdalclitch wrapped it up in a handkerchief, and carried it home in her pocket to keep among other trinkets, of which the girl was very fond, as children at her age usually are.

The King's kitchen is indeed a noble building, vaulted at

---

[5] An open sedan chair, as opposed to the "close chair."
[6] The tallest spire in England, 404 feet high.

top, and about six hundred foot high. The great oven is not so wide by ten paces as the cupola at St. Paul's:[7] for I measured the latter on purpose after my return. But if I should describe the kitchen-grate, the prodigious pots and kettles, the joints of meat turning on the spits, with many other particulars, perhaps I should be hardly believed; at least a severe critic would be apt to think I enlarged a little, as travellers are often suspected to do. To avoid which censure, I fear I have run too much into the other extreme; and that if this treatise should happen to be translated into the language of Brobdingnag (which is the general name of that kingdom) and transmitted thither, the King and his people would have reason to complain that I had done them an injury by a false and diminutive representation.

His Majesty seldom keeps above six hundred horses in his stables: they are generally from fifty-four to sixty foot high. But when he goes abroad on solemn days, he is attended for state by a militia guard of five hundred horse, which indeed I thought was the most splendid sight that could be ever beheld, till I saw part of his army in battalia,[8] whereof I shall find another occasion to speak.

Chapter Five: Several adventures that happened to the author. The execution of a criminal. The author shows his skill in navigation.

I should have lived happy enough in that country, if my littleness had not exposed me to several ridiculous and troublesome accidents, some of which I shall venture to relate. Glumdalclitch often carried me into the gardens of the court in my

[7] The dome of St. Paul's Cathedral, London, has a diameter of 122 feet at its base.
[8] Battle array.

smaller box, and would sometimes take me out of it and hold me in her hand or set me down to walk. I remember, before the dwarf left the Queen, he followed us one day into those gardens, and, my nurse having set me down, he and I being close together near some dwarf apple-trees, I must needs show my wit by a silly allusion between him and the trees, which happens to hold in their language as it doth in ours. Whereupon the malicious rogue, watching his opportunity, when I was walking under one of them, shook it directly over my head, by which a dozen apples, each of them near as large as a Bristol barrel,[1] came tumbling about my ears; one of them hit me on the back as I chanced to stoop and knocked me down flat on my face, but I received no other hurt, and the dwarf was pardoned at my desire, because I had given the provocation.

Another day Glumdalclitch left me on a smooth grass-plot to divert myself while she walked at some distance with her governess. In the meantime there suddenly fell such a violent shower of hail that I was immediately by the force of it struck to the ground: and when I was down, the hailstones gave me such cruel bangs all over the body as if I had been pelted with tennis-balls; however I made a shift to creep on all four and shelter myself by lying flat on my face on the lee-side of a border of lemon thyme, but so bruised from head to foot that I could not go abroad in ten days. Neither is this at all to be wondered at, because nature in that country observing the same proportion through all her operations, a hailstone is near eighteen hundred times as large as one in Europe, which I can assert upon experience, having been so curious to weigh and measure them.

But a more dangerous accident happened to me in the same garden when my little nurse, believing she had put me in a secure place, which I often entreated her to do that I might enjoy my own thoughts, and having left my box at home to

[1] Hogshead, large cask.

avoid the trouble of carrying it, went to another part of the gardens with her governess and some ladies of her acquaintance. While she was absent and out of hearing, a small white spaniel belonging to one of the chief gardeners, having got by accident into the garden, happened to range near the place where I lay. The dog, following the scent, came directly up, and taking me in his mouth ran straight to his master, wagging his tail, and set me gently on the ground. By good fortune he had been so well taught that I was carried between his teeth without the least hurt, or even tearing my clothes. But the poor gardener, who knew me well and had a great kindness for me, was in a terrible fright. He gently took me up in both his hands and asked me how I did; but I was so amazed and out of breath that I could not speak a word. In a few minutes I came to myself, and he carried me safe to my little nurse, who by this time had returned to the place where she left me, and was in cruel agonies when I did not appear nor answer when she called: she severely reprimanded the gardener on account of his dog. But the thing was hushed up and never known at court; for the girl was afraid of the Queen's anger, and truly, as to myself, I thought it would not be for my reputation that such a story should go about.

This accident absolutely determined Glumdalclitch never to trust me abroad for the future out of her sight. I had been long afraid of this resolution, and therefore concealed from her some little unlucky adventures that happened in those times when I was left by myself. Once a kite hovering over the garden made a stoop [2] at me, and if I had not resolutely drawn my hanger, and run under a thick espalier, he would have certainly carried me away in his talons. Another time walking to the top of a fresh mole-hill, I fell to my neck in the hole through which that animal had cast up the earth, and coined some lie not worth remembering, to excuse myself for spoiling my clothes. I likewise broke [3] my right shin against the shell

[2] Dive.
[3] Bruised.

of a snail, which I happened to stumble over as I was walking alone and thinking on poor England.

I cannot tell whether I were more pleased or mortified to observe, in those solitary walks, that the smaller birds did not appear to be at all afraid of me, but would hop about within a yard distance, looking for worms and other food with as much indifference and security as if no creature at all were near them. I remember a thrush had the confidence to snatch out of my hand with his bill a piece of cake that Glumdalclitch had just given me for my breakfast. When I attempted to catch any of these birds, they would boldly turn against me, endevouring to pick my fingers, which I durst not venture within their reach; and then they would hop back unconcerned to hunt for worms or snails as they did before. But one day I took a thick cudgel, and threw it with all my strength so luckily at a linnet that I knocked him down, and seizing him by the neck with both my hands, ran with him in triumph to my nurse. However, the bird, who had only been stunned, recovering himself, gave me so many boxes with his wings on both sides of my head and body, although I held him at arm's length and was out of the reach of his claws, that I was twenty times thinking to let him go. But I was soon relieved by one of our servants, who wrung off the bird's neck, and I had him next day for dinner by the Queen's command. This linnet, as near as I can remember, seemed to be somewhat larger than an English swan.

The maids of honour often invited Glumdalclitch to their apartments, and desired she would bring me along with her, on purpose to have the pleasure of seeing and touching me. They would often strip me naked from top to toe, and lay me at full length in their bosoms; wherewith I was much disgusted; because, to say the truth, a very offensive smell came from their skins; which I do not mention or intend to the disadvantage of those excellent ladies, for whom I have all manner of respect; but I conceive that my sense was more acute in proportion to my littleness, and that those illustrious persons were no more disagreeable to their lovers, or to each other, than people of the same quality are with us in England. And, after all, I found their natural smell was much more supportable than when they used perfumes, under which I immediately swooned away. I cannot forget that an intimate friend of mine in Lilliput took the freedom, in a warm day, when I had used a good deal of exercise, to complain of a strong smell about me, although I am as little faulty that way as most of my sex: but I suppose his faculty of smelling was as nice with regard to me as mine was to that of this people. Upon this point, I cannot forbear doing justice to the Queen my mistress, and Glumdalclitch my nurse, whose persons were as sweet as those of any lady in England.

That which gave me most uneasiness among these maids of honour, when my nurse carried me to visit them, was to see them use me without any manner of ceremony, like a creature who had no sort of consequence. For they would strip themselves to the skin and put on their smocks in my presence, while I was placed on their toilet [4] directly before their naked bodies, which, I am sure, to me was very far from being a tempting sight or from giving me any other emotions than those of horror and disgust. Their skins appeared so coarse and uneven, so variously coloured, when I saw them near, with a mole here and there as broad as a trencher, and hairs hanging from it thicker than pack-threads; to say nothing further concerning the rest of their persons. Neither did they at all scruple while I was by to discharge what they had drunk, to the quantity of at least two hogsheads, in a vessel that held above three tuns. The handsomest among these maids of honour, a pleasant frolicsome girl of sixteen, would sometimes set me astride upon one of her nipples, with many other tricks, wherein the reader will excuse me for not being over particular. But I was so much displeased that I entreated Glumdalclitch to contrive some excuse for not seeing that young lady any more.

[4] Dressing table.

One day a young gentleman, who was nephew to my nurse's governess, came and pressed them both to see an execution. It was of a man who had murdered one of that gentleman's intimate acquaintance. Glumdalclitch was prevailed on to be of the company, very much against her inclination, for she was naturally tender-hearted: and as for myself, although I abhorred such kind of spectacles, yet my curiosity tempted me to see something that I thought must be extraordinary. The malefactor was fixed in a chair upon a scaffold erected for the purpose, and his head cut off at one blow with a sword of about forty foot long. The veins and arteries spouted up such a prodigious quantity of blood, and so high in the air, that the great *jet d'eau* at Versailles [5] was not equal for the time it lasted; and the head, when it fell on the scaffold floor, gave such a bounce as made me start, although I was at least an English mile distant.

The Queen, who often used to hear me talk of my sea-voyages, and took all occasions to divert me when I was melancholy, asked me whether I understood how to handle a sail or an oar, and whether a little exercise of rowing might not be convenient for my health. I answered that I understood both very well. For although my proper employment had been to be surgeon or doctor to the ship, yet often, upon a pinch, I was forced to work like a common mariner. But I could not see how this could be done in their country, where the smallest wherry was equal to a first-rate man-of-war among us, and such a boat as I could manage would never live in any of their rivers: her Majesty said, if I would contrive a boat, her own joiner should make it, and she would provide a place for me to sail in. The fellow was an ingenious workman, and by my instructions in ten days finished a pleasure-boat with all its tackling, able conveniently to hold eight Europeans. When it was finished, the Queen was so delighted that she ran with it

[5] The largest fountain at Versailles spouted water seventy-four feet into the air.

in her lap to the King, who ordered it to be put in a cistern full of water, with me in it, by way of trial, where I could not manage my two sculls or little oars for want of room. But the Queen had before contrived another project. She ordered the joiner to make a wooden trough of three hundred foot long, fifty broad, and eight deep; which being well pitched to prevent leaking, was placed on the floor along the wall in an outer room of the palace. It had a cock near the bottom to let out the water when it began to grow stale, and two servants could easily fill it in half an hour. Here I often used to row for my diversion, as well as that of the Queen and her ladies, who thought themselves agreeably entertained with my skill and agility. Sometimes I would put up my sail, and then my business was only to steer, while the ladies gave me a gale with their fans; and when they were weary, some of the pages would blow my sail forward with their breath, while I showed my art by steering starboard or larboard as I pleased. When I had done, Glumdalclitch always carried back my boat into her closet [6] and hung it on a nail to dry.

In this exercise I once met an accident which had like to have cost me my life. For, one of the pages having put my boat into the trough, the governess who attended Glumdalclitch very officiously lifted me up to place me in the boat, but I happened to slip through her fingers, and should have infallibly fallen down forty foot upon the floor if, by the luckiest chance in the world, I had not been stopped by a corking-pin [7] that stuck in the good gentlewoman's stomacher; the head of the pin passed between my shirt and the waistband of my breeches, and thus I was held by the middle in the air till Glumdalclitch ran to my relief.

Another time one of the servants, whose office it was to fill my trough every third day with fresh water, was so careless to let a huge frog (not perceiving it) slip out of his pail. The

[6] Small private room, like "cabinet."
[7] A very large pin.

frog lay concealed till I was put into my boat, but then seeing a resting place, climbed up, and made it lean so much on one side that I was forced to balance it with all my weight on the other, to prevent overturning. When the frog was got in, it hopped at once half the length of the boat, and then over my head backwards and forwards, daubing my face and clothes with its odious slime. The largeness of its features made it appear the most deformed animal that can be conceived. However, I desired Glumdalclitch to let me deal with it alone. I banged it a good while with one of my sculls, and at last forced it to leap out of the boat.

But the greatest danger I ever underwent in that kingdom was from a monkey, who belonged to one of the clerks of the kitchen. Glumdalclitch had locked me up in her closet while she went somewhere upon business or a visit. The weather being very warm, the closet window was left open, as well as the windows and the door of my bigger box, in which I usually lived because of its largeness and conveniency. As I sat quietly meditating at my table, I heard something bounce in at the closet window and skip about from one side to the other; whereat, although I were much alarmed, yet I ventured to look out, but not stirring from my seat; and then I saw this frolicsome animal frisking and leaping up and down till at last he came to my box, which he seemed to view with great pleasure and curiosity, peeping in at the door and every window. I retreated to the farther corner of my room, or box, but the monkey, looking in at every side, put me into such a fright that I wanted presence of mind to conceal myself under the bed, as I might easily have done. After some time spent in peeping, grinning, and chattering, he at last espied me, and reaching one of his paws in at the door, as a cat does when she plays with a mouse, although I often shifted place to avoid him, he at length seized the lappet of my coat (which being made of that country silk, was very thick and strong) and dragged me out. He took me up in his right forefoot, and held me as a nurse does a child she is going to suckle, just as I have

seen the same sort of creature do with a kitten in Europe: and
when I offered to struggle, he squeezed me so hard that I
thought it more prudent to submit. I have good reason to believe that he took me for a young one of his own species, by
his often stroking my face very gently with his other paw. In
these diversions he was interrupted by a noise at the closet door,
as if somebody were opening it; whereupon he suddenly
leaped up to the window at which he had come in and thence
upon the leads and gutters, walking upon three legs and holding me in the fourth, till he clambered up to a roof that was
next to ours. I heard Glumdalclitch give a shriek at the moment he was carrying me out. The poor girl was almost dis-
tracted: that quarter of the palace was all in an uproar; the
servants ran for ladders; the monkey was seen by hundreds in
the court sitting upon the ridge of a building, holding me like
a baby in one of his fore-paws, and feeding me with the other,
by cramming into my mouth some victuals he had squeezed
out of the bag on one side of his chaps, and patting me when
I would not eat; whereat many of the rabble below could not
forbear laughing; neither do I think they justly ought to be
blamed, for without question the sight was ridiculous enough
to everybody but myself. Some of the people threw up stones,
hoping to drive the monkey down; but this was strictly forbidden, or else very probably my brains had been dashed out.

The ladders were now applied and mounted by several men,
which the monkey observing, and finding himself almost encompassed, not being able to make speed enough with his three
legs, let me drop on a ridge tile, and made his escape. Here I
sat for some time five hundred yards from the ground, expecting every moment to be blown down by the wind, or to fall
by my own giddiness, and come tumbling over and over from
the ridge to the eaves. But an honest lad, one of my nurse's
footmen, climbed up, and putting me into his breeches pocket,
brought me down safe.

I was almost choked with the filthy stuff the monkey had
crammed down my throat; but my dear little nurse picked it

out of my mouth with a small needle, and then I fell a-vomiting, which gave me great relief. Yet I was so weak and bruised in the sides with the squeezes given me by this odious animal that I was forced to keep my bed a fortnight. The King, Queen and all the court sent every day to enquire after my health, and her Majesty made me several visits during my sickness. The monkey was killed, and an order made that no such animal should be kept about the palace.

When I attended the King after my recovery, to return him thanks for his favours, he was pleased to rally me a good deal upon this adventure. He asked me what my thoughts and speculations were while I lay in the monkey's paw, how I liked the victuals he gave me, his manner of feeding, and whether the fresh air on the roof had sharpened my stomach. He desired to know what I would have done upon such an occasion in my own country. I told his Majesty that in Europe we had no monkeys, except such as were brought for curiosities from other places, and so small that I could deal with a dozen of them together, if they presumed to attack me. And as for that monstrous animal with whom I was so lately engaged (it was indeed as large as an elephant), if my fears had suffered me to think so far as to make use of my hanger (looking fiercely and clapping my hand upon the hilt as I spoke) when he poked his paw into my chamber, perhaps I should have given him such a wound as would have made him glad to withdraw it with more haste than he put it in. This I delivered in a firm tone, like a person who was jealous lest his courage should be called in question. However, my speech produced nothing else besides a loud laughter, which all the respect due to his Majesty from those about him could not make them contain. This made me reflect how vain an attempt it is for a man to endeavour doing himself honour among those who are out of all degree of equality or comparison with him. And yet I have seen the moral of my own behaviour very frequent in England since my return, where a little contemptible varlet, without the least title to birth, person, wit, or common sense,

shall presume to look with importance and put himself upon
a foot with the greatest persons of the kingdom.

I was every day furnishing the court with some ridiculous
story; and Glumdalclitch, although she loved me to excess, yet
was arch enough to inform the Queen whenever I committed
any folly that she thought would be diverting to her Majesty.
The girl, who had been out of order, was carried by her governess to take the air about an hour's distance, or thirty miles
from town. They alighted out of the coach near a small footpath in a field, and Glumdalclitch setting down my travelling
box, I went out of it to walk. There was a cow-dung in the
path, and I must needs try my activity by attempting to leap
over it. I took a run, but unfortunately jumped short, and
found myself just in the middle up to my knees. I waded
through with some difficulty, and one of the footmen wiped
me as clean as he could with his handkerchief; for I was filthily
bemired, and my nurse confined me to my box till we returned
home; where the Queen was soon informed of what had passed,
and the footmen spread it about the court, so that all the mirth
for some days was at my expense.

*Chapter Six: Several contrivances of the author to please the King
and Queen. He shows his skill in music. The King enquires into the
state of Europe, which the author relates to him. The King's observations thereon.*

I used to attend the King's levee [1] once or twice a week, and
had often seen him under the barber's hand, which indeed was
at first very terrible to behold. For the razor was almost twice

[1] From the French *lever*, to rise; a formal reception at the King's
rising from bed, attended by the royal household and distinguished
nobility and ministers. The ceremony had been elaborated by
Louis XIV.

as long as an ordinary scythe. His Majesty according to the custom of the country was only shaved twice a week. I once prevailed on the barber to give me some of the suds or lather, out of which I picked forty or fifty of the strongest stumps of hair. I then took a piece of fine wood and cut it like the back of a comb, making several holes in it at equal distance with as small a needle as I could get from Glumdalclitch. I fixed in the stumps so artificially,[2] scraping and sloping them with my knife towards the points, that I made a very tolerable comb; which was a seasonable supply, my own being so much broken in the teeth that it was almost useless: neither did I know any artist in that country so nice and exact as would undertake to make me another.

And this puts me in mind of an amusement wherein I spent many of my leisure hours. I desired the Queen's woman to save for me the combings of her Majesty's hair, whereof in time I got a good quantity, and consulting with my friend the cabinetmaker, who had received general orders to do little jobs for me, I directed him to make two chair-frames no larger than those I had in my box, and then to bore little holes with a fine awl round those parts where I designed the backs and seats; through these holes I wove the strongest hairs I could pick out, just after the manner of cane-chairs in England. When they were finished, I made a present of them to her Majesty, who kept them in her cabinet and used to show them for curiosities, as indeed they were the wonder of everyone who beheld them. The Queen would have had me sit upon one of these chairs, but I absolutely refused to obey her, protesting I would rather die a thousand deaths than place a dishonourable part of my body on those precious hairs that once adorned her Majesty's head. Of these hairs (as I had always a mechanical genius) I likewise made a neat little purse about five foot long, with her Majesty's name deciphered[3] in gold

2 Artfully.
3 Inscribed, woven.

letters, which I gave to Glumdalclitch by the Queen's consent. To say the truth, it was more for show than use, being not of strength to bear the weight of the larger coins, and therefore she kept nothing in it but some little toys that girls are fond of.

The King, who delighted in music, had frequent consorts [4] at court, to which I was sometimes carried and set in my box on a table to hear them: but the noise was so great that I could hardly distinguish the tunes. I am confident that all the drums and trumpets of a royal army, beating and sounding together just at your ears, could not equal it. My practice was to have my box removed from the places where the performers sat as far as I could, then to shut the doors and windows of it and draw the window curtains; after which I found their music not disagreeable.

I had learned in my youth to play a little upon the spinet. Glumdalclitch kept one in her chamber, and a master attended twice a week to teach her: I call it a spinet, because it some-what resembled that instrument and was played upon in the same manner. A fancy came into my head that I would enter-tain the King and Queen with an English tune upon this instru-ment. But this appeared extremely difficult: for the spinet was near sixty foot long, each key being almost a foot wide, so that, with my arms extended, I could not reach to above five keys, and to press them down required a good smart stroke with my fist, which would be too great a labour, and to no purpose. The method I contrived was this. I prepared two round sticks about the bigness of common cudgels; they were thicker at one end than the other, and I covered the thicker ends with a piece of a mouse's skin, that by rapping on them I might neither damage the tops of the keys nor interrupt the sound. Before the spinet a bench was placed about four foot below the keys, and I was put upon the bench. I ran sideling upon it that way and this as fast as I could, banging

[4] Concerts.

the proper keys with my two sticks, and made a shift to play a jig to the great satisfaction of both their Majesties: but it was the most violent exercise I ever underwent, and yet I could not strike above sixteen keys, nor, consequently, play the bass and treble together as other artists do; which was a great disadvantage to my performance.

The King, who, as I before observed, was a prince of excellent understanding, would frequently order that I should be brought in my box and set upon the table in his closet. He would then command me to bring one of my chairs out of the box and sit down within three yards distance upon the top of the cabinet, which brought me almost to a level with his face. In this manner I had several conversations with him. I one day took the freedom to tell his Majesty that the contempt he discovered towards Europe and the rest of the world did not seem answerable to [5] those excellent qualities of mind that he was master of. That reason did not extend itself with the bulk of the body: on the contrary, we observed in our country that the tallest persons were usually least provided with it. That among other animals bees and ants had the reputation of more industry, art, and sagacity than many of the larger kinds. And that, as inconsiderable as he took me to be, I hoped I might live to do his Majesty some signal service. The King heard me with attention and began to conceive a much better opinion of me than he had ever before. He desired I would give him as exact an account of the government of England as I possibly could; because, as fond as princes commonly are of their own customs (for so he conjectured of other monarchs by my former discourses), he should be glad to hear of anything that might deserve imitation.

Imagine with thyself, courteous reader, how often I then wished for the tongue of Demosthenes or Cicero,[6] that might

[5] Consistent with.
[6] Not only as great orators, but as defenders of Greece against Philip of Macedon and of Republican Rome against Mark Antony.

have enabled me to celebrate the praise of my own dear native
country in a style equal to its merits and felicity.

I began my discourse by informing his Majesty that our
dominions consisted of two islands, which composed three
mighty kingdoms under one sovereign, besides our plantations [7]
in America. I dwelt long upon the fertility of our soil and the
temperature [8] of our climate. I then spoke at large upon the
constitution of an English parliament, partly made up of an
illustrious body called the House of Peers, persons of the
noblest blood and of the most ancient and ample patrimonies.
I described that extraordinary care always taken of their education in arts and arms to qualify them for being counsellors
born to the king and kingdom, to have a share in the legislature, to be members of the highest court of judicature from
whence there could be no appeal;[9] and to be champions always
ready for the defence of their prince and country by their
valour, conduct, and fidelity. That these were the ornament
and bulwark of the kingdom, worthy followers of their most
renowned ancestors, whose honour had been the reward of
their virtue, from which their posterity were never once
known to degenerate. To these were joined several holy persons as part of that assembly, under the title of bishops,[10]
whose peculiar business it is to take care of religion and of
those who instruct the people therein. These were searched
and sought out through the whole nation, by the prince and
wisest counsellors, among such of the priesthood as were most
deservedly distinguished by the sanctity of their lives and the
depth of their erudition; who were indeed the spiritual fathers
of the clergy and the people.

That the other part of the parliament consisted of an assembly called the House of Commons, who were all principal

[7] Colonies.
[8] Temperateness.
[9] This was the status of the House of Lords in Swift's day (see
Part Four, Chapter Six, p. 269).
[10] Bishops sit in the House of Lords.

gentlemen,[11] *freely* picked and culled out by the people themselves, for their great abilities and love of their country, to represent the wisdom of the whole nation. And these two bodies make up the most august assembly in Europe, to whom, in conjunction with the prince, the whole legislature[12] is committed.

I then descended to the courts of justice, over which the judges, those venerable sages and interpreters of the law, presided, for determining the disputed rights and properties of men, as well as for the punishment of vice and protection of innocence. I mentioned the prudent management of our treasury, the valour and achievements of our forces by sea and land. I computed the number of our people by reckoning how many millions there might be of each religious sect or political party among us. I did not omit even our sports and pastimes, or any other particular which I thought might redound to the honour of my country. And I finished all with a brief historical account of affairs and events in England for about an hundred years past.

This conversation was not ended under five audiences, each of several hours, and the King heard the whole with great attention, frequently taking notes of what I spoke, as well as memorandums of what questions he intended to ask me.

When I had put an end to these long discourses, his Majesty in a sixth audience, consulting his notes, proposed many doubts, queries, and objections upon every article. He asked what methods were used to cultivate the minds and bodies of our young nobility, and in what kind of business they commonly spent the first and teachable part of their lives. What course was taken to supply that assembly when any noble family became extinct. What qualifications were necessary in those who are to be created new lords: whether the humour of the prince, a sum of money to a court-lady or a prime minister, or a de-

[11] Men of comparatively high social standing, below the nobility but above the tradesmen.
[12] Lawmaking function.

sign of strengthening a party opposite to the public interest ever happened to be motives in those advancements. What share of knowledge these lords had in the laws of their country, and how they came by it, so as to enable them to decide the properties of their fellow-subjects in the last resort. Whether they were always so free from avarice, partialities, or want that a bribe, or some other sinister view, could have no place among them. Whether those holy lords I spoke of were constantly promoted to that rank upon account of their knowledge in religious matters and the sanctity of their lives, had never been compliers with the times while they were common priests, or slavish prostitute chaplains to some nobleman whose opinions they continued servilely to follow after they were admitted into that assembly.

He then desired to know what arts were practised in electing those whom I called commoners. Whether a stranger with a strong purse might not influence the vulgar voters to choose him before their own landlord or the most considerable gentleman in the neighbourhood. How it came to pass that people were so violently bent upon getting into this assembly, which I allowed to be a great trouble and expense, often to the ruin of their families, without any salary or pension: because this appeared such an exalted strain of virtue and public spirit that his Majesty seemed to doubt [13] it might possibly not be always sincere: and he desired to know whether such zealous gentlemen could have any views of refunding themselves for the charges and trouble they were at, by sacrificing the public good to the designs of a weak and vicious prince in conjunction with a corrupted ministry. He multiplied his questions and sifted me thoroughly upon every part of this head, proposing numberless enquiries and objections which I think it not prudent or convenient to repeat.

Upon what I said in relation to our courts of justice, his Majesty desired to be satisfied in several points: and this I was the

[13] Suspect.

better able to do, having been formerly almost ruined by a long suit in Chancery, which was decreed for me with costs. He asked what time was usually spent in determining between right and wrong, and what degree of expense. Whether advocates and orators had liberty to plead in causes manifestly known to be unjust, vexatious, or oppressive. Whether party in religion or politics were observed to be of any weight in the scale of justice. Whether those pleading orators were persons educated in the general knowledge of equity, or only in provincial, national, and other local customs. Whether they or their judges had any part in penning those laws which they assumed the liberty of interpreting and glossing upon at their pleasure. Whether they had ever at different times pleaded for and against the same cause, and cited precedents to prove contrary opinions. Whether they were a rich or a poor corporation. Whether they received any pecuniary reward for pleading or delivering their opinions. And particularly whether they were ever admitted as members in the lower senate.

He fell next upon the management of our treasury, and said he thought my memory had failed me, because I computed our taxes at about five or six millions a year, and when I came to mention the issues, he found they sometimes amounted to more than double; for the notes he had taken were very particular in this point, because he hoped, as he told me, that the knowledge of our conduct might be useful to him, and he could not be deceived in his calculations. But, if what I told him were true, he was still at a loss how a kingdom could run out of its estate like a private person. He asked me who were our creditors, and where we found money to pay them.[14] He wondered to

[14] The national debt (as opposed to personal debts of the sovereign) first became a permanent element of English policy during the wars of William and Mary. It increased substantially during the reign of Queen Anne, and it helped (Swift feared) to create a powerful new "moneyed interest, that might in time vie with the landed" (*The Conduct of the Allies*, 1713). See also Part Three, Chapter Three, Note 5.

hear me talk of such chargeable and extensive wars; that certainly we must be a quarrelsome people or live among very bad neighbours, and that our generals must needs be richer than our kings.[15] He asked what business we had out of our own islands, unless upon the score of trade or treaty or to defend the coasts with our fleet.[16] Above all, he was amazed to hear me talk of a mercenary standing army in the midst of peace and among a free people.[17] He said if we were governed by our own consent in the persons of our representatives, he could not imagine of whom we were afraid or against whom we were to fight, and would hear my opinion whether a private man's house might not better be defended by himself, his children, and family than by a half a dozen rascals picked up at a venture in the streets for small wages, who might get an hundred times more by cutting their throats.

He laughed at my odd kind of arithmetic [18] (as he was pleased to call it) in reckoning the numbers of our people by

[15] The Duke of Marlborough (1650–1722) amassed a great fortune in the course of his triumphs in the War of the Spanish Succession. He had been attacked for his avarice, accused of dishonesty, and finally dismissed from office. In *The Examiner* (No. 17, November 1710) Swift claimed that the Duke had gained the equivalent of £540,000 in rewards for his victories. This included Blenheim Palace, often called the English Versailles, built for the Duke at royal expense but not completed until after his death.

[16] Campaigns in the recent war had extended to Spain, Italy, and the Low Countries as well as to North America. Swift's *The Conduct of the Allies* had argued against the continued expense of "blood and treasure" in behalf of allies who might thereby become new and powerful enemies to England.

[17] A measure opposed by the Tories, and notably by Swift, as the creation of a force that might overthrow English liberties. Compare the militia or "citizen army" of the Brobdingnagians (Part Two, Chapter Seven, pp. 136–137).

[18] The science of statistics or "political arithmetic" was new in Swift's day. Sir William Petty (1623–1687) undertook the study of vital statistics in London and Dublin, classifying and measuring the populations by trade, property holdings, religious affiliation, and so on.

a computation drawn from the several sects among us in religion and politics. He said he knew no reason why those who entertain opinions prejudicial to the public should be obliged to change, or should not be obliged to conceal them.[19] And as it was tyranny in any government to require the first, so it was weakness not to enforce the second: for a man may be allowed to keep poisons in his closets, but not to vend them about as cordials.

He observed, that among the diversions of our nobility and gentry I had mentioned gaming. He desired to know at what age this entertainment was usually taken up and when it was laid down. How much of their time it employed; whether it ever went so high as to affect their fortunes. Whether mean vicious people by their dexterity in that art might not arrive at great riches, and sometimes keep our very nobles in dependence, as well as habituate them to vile companions, wholly take them from the improvement of their minds, and force them, by the losses they received, to learn and practice that infamous dexterity upon others.

He was perfectly astonished with the historical account I gave him of our affairs during the last century, protesting it was only an heap of conspiracies, rebellions, murders, massacres, revolutions, banishments; the very worst effects that avarice, faction, hypocrisy, perfidiousness, cruelty, rage, madness, hatred, envy, lust, malice, and ambition could produce.

His Majesty in another audience was at the pains to recapitulate the sum of all I had spoken, compared the questions he made with the answers I had given; then taking me into his hands, and stroking me gently, delivered himself in these words, which I shall never forget, nor the manner he spoke them in: "My little friend Grildrig, you have made a most admirable panegyric upon your country. You have clearly proved that ignorance, idleness, and vice are the proper ingredients for qualifying a legislator. That laws are best explained, interpreted, and applied by those whose interest and

---

[19] One of the few policies Swift admired in Oliver Cromwell.

abilities lie in perverting, confounding, and eluding them. I observe among you some lines of an institution which in its original might have been tolerable, but these half erased, and the rest wholly blurred and blotted by corruptions. It doth not appear from all you have said how any one perfection is required towards the procurement of any one station among you, much less that men are ennobled on account of their virtue, that priests are advanced for their piety or learning, soldiers for their conduct or valour, judges for their integrity, senators for the love of their country, or counsellors for their wisdom. As for yourself," continued the King, "who have spent the greatest part of your life in travelling, I am well disposed to hope you may hitherto have escaped many vices of your country. But, by what I have gathered from your own relation, and the answers I have with much pains wringed and extorted from you, I cannot but conclude the bulk of your natives to be the most pernicious race of little odious vermin that nature ever suffered to crawl upon the surface of the earth."

Chapter Seven: The author's love of his country. He makes a proposal of much advantage to the King, which is rejected. The King's great ignorance in politics. The learning of that country very imperfect and confined. Their laws and military affairs, and parties in the state.

Nothing but an extreme love of truth could have hindered me from concealing this part of my story. It was in vain to discover my resentments, which were always turned into ridicule; and I was forced to rest with patience while my noble and most beloved country was so injuriously treated. I am heartily sorry as any of my readers can possibly be that such an occasion was given: but this prince happened to be so curious and inquisitive upon every particular that it could not consist either with gratitude or good manners to refuse giving him what satisfaction I was able. Yet thus much I may be allowed to say in my own vindication, that I artfully eluded many of his questions and gave to every point a more favourable turn by many degrees than the strictness of truth would allow. For I have always borne that laudable partiality to my own country which Dionysius Halicarnassensis with so much justice recommends to an historian.[1] I would hide the frailties and deformities of my political mother and place her virtues and beauties in the most advantageous light. This was my sincere endeavour in those many discourses I had with that mighty monarch, although it unfortunately failed of success.

But great allowances should be given to a king who lives wholly secluded from the rest of the world and must therefore be altogether unacquainted with the manners and customs that most prevail in other nations: the want of which knowledge will ever produce many prejudices and a certain narrowness of thinking, from which we and the politer countries of Europe are wholly exempted. And it would be hard indeed if so remote a prince's notions of virtue and vice were to be offered as a standard for all mankind.

To confirm what I have now said, and further to show the miserable effects of a confined education, I shall here insert a passage which will hardly obtain belief. In hopes to ingratiate myself farther into his Majesty's favour, I told him of an invention discovered between three and four hundred years ago, to make a certain powder, into an heap of which the smallest spark of fire falling would kindle the whole in a moment, although it were as big as a mountain, and make it all fly up in the air together, with a noise and agitation greater than thunder. That a proper quantity of this powder rammed into an

[1] Dionysius of Halicarnassus (first century B.C.), who wrote the *Antiquities of Rome* to celebrate his adopted nation and to persuade his Greek countrymen to accept Roman domination. Gulliver's error is significant.

hollow tube of brass or iron, according to its bigness, would drive a ball of iron or lead with such violence and speed as nothing was able to sustain its force. That the largest balls, thus discharged, would not only destroy whole ranks of an army at once but batter the strongest walls to the ground, sink down ships, with a thousand men in each, to the bottom of the sea; and when linked together by a chain, would cut through masts and rigging, divide hundreds of bodies in the middle, and lay all waste before them. That we often put this powder into large hollow balls of iron, and discharged them by an engine into some city we were besieging, which would rip up the pavement, tear the houses to pieces, burst and throw splinters on every side, dashing out the brains of all who came near. That I knew the ingredients very well, which were cheap and common; I understood the manner of compounding them, and could direct his workmen how to make those tubes of a size proportionable to all other things in his Majesty's kingdom, and the largest need not be above two hundred foot long; twenty or thirty of which tubes, charged with the proper quantity of powder and balls, would batter down the walls of the strongest town in his dominions in a few hours or destroy the whole metropolis, if ever it should pretend to dispute his absolute commands. This I humbly offered to his Majesty as a small tribute of acknowledgment in return of so many marks that I had received of his royal favour and protection.

The King was struck with horror at the description I had given of those terrible engines and the proposal I had made. He was amazed how so impotent and groveling an insect as I (these were his expressions) could entertain such inhuman ideas, and in so familiar a manner as to appear wholly unmoved at all the scenes of blood and desolation which I had painted as the common effects of those destructive machines; whereof he said, some evil genius, enemy to mankind, must have been the first contriver. As for himself, he protested that although few things delighted him so much as new discoveries in art or in nature, yet he would rather lose half his kingdom than be privy to such a secret, which he commanded me, as I valued my life, never to mention any more.

A strange effect of narrow principles and short views! that a prince possessed of every quality which procures veneration, love, and esteem; of strong parts, great wisdom, and profound learning, endued with admirable talents for government, and almost adored by his subjects, should from a nice[2] unnecessary scruple, whereof in Europe we can have no conception, let slip an opportunity put into his hands that would have made him absolute master of the lives, the liberties, and the fortunes of his people. Neither do I say this with the least intention to detract from the many virtues of that excellent king, whose character I am sensible will on this account be very much lessened in the opinion of an English reader: but I take this defect among them to have risen from their ignorance, by not having hitherto reduced politics into a science, as the more acute wits of Europe have done.[3] For I remember very well, in a discourse one day with the King, when I happened to say there were several thousand books among us written upon the art of government, it gave him (directly contrary to my intention) a very mean opinion of our understandings. He professed both to abominate and despise all mystery, refinement, and intrigue, either in a prince or a minister. He could not tell what I meant by secrets of state where an enemy or some rival nation were

[2] Foolishly delicate.

[3] The references in this and following sentences are to the followers of Niccolo Machiavelli, who in *The Prince* (1513) studied with scientific detachment methods of winning and maintaining political power. This new "science" of power politics aroused horror by its neglect of moral concerns and its recognition of the efficiency of cruel and deceptive means. One may compare the King's remarks on "justice and lenity" with the "lenity" of the Lilliputian Emperor (Part One, Chapter Seven, p. 62). See Edwin B. Benjamin, "The King of Brobdingnag and Secrets of State," *Journal of the History of Ideas*, XVIII (1957), 572–579.

not in the case. He confined the knowledge of governing within very narrow bounds; to common sense and reason, to justice and lenity, to the speedy determination of civil and criminal causes, with some other obvious topics which are not worth considering. And he gave it for his opinion that whoever could make two ears of corn or two blades of grass to grow upon a spot of ground where only one grew before, would deserve better of mankind, and do more essential service to his country, than the whole race of politicians put together.

The learning of this people is very defective, consisting only in morality, history, poetry, and mathematics, wherein they must be allowed to excel. But the last of these is wholly applied to what may be useful in life, to the improvement of agriculture and all mechanical arts; so that among us it would be little esteemed. And as to ideas, entities, abstractions, and transcendentals,[4] I could never drive the least conception into their heads.

No law of that country must exceed in words the number of letters in their alphabet, which consists only of two and twenty. But indeed few of them extend even to that length. They are expressed in the most plain and simple terms, wherein those people are not mercurial enough to discover above one interpretation. And to write a comment upon any law is a capital crime. As to the decision of civil causes or proceedings against criminals, their precedents are so few that they have little reason to boast of any extraordinary skill in either.

They have had the art of printing, as well as the Chinese, time out of mind. But their libraries are not very large; for that of the King's, which is reckoned the largest, doth not amount to above a thousand volumes, placed in a gallery of twelve hundred foot long, from whence I had liberty to borrow what

[4] Metaphysical terms. This jargon is drawn largely from Platonic and Aristotelian (or Scholastic) philosophy, the technicalities of which Swift, like most of his age, tended to despise.

books I pleased. The Queen's joiner had contrived in one of Glumdalclitch's rooms a kind of wooden machine five and twenty foot high, formed like a standing ladder; the steps were each fifty foot long. It was indeed a moveable pair of stairs, the lowest end placed at ten foot distance from the wall of the chamber. The book I had a mind to read was put up leaning against the wall. I first mounted to the upper step of the ladder and, turning my face towards the book, began at the top of the page, and so walking to the right and left about eight or ten paces, according to the length of the lines, till I had gotten a little below the level of my eyes, and then descending gradually till I came to the bottom: after which I mounted again and began the other page in the same manner, and so turned over the leaf, which I could easily do with both my hands, for it was as thick and stiff as a pasteboard, and in the largest folios not above eighteen or twenty foot long.

Their style is clear, masculine, and smooth, but not florid, for they avoid nothing more than multiplying unnecessary words or using various expressions. I have perused many of their books, especially those in history and morality. Among the latter I was much diverted with a little old treatise which always lay in Glumdalclitch's bedchamber, and belonged to her governess, a grave elderly gentlewoman, who dealt in writings of morality and devotion. The book treats of the weakness of human kind and is in little esteem except among women and the vulgar. However, I was curious to see what an author of that country could say upon such a subject. This writer went through all the usual topics of European moralists, showing how diminutive, contemptible, and helpless an animal was man in his own nature; how unable to defend himself from the inclemencies of the air or the fury of wild beasts. How much he was excelled by one creature in strength, by another in speed, by a third in foresight, by a fourth in industry. He added that nature was degenerated in these latter declining ages of the world, and could now produce only small abortive births in comparison of those in ancient times. He said it was very reasonable to think not only that the species of men were originally much larger, but also that there must have been giants in former ages which, as it is asserted by history and tradition, so it hath been confirmed by huge bones and skulls casually dug up in several parts of the kingdom, far exceeding the common dwindled race of man in our days. He argued that the very laws of nature absolutely required we should have been made, in the beginning, of a size more large and robust, not so liable to destruction from every little accident of a tile falling from an house or a stone cast from the hand of a boy, or of being drowned in a little brook. From this way of reasoning the author drew several moral applications useful in the conduct of life, but needless here to repeat. For my own part, I could not avoid reflecting how universally this talent was spread of drawing lectures in morality, or indeed rather matter of discontent and repining, from the quarrels we raise with Nature. And, I believe, upon a strict enquiry those quarrels might be shown as ill-grounded among us as they are among that people.[5]

As to their military affairs, they boast that the King's army consists of an hundred and seventy-six thousand foot and thirty-two thousand horse, if that may be called an army which is made up of tradesmen in the several cities and farmers in

---

[5] The "little old treatise" falls into the pattern of such well-known works as Godfrey Goodman's *The Fall of Man* (1616), which stressed the universal decay of nature and saw in latter days the growth of corruption and the loss of original stature and powers. (John Donne's *Anniversaries* [1611–1612] are perhaps the finest poetic statement of such a view.) Gulliver's dismissal of the treatise is characteristically complacent. Yet the treatise might be seen as one of those works that overstrains its case and confronts the growing faith in inevitable progress with an equally partial (and in this case somewhat ludicrous) view. For a study of the controversy on the decay of nature, see Victor Harris, *All Coherence Gone* (Chicago, 1949).

the country, whose commanders are only the nobility and gentry without pay or reward. They are indeed perfect enough in their exercises and under very good discipline, wherein I saw no great merit; for how should it be otherwise where every farmer is under the command of his own landlord, and every citizen under that of the principal men in his own city, chosen after the manner of Venice by ballot?[6]

I have often seen the militia of Lorbrulgrud drawn out to exercise in a great field near the city, of twenty miles square. They were in all not above twenty-five thousand foot and six thousand horse; but it was impossible for me to compute their number, considering the space of ground they took up. A cavalier mounted on a large steed might be about ninety foot high. I have seen this whole body of horse upon the word of command draw their swords at once and brandish them in the air. Imagination can figure nothing so grand, so surprising, and so astonishing. It looked as if ten thousand flashes of lightning were darting at the same time from every quarter of the sky.

I was curious to know how this prince, to whose dominions there is no access from any other country, came to think of armies or to teach his people the practice of military discipline. But I was soon informed, both by conversation and reading their histories. For in the course of many ages they have been troubled with the same disease to which the whole race of mankind is subject; the nobility often contending for power, the people for liberty, and the King for absolute dominion. All which, however happily tempered by the laws of that kingdom, have been sometimes violated by each of the three parties, and have more than once occasioned civil wars, the last

[6] The idea of a citizen army or militia was originated by Machiavelli in Florence, but, like the secret ballot used in the Senate and the Great Council of the Republic of Venice, was much admired by the "classical republicans" in England. See Z. S. Fink, "Political Theory in *Gulliver's Travels*," *ELH*, xiv (1947), 151–161, and *The Classical Republicans* (Evanston, 1945).

whereof was happily put an end to by this prince's grandfather in a general composition;[7] and the militia then settled with common consent hath been ever since kept in the strictest duty.

Chapter Eight: The King and Queen make a progress to the frontiers. The author attends them. The manner in which he leaves the country very particularly related. He returns to England.

I had always a strong impulse that I should sometime recover my liberty, although it were impossible to conjecture by what means, or to form any project with the least hope of succeeding. The ship in which I sailed was the first ever known to be driven within sight of that coast, and the King had given strict orders that, if at any time another appeared, it should be taken ashore, and with all its crew and passengers brought in a tumbril[1] to Lorbrulgrud. He was strongly bent to get me a woman of my own size by whom I might propagate the breed:[2] but I think I should rather have died than undergone the disgrace of leaving a posterity to be kept in cages like tame canary birds, and perhaps in time sold about the kingdom to persons of quality for curiosities. I was indeed treated with much kindness; I was the favourite of a great king and queen, and the

[7] Treaty, agreement. Brobdingnag has a "mixed" state: a balance of the powers of the one, the few, and the many. The "pure" states of monarchy, oligarchy, and democracy were believed by Swift and other theorists (who followed the Greek historian Polybius, as did the framers of the American Constitution later) to be unstable, whereas the mixed state gave promise of a comparatively permanent equilibrium. The balance is achieved, it should be noted, in a partyless state, unlike that of Lilliput.

[1] Cart, wagon.

[2] Compare Gulliver's readiness to take Blefuscudian natives as well as sheep (Part One, Chapter Eight, p. 68).

delight of the whole court, but it was upon such a foot as ill became the dignity of humankind. I could never forget those domestic pledges I had left behind me. I wanted to be among people with whom I could converse upon even terms, and walk about the streets and fields without fear of being trod to death like a frog or young puppy. But my deliverance came sooner than I expected, and in a manner not very common: the whole story and circumstances of which I shall faithfully relate.

I had now been two years in this country; and about the beginning of the third, Glumdalclitch and I attended the King and Queen in a progress to the south coast of the kingdom. I was carried as usual in my travelling-box, which, as I have already described, was a very convenient closet of twelve foot wide. I had ordered a hammock to be fixed by silken ropes from the four corners at the top, to break the jolts when a servant carried me before him on horseback, as I sometimes desired; and would often sleep in my hammock while we were upon the road. On the roof of my closet, just over the middle of the hammock, I ordered the joiner to cut out a hole of a foot square to give me air in hot weather as I slept, which hole I shut at pleasure with a board that drew backwards and forwards through a groove.

When we came to our journey's end, the King thought proper to pass a few days at a palace he hath near Flanflasnic, a city within eighteen English miles of the seaside. Glumdalclitch and I were much fatigued; I had gotten a small cold, but the poor girl was so ill as to be confined to her chamber. I longed to see the ocean, which must be the only scene of my escape, if ever it should happen. I pretended to be worse than I really was and desired leave to take the fresh air of the sea, with a page whom I was very fond of and who had sometimes been trusted with me. I shall never forget with what unwillingness Glumdalclitch consented, nor the strict charge she gave the page to be careful of me, bursting at the same time into a flood of tears, as if she had some foreboding of what was to happen. The boy took me out in my box about half an hour's walk from the palace towards the rocks on the seashore. I ordered him to set me down and, lifting up one of my sashes, cast many a wistful melancholy look towards the sea. I found myself not very well, and told the page that I had a mind to take a nap in my hammock, which I hoped would do me good. I got in, and the boy shut the window close down to keep out the cold. I soon fell asleep, and all I can conjecture is that while I slept, the page, thinking no danger could happen, went among the rocks to look for birds' eggs, having before observed him from my window searching about and picking up one or two in the clefts. Be that as it will, I found myself suddenly awaked with a violent pull upon the ring which was fastened at the top of my box for the conveniency of carriage. I felt the box raised very high in the air and then borne forward with prodigious speed. The first jolt had like to have shaken me out of my hammock, but afterwards the motion was easy enough. I called out several times as loud as I could raise my voice, but all to no purpose. I looked towards my windows, and could see nothing but the clouds and sky. I heard a noise just over my head like the clapping of wings, and then began to perceive the woful condition I was in; that some eagle had got the ring of my box in his beak, with an intent to let it fall on a rock like a tortoise in a shell, and then pick out my body and devour it. For the sagacity and smell of this bird enable him to discover his quarry at a great distance, although better concealed than I could be within a two-inch board.

In a little time I observed the noise and flutter of wings to encrease very fast, and my box was tossed up and down like a signpost in a windy day. I heard several bangs or buffets, as I thought, given to the eagle (for such I am certain it must have been that held the ring of my box in his beak), and then all on a sudden felt myself falling perpendicularly down for above a minute, but with such incredible swiftness that I almost lost my breath. My fall was stopped by a terrible squash, that sounded louder to my ears than the cataract of Niagara; after which I was quite in the dark for another minute, and then my box began to rise so high that I could see light from the tops of my windows. I now perceived that I was fallen into the sea. My box, by the weight of my body, the goods that were in, and the broad plates of iron fixed for strength at the four corners of the top and bottom, floated about five foot deep in water. I did then, and do now suppose, that the eagle which flew away with my box was pursued by two or three others, and forced to let me drop while he was defending himself against the rest, who hoped to share in the prey. The plates of iron fastened at the bottom of the box (for those were the strongest) preserved the balance while it fell, and hindered it from being broken on the surface of the water. Every joint of it was well grooved, and the door did not move on hinges, but up and down like a sash, which kept my closet so tight that very little water came in. I got with much difficulty out of my hammock, having first ventured to draw back the slip-board on the roof already mentioned, contrived on purpose to let in air, for want of which I found myself almost stifled.

How often did I then wish myself with my dear Glumdal-clitch, from whom one single hour had so far divided me! And I may say with truth that in the midst of my own misfortune I could not forbear lamenting my poor nurse, the grief she would suffer for my loss, the displeasure of the Queen, and the ruin of her fortune. Perhaps many travellers have not been under greater difficulties and distress than I was at this juncture, expecting every moment to see my box dashed in pieces or at least overset by the first violent blast or a rising wave. A breach in one single pane of glass would have been immediate death: nor could anything have preserved the windows but the strong lattice wires placed on the outside against accidents in travelling. I saw the water ooze in at several crannies, although the leaks were not considerable, and I endeavoured to stop them as well as I could. I was not able to lift up the roof of my closet, which otherwise I certainly should have done and sat on the top of it, where I might at least preserve myself from being shut up, as I may call it, in the hold. Or, if I escaped these dangers for a day or two, what could I expect but a miserable death of cold and hunger! I was four hours under these circumstances, expecting and indeed wishing every moment to be my last.

I have already told the reader that there were two strong staples fixed upon the side of my box which had no window, and into which the servant who used to carry me on horseback would put a leathern belt and buckle it about his waist. Being in this disconsolate state, I heard or at least thought I heard some kind of grating noise on that side of my box where the staples were fixed, and soon after I began to fancy that the box was pulled or towed along in the sea; for I now and then felt a sort of tugging which made the waves rise near the tops of my windows, leaving me almost in the dark. This gave me some faint hopes of relief, although I were not able to imagine how it could be brought about. I ventured to unscrew one of my chairs, which were always fastened to the floor; and having made a hard shift to screw it down again directly under the slipping-board that I had lately opened, I mounted on the chair, and putting my mouth as near as I could to the hole, I called for help in a loud voice and in all the languages I understood. I then fastened my handkerchief to a stick I usually carried and, thrusting it up the hole, waved it several times in the air, that if any boat or ship were near, the seamen might conjecture some unhappy mortal to be shut up in the box.

I found no effect from all I could do, but plainly perceived my closet to be moved along; and in the space of an hour or better, that side of the box where the staples were and had no window struck against something that was hard. I apprehended it to be a rock, and found myself tossed more than ever. I plainly heard a noise upon the cover of my closet like that of a cable, and the grating of it as it passed through the ring. I then found myself hoisted up by degrees at least three foot higher than I was before. Whereupon I again thrust up my stick and handkerchief, calling for help till I was almost hoarse. In return to which I heard a great shout repeated three times, giving me such transports of joy as are not to be conceived but by those who feel them. I now heard a trampling over my head, and somebody calling through the hole with a loud voice in the English tongue, "If there be anybody below let them speak." I answered, I was an Englishman drawn by ill fortune into the greatest calamity that ever any creature underwent, and begged, by all that was moving, to be delivered out of the dungeon I was in. The voice replied, I was safe, for my box was fastened to their ship; and the carpenter should immediately come and saw an hole in the cover large enough to pull me out. I answered, that was needless and would take up too much time, for there was no more to be done but let one of the crew put his finger into the ring and take the box out of the sea into the ship, and so into the captain's cabin. Some of them upon hearing me talk so wildly thought I was mad; others laughed; for indeed it never came into my head that I was now got among people of my own stature and strength. The carpenter came, and in a few minutes sawed a passage about four foot square, then let down a small ladder, upon which I mounted, and from thence was taken into the ship in a very weak condition.

The sailors were all in amazement and asked me a thousand questions, which I had no inclination to answer. I was equally confounded at the sight of so many pigmies, for such I took them to be after having so long accustomed my eyes to the monstrous objects I had left. But the captain, Mr. Thomas Wilcocks, an honest worthy Shropshire man, observing I was ready to faint, took me into his cabin, gave me a cordial to comfort me, and made me turn in upon his own bed, advising me to take a little rest, of which I had great need. Before I went to sleep I gave him to understand that I had some valuable furniture in my box, too good to be lost; a fine hammock, an handsome field-bed, two chairs, a table, and a cabinet: that my closet was hung on all sides, or rather quilted, with silk

and cotton: that if he would let one of the crew bring my
closet into his cabin, I would open it there before him and
show him my goods. The captain, hearing me utter these absurdities, concluded I was raving: however (I suppose to
pacify me), he promised to give order as I desired, and going
upon deck sent some of his men down into my closet, from
whence (as I afterwards found) they drew up all my goods
and stripped off the quilting; but the chairs, cabinet, and bed-
stead, being screwed to the floor, were much damaged by the
ignorance of the seamen, who tore them up by force. Then
they knocked off some of the boards for the use of the ship
and, when they had got all they had a mind for, let the hulk
drop into the sea, which, by reason of many breaches made in
the bottom and sides, sunk to rights. And indeed I was glad
not to have been a spectator of the havoc they made; because
I am confident it would have sensibly touched me, by bringing
former passages into my mind which I had rather forget.

I slept some hours, but perpetually disturbed with dreams of
the place I had left and the dangers I had escaped. However,
upon waking I found myself much recovered. It was now
about eight o'clock at night, and the captain ordered supper
immediately, thinking I had already fasted too long. He entertained me with great kindness, observing me not to look wildly
or talk inconsistently; and when we were left alone, desired I
would give him a relation of my travels, and by what accident
I came to be set adrift in that monstrous wooden chest. He said
that about twelve o'clock at noon, as he was looking through
his glass, he spied it at a distance and thought it was a sail,
which he had a mind to make, being not much out of his
course, in hopes of buying some biscuit, his own beginning to
fall short. That upon coming nearer and finding his error, he
sent out his longboat to discover what I was; that his men came
back in a fright, swearing they had seen a swimming house.
That he laughed at their folly and went himself in the boat,
ordering his men to take a strong cable along with them. That
the weather being calm, he rowed round me several times, ob-

served my windows, and the wire lattices that defended them. That he discovered two staples upon one side, which was all of boards without any passage for light. He then commanded his men to row up to that side, and fastening a cable to one of the staples, ordered his men to tow my chest (as he called it) towards the ship. When it was there, he gave directions to fasten another cable to the ring fixed in the cover, and to raise up my chest with pulleys, which all the sailors were not able to do above two or three foot. He said they saw my stick and handkerchief thrust out of the hole, and concluded that some unhappy man must be shut up in the cavity. I asked whether he or the crew had seen any prodigious birds in the air about the time he first discovered me. To which he answered that, discoursing this matter with the sailors while I was asleep, one of them said he had observed three eagles flying towards the north, but remarked nothing of their being larger than the usual size, which I suppose must be imputed to the great height they were at: and he could not guess the reason of my question. I then asked the captain how far he reckoned we might be from land; he said, by the best computation he could make, we were at least an hundred leagues. I assured him that he must be mistaken by almost half, for I had not left the country from whence I came above two hours before I dropped into the sea. Whereupon he began again to think that my brain was disturbed, of which he gave me a hint, and advised me to go to bed in a cabin he had provided. I assured him I was well refreshed with his good entertainment and company, and as much in my senses as ever I was in my life. He then grew serious, and desired to ask me freely whether I were not troubled in mind by the consciousness of some enormous crime, for which I was punished at the command of some prince by exposing me in that chest, as great criminals in other countries have been forced to sea in a leaky vessel without provisions: for although he should be sorry to have taken so ill a man into his ship, yet he would engage his word to set me safe on shore in the first port where we arrived. He added that his suspicions were much increased by some very absurd speeches I had delivered at first to the sailors and afterwards to himself, in relation to my closet or chest, as well as by my odd looks and behaviour while I was at supper.

I begged his patience to hear me tell my story, which I faithfully did from the last time I left England to the moment he first discovered me. And, as truth always forceth its way into rational minds, so this honest worthy gentleman, who had some tincture of learning and very good sense, was immediately convinced of my candor and veracity. But further to confirm all I had said, I entreated him to give order that my cabinet should be brought, of which I kept the key in my pocket (for he had already informed me how the seamen disposed of my closet); I opened it in his presence, and showed him the small collection of rarities I made in the country from whence I had been so strangely delivered. There was the comb I had contrived out of the stumps of the King's beard, and another of the same materials, but fixed into a paring of her Majesty's thumb-nail which served for the back. There was a collection of needles and pins from a foot to half a yard long. Four wasp-stings, like joiners'[3] tacks; some combings of the Queen's hair; a gold ring which one day she made me a present of in a most obliging manner, taking it from her little finger and throwing it over my head like a collar. I desired the captain would please to accept this ring in return of his civilities, which he absolutely refused. I showed him a corn that I had cut off with my own hand from a maid of honour's toe; it was about the bigness of a Kentish pippin, and grown so hard that, when I returned to England, I got it hollowed into a cup and set in silver. Lastly, I desired him to see the breeches I had then on, which were made of a mouse's skin.

I could force nothing on him but a footman's tooth, which I observed him to examine with great curiosity, and found he had a fancy for it. He received it with abundance of thanks, more than such a trifle could deserve. It was drawn by an

[3] Carpenters'.

unskilful surgeon in a mistake from one of Glumdalclitch's men who was afflicted with the toothache, but it was as sound as any in his head. I got it cleaned and put it into my cabinet. It was about a foot long and four inches in diameter.

The captain was very well satisfied with this plain relation I had given him; and said he hoped, when we returned to England, I would oblige the world by putting it in paper and making it public. My answer was that I thought we were already overstocked with books of travels: that nothing could now pass which was not extraordinary, wherein I doubted some authors less consulted truth than their own vanity or interest or the diversion of ignorant readers. That my story could contain little besides common events, without those ornamental descriptions of strange plants, trees, birds, and other animals, or the barbarous customs and idolatry of savage people, with which most writers abound. However, I thanked him for his good opinion and promised to take the matter into my thoughts.

He said he wondered at one thing very much, which was to hear me speak so loud, asking me whether the King or Queen of that country were thick of hearing. I told him it was what I had been used to for above two years past, and that I admired as much at the voices of him and his men, who seemed to me only to whisper, and yet I could hear them well enough. But when I spoke in that country, it was like a man talking in the street to another looking out from the top of a steeple, unless when I was placed on a table or held in any person's hand. I told him I had likewise observed another thing, that when I first got into the ship and the sailors stood all about me, I thought they were the most little contemptible creatures I had ever beheld. For, indeed, while I was in that prince's country, I could never endure to look in a glass after my eyes had been accustomed to such prodigious objects, because the comparison gave me so despicable a conceit [4] of myself. The captain said that while we were at supper he observed me to look at every-

[4] Conception, image.

thing with a sort of wonder, and that I often seemed hardly
able to contain my laughter, which he knew not well how to
take, but imputed it to some disorder in my brain. I answered,
it was very true, and I wondered how I could forbear, when
I saw his dishes of the size of a silver threepence, a leg of pork
hardly a mouthful, a cup not so big as a nutshell; and so I went
on, describing the rest of his household-stuff and provisions
after the same manner. For although the Queen had ordered a
little equipage of all things necessary for me while I was in
her service, yet my ideas were wholly taken up with what I
saw on every side of me, and I winked at my own littleness as
people do at their own faults. The captain understood my
raillery very well and merrily replied with the old English
proverb, that he doubted my eyes were bigger than my belly,
for he did not observe my stomach so good, although I had
fasted all day; and continuing in his mirth, protested he would
have gladly given an hundred pounds to have seen my closet
in the eagle's bill, and afterwards in its fall from so great an
height into the sea; which would certainly have been a most
astonishing object, worthy to have the description of it transmitted to future ages: and the comparison of Phaeton[5] was so
obvious, that he could not forbear applying it, although I did
not much admire the conceit.

The captain, having been at Tonquin,[6] was in his return to
England driven northeastward to the latitude of 44 degrees and
of longitude 143. But meeting a trade wind two days after I
came on board him, we sailed southward a long time, and coast-
ing New Holland [7] kept our course west-southwest, and then
south-southwest till we doubled the Cape of Good Hope. Our

[5] Phaeton, or Phaethon, tried to drive the chariot of his father,
the Sun, but could not control it and careened through the heavens
until he was struck down by Jupiter's thunderbolt. His fall was
often represented on ancient sarcophagi as a parable of the transi-
toriness of life.

[6] French Indochina or Vietnam.

[7] Australia.

voyage was very prosperous, but I shall not trouble the reader with a journal of it. The captain called in at one or two ports and sent in his longboat for provisions and fresh water, but I never went out of the ship till we came into the Downs, which was on the 3d day of June, 1706, about nine months after my escape. I offered to leave my goods in security for payment of my freight;[8] but the captain protested he would not receive one farthing. We took kind leave of each other, and I made him promise he would come to see me at my house in Redriff. I hired a horse and guide for five shillings, which I borrowed of the captain.

As I was on the road, observing the littleness of the houses, the trees, the cattle, and the people, I began to think myself in Lilliput. I was afraid of trampling on every traveller I met, and often called aloud to have them stand out of the way, so that I had like to have gotten one or two broken heads for my impertinence.

When I came to my own house, for which I was forced to enquire, one of the servants opening the door, I bent down to go in (like a goose under a gate) for fear of striking my head. My wife ran out to embrace me, but I stooped lower than her knees, thinking she could otherwise never be able to reach my mouth. My daughter kneeled to ask me blessing, but I could not see her till she arose, having been so long used to stand with my head and eyes erect to above sixty foot; and then I went to take her up with one hand by the waist. I looked down upon the servants and one or two friends who were in the house, as if they had been pigmies and I a giant. I told my wife she had been too thrifty, for I found she had starved herself and her daughter to nothing. In short, I behaved myself so unaccountably that they were all of the captain's opinion when he first saw me, and concluded I had lost my wits. This I mention as an instance of the great power of habit and prejudice.

In a little time I and my family and friends came to a right

[8] Passage.

understanding: but my wife protested I should never go to sea any more; although my evil destiny so ordered that she had not power to hinder me, as the reader may know hereafter. In the meantime I here conclude the second part of my unfortunate voyages.

The End of the Second Part

Part Three

A Voyage to Laputa, Balnibarbi,
Glubbdubdrib, Luggnagg,
and Japan

The map places Luggnagg too far north and too close to Japan and badly misconceives Balnibarbi, which should be a vast body of land lying in the Pacific southeast of Luggnagg, although possibly extending far into the North Pacific as well (where it would, unfortunately, overlap Brobdingnag). In doing so, it misses the typical pattern of the third voyage: the large, supine (but occasionally rebellious) land and the small, self-engrossed "control center" (at first seen as the literal flying island, later as a travesty of a research institute, still further on as a tyrannous and inhuman court). The reason for the variety of representations may be that Swift is here—massing his forces for the final part—turning the cultural issues of the first two voyages into an exploration of the mind of man itself (as Pope does in the fourth book of *The Dunciad*).

The third voyage has a constant undernote of filth, corruption, or insanity. It presents the divorces of intellect from sense, of theory from practice, and of technical skill from a sense of values. The flying island is a place of "pure" science, but it is also an instrument of tyrannical domination. The world of Balnibarbi is a place of insanely ingenious experiments but is also a society in which the rule of fashion destroys whatever has been stable enough to last. History itself, the movement forward in time, seems to be nothing more than progressive loss: of a sense of responsibility; of healthy simplicity; of the desire for freedom. The final embodiment of this "anti-progressive" movement is in the Struldbruggs, who, with the image of endless decay, confound Gulliver's complacent dream of eternal life.

Parts Unknown

LAND OF
St James Bay
Robbin I
IESSO
SalmonB.
C.Canal
C. Patience
Straits of the Vries

Companys
Land
Stats I

Laputa

BALNIBARBI
Lagada
Dicovered. A. D 1701

Sea of Corea
Sando I
Torpul
Meaco
JA
Asace
Puningo
Iedo
Hwalo
PON
Jaso
Toy Pt
Red Pt
Bosho Pt
Barnevelts
Ongelukig I
South I
Tonsa I
Bungo I
Dimeris Strats
I Tanaxima

LUGN-AGG
Maldopgdul
Clamegnig

Sialo
Glangurn
Maldoneda
I Deserta
Glubdrubdrib
Urac
Timal

I HAD not been at home above ten days, when Captain William Robinson, a Cornish man, commander of the *Hope-well*, a stout ship of three hundred tons, came to my house. I had formerly been surgeon of another ship where he was master, and a fourth part owner, in a voyage to the Levant; he had always treated me more like a brother than an inferior officer, and hearing of my arrival made me a visit, as I apprehended, only out of friendship, for nothing passed more than what is usual after long absence. But repeating his visits often, expressing his joy to find me in good health, asking whether I were now settled for life, adding that he intended a voyage to the East Indies in two months, at last plainly invited me, although with some apologies, to be surgeon of the ship; that I should have another surgeon under me besides our two mates; that my salary should be double to the usual pay; and that having experienced my knowledge in sea-affairs to be at least equal to his, he would enter into any engagement to follow my advice, as much as if I had share in the command.

He said so many other obliging things, and I knew him to be so honest a man, that I could not reject his proposal; the thirst I had of seeing the world, notwithstanding my past misfortunes, continuing as violent as ever. The only difficulty that remained was to persuade my wife, whose consent however I at last obtained, by the prospect of advantage she proposed [1] to her children.

We set out the 5th day of August, 1706, and arrived at Fort St. George [2] the 11th of April, 1707. We stayed there three weeks to refresh our crew, many of whom were sick. From thence we went to Tonquin, where the captain resolved to continue some time, because many of the goods he intended to buy were not ready, nor could he expect to be dispatched in several months. Therefore in hopes to defray some of the

[1] Foresaw.
[2] Madras, on the eastern coast of India.

charges he must be at, he bought a sloop, loaded it with several sorts of goods, wherewith the Tonquinese usually trade to the neighbouring islands; and putting fourteen men on board, whereof three were of the country, he appointed me master of the sloop and gave me power to traffic while he transacted his affairs at Tonquin.

We had not sailed above three days, when, a great storm arising, we were driven five days to the north-northeast, and then to the east, after which we had fair weather, but still with a pretty strong gale from the west. Upon the tenth day we were chased by two pirates, who soon overtook us; for my sloop was so deep loaden, that she sailed very slow, neither were we in a condition to defend ourselves.

We were boarded about the same time by both the pirates, who entered furiously at the head of their men, but finding us all prostrate upon our faces (for so I gave order), they pinioned us with strong ropes and, setting a guard upon us, went to search the sloop.

I observed among them a Dutchman who seemed to be of some authority, although he were not commander of either ship. He knew us by our countenances to be Englishmen and, jabbering to us in his own language, swore we should be tied back to back and thrown into the sea. I spoke Dutch tolerably well; I told him who we were and begged him, in consideration of our being Christians and Protestants, of neighbouring countries in strict alliance, that he would move the captains to take some pity on us.[3] This inflamed his rage, he repeated his threatenings, and turning to his companions, spoke with great vehemence, in the Japanese language, as I suppose, often using the word *Christianos*.

The largest of the two pirate ships was commanded by a Japanese captain, who spoke a little Dutch, but very imper-

---

[3] At the time of which Gulliver writes, England and Holland were allies against France; however, the two nations had previously been at war with one another and maintained a strong mercantile rivalry.

fectly. He came up to me, and, after several questions which I answered in great humility, he said we should not die. I made the captain a very low bow and, then turning to the Dutchman, said I was sorry to find more mercy in a heathen than in a brother Christian. But I had soon reason to repent those foolish words; for that malicious reprobate, having often endeavoured in vain to persuade both the captains that I might be thrown into the sea (which they would not yield to after the promise made me that I should not die), however prevailed so far as to have a punishment inflicted on me worse in all human appearance than death itself. My men were sent by an equal division into both the pirate ships, and my sloop new manned. As to myself, it was determined that I should be set adrift in a small canoe with paddles and a sail and four days' provisions, which last the Japanese captain was so kind to double out of his own stores, and would permit no man to search me. I got down into the canoe, while the Dutchman, standing upon the deck, loaded me with all the curses and injurious terms his language could afford.

About an hour before we saw the pirates, I had taken an observation and found we were in the latitude of 46 N. and of longitude 183. When I was at some distance from the pirates, I discovered by my pocket-glass several islands to the southeast. I set up my sail, the wind being fair, with a design to reach the nearest of those islands, which I made a shift to do in about three hours. It was all rocky; however I got many birds' eggs, and, striking fire, I kindled some heath and dry seaweed, by which I roasted my eggs. I eat no other supper, being resolved to spare my provisions as much as I could. I passed the night under the shelter of a rock, strowing some heath under me, and slept pretty well.

The next day I sailed to another island, and thence to a third and fourth, sometimes using my sail and sometimes my paddles. But not to trouble the reader with a particular account of my distresses, let it suffice that on the 5th day I arrived at the last island in my sight, which lay south-southeast to the former.

This island was at a greater distance than I expected, and I did not reach it in less than five hours. I encompassed it almost round before I could find a convenient place to land in, which was a small creek about three times the wideness of my canoe. I found the island to be all rocky, only a little intermingled with tufts of grass and sweet-smelling herbs. I took out my small provisions, and, after having refreshed myself, I secured the remainder in a cave, whereof there were great numbers. I gathered plenty of eggs upon the rocks and got a quantity of dry seaweed and parched grass, which I designed to kindle the next day, and roast my eggs as well as I could. (For I had about me my flint, steel, match,[4] and burning-glass.) I lay all night in the cave where I had lodged my provisions. My bed was the same dry grass and seaweed which I intended for fuel. I slept very little, for the disquiets of my mind prevailed over my weariness and kept me awake. I considered how impossible it was to preserve my life in so desolate a place, and how miserable my end must be. Yet I found myself so listless and desponding that I had not the heart to rise, and, before I could get spirits enough to creep out of my cave, the day was far advanced. I walked a while among the rocks; the sky was perfectly clear, and the sun so hot that I was forced to turn my face from it: when all on a sudden it became obscured, as I thought, in a manner very different from what happens by the interposition of a cloud. I turned back, and perceived a vast opaque body between me and the sun, moving forwards towards the island: it seemed to be about two miles high, and hid the sun six or seven minutes, but I did not observe the air to be much colder or the sky more darkened than if I had stood under the shade of a mountain. As it approached nearer over the place where I was, it appeared to be a firm substance, the bottom flat, smooth, and shining very bright from the reflection of the sea below. I stood upon a height about two

[4] In Swift's day, a piece of cord or wood dipped in melted sulphur and thus easily ignited by a tinder box.

hundred yards from the shore and saw this vast body descending almost to a parallel with me, at less than an English mile distance. I took out my pocket-perspective and could plainly discover numbers of people moving up and down the sides of it, which appeared to be sloping, but what those people were doing I was not able to distinguish.

The natural love of life gave me some inward motions of joy, and I was ready to entertain a hope that this adventure might some way or other help to deliver me from the desolate place and condition I was in. But at the same time the reader can hardly conceive my astonishment to behold an island in the air, inhabited by men, who were able (as it should seem) to raise, or sink, or put it into a progressive motion, as they pleased. But not being at that time in a disposition to philosophize upon this phenomenon, I rather chose to observe what course the island would take, because it seemed for a while to stand still. Yet soon after it advanced nearer, and I could see the sides of it, encompassed with several gradations of galleries, and stairs at certain intervals to descend from one to the other. In the lowest gallery, I beheld some people fishing with long angling rods, and others looking on. I waved my cap (for my hat was long since worn out) and my handkerchief towards the island; and upon its nearer approach I called and shouted with the utmost strength of my voice; and then looking circumspectly, I beheld a crowd gathered to that side which was most in my view. I found by their pointing towards me and to each other that they plainly discovered me, although they made no return to my shouting. But I could see four or five men running in great haste up the stairs to the top of the island, who then disappeared. I happened rightly to conjecture that these were sent for orders to some person in authority upon this occasion.

The number of people increased, and in less than half an hour the island was moved and raised in such a manner that the lowest gallery appeared in a parallel of less than an hundred yards' distance from the height where I stood. I then put myself into the most supplicating postures and spoke in the humblest accent, but received no answer. Those who stood nearest over-against me seemed to be persons of distinction, as I supposed by their habit. They conferred earnestly with each other, looking often upon me. At length one of them called out in a clear, polite, smooth dialect, not unlike in sound to the Italian; and therefore I returned an answer in that language, hoping at least that the cadence might be more agreeable to his ears. Although neither of us understood the other, yet my meaning was easily known, for the people saw the distress I was in.

They made signs for me to come down from the rock and go towards the shore, which I accordingly did; and the flying island being raised to a convenient height, the verge directly over me, a chain was let down from the lowest gallery, with a seat fastened to the bottom, to which I fixed myself, and was drawn up by pulleys.

Chapter Two: The humours and dispositions of the Laputans described. An account of their learning. Of the King and his court. The author's reception there. The inhabitants subject to fears and disquietudes. An account of the women.

At my alighting I was surrounded by a crowd of people, but those who stood nearest seemed to be of better quality. They beheld me with all the marks and circumstances of wonder; neither indeed was I much in their debt, having never till then seen a race of mortals so singular in their shapes, habits, and countenances. Their heads were all reclined either to the right or the left, one of their eyes turned inward and the other directly up to the zenith. Their outward garments were adorned with the figures of suns, moons, and stars, interwoven with those of fiddles, flutes, harps, trumpets, guitars, harpsichords, and many more instruments of music unknown to us in Europe.[1] I observed here and there many in the habits of servants, with a blown bladder fastened like a flail to the end of a short stick, which they carried in their hands. In each bladder was a small quantity of dried pease or little pebbles (as I was afterwards informed). With these bladders they now and then flapped the mouths and ears of those who stood near them, of which practice I could not then conceive the meaning; it seems, the minds of these people are so taken up with intense speculations, that they neither can speak nor attend to the discourses of others without being roused by some external taction[2] upon the organs of speech and hearing; for which reason those persons who are able to afford it always keep a flapper (the original is *climenole*) in their family as one of their domestics, nor ever walk abroad or make visits without him. And the business of this officer is, when two or more persons are in company, gently to strike with his bladder the mouth of him who is to speak, and the right ear of him or them to whom the speaker addresseth himself. This flapper is likewise employed diligently to attend his master in his walks and upon occasion to give him a soft flap on his eyes, because he is always so wrapped up in cogitation that he is in manifest danger of falling down every precipice and bouncing his head against every post, and in the streets of jostling others or being jostled himself into the kennel.[3]

---

[1] The combination of astronomy and music is an indication of the Laputans' interest in pure science to the degree of neglecting application or even empirical test. Emphasis on the relationship of music and mathematics, with mystical emphasis, goes back at least to the Pythagoreans of ancient Sicily; it was the basis for much speculation about cosmic order throughout the Middle Ages and the Renaissance but came, with the growth of modern science, to be relegated more and more to "occult" thinkers and cranks. George I, who came to the throne at fifty-four, knew little English and showed little concern for literature, but he did patronize opera.

[2] Touch, contact.

[3] Gutter.

It was necessary to give the reader this information, without which he would be at the same loss with me to understand the proceedings of these people, as they conducted me up the stairs to the top of the island, and from thence to the royal palace. While we were ascending, they forgot several times what they were about and left me to myself, till their memories were again roused by their flappers; for they appeared altogether unmoved by the sight of my foreign habit and countenance and by the shouts of the vulgar, whose thoughts and minds were more disengaged.

At last we entered the palace and proceeded into the chamber of presence, where I saw the King seated on his throne, attended on each side by persons of prime quality. Before the throne was a large table filled with globes and spheres, and mathematical instruments of all kinds. His Majesty took not the least notice of us, although our entrance were not without sufficient noise, by the concourse of all persons belonging to the court. But he was then deep in a problem, and we attended at least an hour before he could solve it. There stood by him, on each side, a young page with flaps in their hands; and when they saw he was at leisure, one of them gently struck his mouth and the other his right ear; at which he started like one awaked on the sudden, and looking towards me and the company I was in, recollected the occasion of our coming, whereof he had been informed before. He spoke some words, whereupon immediately a young man with a flap came up to my side and flapped me gently on the right ear; but I made signs as well as I could that I had no occasion for such an instrument; which as I afterwards found gave his Majesty and the whole court a very mean opinion of my understanding. The King, as far as I could conjecture, asked me several questions, and I addressed myself to him in all the languages I had. When it was found that I could neither understand nor be understood, I was conducted by his order to an apartment in his palace (this prince being distinguished above all his predecessors for his hospitality to strangers), where two servants were appointed to attend me. My dinner was brought, and four persons of quality, whom I remembered to have seen very near the King's person, did me the honour to dine with me. We had two courses of three dishes each. In the first course there was a shoulder of mutton cut into an equilateral triangle, a piece of beef into a rhomboides, and a pudding into a cycloid.[4] The second course was two ducks trussed up into the form of fiddles, sausages and puddings resembling flutes and hautboys,[5] and a breast of veal in the shape of a harp. The servants cut our bread into cones, cylinders, parallelograms, and several other mathematical figures.

While we were at dinner I made bold to ask the names of several things in their language, and those noble persons, by the assistance of their flappers, delighted to give me answers, hoping to raise my admiration of their great abilities if I could be brought to converse with them. I was soon able to call for bread and drink or whatever else I wanted.

After dinner my company withdrew, and a person was sent to me by the King's order, attended by a flapper. He brought with him pen, ink, and paper, and three or four books, giving me to understand by signs that he was sent to teach me the language. We sat together four hours, in which time I wrote down a great number of words in columns, with the translations over against them. I likewise made a shift to learn several short sentences. For my tutor would order one of my servants to fetch something, to turn about, to make a bow, to sit or stand or walk and the like. Then I took down the sentence in writing. He showed me also in one of his books the figures of the sun, moon, and stars, the zodiac, the tropics,[6] and polar circles, together with the denominations of many figures of planes and solids. He gave me the names and descriptions of all the musi-

---

[4] That is, rhomboid (a parallelogram with opposite sides equal) and cycloid (circle).

[5] Oboes.

[6] That is, of Cancer and Capricorn.

cal instruments, and the general terms of art[7] in playing on each of them. After he had left me, I placed all my words with their interpretations in alphabetical order. And thus in a few days, by the help of a very faithful memory, I got some insight into their language.

The word which I interpret the *Flying* or *Floating Island* is in the original *Laputa*, whereof I could never learn the true etymology. *Lap* in the old obsolete language signifieth *high*, and *untuh* a *governor*, from which they say by corruption was derived *Laputa*, from *Lapuntuh*. But I do not approve of this derivation, which seems to be a little strained. I ventured to offer to the learned among them a conjecture of my own, that *Laputa* was *quasi*[8] *Lap outed; Lap* signifying properly the dancing of the sunbeams in the sea, and *outed* a wing, which however I shall not obtrude but submit to the judicious reader.[9]

Those to whom the King had entrusted me, observing how ill I was clad, ordered a tailor to come next morning and take my measure for a suit of clothes. This operator did his office after a different manner from those of his trade in Europe. He first took my altitude by a quadrant, and then with rule and compasses described the dimensions and outlines of my whole body, all which he entered upon paper, and in six days brought my clothes very ill made and quite out of shape, by happening to mistake a figure in the calculation.[10] But my comfort was that I observed such accidents very frequent and little regarded.

[7] Technical vocabulary.

[8] Seemingly.

[9] A parody of farfetched pedantic etymology. For recent explanations, see Appendix One.

[10] The weight of error in such highly mathematical procedure (compare the Lilliputians' more successful fitting of Gulliver in Part One, Chapter Six) had been made memorable by a printer's mistaken addition of a zero to Newton's estimate of the distance of the sun from the earth.

During my confinement for want of clothes, and by an in-
disposition that held me some days longer, I much enlarged my
dictionary; and when I went next to court was able to understand many things the King spoke, and to return him some
kind of answers. His Majesty had given orders that the island
should move northeast and by east, to the vertical point over
Lagado, the metropolis of the whole kingdom below upon
the firm earth. It was about ninety leagues distant, and our
voyage lasted four days and a half. I was not in the least sensible of the progressive motion made in the air by the island. On
the second morning about eleven o'clock the King himself in
person, attended by his nobility, courtiers, and officers, having
prepared all their musical instruments, played on them for
three hours without intermission, so that I was quite stunned
with the noise; neither could I possibly guess the meaning till
my tutor informed me. He said that the people of their island
had their ears adapted to hear the music of the spheres,[11]
which always played at certain periods, and the court was now
prepared to bear their part in whatever instrument they most
excelled.

In our journey towards Lagado, the capital city, his Majesty
ordered that the island should stop over certain towns and villages, from whence he might receive the petitions of his
subjects. And to this purpose several packthreads were let down
with small weights at the bottom. On these packthreads the
people strung their petitions, which mounted up directly like
the scraps of paper fastened by schoolboys at the end of the
string that holds their kite. Sometimes we received wine and
victuals from below, which were drawn up by pulleys.

The knowledge I had in mathematics gave me great assistance in acquiring their phraseology, which depended much
upon that science and music; and in the latter I was not un-

[11] The celestial music imagined by Pythagoras to be created by
the movement of the spheres that held the planets and other heavenly bodies. This movement was expressible in mathematical terms,
which corresponded to musical harmonies.

skilled. Their ideas are perpetually conversant [12] in lines and figures. If they would, for example, praise the beauty of a woman or any other animal, they describe it by rhombs, circles, parallelograms, ellipses, and other geometrical terms, or else by words of art drawn from music, needless here to repeat. I observed in the King's kitchen all sorts of mathematical and musical instruments, after the figures of which they cut up the joints that were served to his Majesty's table.

Their houses are very ill built, the walls bevil,[13] without one right angle in any apartment; and this defect ariseth from the contempt they bear for practical geometry, which they despise as vulgar and mechanic; those instructions they give being too refined for the intellectuals of their workmen, which occasions perpetual mistakes. And although they are dextrous enough upon a piece of paper in the management of the rule, the pencil, and the divider, yet in the common actions and behaviour of life I have not seen a more clumsy, awkward, and unhandy people, nor so slow and perplexed in their conceptions upon all other subjects, except those of mathematics and music. They are very bad reasoners and vehemently given to opposition, unless when they happen to be of the right opinion, which is seldom their case. Imagination, fancy, and invention,[14] they are wholly strangers to, nor have any words in their language by which those ideas can be expressed; the whole compass of their thoughts and mind being shut up within the two forementioned sciences.

Most of them, and especially those who deal in the astronomical part, have great faith in judicial astrology,[15] although they are ashamed to own it publicly. But what I chiefly admired, and thought altogether unaccountable, was the strong

[12] Expressed.
[13] Leaning at an angle.
[14] Creation or discovery of new ideas in art or science.
[15] The study of the influence of the stars on human affairs, as opposed to "natural astrology," which foretold natural phenomena such as tides and eclipses.

disposition I observed in them towards news and politics, perpetually enquiring into public affairs, giving their judgments
in matters of state, and passionately disputing every inch of a
party opinion. I have indeed observed the same disposition
among most of the mathematicians I have known in Europe,
although I could never discover the least analogy between the
two sciences; unless those people suppose that, because the
smallest circle hath as many degrees as the largest, therefore
the regulation and management of the world require no more
abilities than the handling and turning of a globe. But I rather
take this quality to spring from a very common infirmity of
human nature, inclining us to be more curious and conceited
in matters where we have least concern, and for which we are
least adapted either by study or nature.

These people are under continual disquietudes, never enjoy-
ing a minute's peace of mind; and their disturbances proceed
from causes which very little affect the rest of mortals. Their
apprehensions arise from several changes they dread in the
celestial bodies. For instance, that the earth, by the continual
approaches of the sun towards it, must in course of time be
absorbed or swallowed up.[16] That the face of the sun will by
degrees be encrusted with its own effluvia, and give no more
light to the world. That the earth very narrowly escaped a
brush from the tail of the last comet, which would have infallibly reduced it to ashes; and that the next, which they have

[16] This and the following fears were expressed or implied by
astronomers of the day, notably Newton and Edmund Halley
(see Part Three, Chapter Three, Note 4). Swift ironically links
the novel scientific speculation of his day with traditional super-
stitions. The crusting of heavenly bodies (of which sun spots were
taken as an example) was included in Descartes' theory of vortices:
once a body lost its expansive force through encrustation, it might
cease to be a sun and become absorbed into the vortex of another
body as a planet, or, if its velocity were great enough, wander
through vortices as a comet. (See Part Three, Chapter Eight, Note
4.)

calculated for one and thirty years hence, will probably destroy us. For, if in its perihelion it should approach within a certain degree of the sun (as by their calculations they have reason to dread), it will conceive a degree of heat ten thousand times more intense than that of red-hot glowing iron; and in its absence from the sun carry a blazing tail ten hundred thousand and fourteen miles long; through which if the earth should pass at the distance of one hundred thousand miles from the nucleus or main body of the comet, it must in its passage be set on fire and reduced to ashes. That the sun, daily spending its rays without any nutriment to supply them, will at last be wholly consumed and annihilated; which must be attended with the destruction of this earth and of all the planets that receive their light from it.

They are so perpetually alarmed with the apprehensions of these and the like impending dangers that they can neither sleep quietly in their beds nor have any relish for the common pleasures or amusements of life. When they meet an acquaintance in the morning the first question is about the sun's health, how he looked at his setting and rising, and what hopes they have to avoid the stroke of the approaching comet. This conversation they are apt to run into with the same temper that boys discover in delighting to hear terrible stories of sprites and hobgoblins, which they greedily listen to and dare not go to bed for fear.

The women of the island have abundance of vivacity; they contemn their husbands and are exceedingly fond of strangers, whereof there is always a considerable number from the continent below, attending at court, either upon affairs of the several towns and corporations or their own particular occasions, but are much despised, because they want the same endowments. Among these the ladies choose their gallants: but the vexation is that they act with too much ease and security, for the husband is always so wrapped in speculation that the mistress and lover may proceed to the greatest familiarities before his face, if he be but provided with paper and implements and without his flapper at his side.

The wives and daughters lament their confinement to the island, although I think it the most delicious spot of ground in the world; and, although they live here in the greatest plenty and magnificence and are allowed to do whatever they please, they long to see the world and take the diversions of the metropolis, which they are not allowed to do without a particular licence from the King; and this is not easy to be obtained because the people of quality have found by frequent experience how hard it is to persuade their women to return from below. I was told that a great court lady, who had several children, is married to the Prime Minister, the richest subject in the kingdom, a very graceful person extremely fond of her, and lives in the finest palace of the island, went down to Lagado on the pretence of health, there hid herself for several months, till the King sent a warrant to search for her; and she was found in an obscure eating house all in rags, having pawned her clothes to maintain an old deformed footman, who beat her every day, and in whose company she was taken much against her will. And although her husband received her with all possible kindness and without the least reproach, she soon after contrived to steal down again with all her jewels to the same gallant, and hath not been heard of since.

This may perhaps pass with the reader rather for an European or English story than for one of a country so remote. But he may please to consider that the caprices of womankind are not limited by any climate or nation and that they are much more uniform than can be easily imagined.

In about a month's time I had made a tolerable proficiency in their language and was able to answer most of the King's questions when I had the honour to attend him. His Majesty discovered not the least curiosity to enquire into the laws, government, history, religion, or manners of the countries where I had been, but confined his questions to the state of mathematics, and received the account I gave him with great contempt and indifference, though often roused by his flapper on each side.

Chapter Three: A phenomenon solved by modern philosophy and astronomy. The Laputans' great improvements in the latter. The King's method of suppressing insurrections.

I desired leave of this prince to see the curiosities of the island, which he was graciously pleased to grant, and ordered my tutor to attend me. I chiefly wanted to know to what cause in art or in nature it owed its several motions, whereof I will now give a philosophical account to the reader.[1]

The Flying or Floating Island is exactly circular, its diameter 7,837 yards, or about four miles and an half, and consequently contains ten thousand acres. It is three hundred yards thick. The bottom or under surface, which appears to those who view it from below, is one even regular plate of adamant, shooting up to the height of about two hundred yards. Above it lie the several minerals in their usual order, and over all is a coat of rich mould ten or twelve foot deep. The declivity of the upper surface, from the circumference to the center, is the natural cause why all the dews and rains which fall upon the island are conveyed in small rivulets towards the middle, where they are emptied into four large basins, each of about half a mile in circuit and two hundred yards distant from the center.

---

[1] What follows is a parody of the style of scientific papers published in the *Transactions of the Royal Society*. For detailed treatment of Swift's close use of actual writings and experiments of the day throughout this voyage, see the articles by Marjorie H. Nicolson and Nora Mohler reprinted in Marjorie Nicolson, *Science and Imagination* (1956).

From these basins the water is continually exhaled by the sun in the daytime, which effectually prevents their overflowing. Besides, as it is in the power of the monarch to raise the island above the region of clouds and vapours, he can prevent the falling of dews and rains whenever he pleases. For the highest clouds cannot rise above two miles, as naturalists agree; at least they were never known to do so in that country.

At the center of the island there is a chasm about fifty yards in diameter, from whence the astronomers descend into a large dome, which is therefore called *Flandona Gagnole,* or the *Astronomer's Cave,* situated at the depth of an hundred yards beneath the upper surface of the adamant. In this cave are twenty lamps continually burning, which from the reflection of the adamant cast a strong light into every part. The place is stored with great variety of sextants, quadrants, telescopes, astrolabes, and other astronomical instruments. But the greatest curiosity, upon which the fate of the island depends, is a lodestone of a prodigious size, in shape resembling a weaver's shuttle. It is in length six yards, and in the thickest part at least three yards over. This magnet is sustained by a very strong axle of adamant passing through its middle, upon which it plays, and is poised so exactly that the weakest hand can turn it. It is hooped round with an hollow cylinder of adamant, four foot deep, as many thick, and twelve yards in diameter, placed horizontally, and supported by eight adamantine feet, each six yards high. In the middle of the concave side there is a groove twelve inches deep, in which the extremities of the axle are lodged, and turned round as there is occasion.

This stone cannot be moved from its place by any force, because the hoop and its feet are one continued piece with that body of adamant which constitutes the bottom of the island.

By means of this lodestone the island is made to rise and fall and move from one place to another. For, with respect to that part of the earth over which the monarch presides, the stone is endued at one of its sides with an attractive power and at the other with a repulsive. Upon placing the magnet erect with its attracting end towards the earth, the island descends; but when the repelling extremity points downwards, the island mounts directly upwards. When the position of the stone is oblique, the motion of the island is so too. For in this magnet the forces always act in lines parallel to its direction.

By this oblique motion the island is conveyed to different parts of the monarch's dominions. To explain the manner of its progress, let *A B* represent a line drawn cross the dominions of Balnibarbi, let the line *c d* represent the lodestone, of which let *d* be the repelling end, and *c* the attracting end, the island being over *C;* let the stone be placed in the position *c d* with its repelling end downwards; then the island will be driven upwards obliquely towards *D*. When it is arrived at *D*, let the stone be turned upon its axle till its attracting end points towards *E*, and then the island will be carried obliquely towards *E;* where if the stone be again turned upon its axle till it stands in the position *E F*, with its repelling point downwards, the island will rise obliquely towards *F*, where by directing the attracting end towards *G*, the island may be carried to *G*, and from *G* to *H*, by turning the stone so as to make its repelling extremity point directly downwards. And thus by changing the situation of the stone as often as there is occasion, the island is made to rise and fall by turns in an oblique direction, and by those alternate risings and fallings (the obliquity being not considerable) is conveyed from one part of the dominions to the other.

But it must be observed that this island cannot move beyond the extent of the dominions below, nor can it rise above the height of four miles. For which the astronomers (who have written large systems concerning the stone) assign the following reason: that the magnetic virtue does not extend beyond the distance of four miles, and that the mineral which acts upon the stone in the bowels of the earth, and in the sea about six leagues distant from the shore, is not diffused through the whole globe, but terminated with the limits of the King's

dominions; and it was easy, from the great advantage of such a superior situation, for a prince to bring under his obedience whatever country lay within the attraction of that magnet.

When the stone is put parallel to the plane of the horizon, the island standeth still; for in that case the extremities of it, being at equal distance from the earth, act with equal force, the one in drawing downwards, the other in pushing upwards, and consequently no motion can ensue.

This lodestone is under the care of certain astronomers, who from time to time give it such positions as the monarch directs. They spend the greatest part of their lives in observing the celestial bodies, which they do by the assistance of glasses far excelling ours in goodness. For although their largest telescopes do not exceed three feet, they magnify much more than those of an hundred-yards among us, and at the same time show the stars with greater clearness. This advantage hath enabled them to extend their discoveries much farther than our astronomers in Europe. They have made a catalogue of ten thousand fixed stars, whereas the largest of ours do not contain above one third part of that number.[2] They have likewise discovered two lesser stars, or *satellites*, which revolve about Mars, whereof the innermost is distant from the center of the primary planet exactly three of his diameters, and the outermost five; the former revolves in the space of ten hours, and the latter in twenty-one and an half; so that the squares of their periodical times are very near in the same proportion with the cubes of their distance from the center of Mars, which evidently shows them to be governed by the same law of gravitation that influences the other heavenly bodies.[3]

They have observed ninety-three different comets, and settled their periods with great exactness. If this be true (and they affirm it with great confidence) it is much to be wished that their observations were made public, whereby the theory

[2] The *British Catalogue* of fixed stars, published in 1725, included less than three thousand.

[3] Two such satellites were in fact observed in 1877.

of comets, which at present is very lame and defective, might be brought to the same perfection with other parts of astronomy.[4]

The King would be the most absolute prince in the universe if he could but prevail on a ministry to join with him; but these having their estates below on the continent and considering that the office of a favourite hath a very uncertain tenure, would never consent to the enslaving their country.

If any town should engage in rebellion or mutiny, fall into violent factions, or refuse to pay the usual tribute, the King hath two methods of reducing them to obedience. The first and the mildest course is by keeping the island hovering over such a town and the lands about it, whereby he can deprive them of the benefit of the sun and the rain, and consequently afflict the inhabitants with dearth and diseases. And if the crime deserve it, they are at the same time pelted from above with great stones, against which they have no defence but by creeping into cellars or caves while the roofs of their houses are beaten to pieces. But if they still continue obstinate or offer to raise insurrections, he proceeds to the last remedy, by letting the island drop directly upon their heads, which makes a universal destruction both of houses and men. However, this is an extremity to which the prince is seldom driven; neither indeed is he willing to put it in execution, nor dare his ministers advise him to an action which, as it would render them odious to the people, so it would be a great damage to their own estates, that lie all below, for the island is the King's demesne.[5]

---

[4] Edmund Halley (1656–1742), who had studied the orbits of twenty-four comets, was the first to calculate a regular orbit for a comet (that of 1682) and predict its return (verified in 1759).

[5] The Flying Island, and particularly its adamantine bottom, suggests the royal prerogative (those privileges of the Crown uncircumscribed by law), with which Swift had been concerned in *The Drapier's Letters* (1724–1725). Swift had fought the sending of great quantities of copper halfpence to Ireland; not only were these a source of profit to royal favorites, but they threatened, in Swift's eyes, to drain gold and silver from Ireland and to promote

But there is still indeed a more weighty reason why the kings of this country have been always averse from executing so terrible an action, unless upon the utmost necessity. For if the town intended to be destroyed should have in it any tall rocks, as it generally falls out in the larger cities, a situation probably chosen at first with a view to prevent such a catastrophe, or if it abound in high spires or pillars of stone, a sudden fall might endanger the bottom or under surface of the island; which although it consist, as I have said, of one entire adamant two hundred yards thick, might happen to crack by too great a shock, or burst by approaching too near the fires from the houses below, as the backs both of iron and stone will often do in our chimneys. Of all this the people are well apprised, and understand how far to carry their obstinacy where their liberty or property is concerned. And the King, when he is highest provoked and most determined to press a city to rubbish, orders the island to descend with great gentleness, out of a pretence of tenderness to his people, but indeed for fear of breaking the adamantine bottom; in which case it is the opinion of all their philosophers, that the lodestone could no longer hold it up, and the whole mass would fall to the ground.

About three years before my arrival among them, while the King was in his progress over his dominions, there happened an extraordinary accident which had like to have put a period to the fate of that monarchy, at least as it is now instituted. Lindalino, the second city in the kingdom,[6] was the first his Majesty visited in his progress. Three days after his departure, the inhabitants, who had often complained of great oppressions, shut the town gates, seized on the governor, and with incredi-

---

a debased and inflationary currency. The imposition of royal power at the expense of the lands below (Great Britain and Ireland) is limited in Laputa only by the interest of those ministers whose landed wealth depends on the prosperity of the country. This reflects Swift's hostility to the growth of a moneyed but landless upper middle class. (See Part Two, Chapter Six, Note 14.)

[6] Dublin, where Swift was Dean of St. Patrick's Cathedral.

ble speed and labour erected four large towers, one at every corner of the city (which is an exact square), equal in height to a strong pointed rock that stands directly in the center of the city. Upon the top of each tower, as well as upon the rock, they fixed a great lodestone; and in case their design should fail, they had provided a vast quantity of the most combustible fuel, hoping to burst therewith the adamantine bottom of the island if the lodestone project should miscarry.

It was eight months before the King had perfect notice that the Lindalinians were in rebellion. He then commanded that the island should be wafted over the city. The people were unanimous and had laid in store of provisions, and a great river runs through the middle of the town. The King hovered over them several days to deprive them of the sun and the rain. He ordered many packthreads to be let down, yet not a person offered to send up a petition, but instead thereof, very bold demands, the redress of all their grievances, great immunities, the choice of their own governor, and other the like exorbitances.[7] Upon which his Majesty commanded all the inhabitants of the island to cast great stones from the lower gallery into the town; but the citizens had provided against this mischief by conveying their persons and effects into the four towers, and other strong buildings, and vaults underground.

The King, being now determined to reduce this proud people, ordered that the island should descend gently within forty yards of the top of the towers and rock. This was accordingly done; but the officers employed in that work found the descent much speedier than usual, and by turning the lodestone could

[7] The Irish resistance to William Wood's halfpence, mobilized by Swift in the anonymous *Drapier's Letters*, led to the offer of a reward of £300 for the identification of the author of "several seditious and scandalous paragraphs" in the Fourth Letter. Everyone knew that Swift had written them, but no one claimed the reward. The Court was finally forced to cancel the patent for the coinage.

not without great difficulty keep it in a firm position, but found the island inclining to fall. They sent the King immediate intelligence of this astonishing event and begged his Majesty's permission to raise the island higher; the King consented, a general council was called, and the officers of the lodestone ordered to attend. One of the oldest and expertest among them obtained leave to try an experiment. He took a strong line of an hundred yards, and the island being raised over the town above the attracting power they had felt, he fastened a piece of adamant to the end of his line which had in it a mixture of iron mineral, of the same nature with that whereof the bottom or lower surface of the island is composed, and from the lower gallery let it down slowly towards the top of the towers. The adamant was not descended four yards before the officer felt it drawn so strongly downwards, that he could hardly pull it back. He then threw down several small pieces of adamant and observed that they were all violently attracted by the top of the tower. The same experiment was made on the other three towers and on the rock with the same effect.

This incident broke entirely the King's measures and (to dwell no longer on other circumstances) he was forced to give the town their own conditions.

I was assured by a great minister, that if the island had descended so near the town as not to be able to raise itself, the citizens were determined to fix it forever, to kill the King and all his servants, and entirely change the government.

By a fundamental law of this realm neither King nor either of his two elder sons are permitted to leave the island, nor the Queen till she is past child-bearing.[8]

---

[8] Such a clause, in the Act of Settlement of 1701, forbade the King to leave England without consent of Parliament. George I, once he secured its repeal, spent much time in his German dominion of Hanover. The ironic point here suggests the danger to the Laputan royal family if they should travel within their own oppressed country.

Chapter Four: The author leaves Laputa, is conveyed to Balnibarbi, arrives at the metropolis. A description of the metropolis and the country adjoining. The author hospitably received by a great lord. His conversation with that lord.

Although I cannot say that I was ill treated in this island, yet I must confess I thought myself too much neglected, not without some degree of contempt. For neither prince nor people appeared to be curious in any part of knowledge, except mathematics and music, wherein I was far their inferior and upon that account very little regarded.

On the other side, after having seen all the curiosities of the island, I was very desirous to leave it, being heartily weary of those people. They were indeed excellent in two sciences for which I have great esteem and wherein I am not unversed, but at the same time so abstracted and involved in speculation that I never met with such disagreeable companions. I conversed only with women, tradesmen, flappers, and court-pages during two months of my abode there, by which at last I rendered myself extremely contemptible; yet these were the only people from whom I could ever receive a reasonable answer.

I had obtained by hard study a good degree of knowledge in their language; I was weary of being confined to an island where I received so little countenance, and resolved to leave it with the first opportunity.

There was a great lord at court, nearly related to the King, and for that reason alone used with respect. He was universally reckoned the most ignorant and stupid person among them. He had performed many eminent services for the crown, had great natural and acquired parts, adorned with integrity and honour, but so ill an ear for music that his detractors reported he had been often known to beat time in the wrong place; neither could his tutors without extreme difficulty teach him to demonstrate the most easy proposition in the mathematics. He was pleased to show me many marks of favour, often did me the honour of a visit, desired to be informed in the affairs of Europe, the laws and customs, the manners and learning of the several countries where I had travelled. He listened to me with great attention and made very wise observations on all I spoke. He had two flappers attending him for state, but never made use of them except at court and in visits of ceremony, and would always command them to withdraw when we were alone together.

I intreated this illustrious person to intercede in my behalf with his Majesty for leave to depart, which he accordingly did, as he was pleased to tell me, with regret: for indeed he had made me several offers very advantageous, which however I refused with expressions of the highest acknowledgment.

On the 16th day of February I took leave of his Majesty and the court. The King made me a present to the value of about two hundred pounds English, and my protector his kinsman as much more, together with a letter of recommendation to a friend of his in Lagado, the metropolis; the island being then hovering over a mountain about two miles from it, I was let down from the lowest gallery in the same manner as I had been taken up.

The continent, as far as it is subject to the monarch of the Flying Island, passes under the general name of Balnibarbi, and the metropolis, as I said before, is called Lagado. I felt some little satisfaction in finding myself on firm ground. I walked to the city without any concern, being clad like one of the natives, and sufficiently instructed to converse with them. I soon found out the person's house to whom I was recommended, presented my letter from his friend, the grandee in the island, and was received with much kindness. This great lord, whose name was Munodi,[1] ordered me an apartment in his own house, where I continued during my stay, and was entertained in a most hospitable manner.

The next morning after my arrival he took me in his chariot to see the town, which is about half the bigness of London, but

[1] From *mundum odi*, "I hate the world."

the houses very strangely built, and most of them out of re-
pair. The people in the streets walked fast, looked wild, their
eyes fixed, and were generally in rags. We passed through one
of the town gates and went about three miles into the country,
where I saw many labourers working with several sorts of
tools in the ground, but was not able to conjecture what they
were about; neither did I observe any expectation either of
corn or grass, although the soil appeared to be excellent. I
could not forbear admiring at these odd appearances both in
town and country, and I made bold to desire my conductor
that he would be pleased to explain to me what could be meant
by so many busy heads, hands, and faces, both in the streets
and the fields, because I did not discover any good effects they
produced; but on the contrary, I never knew a soil so un-
happily cultivated, houses so ill contrived and so ruinous, or
a people whose countenances and habit expressed so much
misery and want.

This Lord Munodi was a person of the first rank and had
been some years Governor of Lagado, but by a cabal of ministers was discharged for insufficiency. However, the King
treated him with tenderness, as a well-meaning man, but of a
low contemptible understanding.

When I gave that free censure of the country and its inhabitants, he made no further answer than by telling me that I had
not been long enough among them to form a judgment and
that the different nations of the world had different customs,
with other common topics to the same purpose. But when we
returned to his palace, he asked me how I liked the building,
what absurdities I observed, and what quarrel I had with the
dress and looks of his domestics. This he might safely do, because everything about him was magnificent, regular, and
polite. I answered that his Excellency's prudence, quality, and
fortune had exempted him from those defects which folly and
beggary had produced in others. He said if I would go with
him to his country house, about twenty miles distant, where
his estate lay, there would be more leisure for this kind of con-

versation. I told his Excellency that I was entirely at his disposal, and accordingly we set out next morning.

During our journey he made me observe the several methods used by farmers in managing their lands, which to me were wholly unaccountable, for, except in some very few places, I could not discover one ear of corn or blade of grass. But in three hours' travelling the scene was wholly altered; we came into a most beautiful country; farmers' houses at small distances, neatly built, the fields enclosed, containing vineyards, corn-grounds, and meadows. Neither do I remember to have seen a more delightful prospect. His Excellency observed my countenance to clear up; he told me with a sigh that there his estate began, and would continue the same till we should come to his house. That his countrymen ridiculed and despised him for managing his affairs no better and for setting so ill an example to the kingdom, which however was followed by very few, such as were old and wilful, and weak like himself.

We came at length to the house, which was indeed a noble structure, built according to the best rules of ancient architecture. The fountains, gardens, walks, avenues, and groves were all disposed with exact judgment and taste. I gave due praises to everything I saw, whereof his Excellency took not the least notice till after supper, when, there being no third companion, he told me with a very melancholy air, that he doubted he must throw down his houses in town and country, to rebuild them after the present mode, destroy all his plantations,[2] and cast others into such a form as modern usage required, and give the same directions to all his tenants, unless he would submit to incur the censure of pride, singularity, affectation, ignorance, caprice, and perhaps encrease his Majesty's displeasure.

That the admiration I appeared to be under would cease or diminish when he had informed me of some particulars, which probably I never heard of at court, the people there being too

[2] Plantings, landscape gardening.

much taken up in their own speculations to have regard to what passed here below.

The sum of his discourse was to this effect. That about forty years ago, certain persons went up to Laputa either upon business or diversion, and after five months continuance came back with a very little smattering in mathematics, but full of volatile spirits acquired in that airy region. That these persons upon their return began to dislike the management of everything below, and fell into schemes of putting all arts, sciences, languages, and mechanics upon a new foot. To this end they procured a Royal patent for erecting an Academy of Projectors in Lagado; [3] and the humour prevailed so strongly among the people that there is not a town of any consequence in the kingdom without such an academy. In these colleges the professors contrive new rules and methods of agriculture and building, and new instruments and tools for all trades and manufactures; whereby, as they undertake, one man shall do the work of ten, a palace may be built in a week of materials so durable as to last forever without repairing. All the fruits of the earth shall come to maturity at whatever season we think fit to choose, and increase an hundred fold more than they do at present, with innumerable other happy proposals. The only inconvenience is that none of these projects are yet brought to perfection, and in the meantime the whole country lies miserably waste, the houses in ruins, and the people without food or clothes. By all which, instead of being discouraged, they are fifty times more violently bent upon prosecuting their schemes, driven equally on by hope and despair; that as for himself, being not of an enterprising spirit, he was content to go on in the old forms, to live in the houses his ancestors had built,

[3] The Royal Society was chartered by Charles II in 1662. Many of the experiments presented in the following chapter are only slight exaggerations or distortions of experiments and proposals published in its *Transactions.* "Projectors" was a term in considerable disrepute by this time, applied to the devisers of ingenious scientific, economic, and political schemes.

and act as they did in every part of life without innovation. That some few other persons of quality and gentry had done the same, but were looked on with an eye of contempt and ill will, as enemies to art, ignorant, and ill commonwealth'smen, preferring their own ease and sloth before the general improvement of their country.

His Lordship added, that he would not by any further particulars prevent[4] the pleasure I should certainly take in viewing the Grand Academy, whither he was resolved I should go. He only desired me to observe a ruined building upon the side of a mountain about three miles distant, of which he gave me this account. That he had a very convenient mill within half a mile of his house, turned by a current from a large river, and sufficient for his own family as well as a great number of his tenants. That about seven years ago a club of those projectors came to him with proposals to destroy this mill and build another on the side of that mountain, on the long ridge whereof a long canal must be cut for a repository of water, to be conveyed up by pipes and engines to supply the mill: because the wind and air upon a height agitated the water, and thereby made it fitter for motion, and because the water descending down a declivity would turn the mill with half the current of a river whose course is more upon a level. He said that, being then not very well with the court and pressed by many of his friends, he complied with the proposal; and after employing an hundred men for two years, the work miscarried, the projectors went off, laying the blame entirely upon him, railing at him ever since, and putting others upon the same experiment, with equal assurance of success, as well as equal disappointment.

In a few days we came back to town, and his Excellency, considering the bad character he had in the Academy, would not go with me himself, but recommended me to a friend of his to bear me company thither. My Lord was pleased to rep-

[4] Anticipate.

resent me as a great admirer of projects and a person of much curiosity and easy belief, which indeed was not without truth, for I had myself been a sort of projector in my younger days.

Chapter Five: The author permitted to see the Grand Academy of Lagado. The Academy largely described. The arts wherein the professors employ themselves.

This academy is not an entire single building, but a continuation of several houses on both sides of a street, which, growing waste, was purchased and applied to that use.

I was received very kindly by the Warden and went for many days to the Academy. Every room hath in it one or more projectors, and I believe I could not be in fewer than five hundred rooms.

The first man I saw was of a meagre aspect, with sooty hands and face, his hair and beard long, ragged, and singed in several places. His clothes, shirt, and skin were all of the same colour. He had been eight years upon a project for extracting sunbeams out of cucumbers, which were to be put into vials hermetically sealed, and let out to warm the air in raw inclement summers. He told me, he did not doubt in eight years more that he should be able to supply the Governor's gardens with sunshine at a reasonable rate; but he complained that his stock was low and entreated me to give him something as an encouragement to ingenuity, especially since this had been a very dear season for cucumbers. I made him a small present, for my Lord had furnished me with money on purpose, because he knew their practice of begging from all who go to see them.

I went into another chamber, but was ready to hasten back, being almost overcome with a horrible stink. My conductor pressed me forward, conjuring me in a whisper to give no offence, which would be highly resented, and therefore I durst not so much as stop my nose. The projector of this cell was the most ancient student of the Academy. His face and beard were of a pale yellow, his hands and clothes daubed over with filth. When I was presented to him, he gave me a very close embrace (a compliment I could well have excused). His employment from his first coming into the Academy was an operation to reduce human excrement to its original food, by separating the several parts, removing the tincture which it receives from the gall, making the odour exhale, and scumming off the saliva. He had a weekly allowance from the society of a vessel filled with human ordure, about the bigness of a Bristol barrel.

I saw another at work to calcine ice into gunpowder, who likewise showed me a treatise he had written concerning the malleability of fire, which he intended to publish.

There was a most ingenious architect who had contrived a new method for building houses, by beginning at the roof and working downwards to the foundation, which he justified to me by the like practice of those two prudent insects, the bee and the spider.

There was a man born blind, who had several apprentices in his own condition: their employment was to mix colours for painters, which their master taught them to distinguish by feeling and smelling. It was indeed my misfortune to find them at that time not very perfect in their lessons, and the professor himself happened to be generally mistaken; this artist is much encouraged and esteemed by the whole fraternity.

In another apartment I was highly pleased with a projector who had found a device of plowing the ground with hogs, to save the charges of plows, cattle, and labour. The method is this: in an acre of ground you bury, at six inches distance and eight deep, a quantity of acorns, dates, chestnuts, and other mast or vegetables whereof these animals are fondest: then you drive six hundred or more of them into the field, where in a few days they will root up the whole ground in search of their food, and make it fit for sowing, at the same time manuring it with their dung; it is true upon experiment they found the charge and trouble very great, and they had little or no crop. However, it is not doubted that this invention may be capable of great improvement.

I went into another room, where the walls and ceiling were all hung round with cobwebs, except a narrow passage for the artist to go in and out. At my entrance he called aloud to me not to disturb his webs. He lamented the fatal mistake the world had been so long in of using silkworms, while we had such plenty of domestic insects who infinitely excelled the former, because they understood how to weave as well as spin. And he proposed farther that by employing spiders the charge of dyeing silks would be wholly saved, whereof I was fully convinced when he showed me a vast number of flies most beautifully coloured, wherewith he fed his spiders, assuring us that the webs would take a tincture from them; and as he had them of all hues, he hoped to fit everybody's fancy as soon as he could find proper food for the flies, of certain gums, oils, and other glutinous matter, to give a strength and consistence to the threads.

There was an astronomer who had undertaken to place a sundial upon the great weathercock on the town-house, by adjusting the annual and diurnal motions of the earth and sun, so as to answer and coincide with all accidental turnings by the wind.

I was complaining of a small fit of the colic, upon which my conductor led me into a room, where a great physician resided, who was famous for curing that disease by contrary operations from the same instrument. He had a large pair of bellows with a long slender muzzle of ivory. This he conveyed eight inches up the anus, and drawing in the wind, he affirmed he could make the guts as lank as a dried bladder. But when the disease was more stubborn and violent, he let in the muzzle while the bellows was full of wind, which he discharged into the body of the patient, then withdrew the instrument to replenish it, clapping his thumb strongly against the orifice of the fundament; and this being repeated three or four times, the adventitious wind would rush out, bringing the noxious along with it (like water put into a pump), and the patient recovers. I saw him try both experiments upon a dog, but could not discern any effect from the former. After the latter, the animal was ready to burst, and made so violent a discharge as was very offensive to me and my companions. The dog died on the spot, and we left the doctor endeavouring to recover him by the same operation.

I visited many other apartments, but shall not trouble my reader with all the curiosities I observed, being studious of brevity.

I had hitherto seen only one side of the Academy, the other being appropriated to the advancers of speculative learning, of whom I shall say something when I have mentioned one illustrious person more, who is called among them "the universal artist." He told us he had been thirty years employing his thoughts for the improvement of human life. He had two large rooms full of wonderful curiosities, and fifty men at work. Some were condensing air into a dry tangible substance, by extracting the nitre and letting the aqueous or fluid particles percolate; others softening marble for pillows and pincushions; others petrifying the hoofs of a living horse to preserve them from foundering. The artist himself was at that time busy upon two great designs; the first, to sow land with chaff, wherein he affirmed the true seminal virtue to be contained, as he demonstrated by several experiments which I was not skilful enough to comprehend. The other was, by a certain composition of gums, minerals, and vegetables outwardly applied, to prevent the growth of wool upon two young lambs; and he hoped in a reasonable time to propagate the breed of naked sheep all over the kingdom.

We crossed a walk to the other part of the Academy, where, as I have already said, the projectors in speculative learning resided.

The first professor I saw was in a very large room, with forty pupils about him. After salutation, observing me to look earnestly upon a frame, which took up the greatest part of both the length and breadth of the room, he said perhaps I might wonder to see him employed in a project for improving speculative knowledge by practical and mechanical operations. But the world would soon be sensible of its usefulness, and he flattered himself that a more noble, exalted thought never sprang in any other man's head. Everyone knows how laborious the usual method is of attaining to arts and sciences; whereas by his contrivance the most ignorant person, at a reasonable charge, and with a little bodily labour, may write books in philosophy, poetry, politics, law, mathematics, and theology, without the least assistance from genius or study. He then led me to the frame, about the sides whereof all his pupils stood in ranks. It was twenty foot square, placed in the middle of the room. The superficies was composed of several bits of wood, about the bigness of a die, but some larger than others. They were all linked together by slender wires. These bits of wood were covered on every square with paper pasted on them, and on these papers were written all the words of their language in their several moods, tenses, and declensions, but without any order. The professor then desired me to observe, for he was going to set his engine at work. The pupils at his command took each of them hold of an iron handle, whereof there were forty fixed round the edges of the frame, and, giving them a sudden turn, the whole disposition of the words was entirely changed. He then commanded six and thirty of the lads to read the several lines softly as they appeared upon the frame; and, where they found three or four words together that might make part of a sentence, they dictated to the four remaining boys who were scribes. This work was repeated three or four times, and at every turn the engine was so contrived that the words shifted into new places as the square bits of wood moved upside down.

Six hours a day the young students were employed in this labour, and the professor showed me several volumes in large folio already collected, of broken sentences which he intended to piece together, and out of those rich materials to give the world a complete body of all arts and sciences; which however might be still improved, and much expedited, if the public would raise a fund for making and employing five hundred such frames in Lagado, and oblige the managers to contribute in common their several collections.

He assured me, that this invention had employed all his thoughts from his youth, that he had emptied the whole vocabulary into his frame, and made the strictest computation of the general proportion there is in books between the numbers of particles, nouns, and verbs, and other parts of speech.

I made my humblest acknowledgments to this illustrious person for his great communicativeness and promised, if ever I had the good fortune to return to my native country, that I would do him justice as the sole inventor of this wonderful machine; the form and contrivance of which I desired leave to delineate upon paper as in the figure here annexed. I told him, although it were the custom of our learned in Europe to steal inventions from each other, who had thereby at least this advantage, that it became a controversy which was the right owner, yet I would take such caution that he should have the honour entire without a rival.

We next went to the School of Languages, where three professors sat in consultation upon improving that of their own country.

The first project was to shorten discourse by cutting polysyllables into one, and leaving out verbs and participles, because in reality all things imaginable are but nouns.

The other was a scheme for entirely abolishing all words whatsoever; and this was urged as a great advantage in point of health as well as brevity. For it is plain that every word we speak is in some degree a diminution of our lungs by corrosion and consequently contributes to the shortening of our lives. An expedient was therefore offered that, since words are only names for *things*, it would be more convenient for all men to carry about them such *things* as were necessary to express the

particular business they are to discourse on.[1] And this invention would certainly have taken place, to the great ease as well as health of the subject, if the women, in conjunction with the vulgar and illiterate, had not threatened to raise a rebellion unless they might be allowed the liberty to speak with their tongues, after the manner of their forefathers; such constant irreconcilable enemies to science are the common people. However, many of the most learned and wise adhere to the new scheme of expressing themselves by *things,* which hath only this inconvenience attending it, that if a man's business be very great and of various kinds, he must be obliged in proportion to carry a greater bundle of *things* upon his back, unless he can afford one or two strong servants to attend him. I have often beheld two of those sages almost sinking under the weight of their packs, like pedlars among us; who when they met in the street would lay down their loads, open their sacks, and hold conversation for an hour together; then put up their implements, help each other to resume their burthens, and take their leave.

But for short conversations a man may carry implements in his pockets and under his arms, enough to supply him, and in his house he cannot be at a loss; therefore the room where

[1] Swift has in mind the Royal Society's interest in the reformation of language or the creation of an artificial language that would avoid the vagueness and confusion of common speech. Although this program was primarily concerned with the language of science, it was part of an effort to avoid needless disputes about ill-defined terms (a constant complaint against religious sects) and to escape the misleading questions created by the very form of traditional language (a complaint against the Scholastics). Thomas Sprat, in his *History of the Royal Society* (1667), asked for a purified language in which men "delivered so many *things,* almost in an equal number of *words.*" Swift, who has already satirized the political manipulation of words in Lilliput (Part One, Chapter Seven, p. 62) and the "ideas, entities, abstractions, and transcendentals" the Brobdingnagians could not comprehend (Part Two, Chapter Seven, p. 134), here gives a satirical version of the other extreme: a "thing" language that, finally, avoids all words.

company meet who practise this art is full of all *things* ready at hand, requisite to furnish matter for this kind of artificial converse.

Another great advantage proposed by this invention was that it would serve as an universal language to be understood in all civilised nations, whose goods and utensils are generally of the same kind or nearly resembling, so that their uses might easily be comprehended. And thus ambassadors would be qualified to treat with foreign princes or ministers of state to whose tongues they were utter strangers.

I was at the Mathematical School, where the master taught his pupils after a method scarce imaginable to us in Europe. The proposition and demonstration were fairly written on a thin wafer, with ink composed of a cephalic tincture.[2] This the student was to swallow upon a fasting stomach, and for three days following eat nothing but bread and water. As the wafer digested, the tincture mounted to his brain, bearing the proposition along with it. But the success hath not hitherto been answerable, partly by some error in the *quantum* or composition, and partly by the perverseness of lads, to whom this bolus is so nauseous that they generally steal aside and discharge it upwards before it can operate; neither have they been yet persuaded to use so long an abstinence as the prescription requires.

Chapter Six: A further account of the Academy. The author proposes some improvements, which are honourably received.

In the School of Political Projectors I was but ill entertained, the professors appearing in my judgment wholly out of their senses, which is a scene that never fails to make me melan-

[2] A solution of brain tissue, which would seek its proper place within the body.

choly. These unhappy people were proposing schemes for persuading monarchs to choose favourites upon the score of their wisdom, capacity and virtue; of teaching ministers to consult the public good; of rewarding merit, great abilities, and eminent services; of instructing princes to know their true interest by placing it on the same foundation with that of their people: of choosing for employments persons qualified to exercise them; with many other wild impossible chimeras that never entered before into the heart of man to conceive, and confirmed in me the old observation that there is nothing so extravagant and irrational which some philosophers have not maintained for truth.

But, however, I shall so far do justice to this part of the Academy as to acknowledge that all of them were not so visionary. There was a most ingenious doctor who seemed to be perfectly versed in the whole nature and system of government. This illustrious person had very usefully employed his studies in finding out effectual remedies for all diseases and corruptions to which the several kinds of public administration are subject by the vices or infirmities of those who govern, as well as by the licentiousness of those who are to obey. For instance: whereas all writers and reasoners have agreed, that there is a strict universal resemblance between the natural and the political body, can there be anything more evident, than that the health of both must be preserved, and the disesases cured, by the same prescriptions? It is allowed that senates and great councils are often troubled with redundant, ebullient, and other peccant humours,[1] with many diseases of the head and more of the heart; with strong convulsions, with grievous

[1] The humors were, traditionally, the four fluids (blood, phlegm, yellow bile, and black bile) whose proper balance within the body constituted health. The excess of any one produced a corresponding temperament (sanguine, phlegmatic, choleric, melancholic); carried very far, this excess made a man "humorsome" or, further, virulently diseased or insane. "Humours" here refers to both the bodily temperaments and to the whimsical and irrational schemes or moods that might affect an assembly.

contractions of the nerves and sinews in both hands, but especially the right; with spleen, flatus, vertigos, and deliriums; with scrofulous tumours full of foetid purulent matter; with sour frothy ructations, with canine [2] appetites and crudeness of digestion, besides many others needless to mention. This doctor therefore proposed, that upon the meeting of a senate certain physicians should attend at the three first days of their sitting, and, at the close of each day's debate, feel the pulses of every senator; after which, having maturely considered and consulted upon the nature of the several maladies and the methods of cure, they should on the fourth day return to the senate house, attended by their apothecaries stored with proper medicines and, before the members sat, administer to each of them lenitives, aperitives, abstersives, corrosives, restringents, palliatives, laxatives, cephalalgics, icterics, apophlegmatics, acoustics,[3] as their several cases required; and according as these medicines should operate, repeat, alter, or omit them at the next meeting.

This project could not be of any great expense to the public, and might, in my poor opinion, be of much use for the dispatch of business in those countries where senates have any share in the legislative power, beget unanimity, shorten debates, open a few mouths which are now closed, and close many more which are now open; curb the petulancy of the young and correct the positiveness of the old; rouse the stupid and damp the pert.

Again, because it is a general complaint that the favourites of princes are troubled with short and weak memories, the same doctor proposed that whoever attended a first minister, after having told his business with the utmost brevity and in the plainest words, should at his departure give the said minister a tweak by the nose or a kick in the belly, or tread on his

[2] Voracious and indiscriminate.
[3] Various medicines for soothing, alerting, cleansing, consuming, curbing, moderating, loosening, relieving headaches, curing jaundice, stirring to action, and improving hearing.

corns, or lug him thrice by both ears, or run a pin into his breech, or pinch his arm black and blue, to prevent forgetfulness; and at every levee day repeat the same operation till the business were done or absolutely refused.

He likewise directed that every senator in the great council of a nation, after he had delivered his opinion and argued in the defence of it, should be obliged to give his vote directly contrary; because if that were done the result would infallibly terminate in the good of the public.

When parties in a state are violent, he offered a wonderful contrivance to reconcile them. The method is this. You take an hundred leaders of each party, you dispose them into couples of such whose heads are nearest of a size; then let two nice [4] operators saw off the occiput of each couple at the same time, in such a manner that the brain may be equally divided. Let the occiputs thus cut off be interchanged, applying each to the head of his opposite party-man. It seems indeed to be a work that requireth some exactness, but the professor assured us, that if it were dextrously performed the cure would be infallible. For he argued thus: that the two half brains, being left to debate the matter between themselves within the space of one skull, would soon come to a good understanding, and produce that moderation as well as regularity of thinking so much to be wished for in the heads of those who imagine they came into the world only to watch and govern its motion: and as to the difference of brains in quantity or quality among those who are directors in faction, the doctor assured us from his own knowledge that it was a perfect trifle.

I heard a very warm debate between two professors about the most commodious and effectual ways and means of raising money without grieving the subject. The first affirmed the justest method would be to lay a certain tax upon vices and folly, and the sum fixed upon every man to be rated after the fairest manner by a jury of his neighbours. The second was of

[4] Delicate.

an opinion directly contrary, to tax those qualities of body and mind for which men chiefly value themselves, the rate to be more or less according to the degrees of excelling, the decision whereof should be left entirely to their own breast. The highest tax was upon men who are the greatest favourites of the other sex, and the assessments according to the number and natures of the favours they have received, for which they are allowed to be their own vouchers. Wit, valour, and politeness were likewise proposed to be largely taxed and collected in the same manner, by every person giving his own word for the quantum of what he possessed. But as to honour, justice, wisdom, and learning, they should not be taxed at all, because they are qualifications of so singular a kind that no man will either allow them in his neighbour or value them in himself.

The women were proposed to be taxed according to their beauty and skill in dressing, wherein they had the same privilege with the men to be determined by their own judgment. But constancy, chastity, good sense, and good nature were not rated, because they would not bear the charge of collecting.

To keep senators in the interest of the crown it was proposed that the members should raffle for employments, every man first taking an oath and giving security that he would vote for the court whether he won or no, after which the losers had in their turn the liberty of raffling upon the next vacancy. Thus hope and expectation would be kept alive, none would complain of broken promises, but impute their disappointments wholly to Fortune, whose shoulders are broader and stronger than those of a ministry.

Another professor showed me a large paper of instructions for discovering plots and conspiracies against the government. He advised great statesmen to examine into the diet of all suspected persons; their times of eating; upon which side they lay in bed; with which hand they wiped their posteriors; to take a strict view of their excrements, and from the colour, the odour, the taste, the consistence, the crudeness or maturity of digestion, form a judgment of their thoughts and designs. Because men are never so serious, thoughtful, and intent, as when they are at stool, which he found by frequent experiment: for in such conjunctures, when he used merely as a trial to consider which was the best way of murdering the King, his ordure would have a tincture of green, but quite different when he thought only of raising an insurrection or burning the metropolis.

The whole discourse was written with great acuteness, containing many observations both curious and useful for politicians, but, as I conceived, not altogether complete. This I ventured to tell the author and offered, if he pleased, to supply him with some additions. He received my proposition with more compliance than is usual among writers, especially those of the projecting species, professing he would be glad to receive farther information.

I told him that in the kingdom of Tribnia, by the natives called Langden,[5] where I had long sojourned, the bulk of the people consisted wholly of discoverers, witnesses, informers, accusers, prosecutors, evidences, swearers, together with their several subservient and subaltern instruments, all under the colours,[6] the conduct, and pay of ministers and their deputies. The plots in that kingdom are usually the workmanship of those persons who desire to raise their own characters of profound politicians, to restore new vigour to a crazy[7] administration, to stifle or divert general discontents, to fill their coffers with forfeitures, and raise or sink the opinion of public credit, as either shall best answer their private advantage. It is first agreed and settled among them what suspected persons shall be accused of a plot: then effectual care is taken to secure all their letters and other papers, and put the owners in chains. These papers are delivered to a set of artists, very dextrous

[5] Anagrams for Britain and England.
[6] In the service of; wearing, like servants, their livery.
[7] Rotten.

in finding out the mysterious meanings of words, syllables, and letters.[8] For instance, they can decipher a close-stool to signify a privy-council, a flock of geese a senate, a lame dog an invader, a codshead a ——, the plague a standing army, a buzzard a prime minister, the gout a high priest, a gibbet a secretary of state, a chamberpot a committee of grandees, a sieve a court lady, a broom a revolution, a mousetrap an employment, a bottomless pit the treasury, a sink a court, a cap and bells a favourite, a broken reed a court of justice, an empty tun a general, a running sore the administration.

When this method fails, they have two others more effectual, which the learned among them call acrostics and anagrams. First, they can decipher all initial letters into political meanings. Thus N shall signify a plot, B a regiment of horse, L a fleet at sea. Or, secondly, by transposing the letters of the alphabet in any suspected paper, they can lay open the deepest designs of a discontented party. So, for example, if I should say in a letter to a friend, "Our brother Tom has just got the piles," a man of skill in this art would discover how the same letters which compose that sentence may be analyzed into the following words: "Resist—a plot is brought home—The Tour."[9] And this is the anagrammatic method.

The professor made me great acknowledgments for communicating these observations and promised to make honourable mention of me in his treatise.

I saw nothing in this country that could invite me to a longer continuance and began to think of returning home to England.

[8] At the trial of Swift's friend, Francis Atterbury, Bishop of Rochester, in 1723, for Jacobite plotting, ingenious readings were offered of possible codes in his correspondence. Swift, of course, gives each of the arbitrary code words a fine satirical aptness: the "codshead a ——" should probably be read as "a blockhead a King."

[9] "La Tour" was a pseudonym used by Swift's friend Bolingbroke when he was exiled to France as a Jacobite plotter.

Chapter Seven: The author leaves Lagado, arrives at Maldonada. No ship ready. He takes a short voyage to Glubbdubdrib. His reception by the Governor.

The continent of which this kingdom is a part extends itself, as I have reason to believe, eastward to that unknown tract of America, westward of California and north to the Pacific Ocean, which is not above an hundred and fifty miles from Lagado, where there is a good port and much commerce with the great island of Luggnagg, situated to the northwest about 29 degrees north latitude and 140 longitude. This island of Luggnagg stands southeastwards of Japan about an hundred leagues distant. There is a strict alliance between the Japanese Emperor and the King of Luggnagg, which affords frequent opportunities of sailing from one island to the other. I determined therefore to direct my course this way in order to direct my return to Europe. I hired two mules with a guide to show me the way and carry my small baggage. I took leave of my noble protector, who had shown me so much favour, and made me a generous present at my departure.

My journey was without any accident or adventure worth relating. When I arrived at the port of Maldonada (for so it is called) there was no ship in the harbour bound for Luggnagg, nor like to be in some time. The town is about as large as Portsmouth.[1] I soon fell into some acquaintance and was very hospitably received. A gentleman of distinction said to me that, since the ships bound for Luggnagg could not be ready in less than a month, it might be no disagreeable amusement for me to take a trip to the little island of Glubbdubdrib, about five leagues off to the southwest. He offered himself and a friend to accompany me, and that I should be provided with a small convenient barque for the voyage.

Glubbdubdrib, as nearly as I can interpret the word, signifies

[1] The great naval base on the south coast had grown enormously in Swift's day because of the wars.

The Island of Sorcerers or Magicians. It is about one third as large as the Isle of Wight,[2] and extremely fruitful: it is governed by the head of a certain tribe who are all magicians. This tribe marries only among each other, and the eldest in succession is prince or governor. He hath a noble palace and a park of about three thousand acres, surrounded by a wall of hewn stone twenty foot high. In this park are several smaller inclosures for cattle, corn, and gardening.

The Governor and his family are served and attended by domestics of a kind somewhat unusual. By his skill in necromancy, he hath power of calling whom he pleaseth from the dead, and commanding their service for twenty-four hours, but no longer; nor can he call the same persons up again in less than three months, except upon very extraordinary occasions.

When we arrived at the island, which was about eleven in the morning, one of the gentlemen who accompanied me went to the Governor and desired admittance for a stranger, who came on purpose to have the honour of attending on his Highness. This was immediately granted, and we all three entered the gate of the palace between two rows of guards, armed and dressed after a very antic [3] manner, and something in their countenances that made my flesh creep with a horror I cannot express. We passed through several apartments between servants of the same sort, ranked on each side as before, till we came to the Chamber of Presence, where, after three profound obeisances and a few general questions, we were permitted to sit on three stools near the lowest step of his Highness's throne. He understood the language of Balnibarbi, although it were different from that of his island. He desired me to give him some account of my travels; and, to let me see that I should be treated without ceremony, he dismissed all his attendants with a turn of his finger, at which to my great astonishment

[2] Therefore, with an area of about fifty square miles.
[3] Odd, fantastic.

they vanished in an instant, like visions in a dream when we awake on a sudden. I could not recover myself in some time, till the Governor assured me that I should receive no hurt; and, observing my two companions to be under no concern, who had been often entertained in the same manner, I began to take courage and relate to his Highness a short history of my several adventures, yet not without some hesitation, and frequently looking behind me to the place where I had seen those domestic spectres. I had the honour to dine with the Governor, where a new set of ghosts served up the meat, and waited at table. I now observed myself to be less terrified than I had been in the morning. I stayed till sunset but humbly desired his Highness to excuse me for not accepting his invitation of lodging in the palace. My two friends and I lay at a private house in the town adjoining, which is the capital of this little island; and the next morning we returned to pay our duty to the Governor, as he was pleased to command us.

After this manner we continued in the island for ten days, most part of every day with the Governor, and at night in our lodging. I soon grew so familiarized to the sight of spirits that after the third or fourth time they gave me no emotion at all; or if I had any apprehensions left, my curiosity prevailed over them. For his Highness the Governor ordered me to call up whatever persons I would choose to name, and in whatever numbers among all the dead from the beginning of the world to the present time, and command them to answer any questions I should think fit to ask; with this condition, that my questions must be confined within the compass of the times they lived in. And one thing I might depend upon, that they would certainly tell me truth, for lying was a talent of no use in the lower world.

I made my humble acknowledgments to his Highness for so great a favour. We were in a chamber, from whence there was a fair prospect into the park. And because my first inclination was to be entertained with scenes of pomp and magnificence, I desired to see Alexander the Great at the head of his army just after the battle of Arbela,[4] which upon a motion of the Governor's finger immediately appeared in a large field under the window where we stood. Alexander was called up into the room: it was with great difficulty that I understood his Greek, and had but little of my own. He assured me upon his honour that he was not poisoned, but died of a fever by excessive drinking.

Next I saw Hannibal passing the Alps, who told me he had not a drop of vinegar in his camp.[5]

I saw Caesar and Pompey at the head of their troops, just ready to engage.[6] I saw the former in his last great triumph. I desired that the Senate of Rome might appear before me in one large chamber, and a modern representative [7] in counter-view in another. The first seemed to be an assembly of heroes and demigods; the other a knot of pedlars, pickpockets, high-waymen, and bullies.

The Governor at my request gave the sign for Caesar and Brutus to advance towards us. I was struck with a profound veneration at the sight of Brutus and could easily discover the most consummate virtue, the greatest intrepidity and firmness of mind, the truest love of his country and general benevolence for mankind in every lineament of his countenance. I observed with much pleasure that these two persons were in good intelligence with each other, and Caesar freely confessed to me that the greatest actions of his own life were not equal by many degrees to the glory of taking it away. I had the honour to have much conversation with Brutus; and was told

[4] Near which he overthrew the empire of Darius in Persia, 331 B.C.

[5] According to Livy, Hannibal removed a rock that blocked his army by heating the rock and saturating it with vinegar, then easily cutting it.

[6] At Pharsala, where Pompey was defeated in 48 B.C., four years before Caesar's death.

[7] Legislature; e.g., the British Parliament.

that his ancestor Junius, Socrates, Epaminondas, Cato the younger, Sir Thomas More, and himself were perpetually together: a *sextumvirate* to which all the ages of the world cannot add a seventh.[8]

It would be tedious to trouble the reader with relating what vast numbers of illustrious persons were called up to gratify that insatiable desire I had to see the world in every period of antiquity placed before me. I chiefly fed my eyes with beholding the destroyers of tyrants and usurpers and the restorers of liberty to oppressed and injured nations. But it is impossible to express the satisfaction I received in my own mind after such a manner as to make it a suitable entertainment to the reader.

Chapter Eight: A further account of Glubbdubdrib. Ancient and modern history corrected.

Having a desire to see those ancients who were most renowned for wit and learning, I set apart one day on purpose. I proposed that Homer and Aristotle might appear at the head of all their commentators; but these were so numerous that some hundreds were forced to attend in the court and outward rooms of the palace. I knew and could distinguish those two

[8] Lucius Junius Brutus (sixth century B.C.), brother of Lucrece, who helped drive the Tarquins from Rome, put his own sons to death for plotting the return of the Tarquins. Marcus Junius Brutus, the friend and assassin of Caesar, committed suicide in 42 B.C. Socrates was put to death for his teachings in 399 B.C. Epaminondas led Thebes against the domination of Sparta and died in the victory at Mantinea, 362 B.C. Cato the Younger, the incorruptible Stoic, fought on against Caesar after Pharsala and committed suicide following his defeat at Thapsus, 46 B.C. Sir Thomas More, now canonized, resisted the tyranny of Henry VIII and was beheaded for treason in 1535. Elsewhere, Swift calls More "a person of the greatest virtue this kingdom ever produced."

heroes at first sight, not only from the crowd, but from each
other. Homer was the taller and comelier person of the two,
walked very erect for one of his age, and his eyes were the
most quick and piercing I ever beheld. Aristotle stooped much
and made use of a staff. His visage was meagre, his hair lank
and thin, and his voice hollow.[1] I soon discovered that both of
them were perfect strangers to the rest of the company and
had never seen or heard of them before. And I had a whisper
from a ghost, who shall be nameless, that these commentators
always kept in the most distant quarters from their principals in
the lower world, through a consciousness of shame and guilt,
because they had so horribly misrepresented the meaning of
those authors to posterity. I introduced Didymus and Eusta-
thius[2] to Homer and prevailed on him to treat them better
than perhaps they deserved, for he soon found they wanted a
genius to enter into the spirit of a poet. But Aristotle was out
of all patience with the account I gave him of Scotus and
Ramus,[3] as I presented them to him, and he asked them whether
the rest of the tribe were as great dunces as themselves.

I then desired the Governor to call up Descartes and Gassendi,[4] with whom I prevailed to explain their systems to

[1] Just as Gulliver destroys the traditional legend of Homer's
blindness, so he confutes the accounts of Aristotle as bald, rather
handsome, foppishly dressed, witty, and having a tendency to lisp.

[2] Homeric commentators of the first and twelfth centuries.

[3] John Duns Scotus (d. 1308) the subtle Doctor (whose name
gives us the word "dunce"), was a major Scholastic philosopher
and commentator on Aristotle. Petrus Ramus (Pierre de la Ramée,
1515–1572) sought to correct Aristotelian logic and rhetoric by
introducing new simplifications; his influence was great, especially
among the Puritans.

[4] René Descartes (1596–1650), the French philosopher and mathematician, propounded the theory of vortices to explain the origin of
motion in all parts of the universe. Descartes held that "attraction"
was an "occult quality" and not fully intelligible in mechanical
terms. Newton's analysis of gravitational movement rejected the
unnecessary Cartesian hypothesis and was acclaimed as a triumph
of empiricism. Pierre Gassendi (1592–1655), French philosopher,

Aristotle. This great philosopher freely acknowledged his own mistakes in natural philosophy, because he proceeded in many things upon conjecture, as all men must do; and he found that Gassendi, who had made the doctrine of Epicurus as palatable as he could, and the *vortices* of Descartes, were equally exploded. He predicted the same fate to *attraction,* whereof the present learned are such zealous asserters. He said, that new systems of nature were but new fashions which would vary in every age; and even those who pretend to demonstrate them from mathematical principles would flourish but a short period of time and be out of vogue when that was determined.[5]

I spent five days in conversing with many others of the ancient learned. I saw most of the first Roman emperors. I prevailed on the Governor to call up Eliogabalus's cooks [6] to dress us a dinner, but they could not show us much of their skill for want of materials. A helot of Agesilaus [7] made us a dish of Spartan broth, but I was not able to get down a second spoonful.

The two gentlemen who conducted me to the island were pressed by their private affairs to return in three days, which I employed in seeing some of the modern dead who had made the greatest figure for two or three hundred years past in our own and other countries of Europe; and having been always a great admirer of old illustrious families, I desired the Governor would call up a dozen or two of kings, with their ancestors in order for eight or nine generations. But my disappointment was grievous and unexpected. For instead of a long train with royal diadems, I saw in one family two fiddlers, three spruce courtiers, and an Italian prelate. In another, a barber, an abbot, and two cardinals. I have too great a veneration for crowned heads

---

scientist, and mathematician, revived and adapted to current science the atomism of the ancient Greek philosopher, Epicurus.

[5] Concluded.

[6] Heliogabalus, Roman emperor of the third century, notorious for profligacy and for his splendid feasts and ceremonies.

[7] King of Sparta, fourth century B.C.

to dwell any longer on so nice a subject. But as to counts, marquesses, dukes, earls, and the like, I was not so scrupulous. And I confess it was not without some pleasure that I found myself able to trace the particular features, by which certain families are distinguished, up to their originals. I could plainly discover from whence one family derives a long chin, why a second hath abounded with knaves for two generations, and fools for two more; why a third happened to be crack-brained, and a fourth to be sharpers. Whence it came what Polydore Virgil says of a certain great house, *Nec vir fortis, nec femina casta*.[8] How cruelty, falsehood, and cowardice grew to be characteristics by which certain families are distinguished as much as by their coat of arms. Who first brought the pox [9] into a noble house, which hath lineally descended in scrofulous tumours to their posterity. Neither could I wonder at all this, when I saw such an interruption of lineages by pages, lackeys, valets, coachmen, gamesters, fiddlers, players, captains, and pickpockets.

I was chiefly disgusted with modern history. For having strictly examined all the persons of greatest name in the courts of princes for an hundred years past, I found how the world had been misled by prostitute writers to ascribe the greatest exploits in war to cowards, the wisest counsel to fools, sincerity to flatterers, Roman virtue to betrayers of their country, piety to atheists, chastity to sodomites, truth to informers. How many innocent and excellent persons had been condemned to death or banishment by the practising of great ministers upon the corruption of judges and the malice of factions. How many villains had been exalted to the highest places of trust, power, dignity, and profit: how great a share in the motions and events of courts, councils, and senates might be challenged by bawds, whores, pimps, parasites, and buffoons: how low an opinion I

[8] "Neither a man of them brave, nor a woman chaste." Polydore Virgil (*c.* 1470–1555) was an Italian churchman who lived in England and in 1534 published his *Historia Anglica*.
[9] Syphilis.

had of human wisdom and integrity when I was truly informed of the springs and motives of great enterprises and revolutions in the world, and of the contemptible accidents to which they owed their success.

Here I discovered the roguery and ignorance of those who pretend to write *anecdotes*, or secret history, who send so many kings to their graves with a cup of poison; will repeat the discourse between a prince and chief minister where no witness was by; unlock the thoughts and cabinets of ambassadors and secretaries of state, and have the perpetual misfortune to be mistaken. Here I discovered the true causes of many great events that have surprised the world, how a whore can govern the back-stairs, the back-stairs a council, and the council a senate. A general confessed in my presence that he got a victory purely by the force of cowardice and ill conduct: and an admiral that for want of proper intelligence he beat the enemy to whom he intended to betray the fleet. Three kings protested to me, that in their whole reigns they did never once prefer any person of merit, unless by mistake or treachery of some minister in whom they confided; neither would they do it if they were to live again; and they showed, with great strength of reason, that the royal throne could not be supported without corruption, because that positive, confident, restive temper, which virtue infused into man, was a perpetual clog to public business.

I had the curiosity to enquire in a particular manner by what method great numbers had procured to themselves high titles of honour and prodigious estates; and I confined my enquiry to a very modern period: however, without grating upon present times, because I would be sure to give no offence even to foreigners (for I hope the reader need not be told that I do not in the least intend my own country in what I say upon this occasion), a great number of persons concerned were called up and, upon a very slight examination, discovered such a scene of infamy that I cannot reflect upon it without some seriousness. Perjury, oppression, subornation, fraud, pandarism, and the like infirmities were amongst the most excusable arts they had to mention, and for these I gave, as it was reasonable, due allowance. But when some confessed they owed their greatness and wealth to sodomy or incest, others to the prostituting of their own wives and daughters; others to the betraying their country or their prince; some to poisoning, more to the perverting of justice in order to destroy the innocent: I hope I may be pardoned if these discoveries inclined me a little to abate of that profound veneration which I am naturally apt to pay to persons of high rank, who ought to be treated with the utmost respect due to their sublime dignity by us their inferiors.

I had often read of some great services done to princes and states and desired to see the persons by whom those services were performed. Upon enquiry I was told that their names were to be found on no record, except a few of them whom history hath represented as the vilest rogues and traitors. As to the rest, I had never once heard of them. They all appeared with dejected looks and in the meanest habit, most of them telling me they died in poverty and disgrace, and the rest on a scaffold or a gibbet.

Among others there was one person whose case appeared a little singular. He had a youth about eighteen years old standing by his side. He told me he had for many years been commander of a ship, and in the sea fight at Actium[10] had the good fortune to break through the enemy's great line of battle, sink three of their capital ships, and take a fourth, which was the sole cause of Antony's flight and of the victory that ensued; that the youth standing by him, his only son, was killed in the action. He added, that upon the confidence of some merit, the war being at an end, he went to Rome, and solicited at the court of Augustus to be preferred to a greater ship, whose commander had been killed; but without any regard to his pretensions, it was given to a boy who had never seen the sea, the

[10] The great battle in which Antony and Cleopatra were defeated by Octavius (later Augustus) Caesar, 31 B.C.

son of a Libertina,[11] who waited on one of the Emperor's mistresses. Returning back to his own vessel, he was charged with neglect of duty, and the ship given to a favourite page of Publicola, the Vice-Admiral;[12] whereupon he retired to a poor farm at a great distance from Rome, and there ended his life. I was so curious to know the truth of this story that I desired Agrippa might be called, who was admiral in that fight.[13] He appeared and confirmed the whole account, but with much more advantage to the captain, whose modesty had extenuated or concealed a great part of his merit.

I was surprised to find corruption grown so high and so quick in that empire, by the force of luxury so lately introduced, which made me less wonder at many parallel cases in other countries, where vices of all kinds have reigned so much longer, and where the whole praise as well as pillage hath been engrossed by the chief commander, who perhaps had the least title to either.

As every person called up made exactly the same appearance he had done in the world, it gave me melancholy reflections to observe how much the race of human kind was degenerate among us within these hundred years past. How the pox under all its consequences and denominations had altered every lineament of an English countenance, shortened the size of bodies, unbraced the nerves, relaxed the sinews and muscles, introduced a sallow complexion, and rendered the flesh loose and rancid.

I descended so low as to desire that some English yeomen [14] of the old stamp might be summoned to appear, once so famous for the simplicity of their manners, diet, and dress; for justice

[11] This presumably fictitious name means "freedwoman" in Latin but carries over the English sense of "licentious."

[12] L. Gellius Publicola commanded the right wing of Antony's (not, as Swift implies, Octavius') fleet at Actium and may have perished in the battle.

[13] Marcus Vipsanius Agrippa (63–12 B.C.), Roman statesman and general, agent of Octavius in his rise to power, commanded the fleet that defeated Antony at Actium.

[14] Freeholders or independent farmers.

in their dealings, for their true spirit of liberty, for their valour and love of their country. Neither could I be wholly unmoved after comparing the living with the dead, when I considered how all these pure native virtues were prostituted for a piece of money by their grandchildren, who, in selling their votes and managing at elections,[15] have acquired every vice and corruption that can possibly be learned in a court.

Chapter Nine: The author's return to Maldonada. Sails to the kingdom of Luggnagg. The author confined. He is sent for to court. The manner of his admittance. The King's great lenity to his subjects.

The day of our departure being come, I took leave of his Highness the Governor of Glubbdubdrib and returned with my two companions to Maldonada, where after a fortnight's waiting a ship was ready to sail for Luggnagg. The two gentlemen and some others were so generous and kind as to furnish me with provisions and see me on board. I was a month in this voyage. We had one violent storm and were under a necessity of steering westward to get into the trade wind, which holds for above sixty leagues. On the 21st of April, 1708, we sailed in the river of Clumegnig, which is a seaport town at the southeast point of Luggnagg. We cast anchor within a league of the town and made a signal for a pilot. Two of them came on

---

[15] The control of votes through bribery, threat, or promise of favors was all but universal in eighteenth-century England and was skilfully employed by Walpole to maintain power. William Hogarth designed four well-known scenes of election practices in the 1750's. For a discussion of the pattern, especially later in the century, see Sir Lewis Namier's *England in the Age of the American Revolution* (London, 1930) and *The Structure of Politics at the Accession of George III* (2nd ed., London, 1957).

board in less than half an hour, by whom we were guided between certain shoals and rocks, which are very dangerous in the passage, to a large basin where a fleet may ride in safety within a cable's length of the town wall.

Some of our sailors, whether out of treachery or inadvertence, had informed the pilots that I was a stranger and a great traveller, whereof these gave notice to a custom-house officer, by whom I was examined very strictly upon my landing. This officer spoke to me in the language of Balnibarbi, which by the force of much commerce is generally understood in that town, especially by seamen and those employed in the customs. I gave him a short account of some particulars, and made my story as plausible and consistent as I could; but I thought it necessary to disguise my country and call myself a Hollander, because my intentions were for Japan, and I knew the Dutch were the only Europeans permitted to enter into that kingdom.[1] I therefore told the officer that, having been shipwrecked on the coast of Balnibarbi and cast on a rock, I was received up into Laputa, or the Flying Island (of which he had often heard), and was now endeavouring to get to Japan, from whence I might find a convenience of returning to my own country. The officer said I must be confined till he could receive orders from court, for which he would write immediately, and hoped to receive an answer in a fortnight. I was carried to a convenient lodging, with a sentry placed at the door; however I had the liberty of a large garden and was treated with humanity enough, being maintained all the time at the King's charge. I was visited by several persons, chiefly out of curiosity, because it was reported I came from countries very remote, of which they had never heard.

I hired a young man who came in the same ship to be an interpreter; he was a native of Luggnagg but had lived some years at Maldonada and was a perfect master of both languages.

[1] The anti-Christian rebellions of 1638 had closed Japan to European traders, but the Dutch were admitted to the port of Nagasaki on stringent and humiliating conditions.

By his assistance I was able to hold a conversation with those that came to visit me; but this consisted only of their questions and my answers.

The dispatch came from court about the time we expected. It contained a warrant for conducting me and my retinue to Traldragdubb or Trildrogdrib, for it is pronounced both ways as near as I can remember, by a party of ten horse. All my retinue was that poor lad for an interpreter, whom I persuaded into my service. At my humble request we had each of us a mule to ride on. A messenger was dispatched half a day's journey before us to give the King notice of my approach, and to desire that his Majesty would please to appoint a day and hour, when it would be his gracious pleasure that I might have the honour to "lick the dust before his footstool." This is the court style, and I found it to be more than matter of form. For upon my admittance two days after my arrival, I was commanded to crawl upon my belly, and lick the floor as I advanced; but on account of my being a stranger, care was taken to have it so clean that the dust was not offensive. However, this was a peculiar grace, not allowed to any but persons of the highest rank, when they desire an admittance. Nay, sometimes the floor is strewed with dust on purpose when the person to be admitted happens to have powerful enemies at court. And I have seen a great lord with his mouth so crammed that, when he had crept to the proper distance from the throne, he was not able to speak a word. Neither is there any remedy, because it is capital for those who receive an audience to spit or wipe their mouths in his Majesty's presence. There is indeed another custom which I cannot altogether approve of. When the King hath a mind to put any of his nobles to death in a gentle indulgent manner, he commands to have the floor strowed with a certain brown powder, of a deadly composition, which being licked up infallibly kills him in twenty-four hours. But in justice to this prince's great clemency, and the care he hath of his subjects' lives (wherein it were much to be wished that the monarchs of Europe would imitate him), it must be mentioned for his honour that strict orders are given to have the infected parts of the floor well washed after every such execution, which if his domestics neglect, they are in danger of incurring his royal displeasure. I myself heard him give directions that one of his pages should be whipped, whose turn it was to give notice about washing the floor after an execution, but maliciously had omitted it, by which neglect a young lord of great hopes coming to an audience, was unfortunately poisoned, although the King at that time had no design against his life. But this good prince was so gracious as to forgive the page his whipping, upon promise that he would do so no more, without special orders.

To return from this digression: when I had crept within four yards of the throne, I raised myself gently upon my knees, and then striking my forehead seven times against the ground, I pronounced the following words, as they had been taught me the night before, *Ickpling Gloffthrobb Squutserumm blhiop Mlashnalt Zwin tnodbalkguffh Slhiophad Gurdlubh Asht.* This is the compliment established by the laws of the land for all persons admitted to the King's presence. It may be rendered into English thus: May your Celestial Majesty outlive the sun, eleven moons and an half. To this the King returned some answer, which although I could not understand, yet I replied as I had been directed: *Fluft drin Yalerick Dwuldum prastrad mirplush,* which properly signifies, "My tongue is in the mouth of my friend," and by this expression was meant that I desired leave to bring my interpreter; whereupon the young man already mentioned was accordingly introduced, by whose intervention I answered as many questions as his Majesty could put in above an hour. I spoke in the Balnibarbian tongue, and my interpreter delivered my meaning in that of Luggnagg.

The King was much delighted with my company, and ordered his *Bliffmarklub* or high chamberlain to appoint a lodging in the court for me and my interpreter, with a daily allowance for my table, and a large purse of gold for my common expenses.

I stayed three months in this country out of perfect obedience to his Majesty, who was pleased highly to favour me, and made me very honourable offers. But I thought it more consistent with prudence and justice to pass the remainder of my days with my wife and family.

Chapter Ten: The Luggnaggians commended. A particular description of the Struldbruggs, with many conversations between the author and some eminent persons upon that subject.

The Luggnaggians are a polite and generous people, and although they are not without some share of that pride which is peculiar to all eastern countries, yet they show themselves courteous to strangers, especially such who are countenanced by the court. I had many acquaintance among persons of the best fashion, and being always attended by my interpreter, the conversation we had was not disagreeable.

One day in much good company I was asked by a person of quality whether I had seen any of their *Struldbruggs* or *immortals*. I said I had not, and desired he would explain to me what he meant by such an appellation applied to a mortal creature. He told me, that sometimes, although very rarely, a child happened to be born in a family with a red circular spot in the forehead, directly over the left eyebrow, which was an infallible mark that it should never die. The spot, as he described it, was about the compass of a silver threepence, but in the course of time grew larger and changed its colour; for at twelve years old it became green, so continued till five and twenty, then turned to a deep blue; at five and forty it grew coal black, and as large as an English shilling, but never admitted any farther alteration. He said these births were so rare that he did not believe there could be above eleven hundred

Struldbruggs of both sexes in the whole kingdom, of which he computed about fifty in the metropolis, and among the rest a young girl born about three years ago. That these productions were not peculiar to any family but a mere effect of chance, and the children of the *Struldbruggs* themselves were equally mortal with the rest of the people.

I freely own myself to have been struck with inexpressible delight upon hearing this account: and the person who gave it me happening to understand the Balnibarbian language, which I spoke very well, I could not forbear breaking out into expressions perhaps a little too extravagant. I cried out as in a rapture: "Happy nation where every child hath at least a chance for being immortal! Happy people who enjoy so many living examples of ancient virtue and have masters ready to instruct them in the wisdom of all former ages! But happiest beyond all comparison are those excellent *Struldbruggs,* who, being born exempt from that universal calamity of human nature, have their minds free and disengaged, without the weight and depression of spirits caused by the continual apprehension of death." I discovered my admiration that I had not observed any of these illustrious persons at court, the black spot on the forehead being so remarkable a distinction that I could not have easily overlooked it and it was impossible that his Majesty, a most judicious prince, should not provide himself with a good number of such wise and able counsellors. Yet perhaps the virtue of those reverend sages was too strict for the corrupt and libertine manners of a court. And we often find by experience that young men are too opinionative and volatile to be guided by the sober dictates of their seniors. However, since the King was pleased to allow me access to his royal person, I was resolved upon the very first occasion to deliver my opinion to him on this matter freely and at large by the help of my interpreter; and whether he would please to take my advice or no, yet in one thing I was determined, that his Majesty having frequently offered me an establishment in this country, I would with great thankfulness accept the favour, and pass my life here in the conversation of those superior beings the *Struld-bruggs*, if they would please to admit me.

The gentleman to whom I addressed my discourse, because (as I have already observed) he spoke the language of Balnibarbi, said to me with a sort of smile, which usually ariseth from pity to the ignorant, that he was glad of any occasion to keep me among them, and desired my permission to explain to the company what I had spoke. He did so, and they talked together for some time in their own language, whereof I understood not a syllable, neither could I observe by their countenances what impression my discourse had made on them. After a short silence the same person told me that his friends and mine (so he thought fit to express himself) were very much pleased with the judicious remarks I had made on the great happiness and advantages of immortal life, and they were desirous to know in a particular manner what scheme of living I should have formed to myself, if it had fallen to my lot to have been born a *Struldbrugg*.

I answered, it was easy to be eloquent on so copious and delightful a subject, especially to me who have been often apt to amuse myself with visions of what I should do if I were a king, a general, or a great lord; and upon this very case I had frequently run over the whole system how I should employ myself and pass the time if I were sure to live forever.

That if it had been my good fortune to come into the world a *Struldbrugg*, as soon as I could discover my own happiness by understanding the difference between life and death, I would first resolve by all arts and methods whatsoever to procure myself riches. In the pursuit of which by thrift and management, I might reasonably expect in about two hundred years to be the wealthiest man in the kingdom. In the second place, I would from my earliest youth apply myself to the study of arts and sciences, by which I should arrive in time to excel all others in learning. Lastly, I would carefully record every action and event of consequence that happened in the public, impartially draw the characters of the several successions of princes and great ministers of state, with my own observations on every point. I would exactly set down the several changes in customs, language,[1] fashion of dress, diet, and diversions. By all which acquirements, I should be a living treasury of knowledge and wisdom, and certainly become the oracle of the nation.

I would never marry after threescore, but live in an hospitable manner, yet still on the saving side. I would entertain myself in forming and directing the minds of hopeful young men, by convincing them from my own remembrance, experience, and observation, fortified by numerous examples, of the usefulness of virtue in public and private life. But my choice and constant companions should be a set of my own immortal brotherhood, among whom I would elect a dozen from the most ancient down to my own contemporaries. Where any of these wanted fortunes, I would provide them with convenient lodges round my own estate and have some of them always at my table, only mingling a few of the most valuable among you mortals, whom length of time would harden me to lose with little or no reluctance, and treat your posterity after the same manner, just as a man diverts himself with the annual succession of pinks and tulips in his garden, without regretting the loss of those which withered the preceding year.

These *Struldbruggs* and I would mutually communicate our observations and memorials through the course of time, remark the several gradations by which corruption steals into the world, and oppose it in every step by giving perpetual warning and instruction to mankind; which, added to the strong influence of our own example, would probably prevent that continual degeneracy of human nature so justly complained of in all ages.

Add to all this, the pleasure of seeing the various revolutions of states and empires, the changes in the lower and upper world,

[1] The sense of change (and consequent corruption) to which language was always subject led Swift to propose an academy for England like that in France; see his *Proposal for Correcting, Improving, and Ascertaining the English Tongue* (1712).

ancient cities in ruins, and obscure villages become the seats of kings. Famous rivers lessening into shallow brooks; the ocean leaving one coast dry and overwhelming another; the discovery of many countries yet unknown. Barbarity overrunning the politest nations, and the most barbarous becoming civilized. I should then see the discovery of the longitude,[2] the perpetual motion, the universal medicine, and many other great inventions brought to the utmost perfection.

What wonderful discoveries should we make in astronomy, by outliving and confirming our own predictions, by observing the progress and returns of comets, with the changes of motion in the sun, moon, and stars.

I enlarged upon many other topics which the natural desire of endless life and sublunary [3] happiness could easily furnish me with. When I had ended, and the sum of my discourse had been interpreted as before to the rest of the company, there was a good deal of talk among them in the language of the country, not without some laughter at my expense. At last the same gentleman who had been my interpreter said, he was desired by the rest to set me right in a few mistakes, which I had fallen into through the common imbecility of human nature, and upon that allowance was less answerable for them. That this breed of *Struldbruggs* was peculiar to their country, for there

[2] Prizes had been offered since 1598 for the discovery of a method of determining the longitude at sea; they ran as high as £20,000 in Swift's day. The Greenwich observatory was founded in 1674 to aid navigation by providing improved lunar tables; Halley, as Astronomer Royal, undertook this task in 1720. The invention of the sextant and the chronometer in the 1730's met the difficulty. Swift thought this pursuit as futile as the old alchemical search for the philosophers' stone or the panacea for all human ills.

[3] Traditionally, all that existed below the sphere of the moon was subject to change and decay. In Christian terms, the sublunary world is the fallen world, doomed to mutability and death since the first sin and the loss of Paradise. (See Part Two, Chapter Seven, Note 4.)

were no such people either in Balnibarbi or Japan, where he
had the honour to be ambassador from his Majesty, and found
the natives in both those kingdoms very hard to believe that
the fact was possible, and it appeared from my astonishment
when he first mentioned the matter to me that I received it as
a thing wholly new and scarcely to be credited. That in the
two kingdoms above mentioned, where during his residence he
had conversed very much, he observed long life to be the
universal desire and wish of mankind. That whoever had one
foot in the grave was sure to hold back the other as strongly
as he could. That the oldest had still hopes of living one day
longer and looked on death as the greatest evil, from which
nature always prompted him to retreat; only in this island of
Luggnagg the appetite for living was not so eager, from the
continual example of the *Struldbruggs* before their eyes.

That the system of living contrived by me was unreasonable
and unjust because it supposed a perpetuity of youth, health,
and vigour, which no man could be so foolish to hope, however extravagant he might be in his wishes. That the question
therefore was not whether a man would choose to be always in
the prime of youth, attended with prosperity and health, but
how he would pass a perpetual life under all the usual disadvantages which old age brings along with it. For although few
men will avow their desires of being immortal upon such hard
conditions, yet in the two kingdoms before-mentioned of
Balnibarbi and Japan he observed that every man desired to
put off death for some time longer, let it approach ever so
late, and he rarely heard of any man who died willingly, except
he were incited by the extremity of grief or torture. And he
appealed to me whether in those countries I had travelled, as
well as my own, I had not observed the same general disposition.

After this preface he gave me a particular account of the
Struldbruggs among them. He said they commonly acted like
mortals till about thirty years old, after which by degrees they

grew melancholy and dejected, increasing in both till they came to fourscore.[4] This he learned from their own confession; for otherwise there not being above two or three of that species born in an age, they were too few to form a general observation by. When they came to fourscore years, which is reckoned the extremity of living in this country, they had not only all the follies and infirmities of other old men, but many more which arose from the dreadful prospect of never dying. They were not only opinionative, peevish, covetous, morose, vain, talkative, but uncapable of friendship and dead to all natural affection, which never descended below their grandchildren. Envy and impotent desires are their prevailing passions. But those objects against which their envy seems principally directed are the vices of the younger sort and the deaths of the old. By reflecting on the former, they find themselves cut off from all possibility of pleasure; and whenever they see a funeral, they lament and repine that others are gone to an harbour of rest to which they themselves never can hope to arrive. They have no remembrance of anything but what they learned and observed in their youth and middle age, and even that is very imperfect. And for the truth or particulars of any fact, it is safer to depend on common traditions than upon their best recollections. The least miserable among them appear to be those who turn to dotage and entirely lose their memories; these

---

[4] The account of the Struldbruggs may have been meant to suggest (to the reader but not to Gulliver) the fallen nature of man. Swift in a letter of 1735 wrote a little allegory about man's "poor little house of clay," for which, after the first thirty years of life, he paid as rent a rose from his cheek each year and a tooth every two or three, until at last "out with me is the word, and I will not be long before my person will be seized. I might have had my lease on much better terms, if it had not been the fault of my great-grandfather. He and his wife" (i.e., Adam and Eve) "with the advice of a bad neighbour, robbed an orchard belonging to the Lord of the Manor, and so forfeited their grand privileges. . . ." (*Correspondence*, V, 246).

meet with more pity and assistance, because they want many bad qualities which abound in others.

If a *Struldbrugg* happen to marry one of his own kind, the marriage is dissolved of course by the courtesy of the kingdom, as soon as the younger of the two comes to be fourscore. For the law thinks it a reasonable indulgence that those who are condemned without any fault of their own to a perpetual continuance in the world should not have their misery doubled by the load of a wife.

As soon as they have completed the term of eighty years, they are looked on as dead in law; their heirs immediately succeed to their estates, only a small pittance is reserved for their support, and the poor ones are maintained at the public charge. After that period they are held incapable of any employment of trust or profit; they cannot purchase lands or take leases, neither are they allowed to be witnesses in any cause, either civil or criminal, not even for the decision of meres and bounds.

At ninety they lose their teeth and hair; they have at that age no distinction of taste, but eat and drink whatever they can get, without relish or appetite. The diseases they were subject to still continue without encreasing or diminishing. In talking they forget the common appellation of things and the names of persons, even of those who are their nearest friends and relations. For the same reason they never can amuse themselves with reading, because their memory will not serve to carry them from the beginning of a sentence to the end; and by this defect they are deprived of the only entertainment whereof they might otherwise be capable.

The language of this country being always upon the flux, the *Struldbruggs* of one age do not understand those of another, neither are they able after two hundred years to hold any conversation (farther than by a few general words) with their neighbours the mortals, and thus they lie under the disadvantage of living like foreigners in their own country.

This was the account given me of the *Struldbruggs*, as near as I can remember. I afterwards saw five or six of different ages, the youngest not above two hundred years old, who were brought to me at several times by some of my friends; but although they were told that I was a great traveller and had seen all the world, they had not the least curiosity to ask me a question; only desired I would give them *slumskudask*, or a token of remembrance, which is a modest way of begging, to avoid the law that strictly forbids it, because they are provided for by the public, although indeed with a very scanty allowance.

They are despised and hated by all sorts of people; when one of them is born, it is reckoned ominous, and their birth is recorded very particularly; so that you may know their age by consulting the registry, which however hath not been kept above a thousand years past, or at least hath been destroyed by time or public disturbances. But the usual way of computing how old they are is by asking them what kings or great persons they can remember, and then consulting history, for infallibly the last prince in their mind did not begin his reign after they were fourscore years old.

They were the most mortifying sight I ever beheld, and the women more horrible than the men. Besides the usual deformities in extreme old age, they acquired an additional ghastliness in proportion to their number of years, which is not to be described, and among half a dozen I soon distinguished which was the eldest, although there was not above a century or two between them.

The reader will easily believe, that from what I had heard and seen my keen appetite for perpetuity of life was much abated. I grew heartily ashamed of the pleasing visions I had formed and thought no tyrant could invent a death into which I would not run with pleasure from such a life. The King heard of all that had passed between me and my friends upon this occasion, and rallied me very pleasantly, wishing I would send a couple of *Struldbruggs* to my own country to arm our people against the fear of death; but this it seems is forbidden by the fundamental laws of the kingdom, or else I should have been well content with the trouble and expense of transporting them.

I could not but agree that the laws of this kingdom, relating to the *Struldbruggs*, were founded upon the strongest reasons, and such as any other country would be under the necessity of enacting in the like circumstances. Otherwise, as avarice is the necessary consequent of old age, those immortals would in time become proprietors of the whole nation and engross the civil power, which, for want of abilities to manage, must end in the ruin of the public.

Chapter Eleven: The author leaves Luggnagg, and sails to Japan. From thence he returns in a Dutch ship to Amsterdam, and from Amsterdam to England.

I thought this account of the *Struldbruggs* might be some entertainment to the reader, because it seems to be a little out of the common way; at least, I do not remember to have met the like in any book of travels that hath come to my hands: and if I am deceived, my excuse must be that it is necessary for travellers who describe the same country very often to agree in dwelling on the same particulars, without deserving the censure of having borrowed or transcribed from those who wrote before them.

There is indeed a perpetual commerce between this kingdom and the great empire of Japan, and it is very probable that the Japanese authors may have given some account of the *Struldbruggs;* but my stay in Japan was so short, and I was so entirely a stranger to the language, that I was not qualified to make any enquiries. But I hope the Dutch upon this notice will be curious and able enough to supply my defects.

His Majesty having often pressed me to accept some employment in his court, and finding me absolutely determined to return to my native country, was pleased to give me his licence to depart, and honoured me with a letter of recommendation under his own hand to the Emperor of Japan. He likewise presented me with four hundred forty-four large pieces of gold (this nation delighting in even numbers) and a red diamond which I sold in England for eleven hundred pounds.

On the 6th day of May, 1709, I took a solemn leave of his Majesty, and all my friends. This prince was so gracious as to order a guard to conduct me to Glanguenstald, which is a royal port to the southwest part of the island. In six days I found a vessel ready to carry me to Japan, and spent fifteen days in the voyage. We landed at a small port-town called Xamoschi, situated on the southeast part of Japan. The town lies on the western point, where there is a narrow strait leading northward into a long arm of the sea, upon the northwest part of which Yedo,[1] the metropolis, stands. At landing I showed the custom-house officers my letter from the King of Luggnagg to his Imperial Majesty. They knew the seal perfectly well; it was as broad as the palm of my hand. The impression was, *a king lifting up a lame beggar from the earth*. The magistrates of the town, hearing of my letter, received me as a public minister; they provided me with carriages and servants and bore my charges to Yedo, where I was admitted to an audience and delivered my letter, which was opened with great ceremony and explained to the Emperor by an interpreter, who gave me notice of his Majesty's order that I should signify my request, and whatever it were, it should be granted for the sake of his royal brother of Luggnagg. This interpreter was a person employed to transact affairs with the Hollanders; he soon conjectured by my countenance that I was an European, and therefore repeated his Majesty's commands in Low Dutch, which he spoke perfectly well. I answered (as I had before

[1] Tokyo.

determined) that I was a Dutch merchant, shipwrecked in a
very remote country, from whence I travelled by sea and land
to Luggnagg, and then took shipping for Japan, where I knew
my countrymen often traded, and with some of these I hoped
to get an opportunity of returning into Europe: I therefore
most humbly entreated his royal favour to give order, that I
should be conducted in safety to Nangasac:[2] to this I added
another petition, that for the sake of my patron the King of
Luggnagg his Majesty would condescend to excuse my performing the ceremony imposed on my countrymen of *trampling upon the crucifix*,[3] because I had been thrown into his
kingdom by my misfortunes without any intention of trading.
When this latter petition was interpreted to the Emperor, he
seemed a little surprised and said he believed I was the first
of my countrymen who ever made any scruple in this point,
and that he began to doubt whether I was a real Hollander or
no, but rather suspected I must be a Christian.[4] However, for
the reasons I had offered, but chiefly to gratify the King of
Luggnagg, by an uncommon mark of his favour, he would
comply with the singularity of my humour; but the affair must
be managed with dexterity, and his officers should be commanded to let me pass as it were by forgetfulness. For he
assured me, that if the secret should be discovered by my
countrymen, the Dutch, they would cut my throat in the
voyage. I returned my thanks by the interpreter for so unusual a favour, and, some troops being at that time on their
march to Nangasac, the commanding officer had orders to

[2] Nagasaki.
[3] A test applied to Japanese suspected of being Christians, but
not—so far as is known—to foreigners.
[4] The satire on the Dutch arises in part from their national practice of religious toleration and their friendliness to liberal, rationalistic church movements. Swift's antipathy, which goes back at least
to his dislike of William of Orange, seems also to be based upon his
feeling that they were a wholeheartedly commercial people, ruth-
less in their pursuits. See Ellen Douglass Leyburn, "Swift's Views
on the Dutch," *PMLA*, LXVI (1951), 734–745.

convey me safe thither, with particular instructions about the business of the crucifix.

On the 9th day of June, 1709, I arrived at Nangasac, after a very long and troublesome journey. I soon fell into company of some Dutch sailors belonging to the *Amboyna* of Amsterdam, a stout ship of 450 tons. I had lived long in Holland, pursuing my studies at Leyden, and I spoke Dutch well. The seamen soon knew from whence I came last; they were curious to enquire into my voyage and course of life. I made up a story as short and probable as I could, but concealed the greatest part. I knew many persons in Holland; I was able to invent names for my parents, whom I pretended to be obscure people in the province of Gelderland. I would have given the captain (one Theodorus Vangrult) what he pleased to ask for my voyage to Holland; but, understanding I was a surgeon, he was contented to take half the usual rate, on condition that I would serve him in the way of my calling. Before we took shipping I was often asked by some of the crew whether I had performed the ceremony above-mentioned. I evaded the question by general answers that I had satisfied the Emperor and court in all particulars. However, a malicious rogue of a skipper [5] went to an officer and, pointing to me, told him I had not yet *trampled on the crucifix;* but the other, who had received instructions to let me pass, gave the rascal twenty strokes on the shoulders with a bamboo, after which I was no more troubled with such questions.

Nothing happened worth mentioning in this voyage. We sailed with a fair wind to the Cape of Good Hope, where we stayed only to take in fresh water. On the 6th of April we arrived safe at Amsterdam, having lost only three men by sickness in the voyage, and a fourth who fell from the foremast into the sea, not far from the coast of Guinea. From Amsterdam I soon after set sail for England in a small vessel belonging to that city.

[5] Seaman, not captain.

On the 10th of April, 1710, we put in at the Downs. I landed the next morning and saw once more my native country after an absence of five years and six months complete. I went straight to Redriff, whither I arrived the same day at two in the afternoon, and found my wife and family in good health.

The End of the Third Part

Part Four

A Voyage to the Country of the Houyhnhnms

The map moves Houyhnhnmland somewhat west and north of the position indicated in the text, which would be due west of the southern end of Tasmania.

Since this voyage is discussed at some length in the Introduction, it may suffice here to call attention to the way in which it pulls together themes that have run through the first three voyages. Gulliver is embarrassed by the claims of his body in the First Voyage; in the Second Voyage, he gains a microscopic view of the vast bodies of the Brobdingnagians, and his response is disgust. In the Third Voyage there are many ugly assertions of the physical, especially those diseases which are a symptom of moral and social decay. All these strains are brought together in the Yahoos.

The Houyhnhnms, in turn, bring together those patterns of rationality we have seen in the original institutions of Lilliput, in the self-reform of the Brobdingnagians, and in Lord Munodi's integrity. The Houyhnhnms and Yahoos serve not only to sum up central patterns but also to extend those patterns to new extremes. Gulliver's response to these extremes is the first strong moral reaction he has shown in the book; he recoils at last from what he has earlier condoned or espoused, but only into the vain dream of becoming a Houyhnhnm.

Nuyts Land

Edels Land
Lewins Land

I St. Francot

I St. Pieter

Siveers I

I Maelsuyker
De Wits I

HOUYHNHNMS
LAND

Discovered A D 1711

Chapter One: The author sets out as captain of a ship. His men conspire against him, confine him a long time to his cabin. Set him on shore in an unknown land. He travels up into the country. The Yahoos, a strange sort of animal, described. The author meets two Houyhnhnms.

I CONTINUED at home with my wife and children about five months in a very happy condition, if I could have learned the lesson of knowing when I was well. I left my poor wife big with child, and accepted an advantageous offer made me to be captain of the *Adventure*, a stout merchantman of 350 tons: for I understood navigation well, and being grown weary of a surgeon's employment at sea, which however I could exercise upon occasion, I took a skilful young man of that calling, one Robert Purefoy, into my ship. We set sail from Portsmouth upon the 7th day of September, 1710; on the 14th, we met with Captain Pocock of Bristol, at Teneriffe,[1] who was going to the bay of Campechy, to cut logwood.[2] On the 16th, he was parted from us by a storm; I heard since my return that his ship foundered, and none escaped but one cabin-boy. He was an honest man and a good sailor, but a little too positive in his own opinions, which was the cause of his destruction, as it hath been of several others. For if he had followed my advice, he might at this time have been safe at home with his family as well as myself.

I had several men died in my ship of calentures,[3] so that I was forced to get recruits out of Barbadoes and the Leeward Islands,[4] where I touched by the direction of the merchants who employed me, which I had soon too much cause to repent; for I found afterwards that most of them had been buccaneers. I had fifty hands on board, and my orders were that I should trade with the Indians in the South Sea and make what discoveries I could. These rogues whom I had picked up debauched my other men, and they all formed a conspiracy to

[1] The largest of the Canary Islands.
[2] "Campeachy wood," used for dyes, found in Yucatán on the Gulf of Mexico.
[3] Tropical fevers.
[4] In the West Indies.

seize the ship and secure me; which they did one morning, rushing into my cabin and binding me hand and foot, threatening to throw me overboard if I offered to stir. I told them I was their prisoner and would submit. This they made me swear to do, and then unbound me, only fastening one of my legs with a chain near my bed, and placed a sentry at my door with his piece charged, who was commanded to shoot me dead if I attempted my liberty. They sent me down victuals and drink, and took the government of the ship to themselves. Their design was to turn pirates and plunder the Spaniards, which they could not do till they got more men. But first they resolved to sell the goods in the ship, and then go to Madagascar for recruits, several among them having died since my confinement. They sailed many weeks, and traded with the Indians, but I knew not what course they took, being kept close prisoner in my cabin, and expecting nothing less than to be murdered, as they often threatened me.

Upon the 9th day of May, 1711, one James Welch came down to my cabin and said he had orders from the captain to set me ashore. I expostulated with him, but in vain; neither would he so much as tell me who their new captain was. They forced me into the long-boat, letting me put on my best suit of clothes, which were as good as new, and a small bundle of linen, but no arms except my hanger; and they were so civil as not to search my pockets, into which I conveyed what money I had, with some other little necessaries. They rowed about a league, and then set me down on a strand. I desired them to tell me what country it was. They all swore they knew no more than myself, but said that the captain (as they called him) was resolved, after they had sold the lading, to get rid of me in the first place where they discovered land. They pushed off immediately, advising me to make haste, for fear of being overtaken by the tide, and bade me farewell.

In this desolate condition I advanced forward and soon got upon firm ground, where I sat down on a bank to rest myself and consider what I had best to do. When I was a little refreshed

I went up into the country, resolving to deliver myself to the first savages I should meet, and purchase my life from them by some bracelets, glass rings, and other toys, which sailors usually provide themselves with in those voyages, and whereof I had some about me: the land was divided by long rows of trees, not regularly planted, but naturally growing; there was great plenty of grass, and several fields of oats. I walked very circumspectly for fear of being surprised, or suddenly shot with an arrow from behind or on either side. I fell into a beaten road, where I saw many tracks of human feet, and some of cows, but most of horses. At last I beheld several animals in a field, and one or two of the same kind sitting in trees. Their shape was very singular and deformed, which a little discomposed me, so that I lay down behind a thicket to observe them better.[5] Some of them coming forward near the place where I lay, gave me an opportunity of distinctly marking their form. Their heads and breasts were covered with a thick hair, some frizzled and others lank; they had beards like goats, and a long ridge of hair down their backs and the foreparts of their legs and feet, but the rest of their bodies were bare, so that I might see their skins, which were of a brown buff colour. They had no tails, nor any hair at all on their buttocks, except about the anus; which, I presume, nature had placed there to defend them as they sat on the ground; for this posture they used, as well as lying down, and often stood on their hind feet. They climbed high trees as nimbly as a squirrel, for they had strong extended claws before and behind, terminating in sharp points,

---

[5] The details Swift gives of Yahoo animality recall travelers' accounts of primates or of primitive peoples such as the Hottentots, as well as the imagery often used in sermons to render vivid the nastiness and bestiality of man in a sinful condition. For interesting discussions of this, see Ray W. Frantz, "Swift's Yahoos and the Voyagers," *Modern Philology*, XXIX (1931), 49–58; Clarence M. Webster, "Notes on the Yahoos," *Modern Language Notes*, XLVII (1932), 451–459; and Roland M. Frye, "Swift's Yahoos and the Christian Symbols for Sin," *Journal of the History of Ideas*, XV (1954), 201–217.

and hooked. They would often spring and bound and leap with prodigious agility. The females were not so large as the males; they had long lank hair on their heads, but none on their faces, nor anything more than a sort of down on the rest of their bodies, except about the anus and pudenda. Their dugs hung between their fore-feet and often reached almost to the ground as they walked. The hair of both sexes was of several colours, brown, red, black, and yellow. Upon the whole, I never beheld in all my travels so disagreeable an animal, or one against which I naturally conceived so strong an antipathy. So that thinking I had seen enough, full of contempt and aversion, I got up and pursued the beaten road, hoping it might direct me to the cabin of some Indian. I had not gone far when I met one of these creatures full in my way, and coming up directly to me. The ugly monster, when he saw me, distorted several ways every feature of his visage, and stared as at an object he had never seen before; then approaching nearer, lifted up his forepaw, whether out of curiosity or mischief, I could not tell. But I drew my hanger and gave him a good blow with the flat side of it, for I durst not strike him with the edge, fearing the inhabitants might be provoked against me, if they should come to know that I had killed or maimed any of their cattle. When the beast felt the smart, he drew back and roared so loud that a herd of at least forty came flocking about me from the next field, howling and making odious faces; but I ran to the body of a tree and, leaning my back against it, kept them off by waving my hanger. Several of this cursed brood, getting hold of the branches behind, leaped up into the tree, from whence they began to discharge their excrements on my head: however, I escaped pretty well by sticking close to the stem of the tree, but was almost stifled with the filth, which fell about me on every side.

In the midst of this distress, I observed them all to run away on a sudden as fast as they could, at which I ventured to leave the tree and pursue the road, wondering what it was that could put them into this fright. But looking on my left hand, I saw a horse walking softly in the field, which, my persecutors having sooner discovered, was the cause of their flight. The horse started a little when he came near me but, soon recovering himself, looked full in my face with manifest tokens of wonder: he viewed my hands and feet, walking round me several times. I would have pursued my journey, but he placed himself directly in the way, yet looking with a very mild aspect, never offering the least violence. We stood gazing at each other for some time; at last I took the boldness to reach my hand towards his neck with a design to stroke it, using the common style and whistle of jockeys when they are going to handle a strange horse. But this animal, seeming to receive my civilities with disdain, shook his head and bent his brows, softly raising up his left forefoot to remove my hand. Then he neighed three or four times, but in so different a cadence that I almost began to think he was speaking to himself in some language of his own.

While he and I were thus employed, another horse came up; who applying himself to the first in a very formal manner, they gently struck each other's right hoof before, neighing several times by turns and varying the sound, which seemed to be almost articulate. They went some paces off, as if it were to confer together, walking side by side, backward and forward, like persons deliberating upon some affair of weight, but often turning their eyes towards me as it were to watch that I might not escape. I was amazed to see such actions and behaviour in brute beasts, and concluded with myself that, if the inhabitants of this country were endued with a proportionable degree of reason, they must needs be the wisest people upon earth. This thought gave me so much comfort that I resolved to go forward until I could discover some house or village or meet with any of the natives, leaving the two horses to discourse together as they pleased. But the first, who was a dapple grey, observing me to steal off, neighed after me in so expressive a tone that I fancied myself to understand what he meant; whereupon I turned back and came near him, to expect his farther commands: but concealing my fear as much as I could, for I began to be in some pain how this adventure might terminate; and the reader will easily believe I did not much like my present situation.

The two horses came up close to me, looking with great earnestness upon my face and hands. The grey steed rubbed my hat all around with his right fore-hoof, and discomposed it so much that I was forced to adjust it better by taking it off and settling it again; whereat both he and his companion (who was a brown bay) appeared to be much surprised; the latter felt the lappet of my coat, and finding it to hang loose about me, they both looked with new signs of wonder. He stroked my right hand, seeming to admire the softness and colour; but he squeezed it so hard between his hoof and his pastern that I was forced to roar; after which they both touched me with all possible tenderness. They were under great perplexity about my shoes and stockings, which they felt very often, neighing to each other and using various gestures, not unlike those of a philosopher when he would attempt to solve some new and difficult phenomenon.

Upon the whole, the behaviour of these animals was so orderly and rational, so acute and judicious, that I at last concluded they must needs be magicians who had thus metamorphosed themselves upon some design, and, seeing a stranger in the way, were resolved to divert themselves with him; or perhaps were really amazed at the sight of a man so very different in habit, feature, and complexion from those who might probably live in so remote a climate. Upon the strength of this reasoning, I ventured to address them in the following manner: "Gentlemen, if you be conjurers, as I have good cause to believe, you can understand any language; therefore I make bold to let your Worships know that I am a poor distressed Englishman driven by his misfortunes upon your coast, and I entreat one of you, to let me ride upon his back, as if he were a real horse, to some house or village where I can be relieved. In return of which favour, I will make you a present of this knife and bracelet" (taking them out of my pocket). The two creatures stood silent while I spoke, seeming to listen with great attention; and when I had ended they neighed frequently towards each other, as if they were engaged in serious conversation. I plainly observed that their language expressed the passions very well, and the words might with little pains be resolved into an alphabet more easily than the Chinese.

I could frequently distinguish the word *Yahoo*, which was repeated by each of them several times; and, although it was impossible for me to conjecture what it meant, yet while the two horses were busy in conversation I endeavoured to practice this word upon my tongue; and as soon as they were silent, I boldly pronounced *Yahoo* in a loud voice, imitating, at the same time, as near as I could, the neighing of a horse; at which they were both visibly surprised, and the grey repeated the same word twice, as if he meant to teach me the right accent, wherein I spoke after him as well as I could and found myself perceivably to improve every time, although very far from any degree of perfection. Then the bay tried me with a second word much harder to be pronounced; but reducing it to the English orthography, may be spelt thus, *Houyhnhnm*. I did not succeed in this so well as the former, but after two or three farther trials I had better fortune; and they both appeared amazed at my capacity.

After some farther discourse, which I then conjectured might relate to me, the two friends took their leaves, with the same compliment of striking each other's hoof; and the grey made me signs that I should walk before him, wherein I thought it prudent to comply till I could find a better director. When I offered to slacken my pace, he would cry *Hhuun, Hhuun;* I guessed his meaning and gave him to understand, as well as I could, that I was weary and not able to walk faster; upon which he would stand a while to let me rest.

Chapter Two: The author conducted by a Houyhnhnm to his house. The house described. The author's reception. The food of the Houyhnhnms. The author, in distress for want of meat, is at last relieved. His manner of feeding in that country.

Having travelled about three miles, we came to a long kind of building, made of timber stuck in the ground and wattled across; the roof was low and covered with straw. I now began to be a little comforted and took out some toys, which travellers usually carry for presents to the savage Indians of America and other parts, in hopes the people of the house would be thereby encouraged to receive me kindly. The horse made me a sign to go in first; it was a large room with a smooth clay floor and a rack and manger extending the whole length on one side. There were three nags and two mares, not eating, but some of them sitting down upon their hams, which I very much wondered at; but wondered more to see the rest employed in domestic business. The last seemed but ordinary cattle; however, this confirmed my first opinion, that a people who could so far civilize brute animals must needs excel in wisdom all the nations of the world. The grey came in just after, and thereby prevented any ill treatment which the others might have given me. He neighed to them several times in a style of authority, and received answers.

Beyond this room there were three others, reaching the length of the house, to which you passed through three doors, opposite to each other in the manner of a vista; we went through the second room towards the third; here the grey walked in first, beckoning me to attend: I waited in the second room, and got ready my presents for the master and mistress of the house: they were two knives, three bracelets of false pearl, a small looking-glass, and a bead necklace. The horse neighed three or four times, and I waited to hear some answers in human voice; but I heard no other returns than in the same dialect, only one or two a little shriller than his. I began to think that this house must belong to some person of great note among them, because there appeared so much ceremony before I could gain admittance. But that a man of quality should be served all by horses was beyond my comprehension. I feared my brain was disturbed by my sufferings and misfortunes: I roused myself, and looked about me in the room where I was left alone; this was furnished as the first, only after a more elegant manner. I rubbed my eyes often, but the same objects still occurred. I pinched my arms and sides to awake myself, hoping I might be in a dream. I then absolutely concluded that all these appearances could be nothing else but necromancy and magic. But I had no time to pursue these reflections; for the grey horse came to the door and made me a sign to follow him into the third room, where I saw a very comely mare, together with a colt and foal, sitting on their haunches, upon mats of straw not unartfully made and perfectly neat and clean.

The mare, soon after my entrance, rose from her mat, and coming up close, after having nicely observed my hands and face, gave me a most contemptuous look; then turning to the horse, I heard the word *Yahoo* often repeated betwixt them; the meaning of which word I could not then comprehend, although it were the first I had learned to pronounce; but I was soon better informed, to my everlasting mortification: for the horse beckoning to me with his head, and repeating the word *Hhuun, Hhuun*, as he did upon the road, which I understood was to attend him, led me out into a kind of court, where was another building at some distance from the house. Here we entered, and I saw three of those detestable creatures which I first met after my landing, feeding upon roots and the flesh of some animals, which I afterwards found to be that of asses and dogs, and now and then a cow dead by accident or disease. They were all tied by the neck with strong withes fastened to a beam; they held their food between the claws of their forefeet and tore it with their teeth.

The master horse ordered a sorrel nag, one of his servants, to untie the largest of these animals and take him into the yard. The beast and I were brought close together, and our countenances diligently compared both by master and servant, who thereupon repeated several times the word *Yahoo*. My horror and astonishment are not to be described, when I observed, in this abominable animal, a perfect human figure; the face of it indeed was flat and broad, the nose depressed, the lips large, and the mouth wide. But these differences are common to all savage nations, where the lineaments of the countenance are distorted by the natives suffering their infants to lie grovelling on the earth, or by carrying them on their backs, nuzzling with their face against the mother's shoulders. The forefeet of the Yahoo differed from my hands in nothing else but the length of the nails, the coarseness and brownness of the palms, and the hairiness on the backs. There was the same resemblance between our feet, with the same differences, which I knew very well, although the horses did not, because of my shoes and stockings; the same in every part of our bodies, except as to hairiness and colour, which I have already described.

The great difficulty that seemed to stick with the two horses, was to see the rest of my body so very different from that of a Yahoo, for which I was obliged to my clothes, whereof they had no conception: the sorrel nag offered me a root, which he held (after their manner, as we shall describe in its proper place) between his hoof and pastern; I took it in my hand and, having smelt it, returned it to him as civilly as I could. He brought out of the Yahoo's kennel a piece of ass's flesh, but it smelt so offensively that I turned from it with loathing: he then threw it to the Yahoo, by whom it was greedily devoured. He afterwards showed me a wisp of hay and a fetlock full of oats; but I shook my head to signify that neither of these were food for me. And indeed, I now apprehended that I must absolutely starve if I did not get to some of my own species: for as to those filthy Yahoos, although there were few greater lovers of mankind, at that time, than myself, yet I confess I never saw any sensitive being so detestable on all accounts; and the more I came near them, the more hateful they grew, while I stayed in that country. This the master horse observed by my behaviour, and therefore sent the Yahoo back to his kennel. He then put his fore-hoof to his mouth, at which I was much surprised, although he did it with ease and with a motion that appeared perfectly natural, and made other signs to know what I would eat; but I could not return him such an answer as he was able to apprehend; and if he had understood me, I did not see how it was possible to contrive any way for finding myself nourishment. While we were thus engaged, I observed a cow passing by, whereupon I pointed to her and expressed a desire to let me go and milk her. This had its effect; for he led me back into the house and ordered a mare-servant to open a room where a good store of milk lay in earthen and wooden vessels, after a very orderly and cleanly manner. She gave me a large bowl full, of which I drank very heartily, and found myself well refreshed.

About noon I saw coming towards the house a kind of vehicle drawn like a sledge by four Yahoos. There was in it an old steed, who seemed to be of quality; he alighted with his hind feet forward, having by accident got a hurt in his left forefoot. He came to dine with our horse, who received him with great civility. They dined in the best room and had oats boiled in milk for the second course, which the old horse eat warm, but the rest cold. Their mangers were placed circular in the middle of the room, and divided into several partitions, round which they sat on their haunches upon bosses [1] of straw. In the middle was a large rack with angles answering to every partition of the manger. So that each horse and mare eat their own hay and their own mash of oats and milk, with much decency and regularity. The behaviour of the young colt and foal appeared very modest, and that of the master and mistress extremely cheerful and complaisant to their guest. The grey ordered me to stand by him, and much discourse passed be-

---

[1] Seats or hassocks of straw.

tween him and his friend concerning me, as I found by the stranger's often looking on me, and the frequent repetition of the word *Yahoo*.

I happened to wear my gloves, which the master grey observing, seemed perplexed, discovering signs of wonder what I had done to my forefeet; he put his hoof three or four times to them, as if he would signify that I should reduce them to their former shape, which I presently did, pulling off both my gloves and putting them into my pocket. This occasioned farther talk, and I saw the company was pleased with my behaviour, whereof I soon found the good effects. I was ordered to speak the few words I understood, and while they were at dinner, the master taught me the names for oats, milk, fire, water, and some others: which I could readily pronounce after him, having from my youth a great facility in learning languages.

When dinner was done, the master horse took me aside, and by signs and words made me understand the concern he was in that I had nothing to eat. Oats in their tongue are called *hlunnh*. This word I pronounced two or three times; for although I had refused them at first, yet upon second thoughts, I considered that I could contrive to make of them a kind of bread, which might be sufficient with milk to keep me alive till I could make my escape to some other country, and to creatures of my own species. The horse immediately ordered a white mare-servant of his family to bring me a good quantity of oats in a sort of wooden tray. These I heated before the fire as well as I could, and rubbed them till the husks came off, which I made a shift to winnow from the grain; I ground and beat them between two stones, then took water and made them into a paste or cake, which I toasted at the fire and eat warm with milk. It was at first a very insipid diet, although common enough in many parts of Europe, but grew tolerable by time; and having been often reduced to hard fare in my life, this was not the first experiment I had made how easily nature is satisfied. And I cannot but observe that I never had one hour's sickness while I stayed in this island. It is true, I sometimes made a shift to catch a rabbit, or bird, by springes [2] made of Yahoos' hairs, and I often gathered wholesome herbs, which I boiled or eat as salads with my bread, and now and then, for a rarity, I made a little butter and drank the whey. I was at first at a great loss for salt; but custom soon reconciled the want of it; and I am confident that the frequent use of salt among us is an effect of luxury, and was first introduced only as a provocative to drink; except where it is necessary for preserving of flesh in long voyages or in places remote from great markets. For we observe no animal to be fond of it but man: [3] and as to myself, when I left this country, it was a great while before I could endure the taste of it in anything that I eat.

This is enough to say upon the subject of my diet, where-with other travellers fill their books, as if the readers were personally concerned whether we fare well or ill. However, it was necessary to mention this matter lest the world should think it impossible that I could find sustenance for three years in such a country and among such inhabitants.

When it grew towards evening, the master horse ordered a place for me to lodge in; it was but six yards from the house, and separated from the stable of the Yahoos. Here I got some straw and, covering myself with my own clothes, slept very sound. But I was in a short time better accommodated, as the reader shall know hereafter, when I come to treat more particularly about my way of living.

[2] Snares.

[3] An error, resulting from Swift's ignorance or (if deliberate) from Gulliver's enthusiasm for the simple, "natural" life.

Chapter Three: The author studious to learn the language, the Houyhnhnm his master assists in teaching him. The language described. Several Houyhnhnms of quality come out of curiosity to see the author. He gives his master a short account of his voyage.

My principal endeavour was to learn the language, which my master (for so I shall henceforth call him) and his children, and every servant of his house, were desirous to teach me. For they looked upon it as a prodigy that a brute animal should discover such marks of a rational creature. I pointed to everything and enquired the name of it, which I wrote down in my journal-book when I was alone, and corrected my bad accent by desiring those of the family to pronounce it often. In this employment a sorrel nag, one of the under servants, was very ready to assist me.

In speaking, they pronounce through the nose and throat, and their language approaches nearest to the High Dutch or German of any I know in Europe; but is much more graceful and significant. The Emperor Charles V made almost the same observation, when he said that, if he were to speak to his horse, it should be in High Dutch.[1]

The curiosity and impatience of my master were so great that he spent many hours of his leisure to instruct me. He was convinced (as he afterwards told me) that I must be a Yahoo, but my teachableness, civility, and cleanliness astonished him; which were qualities altogether so opposite to those animals. He was most perplexed about my clothes, reasoning sometimes with himself whether they were a part of my body; for I never pulled them off till the family were asleep, and got them on before they waked in the morning. My master was eager to learn from whence I came, how I acquired those appearances of reason which I discovered in all my actions, and to know my story from my own mouth, which he hoped he should soon do

---

[1] Charles V (1500–1558), King of Spain and ruler of the Holy Roman Empire, is reputed to have said that he would address his God in Spanish, his mistress in Italian, and his horse in German.

by the great proficiency I made in learning and pronouncing their words and sentences. To help my memory, I formed all I learned into the English alphabet and writ the words down with the translations. This last, after some time, I ventured to do in my master's presence. It cost me much trouble to explain to him what I was doing; for the inhabitants have not the least idea of books or literature.

In about ten weeks time I was able to understand most of his questions, and in three months could give him some tolerable answers. He was extremely curious to know from what part of the country I came and how I was taught to imitate a rational creature, because the Yahoos (whom he saw I exactly resembled in my head, hands, and face, that were only visible), with some appearance of cunning, and the strongest disposition to mischief, were observed to be the most unteachable of all brutes. I answered, that I came over the sea, from a far place, with many others of my own kind, in a great hollow vessel made of the bodies of trees; that my companions forced me to land on this coast, and then left me to shift for myself. It was with some difficulty and by the help of many signs that I brought him to understand me. He replied that I must needs be mistaken, or that I "said the thing which was not." (For they have no words in their language to express lying or falsehood.) He knew it was impossible that there could be a country beyond the sea, or that a parcel of brutes could move a wooden vessel whither they pleased upon water. He was sure no Houyhnhnm alive could make such a vessel or would trust Yahoos to manage it.

The word *Houyhnhnm*, in their tongue, signifies a *horse*, and in its etymology, *the Perfection of Nature*.[2] I told my master, that I was at a loss for expression, but would improve

[2] Just as man calls himself the lord of nature, so the Houyhnhnms regard their kind as the culmination and masters of all natural creation. Unlike man, however, they have no awareness of anything beyond the realm of nature; that is, of the supernatural or divine.

as fast as I could; and hoped in a short time I should be able
to tell him wonders: he was pleased to direct his own mare,
his colt and foal, and the servants of the family to take all
opportunities of instructing me, and every day for two or
three hours he was at the same pains himself: several horses
and mares of quality in the neighbourhood came often to our
house upon the report spread of a wonderful Yahoo that could
speak like a Houyhnhnm, and seemed in his words and actions
to discover some glimmerings of reason. These delighted to
converse with me; they put many questions and received such
answers as I was able to return. By all which advantages I
made so great a progress that in five months from my arrival
I understood whatever was spoke, and could express myself
tolerably well.

The Houyhnhnms who came to visit my master, out of a
design of seeing and talking with me, could hardly believe me
to be a right Yahoo, because my body had a different covering
from others of my kind. They were astonished to observe me
without the usual hair or skin except on my head, face, and
hands; but I discovered that secret to my master, upon an accident, which happened about a fortnight before.

I have already told the reader that every night, when the
family were gone to bed, it was my custom to strip and cover
myself with clothes: it happened one morning early that my
master sent for me by the sorrel nag, who was his valet; when
he came, I was fast asleep, my clothes fallen off on one side
and my shirt above my waist. I awaked at the noise he made
and observed him to deliver his message in some disorder; after
which he went to my master and in a great fright gave him
a very confused account of what he had seen: this I presently
discovered; for going, as soon as I was dressed, to pay my
attendance upon his Honour, he asked me the meaning of what
his servant had reported, that I was not the same thing when
I slept as I appeared to be at other times; that his valet assured
him some part of me was white, some yellow, at least not so
white, and some brown.

I had hitherto concealed the secret of my dress in order to distinguish myself as much as possible from that cursed race of Yahoos; but now I found it in vain to do so any longer. Besides, I considered that my clothes and shoes would soon wear out, which already were in a declining condition, and must be supplied by some contrivance from the hides of Yahoos or other brutes; whereby the whole secret would be known: I therefore told my master that, in the country from whence I came, those of my kind always covered their bodies with the hairs of certain animals prepared by art, as well for decency as to avoid inclemencies of air both hot and cold; of which, as to my own person, I would give him immediate conviction if he pleased to command me; only desiring his excuse if I did not expose those parts that nature taught us to conceal. He said my discourse was all very strange, but especially the last part; for he could not understand why nature should teach us to conceal what nature had given. That neither himself nor family were ashamed of any parts of their bodies; but however I might do as I pleased. Whereupon, I first unbuttoned my coat and pulled it off. I did the same with my waistcoat; I drew off my shoes, stockings, and breeches. I let my shirt down to my waist, and drew up the bottom, fastening it like a girdle about my middle to hide my nakedness.

My master observed the whole performance with great signs of curiosity and admiration. He took up all my clothes in his pastern, one piece after another, and examined them diligently; he then stroked my body very gently and looked around me several times after which he said, it was plain I must be a perfect Yahoo; but that I differed very much from the rest of my species in the whiteness and smoothness of my skin, my want of hair in several parts of my body, the shape and shortness of my claws behind and before, and my affectation of walking continually on my two hinder feet. He desired to see no more and gave me leave to put on my clothes again, for I was shuddering with cold.

I expressed my uneasiness at his giving me so often the appellation of *Yahoo*, an odious animal for which I had so utter an hatred and contempt; I begged he would forbear applying that word to me, and take the same order in his family and among his friends whom he suffered to see me. I requested likewise that the secret of my having a false covering to my body might be known to none but himself, at least as long as my present clothing should last; for as to what the sorrel nag his valet had observed, his Honour might command him to conceal it.

All this my master very graciously consented to, and thus the secret was kept till my clothes began to wear out, which I was forced to supply by several contrivances that shall hereafter be mentioned. In the meantime he desired I would go on with my utmost diligence to learn their language, because he was more astonished at my capacity for speech and reason than at the figure of my body, whether it were covered or no; adding that he waited with some impatience to hear the wonders which I promised to tell him.

From thenceforward he doubled the pains he had been at to instruct me; he brought me into all company and made them treat me with civility, because, as he told them privately, this would put me into good humour and make me more diverting.

Every day when I waited on him, beside the trouble he was at in teaching, he would ask me several questions concerning myself, which I answered as well as I could; and by those means he had already received some general ideas, although very imperfect. It would be tedious to relate the several steps by which I advanced to a more regular conversation: but the first account I gave of myself in any order and length was to this purpose:

That I came from a very far country, as I already had attempted to tell him, with about fifty more of my own species; that we travelled upon the seas, in a great hollow vessel made of wood and larger than his Honour's house. I described the ship to him in the best terms I could, and explained by the help of my handkerchief displayed how it was driven forward by the wind. That upon a quarrel among us, I was set on shore on this coast, where I walked forward without knowing whither, till he delivered me from the persecution of those execrable Yahoos. He asked me who made the ship, and how it was possible that the Houyhnhnms of my country would leave it to the management of brutes? My answer was that I durst proceed no farther in my relation unless he would give me his word and honour that he would not be offended, and then I would tell him the wonders I had so often promised. He agreed; and I went on by assuring him that the ship was made by creatures like myself, who in all the countries I had travelled, as well as in my own, were the only governing, rational animals; and that upon my arrival hither I was as much astonished to see the Houyhnhnms act like rational beings, as he or his friends could be in finding some marks of reason in a creature he was pleased to call a Yahoo, to which I owned my resemblance in every part, but could not account for their degenerate and brutal nature. I said farther, that if good fortune ever restored me to my native country to relate my travels hither, as I resolved to do, everybody would believe that I "said the thing which was not;" that I invented the story out of my own head; and with all possible respect to himself, his family and friends, and under his promise of not being offended, our countrymen would hardly think it probable that a Houyhnhnm should be the presiding creature of a nation and a Yahoo the brute.

Chapter Four: The Houyhnhnms' notion of truth and falsehood. The author's discourse disapproved by his master. The author gives a more particular account of himself and the accidents of his voyage.

My master heard me with great appearances of uneasiness in his countenance, because *doubting* or *not believing*, are so little known in this country that the inhabitants cannot tell how to behave themselves under such circumstances. And I remember in frequent discourses with my master concerning the nature of manhood in other parts of the world, having occasion to talk of *lying* and *false representation*, it was with much difficulty that he comprehended what I meant, although he had otherwise a most acute judgment. For he argued thus: that the use of speech was to make us understand one another and to receive information of facts; now if any one *said the thing which was not*, these ends were defeated; because I cannot properly be said to understand him, and I am so far from receiving information that he leaves me worse than in ignorance, for I am led to believe a thing *black* when it is *white*, and *short* when it is *long*. And these were all the notions he had concerning that faculty of *lying*, so perfectly well understood and so universally practised among human creatures.

To return from this digression, when I asserted that the Yahoos were the only governing animals in my country, which my master said was altogether past his conception, he desired to know whether we had Houyhnhnms among us and what was their employment: I told him, we had great numbers, that in summer they grazed in the fields and in winter were kept in houses with hay and oats, where Yahoo servants were employed to rub their skins smooth, comb their manes, pick their feet, serve them with food, and make their beds. "I understand you well," said my master, "it is now very plain from all you have spoken that, whatever share of reason the Yahoos pretend to, the Houyhnhnms are your masters; I heartily wish our Yahoos would be so tractable. I begged his Honour would please to excuse me from proceeding any farther, because I was very certain that the account he expected from me would be highly displeasing. But he insisted in commanding me to let him know the best and the worst: I told him he should be obeyed. I owned that the Houyhnhnms among us, whom we called horses, were the most generous [1] and comely animal we had, that they excelled in strength and swiftness; and when

[1] Noble.

they belonged to persons of quality, employed in travelling, racing, and drawing chariots, they were treated with much kindness and care, till they fell into diseases or became foundered in the feet; but then they were sold and used to all kind of drudgery till they died; after which their skins were stripped and sold for what they were worth, and their bodies left to be devoured by dogs and birds of prey. But the common race of horses had not so good fortune, being kept by farmers and carriers and other mean people, who put them to greater labour and feed them worse. I described, as well as I could, our way of riding, the shape and use of a bridle, a saddle, a spur, and a whip, of harness and wheels. I added, that we fastened plates of a certain hard substance called *iron* at the bottom of their feet, to preserve their hoofs from being broken by the stony ways on which we often travelled.

My master, after some expressions of great indignation, wondered how we dared to venture upon a Houyhnhnm's back, for he was sure that the weakest servant in his house would be able to shake off the strongest Yahoo, or by lying down and rolling upon his back squeeze the brute to death. I answered that our horses were trained up from three or four years old to the several uses we intended them for; that if any of them proved intolerably vicious, they were employed for carriages; that they were severely beaten while they were young for any mischievous tricks; that the males, designed for the common use of riding or draught, were generally castrated about two years after their birth to take down their spirits and make them more tame and gentle; that they were indeed sensible of [2] rewards and punishments; but his Honour would please to consider that they had not the least tincture of reason any more than the Yahoos in this country.

It put me to the pains of many circumlocutions to give my master a right idea of what I spoke; for their language doth not abound in variety of words, because their wants and pas-

---

[2] Responsive to.

sions are fewer than among us. But it is impossible to express his noble resentment at our savage treatment of the Houyhnhnm race, particularly after I had explained the manner and use of castrating horses among us to hinder them from propagating their kind and to render them more servile. He said, if it were possible there could be any country where Yahoos alone were endued with reason, they certainly must be the governing animal, because reason will in time always prevail against brutal strength. But, considering the frame of our bodies, and especially of mine, he thought no creature of equal bulk was so ill contrived for employing that reason in the common offices of life; whereupon he desired to know whether those among whom I lived resembled me or the Yahoos of his country. I assured him that I was as well shaped as most of my age: but the younger and the females were much more soft and tender, and the skins of the latter generally as white as milk. He said I differed indeed from other Yahoos, being much more cleanly and not altogether so deformed, but in point of real advantage he thought I differed for the worse. That my nails were of no use either to my fore or hinder feet; as to my forefeet, he could not properly call them by that name, for he never observed me to walk upon them; that they were too soft to bear the ground; that I generally went with them uncovered, neither was the covering I sometimes wore on them of the same shape or so strong as that on my feet behind. That I could not walk with any security, for if either of my hinder feet slipped, I must inevitably fall. He then began to find fault with other parts of my body, the flatness of my face, the prominence of my nose, my eyes placed directly in front, so that I could not look on either side without turning my head: that I was not able to feed myself without lifting one of my forefeet to my mouth: and therefore nature had placed those joints to answer that necessity. He knew not what could be the use of those several clefts and divisions in my feet behind; that these were too soft to bear the hardness and sharpness of stones without a covering made from the skin of some other brute; that my whole body wanted a fence against heat and cold, which I was forced to put on and off every day with tediousness and trouble. And lastly that he observed every animal in this country naturally to abhor the Yahoos, whom the weaker avoided and the stronger drove from them. So that supposing us to have the gift of reason, he could not see how it were possible to cure that natural antipathy which every creature discovered against us; nor consequently how we could tame and render them serviceable. However, he would (as he said) debate the matter no farther, because he was more desirous to know my own story, the country where I was born, and the several actions and events of my life before I came hither.

I assured him how extremely desirous I was that he should be satisfied in every point; but I doubted much whether it would be possible for me to explain myself on several subjects whereof his Honour could have no conception, because I saw nothing in his country to which I could resemble them. That, however, I would do my best and strive to express myself by similitudes, humbly desiring his assistance when I wanted proper words, which he was pleased to promise me.

I said my birth was of honest parents, in an island called England, which was remote from this country as many days' journey as the strongest of his Honour's servants could travel in the annual course of the sun. That I was bred a surgeon, whose trade it is to cure wounds and hurts in the body, got by accident or violence; that my country was governed by a female man, whom we called a *queen*. That I left it to get riches, whereby I might maintain myself and family when I should return. That in my last voyage I was commander of the ship, and had about fifty Yahoos under me, many of which died at sea, and I was forced to supply them by others picked out from several nations. That our ship was twice in danger of being sunk; the first time by a great storm, and the second by striking against a rock. Here my master interposed by asking me how I could persuade strangers out of different countries to venture with me, after the losses I had sustained and the hazards I had run. I said, they were fellows of desperate fortunes, forced to fly from the places of their birth on account of their poverty or their crimes. Some were undone by lawsuits; others spent all they had in drinking, whoring, and gaming; others fled for treason; many for murder, theft, poisoning, robbery, perjury, forgery, coining false money, for committing rapes or sodomy, for flying from their colours, or deserting to the enemy, and most of them had broken prison; none of these durst return to their native countries for fear of being hanged or of starving in a jail; and therefore were under a necessity of seeking a livelihood in other places.

During this discourse, my master was pleased often to interrupt me; I had made use of many circumlocutions in describing to him the nature of the several crimes for which most of our crew had been forced to fly their country. This labour took up several days' conversation before he was able to comprehend me. He was wholly at a loss to know what could be the use or necessity of practising those vices. To clear up which I endeavoured to give him some ideas of the desire of power and riches, of the terrible effects of lust, intemperance, malice, and envy. All this I was forced to define and describe by putting of cases and making suppositions. After which, like one whose imagination was struck with something never seen or heard of before, he would lift up his eyes with amazement and indignation. Power, government, war, law, punishment, and a thousand other things had no terms wherein that language could express them, which made the difficulty almost insuperable to give my master any conception of what I meant. But being of an excellent understanding, much improved by contemplation and converse, he at last arrived at a competent knowledge of what human nature in our parts of the world is capable to perform, and desired I would give him some particular account of that land which we call Europe, especially of my own country.

Chapter Five: The author at his master's command informs him of the state of England. The causes of war among the princes of Europe. The author begins to explain the English constitution.

The reader may please to observe, that the following extract of many conversations I had with my master contains a summary of the most material points which were discoursed at several times for above two years; his Honour often desiring fuller satisfaction as I farther improved in the Houyhnhnm tongue. I laid before him, as well as I could, the whole state of Europe; I discoursed of trade and manufactures, of arts and sciences; and the answers I gave to all the questions he made, as they arose upon several subjects, were a fund of conversation not to be exhausted. But I shall here only set down the substance of what passed between us concerning my own country, reducing it into order as well as I can, without any regard to time or other circumstances, while I strictly adhere to truth. My only concern is that I shall hardly be able to do justice to my master's arguments and expressions, which must needs suffer by any want of capacity, as well as by a translation into our barbarous English.

In obedience therefore to his Honour's commands, I related to him the Revolution under the Prince of Orange; the long war with France entered into by the said prince, and renewed by his successor the present queen, wherein the greatest powers of Christendom were engaged, and which still continued:[1] I computed, at his request, that about a million of Yahoos might have been killed in the whole progress of it, and perhaps a hundred or more cities taken, and five times as many ships burnt or sunk.

[1] William of Orange (1650–1702) became William III of England in the Glorious Revolution of 1688. He was engaged in wars with France until 1697, when Louis XIV recognized him as King of England; and he resumed war in 1701 when Louis gave his recognition to the Stuart Pretender. Anne (1665–1714) carried on the War of the Spanish Succession, which ended in 1713, while Gulliver was still in Houyhnhnmland.

He asked me what were the usual causes or motives that made one country go to war with another. I answered they were innumerable, but I should only mention a few of the chief. Sometimes the ambition of princes, who never think they have land or people enough to govern: sometimes the corruption of ministers, who engage their master in a war in order to stifle or divert the clamor of the subjects against their evil administration. Difference in opinions[2] hath cost many millions of lives: for instance, whether *flesh* be *bread* or *bread* be *flesh;* whether the juice of a certain *berry* be *blood* or *wine;* whether *whistling* be a vice or a virtue; whether it be better to *kiss a post* or throw it into the fire; what is the best colour for a *coat*, whether *black, white, red,* or *grey;* and whether it should be *long* or *short, narrow* or *wide, dirty* or *clean,* with many more. Neither are any wars so furious and bloody or of so long continuance, as those occasioned by difference in opinion, especially if it be in things indifferent.[3]

Sometimes the quarrel between two princes is to decide which of them shall dispossess a third of his dominions, where neither of them pretend to any right. Sometimes one prince quarrelleth with another for fear the other should quarrel with him. Sometimes a war is entered upon because the enemy is too *strong*, and sometimes because he is too *weak*. Sometimes our neighbours *want* the things which we *have*, or *have* the things which we *want;* and we both fight till they take ours or give us theirs. It is a very justifiable cause of war to invade a country after the people have been wasted by famine, destroyed by pestilence, or embroiled by factions amongst themselves. It is justifiable to enter into a war against our nearest ally when one of his towns lies convenient for us, or a territory of land that would render our dominions round and compact. If a

---

[2] These are quarrels among the churches about the transubstantiation of the Eucharistic bread and wine, the use of music in worship, the veneration of the crucifix, and the proper use of church vestments.

[3] Matters inessential to belief.

prince send forces into a nation where the people are poor and ignorant, he may lawfully put half of them to death and make slaves of the rest, in order to civilize and reduce them from their barbarous way of living. It is a very kingly, honourable, and frequent practice, when one prince desires the assistance of another to secure him against an invasion, that the assistant, when he hath driven out the invader, should seize on the dominions himself, and kill, imprison, or banish the prince he came to relieve. Alliance by blood or marriage is a sufficient cause of war between princes, and, the nearer the kindred is, the greater is their disposition to quarrel: *poor* nations are *hungry* and *rich* nations are *proud*, and pride and hunger will ever be at variance. For these reasons, the trade of a soldier is held the most honourable of all others: because a soldier is a Yahoo hired to kill in cold blood as many of his own species, who have never offended him, as possibly he can.

There is likewise a kind of beggarly princes in Europe, not able to make war by themselves, who hire out their troops to richer nations, for so much a day to each man; [4] of which they keep three-fourths to themselves, and it is the best part of their maintenance; such are those in Germany and many northern parts of Europe.

What you have told me (said my master) upon the subject of war does indeed discover most admirably the effects of that reason you pretend to: however, it is happy that the *shame* is greater than the *danger*, and that nature hath left you utterly uncapable of doing much mischief. For your mouths lying flat with your faces, you can hardly bite each other to any purpose unless by consent. Then as to the claws upon your feet before and behind, they are so short and tender that one of our Yahoos would drive a dozen of yours before him. And therefore in recounting the numbers of those who have been killed in battle, I cannot but think that you have *said the thing which is not.*

---

[4] George I of England, while still Elector of Hanover, supplied mercenaries to warring nations.

I could not forbear shaking my head and smiling a little at his ignorance. And being no stranger to the art of war, I gave him a description of cannons, culverins, muskets, carabines, pistols, bullets, powder, swords, bayonets, battles, sieges, retreats, attacks, undermines, countermines, bombardments, seafights; ships sunk with a thousand men; twenty thousand killed on each side; dying groans, limbs flying in the air, smoke, noise, confusion, trampling to death under horses' feet; flight, pursuit, victory; fields strewed with carcasses left for food to dogs and wolves and birds of prey; plundering, stripping, ravishing, burning, and destroying. And to set forth the valour of my own dear countrymen, I assured him, that I had seen them blow up a hundred enemies at once in a siege, and as many in a ship, and beheld the dead bodies drop down in pieces from the clouds, to the great diversion of all the spectators.

I was going on to more particulars when my master commanded me silence. He said whoever understood the nature of Yahoos might easily believe it possible for so vile an animal to be capable of every action I had named, if their strength and cunning equalled their malice. But as my discourse had increased his abhorrence of the whole species, so he found it gave him a disturbance in his mind, to which he was wholly a stranger before. He thought his ears being used to such abominable words might by degrees admit them with less detestation. That although he hated the Yahoos of this country, yet he no more blamed them for their odious qualities, than he did a *gnnayh* (a bird of prey) for its cruelty, or a sharp stone for cutting his hoof. But when a creature pretending to reason could be capable of such enormities, he dreaded lest the corruption of that faculty might be worse than brutality itself. He seemed therefore confident that, instead of reason, we were only possessed of some quality fitted to increase our natural vices; as the reflection from a troubled stream returns the image of an ill-shapen body, not only *larger* but more *distorted*.

He added that he had heard too much upon the subject of war, both in this and some former discourses. There was another point which a little perplexed him at present. I had said, that some of our crew left their country on account of being ruined by *law;* that I had already explained the meaning of the word; but he was at loss how it should come to pass that the *law,* which was intended for *every* man's preservation, should be any man's ruin. Therefore he desired to be farther satisfied what I meant by *law,* and the dispensers thereof according to the present practice in my own country; because he thought nature and reason were sufficient guides for a reasonable animal, as we pretended to be, in showing us what we ought to do, and what to avoid.

I assured his Honour, that law was a science wherein I had not much conversed, further than by employing advocates, in vain, upon some injustices that had been done me. However, I would give him all the satisfaction I was able.

I said there was a society of men among us bred up from their youth in the art of proving by words multiplied for the purpose, that white is black and black is white, according as they are paid. To this society all the rest of the people are slaves.

For example, if my neighbour hath a mind to my cow, he hires a lawyer to prove that he ought to have my cow from me. I must then hire another to defend my right, it being against all rules of law that any man should be allowed to speak for himself. Now in this case, I who am the true owner lie under two great disadvantages. First, my lawyer, being practiced almost from his cradle in defending falsehood, is quite out of his element when he would be an advocate for justice, which as an office unnatural he always attempts with great awkwardness, if not with ill will. The second disadvantage is, that my lawyer must proceed with great caution, or else he will be reprimanded by the judges, and abhorred by his brethren, as one that would lessen the practice of the law. And therefore I have but two methods to preserve my cow. The first is to gain over my adversary's lawyer with a double fee, who will then betray his client by insinuating that he hath justice on his side.

The second way is for my lawyer to make my cause appear as unjust as he can, by allowing the cow to belong to my adversary; and this if it be skilfully done will certainly bespeak the favour of the bench.

Now, your Honour is to know that these judges are persons appointed to decide all controversies of property, as well as for the trial of criminals, and picked out from the most dextrous lawyers who are grown old or lazy and, having been biassed all their lives against truth and equity, lie under such a fatal necessity of favouring fraud, perjury, and oppression, that I have known some of them to have refused a large bribe from the side where justice lay, rather than injure the faculty [5] by doing anything unbecoming their nature or their office.

It is a maxim among these lawyers that whatever hath been done before may legally be done again: and therefore they take special care to record all the decisions formerly made against common justice and the general reason of mankind. These, under the name of *precedents,* they produce as authorities, to justify the most iniquitous opinions; and the judges never fail of decreeing accordingly.

In pleading, they studiously avoid entering into the *merits* of the cause, but are loud, violent, and tedious in dwelling upon all *circumstances* which are not to the purpose. For instance, in the case already mentioned; they never desire to know what claim or title my adversary hath to my cow, but whether the said cow were red or black, her horns long or short; whether the field I graze her in be round or square, whether she were milked at home or abroad, what diseases she is subject to, and the like; after which they consult precedents, adjourn the cause from time to time, and in ten, twenty, or thirty years come to an issue.

It is likewise to be observed that this society hath a peculiar cant and jargon of their own, that no other mortal can understand and wherein all their laws are written, which they take

[5] Profession.

special care to multiply; whereby they have wholly confounded the very essence of truth and falsehood, of right and wrong; so that it will take thirty years to decide whether the field left me by my ancestors for six generations belongs to me or to a stranger three hundred miles off.

In the trial of persons accused for crimes against the state the method is much more short and commendable: the judge first sends to sound the disposition of those in power, after which he can easily hang or save the criminal, strictly preserving all due forms of law.

Here my master, interposing, said it was a pity that creatures endowed with such prodigious abilities of mind as these lawyers, by the description I gave of them, must certainly be, were not rather encouraged to be instructors of others in wisdom and knowledge. In answer to which I assured his Honour, that in all points out of their own trade they were usually the most ignorant and stupid generation among us, the most despicable in common conversation, avowed enemies to all knowledge and learning, and equally disposed to pervert the general reason of mankind in every other subject of discourse as in that of their own profession.

Chapter Six: A continuation of the state of England. The character of a first minister.

My master was yet wholly at a loss to understand what motives could incite this race of lawyers to perplex, disquiet, and weary themselves by engaging in a confederacy of injustice, merely for the sake of injuring their fellow-animals; neither could he comprehend what I meant in saying they did it for hire. Whereupon I was at much pains to describe to him the use of money, the materials it was made of, and the value of the metals; that when a Yahoo had got a great store of this precious substance, he was able to purchase whatever he had a mind to, the finest clothing, the noblest houses, great tracts of land, the most costly meats and drinks, and have his choice of the most beautiful females. Therefore since money alone was able to perform all these feats, our Yahoos thought they could never have enough of it to spend or to save, as they found themselves inclined from their natural bent either to profusion or avarice. That the rich man enjoyed the fruit of the poor man's labour, and the latter were a thousand to one in proportion to the former. That the bulk of our people was forced to live miserably, by labouring every day for small wages to make a few live plentifully. I enlarged myself much on these and many other particulars to the same purpose: but his Honour was still to seek; [1] for he went upon a supposition that all animals had a title to their share in the productions of the earth, and especially those who presided over the rest.[2] Therefore he desired I would let him know what these costly meats were, and how any of us happened to want [3] them. Whereupon I enumerated as many sorts as came into my head, with the various methods of dressing them, which could not be done without sending vessels by sea to every part of the world, as well for liquors to drink as for sauces and innumerable other conveniencies. I assured him, that this whole globe of earth must be at least three times gone round before one of our better female Yahoos could get her breakfast or a cup to put it in. He said that must needs be a miserable country which cannot furnish food for its own inhabitants. But what he chiefly wondered at was how such vast tracts of ground as I described should be wholly without fresh water, and the people put to the necessity of sending over the sea for drink. I replied that England (the dear place of my nativity) was

[1] At a loss to understand.
[2] That is, over the rest of the species of animals; outside Houyhnhnmland, this would mean mankind.
[3] Lack.

computed to produce three times the quantity of food more than its inhabitants are able to consume, as well as liquors extracted from grain or pressed out of the fruit of certain trees, which made excellent drink, and the same proportion in every other convenience of life. But in order to feed the luxury and intemperance of the males and the vanity of the females, we sent away the greatest part of our necessary things to other countries, from whence in return we brought the materials of diseases, folly, and vice, to spend among ourselves. Hence it follows of necessity that vast numbers of our people are compelled to seek their livelihood by begging, robbing, stealing, cheating, pimping, forswearing, flattering, suborning, forging, gaming, lying, fawning, hectoring, voting, scribbling, stargazing, poisoning, whoring, canting, libelling, free-thinking, and the like occupations: every one of which terms I was at much pains to make him understand.

That wine was not imported among us from foreign countries to supply the want of water or other drinks, but because it was a sort of liquid which made us merry by putting us out of our senses; diverted all melancholy thoughts, begat wild extravagant imaginations in the brain, raised our hopes, and banished our fears, suspended every office of reason for a time, and deprived us of the use of our limbs, until we fell into a profound sleep; although it must be confessed that we always awaked sick and dispirited, and that the use of this liquor filled us with diseases which made our lives uncomfortable and short.

But beside all this, the bulk of our people supported themselves by furnishing the necessities or conveniences of life to the rich and to each other. For instance, when I am at home and dressed as I ought to be, I carry on my body the workmanship of an hundred tradesmen; the building and furniture of my house employ as many more, and five times the number to adorn my wife.

I was going on to tell him of another sort of people who get their livelihood by attending the sick, having upon some occasions informed his Honour that many of my crew had died of diseases. But here it was with the utmost difficulty that I brought him to apprehend what I meant. He could easily conceive that a Houyhnhnm grew weak and heavy a few days before his death, or by some accident might hurt a limb. But that Nature, who works all things to perfection, should suffer any pains to breed in our bodies, he thought impossible, and desired to know the reason of so unaccountable an evil. I told him we fed on a thousand things which operated contrary to each other; that we eat when we were not hungry and drank without the provocation of thirst; that we sat whole nights drinking strong liquors without eating a bit, which disposed us to sloth, enflamed our bodies, and precipitated or prevented digestion. That prostitute female Yahoos acquired a certain malady, which bred rottenness in the bones of those who fell into their embraces; that this and many other diseases were propagated from father to son, so that great numbers come into the world with complicated maladies upon them; that it would be endless to give him a catalogue of all diseases incident to human bodies; for they could not be fewer than five or six hundred, spread over every limb and joint; in short, every part, external and intestine, having diseases appropriated to each. To remedy which, there was a sort of people bred up among us in the profession or pretence of curing the sick. And because I had some skill in the faculty, I would, in gratitude to his Honour, let him know the whole mystery and method by which they proceed.

Their fundamental is that all diseases arise from repletion, from whence they conclude that a great evacuation of the body is necessary, either through the natural passage or upwards at the mouth. Their next business is, from herbs, minerals, gums, oils, shells, salts, juices, seaweed, excrements, barks of trees, serpents, toads, frogs, spiders, dead men's flesh and bones, birds, beasts, and fishes, to form a composition for smell and taste the most abominable, nauseous, and detestable that they can possibly contrive, which the stomach immediately rejects with loathing; and this they call a vomit; or else from the same storehouse, with some other poisonous additions, they command us to take in at the orifice above or below (just as the physician then happens to be disposed) a medicine equally annoying and disgustful to the bowels, which, relaxing the belly, drives down all before it, and this they call a purge or a clyster. For nature (as the physicians allege) having intended the superior anterior orifice only for the intromission of solids and liquids and the inferior posterior for ejection, these artists, ingeniously considering that in all diseases Nature is forced out of her seat, therefore to replace her in it, the body must be treated in a manner directly contrary, by interchanging the use of each orifice, forcing solids and liquids in at the anus and making evacuations at the mouth.

But besides real diseases we are subject to many that are only imaginary, for which the physicians have invented imaginary cures; these have their several names, and so have the drugs that are proper for them, and with these our female Yahoos are always infested.

One great excellency in this tribe is their skill at prognostics, wherein they seldom fail; their predictions in real diseases, when they rise to any degree of malignity, generally portending death, which is always in their power when recovery is not: and therefore, upon any unexpected signs of amendment, after they have pronounced their sentence, rather than be accused as false prophets, they know how to approve [4] their sagacity to the world by a seasonable dose.

They are likewise of special use to husbands and wives who are grown weary of their mates, to eldest sons, to great ministers of state, and often to princes.

I had formerly upon occasion discoursed with my master upon the nature of our government in general, and particularly of our own excellent constitution, deservedly the wonder and envy of the whole world. But having here accidentally men-

[4] Prove.

tioned a *minister of state,* he commanded me some time after to inform him, what species of Yahoo I particularly meant by that appellation.

I told him that a *first* or *chief minister of state,* whom I intended to describe, was a creature wholly exempt from joy and grief, love and hatred, pity and anger; at least makes use of no other passions but a violent desire of wealth, power, and titles; that he applies his words to all uses except to the indication of his mind; that he never tells a *truth* but with an intent that you should take it for a *lie;* nor a *lie* but with a design that you should take it for a *truth;* that those he speaks worst of behind their backs are in the surest way to preferment; and whenever he begins to praise you to others or to yourself, you are from that day forlorn. The worst mark you can receive is a *promise,* especially when it is confirmed with an oath; after which every wise man retires and gives over all hopes.

There are three methods by which a man may rise to be chief minister: the first is by knowing how with prudence to dispose of a wife, a daughter, or a sister: the second, by betraying or undermining his predecessor: and the third is by a *furious zeal* in public assemblies against the corruptions of the court. But a wise prince would rather choose to employ those who practise the last of these methods; because such zealots prove always the most obsequious and subservient to the will and passions of their master. That these *ministers,* having all employments at their disposal, preserve themselves in power by bribing the majority of a senate or great council; and at last, by an expedient called an *act of indemnity* (whereof I described the nature to him) they secure themselves from after reckonings, and retire from the public laden with the spoils of the nation.[5]

[5] Such acts were often passed to free ministers from criminal prosecution by their successors to power. The Indemnity Act of 1708 Swift called "a law enacted to take away the force of all laws whatsoever, by which a man may safely commit upon the last of June what he would infallibly be hanged for if he committed on

The palace of a chief minister is a seminary to breed up others in his own trade: the pages, lackeys, and porter, by imitating their master, become ministers of state in their several districts, and learn to excel in the three principal ingredients, of *insolence, lying,* and *bribery.* Accordingly, they have a subaltern court paid to them by persons of the best rank, and sometimes by the force of dexterity and impudence arrive through several gradations to be successors to their lord.

He is usually governed by a decayed wench or favourite footman, who are the tunnels through which all graces are conveyed and may properly be called, *in the last resort,* the governors of the kingdom.

One day my master, having heard me mention the nobility of my country, was pleased to make me a compliment which I could not pretend to deserve: that he was sure I must have been born of some noble family, because I far exceeded in shape, colour, and cleanliness all the Yahoos of his nation, although I seemed to fail in strength and agility, which must be imputed to my different way of living from those other brutes; and, besides, I was not only endowed with the faculty of speech, but likewise with some rudiments of reason, to a degree that with all his acquaintance I passed for a prodigy.

He made me observe, that among the Houyhnhnms, the *white,* the *sorrel,* and the *iron-grey,* were not so exactly shaped as the *bay,* the *dapple-grey,* and the *black;* nor born with equal talents of mind or a capacity to improve them; and therefore continued always in the condition of servants, without ever aspiring to match out of their own race, which in that country would be reckoned monstrous and unnatural.

I made his Honour my most humble acknowledgments for the good opinion he was pleased to conceive of me; but assured him at the same time that my birth was of the lower sort, having been born of plain honest parents who were just able to give me a tolerable education: that *nobility* among us was alto-

---

the first of July" (*Examiner,* No. 18, November 1710). The Earl of Wharton was proved to have sold his influence to an office-seeker for £1,000 but was saved by the act of 1708.

gether a different thing from the idea he had of it; that our young noblemen are bred from their childhood in idleness and luxury; that as soon as years will permit, they consume their vigor and contract odious diseases among lewd females; and when their fortunes are almost ruined, they marry some woman of mean birth, disagreeable person, and unsound constitution, merely for the sake of money, whom they hate and despise. That the productions of such marriages are generally scrofulous, rickety, or deformed children, by which means the family seldom continues above three generations, unless the wife take care to provide a healthy father among her neighbours or domestics, in order to improve and continue the breed. That a weak diseased body, a meagre countenance, and sallow complexion are the true marks of noble blood; and a healthy robust appearance is so disgraceful in a man of quality that the world concludes his real father to have been a groom or a coachman. The imperfections of his mind run parallel with those of his body, being a composition of spleen,[6] dulness, ignorance, caprice, sensuality, and pride.

Without the consent of this illustrious body [7] no law can be enacted, repealed, or altered, and these nobles have likewise the decision of all our possessions without appeal.

Chapter Seven: The author's great love of his native country. His master's observations upon the constitution and administration of England, as described by the author, with parallel cases and comparisons. His master's observations upon human nature.

The reader may be disposed to wonder how I could prevail on myself to give so free a representation of my own species among a race of mortals who were already too apt to conceive the

[6] Fits of temper or passion (see Part Four, Chapter Seven, Note 2).

[7] The House of Lords.

vilest opinion of humankind from the entire congruity betwixt me and their Yahoos. But I must freely confess that the many virtues of those excellent quadrupeds, placed in opposite view to human corruptions, had so far opened my eyes and enlarged my understanding, that I began to view the actions and passions of man in a very different light, and to think the honour of my own kind not worth managing,[1] which, besides, it was impossible for me to do before a person of so acute a judgment as my master, who daily convinced me of a thousand faults in myself, whereof I had not the least perception before, and which with us would never be numbered even among human infirmities: I had likewise learned from his example an utter detestation of all falsehood or disguise; and truth appeared so amiable to me that I determined upon sacrificing everything to it.

Let me deal so candidly with the reader as to confess that there was yet a much stronger motive for the freedom I took in my representation of things. I had not been a year in this country before I contracted such a love and veneration for the inhabitants that I entered on a firm resolution never to return to humankind, but to pass the rest of my life among these admirable Houyhnhnms in the contemplation and practice of every virtue; where I could have no example or incitement to vice. But it was decreed by Fortune, my perpetual enemy, that so great a felicity should not fall to my share. However, it is now some comfort to reflect, that in what I said of my countrymen I extenuated their faults as much as I durst before so strict an examiner, and upon every article gave as favourable a turn as the matter would bear. For, indeed, who is there alive that will not be swayed by his bias and partiality to the place of his birth?

I have related the substance of several conversations I had with my master, during the greatest part of the time I had the honour to be in his service, but have indeed for brevity sake omitted much more than is here set down.

[1] Protecting.

When I had answered all his questions, and his curiosity seemed to be fully satisfied, he sent for me one morning early and, commanding me to sit down at some distance (an honour which he had never before conferred upon me), he said he had been very seriously considering my whole story, as far as it related both to myself and my country: that he looked upon us as a sort of animals to whose share, by what accident he could not conjecture, some small pittance of *reason* had fallen, whereof we made no other use than by its assistance to aggravate our *natural* corruptions, and to acquire new ones which Nature had not given us. That we disarmed ourselves of the few abilities she had bestowed, had been very successful in multiplying our original wants, and seemed to spend our whole lives in vain endeavours to supply them by our own inventions. That as to myself, it was manifest I had neither the strength or agility of a common Yahoo, that I walked infirmly on my hinder feet, had found out a contrivance to make my claws of no use or defence, and to remove the hair from my chin, which was intended as a shelter from the sun and the weather. Lastly, that I could neither run with speed, nor climb trees like my brethren (as he called them), the Yahoos in this country.

That our institutions of government and law were plainly owing to our gross defects in *reason* and, by consequence, in *virtue*; because *reason* alone is sufficient to govern a *rational* creature; which was therefore a character we had no pretence to challenge, even from the account I had given of my own people, although he manifestly perceived that in order to favour them I had concealed many particulars and often *said the thing which was not*.

He was the more confirmed in this opinion because he observed that, as I agreed in every feature of my body with other Yahoos, except where it was to my real disadvantage in point of strength, speed, and activity, the shortness of my claws, and some other particulars where nature had no part; so from the representation I had given him of our lives, our manners, and our actions, he found as near a resemblance in the disposition of our minds. He said the Yahoos were known to hate

one another more than they did any different species of animals; and the reason usually assigned was the odiousness of
their own shapes, which all could see in the rest, but not in
themselves. He had therefore begun to think it not unwise in
us to cover our bodies and, by that invention, conceal many of
our deformities from each other, which would else be hardly
supportable. But he now found he had been mistaken, and that
the dissensions of those brutes in his country were owing to the
same cause with ours, as I had described them. For if (said he)
you throw among five Yahoos as much food as would be sufficient for fifty, they will, instead of eating peaceably, fall
together by the ears, each single one impatient to have all to
itself, and therefore a servant was usually employed to stand
by while they were feeding abroad, and those kept at home
were tied at a distance from each other; that if a cow died of
age or accident, before a Houyhnhnm could secure it for his
own Yahoos, those in the neighbourhood would come in herds
to seize it, and then would ensue such a battle as I had described, with terrible wounds made by their claws on both sides,
although they seldom were able to kill one another, for want of
such convenient instruments of death as we had invented. At
other times the like battles have been fought between the Yahoos
of several neighbourhoods without any visible cause; those of
one district watching all opportunities to surprise the next before they are prepared. But if they find their project hath miscarried, they return home, and, for want of enemies, engage in
what I call a civil war among themselves.

That in some fields of this country there are certain shining
stones of several colours, whereof the Yahoos are violently
fond, and when part of these stones are fixed in the earth, as
it sometimes happeneth, they will dig with their claws for
whole days to get them out, and carry them away, and hide
them by heaps in their kennels; but still looking round with
great caution for fear their comrades should find out their
treasure. My master said he could never discover the reason
of this unnatural appetite, or how these stones could be of any

use to a Yahoo; but now he believed it might proceed from the same principle of avarice which I had ascribed to mankind; that he had once, by way of experiment, privately removed a heap of these stones from the place where one of his Yahoos had buried it: whereupon the sordid animal, missing his treasure, by his loud lamenting brought the whole herd to the place, there miserably howled, then fell to biting and tearing the rest, began to pine away, would neither eat, nor sleep, nor work, till he ordered a servant privately to convey the stones into the same hole and hide them as before; which when his Yahoo had found, he presently recovered his spirits and good humour, but took care to remove them to a better hiding-place, and hath ever since been a very serviceable brute.

My master farther assured me, which I also observed myself, that in the fields where these shining stones abound, the fiercest and most frequent battles are fought, occasioned by perpetual inroads of the neighbouring Yahoos.

He said it was common, when two Yahoos discovered such a stone in a field and were contending which of them should be the proprietor, a third would take the advantage and carry it away from them both; which my master would needs contend to have some resemblance with our *suits at law;* wherein I thought it for our credit not to undeceive him; since the decision he mentioned was much more equitable than many decrees among us: because the plaintiff and defendant there lost nothing beside the stone they contended for, whereas our *courts of equity* would never have dismissed the cause while either of them had anything left.

My master, continuing his discourse, said, there was nothing that rendered the Yahoos more odious than their undistinguishing appetite to devour everything that came in their way, whether herbs, roots, berries, corrupted flesh of animals, or all mingled together: and it was peculiar in their temper that they were fonder of what they could get by rapine or stealth at a greater distance than much better food provided for them at home. If their prey held out, they would eat till they were ready to burst, after which Nature had pointed out to them a certain root that gave them a general evacuation.

There was also another kind of root very juicy, but something rare and difficult to be found, which the Yahoos sought for with much eagerness and would suck it with great delight; and it produced in them the same effects that wine hath upon us. It would make them sometimes hug and sometimes tear one another; they would howl and grin, and chatter, and reel, and tumble, and then fall asleep in the mud.

I did indeed observe that the Yahoos were the only animals in this country subject to any diseases; which, however, were much fewer than horses have among us, and contracted not by any ill treatment they meet with, but by the nastiness and greediness of that sordid brute. Neither has their language any more than a general appellation for those maladies, which is borrowed from the name of the beast, and called *Hnea Yahoo*, or the *Yahoo's Evil*, and the cure prescribed is a mixture of their own dung and urine forcibly put down the Yahoo's throat. This I have since often known to have been taken with success, and do here freely recommend it to my countrymen for the public good, as an admirable specific against all diseases produced by repletion.

As to learning, government, arts, manufactures, and the like, my master confessed he could find little or no resemblance between the Yahoos of that country and those in ours. For he only meant to observe what parity there was in our natures. He had heard indeed some curious Houyhnhnms observe that in most herds there was a sort of ruling Yahoo (as among us there is generally some leading or principal stag in a park), who was always more deformed in body, and mischievous in disposition, than any of the rest. That this leader had usually a favourite as like himself as he could get, whose employment was to lick his master's feet and posteriors, and drive the female Yahoos to his kennel; for which he was now and then rewarded with a piece of ass's flesh. This favourite is hated by the whole herd, and therefore to protect himself keeps always near the person of his leader. He usually continues in office till a worse can be found; but the very moment he is discarded, his successor, at the head of all the Yahoos in that district, young and old, male and female, come in a body and discharge their excrements upon him from head to foot. But how far this might be applicable to our *courts* and *favourites*, and *ministers of state*, my master said I could best determine.

I durst make no return to this malicious insinuation, which debased human understanding below the sagacity of a common *hound*, who has judgment enough to distinguish and follow the cry of the ablest dog in the pack, without being ever mistaken.

My master told me there were some qualities remarkable in the Yahoos which he had not observed me to mention, or at least very slightly, in the accounts I had given him of humankind; he said those animals, like other brutes, had their females in common; but in this they differed, that the she-Yahoo would admit the male while she was pregnant and that the hees would quarrel and fight with the females as fiercely as with each other. Both which practices were such degrees of infamous brutality that no other sensitive creature ever arrived at.

Another thing he wondered at in the Yahoos was their strange disposition to nastiness and dirt, whereas there appears to be a natural love of cleanliness in all other animals. As to the two former accusations, I was glad to let them pass without any reply, because I had not a word to offer upon them in defence of my species, which otherwise I certainly had done from my own inclinations. But I could have easily vindicated humankind from the imputation of singularity upon the last article, if there had been any *swine* in that country (as unluckily for me there were not), which, although it may be a sweeter quadruped than a Yahoo cannot, I humbly conceive, in justice pretend to more cleanliness; and so his Honour himself must have owned, if he had seen their filthy way of feeding and their custom of wallowing and sleeping in the mud.

My master likewise mentioned another quality which his servants had discovered in several Yahoos, and to him was wholly unaccountable. He said a fancy would sometimes take a Yahoo to retire into a corner, to lie down and howl, and groan, and spurn away all that came near him, although he were young and fat, and wanted neither food nor water; nor did the servants imagine what could possibly ail him. And the only remedy they found was to set him to hard work, after which he would infallibly come to himself. To this I was silent out of partiality to my own kind; yet here I could plainly discover the true seeds of *spleen*,[2] which only seizeth on the *lazy*, the *luxurious*, and the *rich*; who, if they were forced to undergo the same regimen, I would undertake for the cure.

His Honour had farther observed that a female Yahoo would often stand behind a bank or a bush, to gaze on the young males passing by, and then appear and hide, using many antic gestures and grimaces, at which time it was observed that she had a most offensive smell; and when any of the males advanced, would slowly retire, looking often back, and with a counterfeit show of fear run off into some convenient place where she knew the male would follow her.

At other times if a female stranger came among them, three or four of her own sex would get about her and stare and chatter, and grin, and smell her all over, and then turn off with gestures that seemed to express contempt and disdain.

Perhaps my master might refine a little in these speculations, which he had drawn from what he observed himself or had been told him by others: however, I could not reflect without some amazement, and much sorrow, that the rudiments of *lewdness, coquetry, censure,* and *scandal* should have place by instinct in womankind.

I expected every moment that my master would accuse the

[2] The fashionable psychosomatic disease of the day, suitably vague in physical diagnosis because the function of the spleen was not known. It was revealed in fits of melancholy, gloom, ennui, hypochondria; enjoyed by those who could afford it; and frequently described in the literature of the day.

Yahoos of those unnatural appetites in both sexes so common among us. But Nature, it seems, hath not been so expert a schoolmistress; and these politer pleasures are entirely the productions of art and reason, on our side of the globe.

Chapter Eight: The author relateth several particulars of the Yahoos. The great virtues of the Houyhnhnms. The education and exercise of their youth. Their General Assembly.

As I ought to have understood human nature much better than I supposed it possible for my master to do, so it was easy to apply the character he gave of the Yahoos to myself and my countrymen, and I believed I could yet make farther discoveries from my own observation. I therefore often begged his Honour to let me go among the herds of Yahoos in the neighbourhood, to which he always very graciously consented, being perfectly convinced that the hatred I bore those brutes would never suffer me to be corrupted by them; and his Honour ordered one of his servants, a strong sorrel nag, very honest and good-natured, to be my guard, without whose protection I durst not undertake such adventures. For I have already told the reader how much I was pestered by those odious animals upon my first arrival. And I afterwards failed very narrowly three or four times of falling into their clutches, when I happened to stray at any distance without my hanger. And I have reason to believe they had some imagination that I was of their own species, which I often assisted myself, by stripping up my sleeves, and showing my naked arms and breast in their sight, when my protector was with me. At which times they would approach as near as they durst and imitate my actions after the manner of monkeys, but ever with great signs of hatred, as a tame jackdaw, with cap and stockings, is always persecuted by the wild ones, when he happens to be got among them.

They are prodigiously nimble from their infancy; however, I once caught a young male of three years old, and endeavoured by all marks of tenderness to make it quiet; but the little imp fell a-squalling, and scratching, and biting with such violence, that I was forced to let it go, and it was high time, for a whole troop of old ones came about us at the noise, but finding the cub was safe (for away it ran), and my sorrel nag being by, they durst not venture near us. I observed the young animal's flesh to smell very rank, and the stink was somewhat between a weasel and a fox, but much more disagreeable. I forgot another circumstance (and perhaps I might have the reader's pardon if it were wholly omitted) that while I held the odious vermin in my hands, it voided its filthy excrement of a yellow liquid substance all over my clothes; but by good fortune there was a small brook hard by where I washed myself as clean as I could, although I durst not come into my master's presence until I were sufficiently aired.

By what I could discover, the Yahoos appear to be the most unteachable of all animals, their capacities never reaching higher than to draw or carry burthens. Yet I am of opinion this defect ariseth chiefly from a perverse, restive disposition. For they are cunning, malicious, treacherous, and revengeful. They are strong and hardy, but of a cowardly spirit, and by consequence insolent, abject, and cruel. It is observed, that the red-haired of both sexes are more libidinous and mischievious than the rest, whom yet they much exceed in strength and activity.

The Houyhnhnms keep the Yahoos for present use in huts not far from the house; but the rest are sent abroad to certain fields where they dig up roots, eat several kinds of herbs, and search about for carrion, or sometimes catch weasels and *luhimuhs* (a sort of wild rat), which they greedily devour. Nature hath taught them to dig deep holes with their nails on the side of a rising ground, wherein they lie by themselves, only the kennels of the females are larger, sufficient to hold two or three cubs.

They swim from their infancy like frogs and are able to continue long under water, where they often take fish, which the females carry home to their young. And upon this occasion, I hope the reader will pardon my relating an odd adventure.

Being one day abroad with my protector the sorrel nag, and the weather exceeding hot, I entreated him to let me bathe in a river that was near. He consented, and I immediately stripped myself stark naked and went down softly into the stream. It happened that a young female Yahoo, standing behind a bank, saw the whole proceeding and, inflamed by desire, as the nag and I conjectured, came running with all speed and leaped into the water within five yards of the place where I bathed. I was never in my life so terribly frighted; the nag was grazing at some distance, not suspecting any harm. She embraced me after a most fulsome manner; I roared as loud as I could, and the nag came galloping towards me, whereupon she quitted her grasp, with the utmost reluctancy, and leaped upon the opposite bank, where she stood gazing and howling all the time I was putting on my clothes.

This was matter of diversion to my master and his family, as well as of mortification to myself. For now I could no longer deny that I was a real Yahoo in every limb and feature, since the females had a natural propensity to me as one of their own species: neither was the hair of this brute of a red colour (which might have been some excuse for an appetite a little irregular) but black as a sloe, and her countenance did not make an appearance altogether so hideous as the rest of the kind; for I think she could not be above eleven years old.

Having already lived three years in this country, the reader I suppose will expect that I should, like other travellers, give him some account of the manners and customs of its inhabitants, which it was indeed my principal study to learn.

As these noble Houyhnhnms are endowed by Nature with a

general disposition to all virtues and have no conceptions or ideas of what is evil in a rational creature, so their grand maxim is to cultivate *reason* and to be wholly governed by it. Neither is *reason* among them a point problematical as with us, where men can argue with plausibility on both sides of a question; but strikes you with immediate conviction; as it must needs do where it is not mingled, obscured, or discoloured by passion and interest. I remember it was with extreme difficulty that I could bring my master to understand the meaning of the word *opinion*, or how a point could be disputable; because *reason* taught us to affirm or deny only where we are certain; and beyond our knowledge we cannot do either. So that controversies, wranglings, disputes, and positiveness in false or dubious propositions are evils unknown among the Houyhnhnms. In the like manner, when I used to explain to him our several systems of *natural philosophy*, he would laugh that a creature pretending to *reason* should value itself upon the knowledge of other people's conjectures, and in things where that knowledge, if it were certain, could be of no use. Wherein he agreed entirely with the sentiments of Socrates, as Plato delivers them;[1] which I mention as the highest honour I can do that prince of philosophers. I have often since reflected what destruction such a doctrine would make in the libraries of Europe, and how many paths to fame would be then shut up in the learned world.

Friendship and *benevolence* are the two principal virtues among the Houyhnhnms, and these not confined to particular objects, but universal to the whole race. For a stranger from the remotest part is equally treated with the nearest neighbour, and wherever he goes looks upon himself as at home. They preserve *decency* and *civility* in the highest degrees, but are altogether ignorant of *ceremony*. They have no fondness [2] for

---

[1] In Plato's *Phaedo*, 97–98, Socrates describes his great expectations upon hearing Anaxagoras' doctrines read aloud and his great disappointment upon reading further himself.

[2] Indulgent or doting tenderness.

their colts or foals, but the care they take in educating them proceeds entirely from the dictates of *reason*. And I observed my master to show the same affection to his neighbour's issue that he had for his own. They will have it that Nature teaches them to love the whole species, and it is *reason* only that maketh a distinction of persons, where there is a superior degree of virtue.

When the matron Houyhnhnms have produced one of each sex, they no longer accompany with their consorts, except they lose one of their issue by some casualty, which very seldom happens: but in such a case they meet again, or, when the like accident befalls a person whose wife is past bearing, some other couple bestows on him one of their own colts, and then go together a second time till the mother be pregnant. This caution is necessary to prevent the country from being over-burthened with numbers. But the race of inferior Houyhnhnms bred up to be servants is not so strictly limited upon this article; these are allowed to produce three of each sex to be domestics in the noble families.

In their marriages they are exactly careful to choose such colours as will not make any disagreeable mixture in the breed. *Strength* is chiefly valued in the male, and *comeliness* in the female, not upon the account of *love*, but to preserve the race from degenerating; for where a female happens to excel in *strength*, a consort is chosen with regard to *comeliness*. Courtship, love, presents, jointures, settlements, have no place in their thoughts or terms whereby to express them in their language. The young couple meet and are joined merely because it is the determination of their parents and friends: it is what they see done every day, and they look upon it as one of the necessary actions in a reasonable being. But the violation of marriage, or any other unchastity, was never heard of: and the married pair pass their lives with the same friendship and mutual benevolence that they bear to all others of the same species who come in their way; without jealousy, fondness, quarrelling, or discontent.

In educating the youth of both sexes, their method is admirable and highly deserves our imitation. These are not suffered to taste a grain of oats, except upon certain days, till eighteen years old; nor milk but very rarely; and in summer they graze two hours in the morning and as many in the evening, which their parents likewise observe, but the servants are not allowed above half that time, and a great part of their grass is brought home, which they eat at the most convenient hours, when they can be best spared from work.

Temperance, industry, exercise and *cleanliness,* are the lessons equally enjoined to the young ones of both sexes: and my master thought it monstrous in us to give the females a different kind of education from the males except in some articles of domestic management; whereby, as he truly observed, one half of our natives were good for nothing but bringing children into the world: and to trust the care of their children to such useless animals, he said, was yet a greater instance of brutality.

But the Houyhnhnms train up their youth to strength, speed, and hardiness by exercising them in running races up and down steep hills or over hard stony grounds; and when they are all in a sweat, they are ordered to leap over head and ears into a pond or a river. Four times a year the youth of certain districts meet to show their proficiency in running and leaping and other feats of strength or agility, where the victor is rewarded with a song made in his or her praise. On this festival the servants drive a herd of Yahoos into the field, laden with hay and oats and milk for a repast to the Houyhnhnms; after which these brutes are immediately driven back again for fear of being noisome to the assembly.

Every fourth year, at the vernal equinox, there is a representative council of the whole nation, which meets in a plain about twenty miles from our house, and continues about five or six days. Here they inquire into the state and condition of the several districts; whether they abound or be deficient in hay or oats, or cows or Yahoos. And wherever there is any want (which is but seldom) it is immediately supplied by unanimous consent and contribution. Here likewise the regulation of children is settled: as for instance, if a Houyhnhnm hath two males, he changeth one of them with another who hath two females: and when a child hath been lost by any casualty, where the mother is past breeding, it is determined what family in the district shall breed another to supply the loss.

Chapter Nine: A grand debate at the General Assembly of the Houyhnhnms, and how it was determined. The learning of the Houyhnhnms. Their buildings. Their manner of burials. The defectiveness of their language.

One of these grand assemblies was held in my time, about three months before my departure, whither my master went as the representative of our district. In this council was resumed their old debate, and indeed the only debate that ever happened in their country; whereof my master after his return gave me a very particular account.

The question to be debated was whether the Yahoos should be exterminated from the face of the earth. One of the members for the affirmative offered several arguments of great strength and weight, alleging that, as the Yahoos were the most filthy, noisome, and deformed animal which nature ever produced, so they were the most restive and indocible, mischievous and malicious: they would privately suck the teats of the Houyhnhnms' cows, kill and devour their cats, trample down their oats and grass, if they were not continually watched, and commit a thousand other extravagancies. He took notice of a general tradition that Yahoos had not been always in their country: but that many ages ago two of these brutes appeared together upon a mountain, whether produced by the heat of the sun upon corrupted mud and slime or from the ooze and froth of the sea was never known. That these Yahoos engendered, and their brood in a short time grew so numerous as to overrun and infest the whole nation. That the Houyhnhnms, to get rid of this evil, made a general hunting, and at last enclosed the whole herd; and destroying the elder, every Houyhnhnm kept two young ones in a kennel, and brought them to such a degree of tameness as an animal so savage by nature can be capable of acquiring, using them for draught and carriage. That there seemed to be much truth in this tradition, and that those creatures could not be *ylnhniamshy* (or *aborigines* of the land) because of the violent hatred the Houyhnhnms, as well as all other animals, bore them; which although their evil disposition sufficiently deserved, could never have arrived at so high a degree if they had been aborigines, or else they would have long since been rooted out. That the inhabitants taking a fancy to use the service of the Yahoos, had very imprudently neglected to cultivate the breed of asses, which were a comely animal, easily kept, more tame and orderly, without any offensive smell, strong enough for labour, although they yield to the other in agility of body; and if their braying be no agreeable sound, it is far preferable to the horrible howlings of the Yahoos.

Several others declared their sentiments to the same purpose, when my master proposed an expedient to the assembly, whereof he had indeed borrowed the hint from me. He approved of the tradition, mentioned by the honourable member who spoke before, and affirmed that the two Yahoos said to be first seen among them had been driven thither over the sea; that coming to land and being forsaken by their companions, they retired to the mountains and, degenerating by degrees, became in process of time much more savage than those of their own species in the country from whence these two originals came. The reason of his assertion was that he had now in his possession a certain wonderful Yahoo (meaning myself) which most of them had heard of and many of them had seen. He then related to them how he first found me; that my body was all covered with an artificial composure of the skins and hairs of other animals: that I spoke in a language of my own and had thoroughly learned theirs: that I had related to him the accidents which brought me thither: that when he saw me without my covering, I was an exact Yahoo in every part, only of a whiter colour, less hairy, and with shorter claws. He added, how I had endeavoured to persuade him that in my own and other countries the Yahoos acted as the governing, rational animal, and held the Houyhnhnms in servitude: that he observed in me all the qualities of a Yahoo, only a little more civilized by some tincture of reason, which however was in a degree as far inferior to the Houyhnhnm race as the Yahoos of their country were to me: that, among other things, I mentioned a custom we had of castrating Houyhnhnms when they were young in order to render them tame; that the operation was easy and safe; that it was no shame to learn wisdom from brutes, as industry is taught by the ant and building by the swallow. (For so I translate the word *lyhannh*, although it be a much larger fowl.) That this invention might be practised upon the younger Yahoos here, which, besides rendering them tractable and fitter for use, would in an age put an end to the whole species without destroying life. That in the meantime the Houyhnhnms should be *exhorted* to cultivate the breed of asses, which, as they are in all respects more valuable brutes, so they have this advantage, to be fit for service at five years old, which the others are not till twelve.

This was all my master thought fit to tell me at that time of what passed in the grand council. But he was pleased to conceal one particular which related personally to myself, whereof I soon felt the unhappy effect, as the reader will know in its proper place, and from whence I date all the succeeding misfortunes of my life.

The Houyhnhnms have no letters, and consequently their knowledge is all traditional. But there happening few events of any moment among a people so well united, naturally disposed to every virtue, wholly governed by reason, and cut off from all commerce with other nations, the historical part is easily preserved without burthening their memories. I have already observed that they are subject to no diseases, and therefore can have no need of physicians. However, they have excellent medicines composed of herbs, to cure accidental bruises and cuts in the pastern or frog [1] of the foot by sharp stones, as well as other maims and hurts in the several parts of the body.

They calculate the year by the revolution of the sun and the moon, but use no subdivisions into weeks. They are well enough acquainted with the motions of those two luminaries and understand the nature of eclipses; and this is the utmost progress of their astronomy.

In poetry they must be allowed to excel all other mortals; wherein the justness of their similes and the minuteness as well as exactness of their descriptions, are indeed inimitable. Their verses abound very much in both of these, and usually contain either some exalted notions of friendship and benevolence, or the praises of those who were victors in races and other bodily exercises. Their buildings, although very rude and simple, are not inconvenient, but well contrived to defend them from all injuries of cold and heat. They have a kind of tree which at forty years old loosens in the root and falls with the first storm; it grows very straight and, being pointed like stakes with a sharp stone (for the Houyhnhnms know not the use of iron), they stick them erect in the ground about ten inches asunder, and then weave in oat-straw or sometimes wattles betwixt them. The roof is made after the same manner and so are the doors.

The Houyhnhnms use the hollow part between the pastern and the hoof of their forefeet as we do our hands, and this with greater dexterity than I could at first imagine. I have seen a white mare of our family thread a needle (which I lent her on purpose) with that joint. They milk their cows, reap their

[1] That is, either the portion of the foot between hoof and fetlock or the horny sole of the foot.

oats, and do all the work which requires hands, in the same manner. They have a kind of hard flints, which, by grinding against other stones, they form into instruments that serve instead of wedges, axes, and hammers. With tools made of these flints they likewise cut their hay and reap their oats, which there groweth naturally in several fields: the Yahoos draw home the sheaves in carriages, and the servants tread them in certain covered huts, to get out the grain, which is kept in stores. They make a rude kind of earthen and wooden vessels and bake the former in the sun.

If they can avoid casualties, they die only of old age, and are buried in the obscurest places that can be found, their friends and relations expressing neither joy nor grief at their departure; nor does the dying person discover the least regret that he is leaving the world, any more than if he were upon returning home from a visit to one of his neighbours; I remember my master having once made an appointment with a friend and his family to come to his house upon some affair of importance; on the day fixed, the mistress and her two children came very late; she made two excuses, first for her husband, who, as she said, happened that very morning to *lhnuwnh*. The word is strongly expressive in their language but not easily rendered into English; it signifies, *to retire to his first mother*. Her excuse for not coming sooner was that, her husband dying late in the morning, she was a good while consulting her servants about a convenient place where his body should be laid; and I observed she behaved herself at our house as cheerfully as the rest: she died about three months after.

They live generally to seventy or seventy-five years, very seldom to fourscore: some weeks before their death they feel a gradual decay, but without pain. During this time they are much visited by their friends because they cannot go abroad with their usual ease and satisfaction. However, about ten days before their death, which they seldom fail in computing, they return the visits that have been made them by those who are nearest in the neighbourhood, being carried in a convenient sledge drawn by Yahoos, which vehicle they use, not only

upon this occasion, but when they grow old, upon long journeys, or when they are lamed by any accident. And therefore
when the dying Houyhnhnms return those visits, they take a
solemn leave of their friends, as if they were going to some
remote part of the country where they designed to pass the
rest of their lives.

I know not whether it may be worth observing that the
Houyhnhnms have no word in their language to express anything that is evil, except what they borrow from the deformities or ill qualities of the Yahoos. Thus they denote the folly
of a servant, an omission of a child, a stone that cuts their feet,
a continuance of foul or unseasonable weather, and the like,
by adding to each the epithet of *yahoo*. For instance, *hhnm
yahoo, whnaholm yahoo, ynlhmnawihlma yahoo,* and an ill-
contrived house *ynholmhnmrohlnw yahoo.*

I could with great pleasure enlarge farther upon the manners and virtues of this excellent people; but, intending in a
short time to publish a volume by itself expressly upon that
subject, I refer the reader thither.[2] And in the meantime, proceed to relate my own sad catastrophe.

*Chapter Ten: The author's economy and happy life among the
Houyhnhnms. His great improvement in virtue by conversing with
them. Their conversations. The author hath notice given him by
his master that he must depart from the country. He falls into a
swoon for grief, but submits. He contrives and finishes a canoe, by
the help of a fellow servant, and puts to sea at a venture.*

I had settled my little economy to my own heart's content. My
master had ordered a room to be made for me after their manner, about six yards from the house, the sides and floors of

[2] This was a typical promise of travel writers, and Gulliver's remained, typically, unfulfilled.

which I plastered with clay, and covered with rush mats of my own contriving; I had beaten hemp, which there grows wild, and made of it a sort of ticking: this I filled with the feathers of several birds I had taken with springes made of Yahoos' hairs, and were excellent food. I had worked two chairs with my knife, the sorrel nag helping me in the grosser and more laborious part. When my clothes were worn to rags, I made myself others with the skins of rabbits, and of a certain beautiful animal about the same size, called *nnuhnoh*, the skin of which is covered with a fine down. Of these I likewise made very tolerable stockings. I soled my shoes with wood which I cut from a tree, and fitted to the upper leather, and when this was worn out, I supplied it with the skins of Yahoos dried in the sun. I often got honey out of hollow trees, which I mingled with water, or eat it with my bread. No man could more verify the truth of these two maxims, *That nature is very easily satisfied;* and *That necessity is the mother of invention.* I enjoyed perfect health of body and tranquillity of mind; I did not feel the treachery or inconstancy of a friend, nor the injuries of a secret or open enemy. I had no occasion of bribing, flattering, or pimping to procure the favour of any great man or of his minion. I wanted no fence against fraud or oppression; here was neither physician to destroy my body, nor lawyer to ruin my fortune; no informer to watch my words and actions, or forge accusations against me for hire: here were no gibers, censurers, backbiters, pickpockets, highwaymen, housebreakers, attorneys, bawds, buffoons, gamesters, politicians, wits, splenetics, tedious talkers, controvertists, ravishers, murderers, robbers, virtuosos: no leaders or followers of party and faction: no encouragers to vice by seducement or examples: no dungeon, axes, gibbets, whipping-posts, or pillories: no cheating shopkeepers or mechanics: no pride, vanity, or affectation: no fops, bullies, drunkards, strolling whores, or poxes: no ranting, lewd, expensive wives: no stupid, proud pedants: no importunate, overbearing, quarrelsome, noisy, roaring, empty, conceited, swearing companions: no scoun-

drels raised from the dust upon the merit of their vices, or
nobility thrown into it on account of their virtues: no lords,
fiddlers, judges, or dancing-masters.

I had the favour of being admitted to several Houyhnhnms
who came to visit or dine with my master; where his Honour
graciously suffered me to wait in the room and listen to their
discourse. Both he and his company would often descend to
ask me questions and receive my answers. I had also sometimes
the honour of attending my master in his visits to others. I
never presumed to speak except in answer to a question, and
then I did it with inward regret, because it was a loss of so
much time for improving myself: but I was infinitely delighted
with the station of an humble auditor in such conversations,
where nothing passed but what was useful, expressed in the
fewest and most significant words: where (as I have already said)
the greatest decency was observed, without the least degree of
ceremony; where no person spoke without being pleased himself and pleasing his companions; where there was no interrup-
tions, tediousness, heat, or difference of sentiments. They have
a notion that, when people are met together, a short silence
doth much improve conversation: this I found to be true; for
during those little intermissions of talk, new ideas would arise
in their minds, which very much enlivened the discourse.
Their subjects are generally on friendship and benevolence,
on order and economy, sometimes upon the visible operations
of nature, or ancient traditions, upon the bounds and limits of
virtue, upon the unerring rules of reason, or upon some determinations to be taken at the next Great Assembly, and
often upon the various excellencies of poetry. I may add without vanity that my presence often gave them sufficient matter
for discourse, because it afforded my master an occasion of
letting his friends into the history of me and my country,
upon which they were all pleased to descant in a manner not
very advantageous to humankind; and for that reason I shall
not repeat what they said: only I may be allowed to observe,
that his Honour, to my great admiration, appeared to under-

stand the nature of Yahoos much better than myself. He went through all our vices and follies, and discovered many which I had never mentioned to him, by only supposing what qualities a Yahoo of their country, with a small proportion of reason, might be capable of exerting; and concluded, with too much probability, how vile as well as miserable such a creature must be.

I freely confess that all the little knowledge I have of any value was acquired by the lectures I received from my master and from hearing the discourses of him and his friends; to which I should be prouder to listen, than to dictate to the greatest and wisest assembly in Europe. I admired the strength, comeliness, and speed of the inhabitants; and such a constellation of virtues in such amiable persons produced in me the highest veneration. At first, indeed, I did not feel that natural awe which the Yahoos and all other animals bear towards them; but it grew upon me by degrees, much sooner than I imagined, and was mingled with a respectful love and gratitude, that they would condescend to distinguish me from the rest of my species.

When I thought of my family, my friends, my countrymen, or human race in general, I considered them as they really were, Yahoos in shape and disposition, perhaps a little more civilized, and qualified with the gift of speech, but making no other use of reason than to improve and multiply those vices whereof their brethren in this country had only the share that Nature allotted them. When I happened to behold the reflection of my own form in a lake or fountain, I turned away my face in horror and detestation of myself, and could better endure the sight of a common Yahoo, than of my own person. By conversing with the Houyhnhnms, and looking upon them with delight, I fell to imitate their gait and gesture, which is now grown into a habit, and my friends often tell me in a blunt way that I *trot like a horse;* which, however, I take for a great compliment: neither shall I disown that in speaking I am apt to fall into the voice and manner of the Houyhnhnms, and hear myself ridiculed on that account without the least mortification.

In the midst of this happiness, when I looked upon myself to be fully settled for life, my master sent for me one morning a little earlier than his usual hour. I observed by his countenance that he was in some perplexity and at a loss how to begin what he had to speak. After a short silence he told me he did not know how I would take what he was going to say; that in the last General Assembly, when the affair of the Yahoos was entered upon, the representatives had taken offence at his keeping a Yahoo (meaning myself) in his family more like a Houyhnhnm than a brute animal. That he was known frequently to converse with me, as if he could receive some advantage or pleasure in my company: that such a practice was not agreeable to reason or nature, or a thing ever heard of before among them. The assembly did therefore *exhort* him either to employ me like the rest of my species, or command me to swim back to the place from whence I came. That the first of these expedients was utterly rejected by all the Houyhnhnms who had ever seen me at his house or their own: for they alleged that, because I had some rudiments of reason, added to the natural pravity of those animals, it was to be feared I might be able to seduce them into the woody and mountainous parts of the country, and bring them in troops by night to destroy the Houyhnhnms' cattle, as being naturally of the ravenous kind and averse from labour.

My master added that he was daily pressed by the Houyhnhnms of the neighbourhood to have the assembly's *exhortation* executed, which he could not put off much longer. He doubted it would be impossible for me to swim to another country, and therefore wished I would contrive some sort of vehicle resembling those I had described to him, that might carry me on the sea, in which work I should have the assistance of his own servants, as well as those of his neighbours. He concluded that for his own part he could have been content to keep me in his service as long as I lived, because he found

I had cured myself of some bad habits and dispositions by endeavouring, as far as my inferior nature was capable, to imitate the Houyhnhnms.

I should here observe to the reader that a decree of the General Assembly in this country is expressed by the word *hnhloayn*, which signifies an *exhortation*, as near as I can render it: for they have no conception how a rational creature can be *compelled*, but only advised or *exhorted*, because no person can disobey reason without giving up his claim to be a rational creature.

I was struck with the utmost grief and despair at my master's discourse, and, being unable to support the agonies I was under, I fell into a swoon at his feet; when I came to myself he told me that he concluded I had been dead. (For these people are subject to no such imbecilities of nature.) I answered, in a faint voice, that death would have been too great an happiness; that although I could not blame the assembly's *exhortation*, or the urgency of his friends, yet, in my weak and corrupt judgment, I thought it might consist with reason to have been less rigorous. That I could not swim a league, and probably the nearest land to theirs might be distant above an hundred; that many materials, necessary for making a small vessel to carry me off, were wholly wanting in this country, which, however, I would attempt in obedience and gratitude to his Honour, although I concluded the thing to be impossible, and therefore looked on myself as already devoted [1] to destruction. That the certain prospect of an unnatural death was the least of my evils: for, supposing I should escape with life by some strange adventure, how could I think with temper [2] of passing my days among Yahoos and relapsing into my old corruptions for want of examples to lead and keep me within the paths of virtue? That I knew too well upon what solid reasons all the determinations of the wise Houyhnhnms

---

[1] Doomed.
[2] Equanimity.

were founded not to be shaken by arguments of mine, a miserable Yahoo; and therefore, after presenting him with my
humble thanks for the offer of his servants' assistance in making a vessel and desiring a reasonable time for so difficult a
work, I told him I would endeavour to preserve a wretched
being; and, if ever I returned to England, was not without
hopes of being useful to my own species by celebrating the
praises of the renowned Houyhnhnms and proposing their
virtues to the imitation of mankind.

My master in a few words made me a very gracious reply,
allowed me the space of two months to finish my boat, and
ordered the sorrel nag, my fellow-servant (for so at this distance I may presume to call him) to follow my instructions,
because I told my master that his help would be sufficient, and
I knew he had a tenderness for me.

In his company my first business was to go to that part of
the coast where my rebellious crew had ordered me to be set
on shore. I got upon a height and, looking on every side into
the sea, fancied I saw a small island towards the northeast: I
took out my pocket-glass and could then clearly distinguish it
about five leagues off, as I computed; but it appeared to the
sorrel nag to be only a blue cloud: for, as he had no conception of any country beside his own, so he could not be as expert in distinguishing remote objects at sea as we who so much
converse in that element.

After I had discovered this island, I considered no farther;
but resolved it should, if possible, be the first place of my
banishment, leaving the consequence to fortune.

I returned home and, consulting with the sorrel nag, we
went into a copse at some distance, where I with my knife,
and he with a sharp flint fastened very artificially, after their
manner, to a wooden handle, cut down several oak wattles
about the thickness of a walking-staff, and some larger pieces.
But I shall not trouble the reader with a particular description
of my own mechanics; let it suffice to say that in six weeks'
time, with the help of the sorrel nag, who performed the parts

that required most labour, I finished a sort of Indian canoe, but much larger, covering it with the skins of Yahoos well stitched together with hempen threads of my own making. My sail was likewise composed of the skins of the same animal; but I made use of the youngest I could get, the older being too tough and thick, and I likewise provided myself with four paddles. I laid in a stock of boiled flesh of rabbits and fowls, and took with me two vessels, one filled with milk and the other with water.

I tried my canoe in a large pond near my master's house and then corrected in it what was amiss; stopping all the chinks with Yahoos' tallow till I found it staunch and able to bear me and my freight. And when it was as complete as I could possibly make it, I had it drawn on a carriage very gently by Yahoos to the seaside, under the conduct of the sorrel nag and another servant.

When all was ready and the day came for my departure, I took leave of my master and lady and the whole family, my eyes flowing with tears and my heart quite sunk with grief. But his Honour, out of curiosity, and perhaps (if I may speak it without vanity) partly out of kindness, was determined to see me in my canoe and got several of his neighbouring friends to accompany him. I was forced to wait above an hour for the tide, and then observing the wind very fortunately bearing towards the island to which I intended to steer my course, I took a second leave of my master: but as I was going to prostrate myself to kiss his hoof, he did me the honour to raise it gently to my mouth. I am not ignorant how much I have been censured for mentioning this last particular. Detractors are pleased to think it improbable that so illustrious a person should descend to give so great a mark of distinction to a creature so inferior as I. Neither have I forgot how apt some travellers are to boast of extraordinary favours they have received. But if these censurers were better acquainted with the noble and courteous disposition of the Houyhnhnms, they would soon change their opinion.

I paid my respects to the rest of the Houyhnhnms in his Honour's company; then getting into my canoe, I pushed off from shore.

Chapter Eleven: The author's dangerous voyage. He arrives at New Holland, hoping to settle there. Is wounded with an arrow by one of the natives. Is seized and carried by force into a Portuguese ship. The great civilities of the captain. The author arrives at England.

I began this desperate voyage on February 15, 1714–5;[1] at 9 o'clock in the morning. The wind was very favourable; however, I made use at first only of my paddles, but considering I should soon be weary and that the wind might probably chop about, I ventured to set up my little sail; and thus with the help of the tide I went at the rate of a league and a half an hour, as near as I could guess. My master and his friends continued on the shore till I was almost out of sight; and I often heard the sorrel nag (who always loved me) crying out, *Hnuy illa nyha maiah Yahoo*, Take care of thyself, gentle Yahoo.

My design was, if possible, to discover some small island uninhabited, yet sufficient by my labour to furnish me with necessaries of life, which I would have thought a greater happiness than to be first minister in the politest court of Europe; so horrible was the idea I conceived of returning to live in the society and under the government of Yahoos. For in such a solitude as I desired, I could at least enjoy my own thoughts and reflect with delight on the virtues of those inimitable Houyhnhnms, without any opportunity of degenerating into the vices and corruptions of my own species.

The reader may remember what I related when my crew

[1] That is, 1715; in England, New Year's Day remained March 25th until 1753.

conspired against me and confined me to my cabin. How I continued there several weeks, without knowing what course we took, and when I was put ashore in the long-boat, how the sailors told me with oaths, whether true or false, that they knew not in what part of the world we were. However, I did then believe us to be about ten degrees southward of the Cape of Good Hope, or about 45 degrees southern latitude, as I gathered from some general words I overheard among them, being, I supposed, to the southeast in their intended voyage to Madagascar. And although this were but little better than conjecture, yet I resolved to steer my course eastward, hoping to reach the southwest coast of New Holland, and perhaps some such island as I desired lying westward of it. The wind was full west, and by six in the evening I computed I had gone eastward at least eighteen leagues, when I spied a very small island about half a league off, which I soon reached. It was nothing but a rock, with one creek, naturally arched by the force of tempests. Here I put in my canoe and, climbing a part of the rock, I could plainly discover land to the east, extending from south to north. I lay all night in my canoe and, repeating my voyage early in the morning, I arrived in seven hours to the southeast point of New Holland. This confirmed me in the opinion I have long entertained that the maps and charts place this country at least three degrees more to the east than it really is; which thought I communicated many years ago to my worthy friend Mr. Herman Moll,[2] and gave him my reasons for it, although he hath rather chosen to follow other authors.

I saw no inhabitants in the place where I landed and, being unarmed, I was afraid of venturing far into the country. I found some shellfish on the shore and eat them raw, not daring to kindle a fire for fear of being discovered by the natives. I

[2] Herman Moll (d. 1732), a Dutchman who settled in England about 1698. His many maps became widely accepted in England, and his map of the world (1719) was the basis of those designed for *Gulliver's Travels*.

continued three days feeding on oysters and limpets, to save my own provisions, and I fortunately found a brook of excellent water, which gave me great relief.

On the fourth day, venturing out early a little too far, I saw twenty or thirty natives upon a height not above five hundred yards from me. They were stark naked, men, women, and children, round a fire, as I could discover by the smoke. One of them spied me and gave notice to the rest; five of them advanced towards me, leaving the women and children at the fire. I made what haste I could to the shore and, getting into my canoe, shoved off: the savages, observing me retreat, ran after me; and before I could get far enough into the sea, discharged an arrow which wounded me deeply on the inside of my left knee (I shall carry the mark to my grave). I apprehended the arrow might be poisoned and, paddling out of the reach of their darts (being a calm day), I made a shift to suck the wound and dress it as well as I could.

I was at a loss what to do, for I durst not return to the same landing-place, but stood to the north, and was forced to paddle; for the wind, although very gentle, was against me, blowing northwest. As I was looking about for a secure landing-place, I saw a sail to the north-northeast, which appearing every minute more visible, I was in some doubt whether I should wait for them or no; but at last my detestation of the Yahoo race prevailed, and turning my canoe, I sailed and paddled together to the south, and got into the same creek from whence I set out in the morning, choosing rather to trust myself among these barbarians than live with European Yahoos. I drew up my canoe as close as I could to the shore and hid myself behind a stone by the little brook, which, as I have already said, was excellent water.

The ship came within a half a league of this creek, and sent out her long-boat with vessels to take in fresh water (for the place it seems was very well known), but I did not observe it until the boat was almost on shore, and it was too late to seek another hiding-place. The seamen at their landing observed my canoe and, rummaging it all over, easily conjectured that the owner could not be far off. Four of them well armed searched every cranny and lurking-hole, till at last they found me flat on my face behind the stone. They gazed a while in admiration at my strange uncouth dress, my coat made of skins, my wooden-soled shoes, and my furred stockings; from whence, however, they concluded I was not a native of the place, who all go naked. One of the seamen in Portuguese bid me rise, and asked who I was. I understood that language very well and, getting upon my feet, said I was a poor Yahoo, banished from the Houyhnhnms, and desired they would please to let me depart. They admired to hear me answer them in their own tongue, and saw by my complexion I must be an European; but were at loss to know what I meant by Yahoos and Houyhnhnms, and at the same time fell a-laughing at my strange tone in speaking, which resembled the neighing of a horse. I trembled all the while betwixt fear and hatred: I again desired leave to depart and was gently moving to my canoe; but they laid hold on me, desiring to know what country I was of, whence I came, with many other questions. I told them I was born in England, from whence I came about five years ago, and then their country and ours were at peace. I therefore hoped they would not treat me as an enemy, since I meant them no harm, but was a poor Yahoo, seeking some desolate place where to pass the remainder of his unfortunate life.

When they began to talk, I thought I never heard or saw anything so unnatural; for it appeared to me as monstrous as if a dog or a cow should speak in England, or a Yahoo in Houyhnhnmland. The honest Portuguese were equally amazed at my strange dress and the odd manner of delivering my words, which however they understood very well. They spoke to me with great humanity and said they were sure their captain would carry me *gratis* to Lisbon, from whence I might return to my own country; that two of the seamen would go back to the ship, inform the captain of what they had seen, and receive his orders; in the meantime, unless I would give my solemn oath not to fly, they would secure me by force. I thought it best to comply with their proposal. They were very curious to know my story, but I gave them very little satisfaction; and they all conjectured that my misfortunes had impaired my reason. In two hours the boat, which went loaden with vessels of water, returned with the captain's commands to fetch me on board. I fell on my knees to preserve my liberty; but all was in vain, and the men, having tied me with cords, heaved me into the boat, from whence I was taken into the ship, and from thence into the captain's cabin.

His name was Pedro de Mendez; he was a very courteous and generous person; he entreated me to give some account of myself, and desired to know what I would eat or drink; said I should be used as well as himself, and spoke so many obliging things that I wondered to find such civilities from a Yahoo. However, I remained silent and sullen; I was ready to faint at the very smell of him and his men. At last I desired something to eat out of my own canoe; but he ordered me a chicken and some excellent wine, and then directed that I should be put to bed in a very clean cabin. I would not undress myself, but lay on the bed-clothes, and in half an hour stole out, when I thought the crew was at dinner, and getting to the side of the ship was going to leap into the sea, and swim for my life rather than continue among Yahoos. But one of the seamen prevented me, and having informed the captain, I was chained to my cabin.

After dinner Don Pedro came to me, and desired to know my reason for so desperate an attempt: assured me he only meant to do me all the service he was able, and spoke so very movingly that at last I descended to treat him like an animal which had some little portion of reason. I gave him a very short relation of my voyage, of the conspiracy against me by my own men, of the country where they set me on shore, and of my three years' residence there. All which he looked upon as if it were a dream or a vision; whereat I took great offence; for I had quite forgot the faculty of lying, so peculiar to

Yahoos in all countries where they preside, and, consequently, the disposition of suspecting truth in others of their own species. I asked him, whether it were the custom of his country to *say the thing that was not*. I assured him I had almost forgot what he meant by falsehood, and, if I had lived a thousand years in Houyhnhnmland, I should never have heard a lie from the meanest servant; that I was altogether indifferent whether he believed me or no; but however, in return for his favours, I would give so much allowance to the corruption of his nature as to answer any objection he would please to make, and he might easily discover the truth.

The captain, a wise man, after many endeavours to catch me tripping in some part of my story, at last began to have a better opinion of my veracity, and the rather because, he confessed, he met with a Dutch skipper, who pretended to have landed with five others of his crew upon a certain island or continent south of New Holland, where they went for fresh water, and observed a horse driving before him several animals exactly resembling those I described under the name of Yahoos, with some other particulars, which the captain said he had forgot, because he then concluded them all to be lies. But he added that since I professed so inviolable an attachment to truth, I must give him my word of honour to bear him company in this voyage without attempting anything against my life, or else he would continue me a prisoner till we arrived in Lisbon. I gave him the promise he required; but at the same time protested that I would suffer the greatest hardships rather than return to live among Yahoos.

Our voyage passed without any considerable accident. In gratitude to the captain I sometimes sat with him at his earnest request, and strove to conceal my antipathy against humankind, although it often broke out, which he suffered to pass without observation. But the greatest part of the day I confined myself to my cabin, to avoid seeing any of the crew. The captain had often entreated me to strip myself of my savage dress, and offered to lend me the best suit of clothes he had. This I would not be prevailed on to accept, abhorring to cover myself with anything that had been on the back of a Yahoo. I only desired he would lend me two clean shirts, which having been washed since he wore them, I believed would not so much defile me. These I changed every second day, and washed them myself.

We arrived at Lisbon, Nov. 5, 1715. At our landing the captain forced me to cover myself with his cloak, to prevent the rabble from crowding about me. I was conveyed to his own house, and, at my earnest request, he led me up to the highest room backwards.[3] I conjured him to conceal from all persons what I had told him of the Houyhnhnms, because the least hint of such a story would not only draw numbers of people to see me, but probably put me in danger of being imprisoned, or burnt by the Inquisition. The captain persuaded me to accept a suit of clothes newly made, but I would not suffer the tailor to take my measure; however, Don Pedro being almost of my size, they fitted me well enough. He accoutred me with other necessaries all new, which I aired for twenty-four hours before I would use them.

The captain had no wife, nor above three servants, none of which were suffered to attend at meals, and his whole deportment was so obliging, added to very good *human* understanding, that I really began to tolerate his company. He gained so far upon me that I ventured to look out of the back window. By degrees I was brought into another room, from whence I peeped into the street, but drew my head back in a fright. In a week's time he seduced me down to the door. I found my terror gradually lessened, but my hatred and contempt seemed to increase. I was at last bold enough to walk the street in his company, but kept my nose well stopped with rue, or sometimes with tobacco.

In ten days Don Pedro, to whom I had given some account of my domestic affairs, put it upon me as a point of honour and conscience that I ought to return to my native country and

---

[3] At the back of the house.

live at home with my wife and children. He told me there was an English ship in the port just ready to sail, and he would furnish me with all things necessary. It would be tedious to repeat his arguments and my contradictions. He said it was altogether impossible to find such a solitary island as I had desired to live in; but I might command in my own house, and pass my time in a manner as recluse as I pleased.

I complied at last, finding I could not do better. I left Lisbon the 24th day of November in an English merchantman, but who was the master I never inquired. Don Pedro accompanied me to the ship and lent me twenty pounds. He took kind leave of me and embraced me at parting, which I bore as well as I could. During this last voyage I had no commerce with the master or any of his men, but pretending I was sick kept close in my cabin. On the fifth of December, 1715, we cast anchor in the Downs about nine in the morning, and at three in the afternoon I got safe to my house at Redriff.

My wife and family received me with great surprise and joy, because they concluded me certainly dead; but I must freely confess the sight of them filled me only with hatred, disgust, and contempt, and the more by reflecting on the near alliance I had to them. For although, since my unfortunate exile from the Houyhnhnm country, I had compelled myself to tolerate the sight of Yahoos, and to converse with Don Pedro de Mendez, yet my memory and imaginations were perpetually filled with the virtues and ideas of those exalted Houyhnhnms. And when I began to consider that by copulating with one of the Yahoo species I had become a parent of more, it struck me with the utmost shame, confusion, and horror.

As soon as I entered the house, my wife took me in her arms and kissed me, at which, having not been used to the touch of that odious animal for so many years, I fell in a swoon for almost an hour. At the time I am writing it is five years since my last return to England: during the first year I could not endure my wife or children in my presence; the very smell of them was intolerable, much less could I suffer them to eat in

the same room. To this hour they dare not presume to touch
my bread or drink out of the same cup, neither was I ever able
to let one of them take me by the hand. The first money I laid
out was to buy two young stone-horses;[4] which I keep in a
good stable, and next to them the groom is my greatest favourite; for I feel my spirits revived by the smell he contracts
in the stable. My horses understand me tolerably well; I converse with them at least four hours every day. They are
strangers to bridle or saddle; they live in great amity with me
and friendship to each other.

*Chapter Twelve: The author's veracity. His design in publishing
this work. His censure of those travellers who swerve from the
truth. The author clears himself from any sinister ends in writing.
An objection answered. The method of planting colonies. His native
country commended. The right of the Crown to those countries
described by the author is justified. The difficulty of conquering
them. The author takes his last leave of the reader, proposeth his
manner of living for the future, gives good advice, and concludeth.*

Thus, gentle reader, I have given thee a faithful history of my
travels for sixteen years and above seven months, wherein I
have not been so studious of ornament as of truth. I could perhaps like others have astonished thee with strange improbable
tales; but I rather chose to relate plain matter of fact in the
simplest manner and style, because my principal design was to
inform and not to amuse thee.

It is easy for us who travel into remote countries, which are
seldom visited by Englishmen or other Europeans, to form descriptions of wonderful animals both at sea and land. Whereas
a traveller's chief aim should be to make men wiser and better,

---

[4] Stallions.

and to improve their minds by the bad as well as good example of what they deliver concerning foreign places.

I could heartily wish a law were enacted that every traveller, before he were permitted to publish his voyages, should be obliged to make oath before the Lord High Chancellor that all he intended to print was absolutely true to the best of his knowledge; for then the world would no longer be deceived as it usually is while some writers, to make their works pass the better upon the public, impose the grossest falsities on the unwary reader. I have perused several books of travels with great delight in my younger days; but having since gone over most parts of the globe and been able to contradict many fabulous accounts from my own observation, it hath given me a great disgust against this part of reading, and some indignation to see the credulity of mankind so impudently abused. Therefore since my acquaintance were pleased to think my poor endeavours might not be unacceptable to my country, I imposed on myself as a maxim, never to be swerved from, that I would *strictly adhere to truth;* neither indeed can I be ever under the least temptation to vary from it, while I retain in my mind the lectures and example of my noble master and the other illustrious Houyhnhnms, of whom I had so long the honour to be an humble hearer.

> —*Nec si miserum Fortuna Sinonem*
> *Finxit, vanum etiam mendacemque improba finget.*[1]

I know very well how little reputation is to be got by writings which require neither genius nor learning, nor indeed any other talent, except a good memory or an exact journal. I know likewise that writers of travels, like dictionary-makers, are

[1] "Nor, if false Fortune has made Sinon wretched, will she make him empty and untruthful as well" (Virgil, *Aeneid* II, 79–80). But Sinon is the treacherous Greek who is about to persuade the Trojans to admit the horse into their city.

sunk into oblivion by the weight and bulk of those who come last and therefore lie uppermost. And it is highly probable that such travellers who shall hereafter visit the countries described in this work of mine, may, by detecting my errors (if there be any) and adding many new discoveries of their own, jostle me out of vogue and stand in my place, making the world forget that ever I was an author. This indeed would be too great a mortification if I wrote for fame: but, as my sole intention was the PUBLIC GOOD, I cannot be altogether disappointed. For who can read of the virtues I have mentioned in the glorious Houyhnhnms without being ashamed of his own vices, when he considers himself as the reasoning, governing animal of his country? I shall say nothing of those remote nations where Yahoos preside, amongst which the least corrupted are the Brobdingnagians, whose wise maxims in morality and government it would be our happiness to observe. But I forbear descanting further, and rather leave the judicious reader to his own remarks and applications.

I am not a little pleased that this work of mine can possibly meet with no censurers: for what objections can be made against a writer who relates only plain facts that happened in such distant countries, where we have not the least interest with respect either to trade or negotiations? I have carefully avoided every fault with which common writers of travels are often too justly charged. Besides, I meddle not the least with any *party*, but write without passion, prejudice, or ill-will against any man or number of men whatsoever. I write for the noblest end, to inform and instruct mankind, over whom I may, without breach of modesty, pretend to some superiority from the advantages I received by conversing so long among the most accomplished Houyhnhnms. I write without any view towards profit or praise. I never suffer a word to pass that may look like reflection, or possibly give the least offence even to those who are most ready to take it. So that I hope I may with justice pronounce myself an author perfectly blameless, against whom the tribes of answerers, considerers, observers, reflecters, detecters, remarkers, will never be able to find matter for exercising their talents.

I confess, it was whispered to me that I was bound in duty, as a subject of England, to have given in a memorial to a secretary of state at my first coming over; because whatever lands are discovered by a subject belong to the Crown. But I doubt whether our conquests in the countries I treat of would be as easy as those of Ferdinando Cortez over the naked Americans.[2] The Lilliputians, I think, are hardly worth the charge of a fleet and army to reduce them, and I question whether it might be prudent or safe to attempt the Brobdingnagians. Or whether an English army would be much at their ease with the Flying Island over their heads. The Houyhnhnms, indeed, appear not to be so well prepared for war, a science to which they are perfect strangers, and especially against missive weapons.[3] However, supposing myself to be a minister of state, I could never give my advice for invading them. Their prudence, unanimity, unacquaintedness with fear, and their love of their country would amply supply all defects in the military art. Imagine twenty thousand of them breaking into the midst of an European army, confounding the ranks, overturning the carriages,[4] battering the warriors' faces into mummy [5] by terrible yerks from their hinder hoofs. For they would well deserve the character given to Augustus: *Recalcitrat undique tutus*.[6] But instead of proposals for conquering that magnanimous [7] nation, I rather wish they were in a capacity or disposition to send a sufficient number of their inhabitants for

[2] Cortez easily subdued the Aztecs in 1519 because Montezuma received him as the descendant of the Sun. The Aztecs were awed by the ships and firearms of the Spaniards and also by the fact that they were mounted on horses.

[3] Weapons thrown or shot rather than wielded by hand.

[4] Gun carriages.

[5] A pulpy mass.

[6] "He kicks, with safety, in all directions" (Horace, *Satires* II, i, 20).

[7] High-souled, noble.

civilizing Europe, by teaching us the first principles of honour, justice, truth, temperance, public spirit, fortitude, chastity, friendship, benevolence, and fidelity. The *names* of all which virtues are still retained among us in most languages, and are to be met with in modern as well as ancient authors; which I am able to assert from my own small reading.

But I had another reason which made me less forward to enlarge his Majesty's dominions by my discoveries. To say the truth, I had conceived a few scruples with relation to the distributive justice of princes upon those occasions. For instance, a crew of pirates are driven by a storm they know not whither, at length a boy discovers land from the topmast, they go on shore to rob and plunder, they see an harmless people, are entertained with kindness, they give the country a new name, they take formal possession of it for the king, they set up a rotten plank or a stone for a memorial, they murder two or three dozen of the natives, bring away a couple more by force for a sample, return home, and get their pardon. Here commences a new dominion acquired with a title by *divine right*.[8] Ships are sent with the first opportunity, the natives driven out or destroyed, their princes tortured to discover their gold, a free license given to all acts of inhumanity and lust, the earth reeking with the blood of its inhabitants: and this execrable crew of butchers employed in so pious an expedition is a *modern colony* sent to convert and civilize an idolatrous and barbarous people.

But this description, I confess, doth by no means affect the British nation, who may be an example to the whole world for their wisdom, care, and justice in planting colonies; their liberal endowments for the advancement of religion and learn-

---

[8] The doctrine of divine right of rulers had been emphasized in England by James I and held currency, not without debate, as long as the Stuarts were on the throne. The chief defense of divine right in later seventeenth-century England, that of Sir Robert Filmer in his *Patriarcha* (published in 1680), traced it to the benevolent rule of family and tribe by the Biblical patriarchs.

ing; their choice of devout and able pastors to propagate Christianity; their caution in stocking their provinces with people of sober lives and conversations from this, the mother kingdom; [9] their strict regard to the distribution of justice in supplying the civil administration through all their colonies with officers of the greatest abilities, utter strangers to corruption; and to crown all, by sending the most vigilant and virtuous governors, who have no other views than the happiness of the people over whom they preside, and the honour of the king their master.

But as those countries which I have described do not appear to have any desire of being conquered, and enslaved, murdered, or driven out by colonies, nor abound either in gold, silver, sugar, or tobacco; I did humbly conceive they were by no means proper objects of our zeal, our valour, or our interest. However, if those whom it more concerns think fit to be of another opinion, I am ready to depose, when I shall be lawfully called, that no European did ever visit these countries before me. I mean, if the inhabitants ought to be believed; unless a dispute may arise about the two Yahoos, said to have been seen many ages ago on a mountain in Houyhnhnmland, from whence, the opinion is, that the race of those brutes hath descended; and these, for anything I know, may have been English, which indeed I was apt to suspect from the lineaments of their posterity's countenances, although very much defaced. But how far that will go to make out a title, I leave to the learned in colony-law.

But as to the formality of taking possession in my sovereign's name, it never came once into my thoughts; and if it had, yet as my affairs then stood, I should perhaps, in point of prudence and self-preservation, have put it off to a better opportunity.

[9] Criminals and prostitutes were often "transported" to the colonies rather than punished in England. Transportation was an alternative to hanging for all but the worst crimes, and it supplied the colonies with a needed labor force.

Having thus answered the *only* objection that can be raised against me as a traveller, I here take a final leave of my courteous readers, and return to enjoy my own speculations in my little garden at Redriff, to apply those excellent lessons of virtue which I learned among the Houyhnhnms, to instruct the Yahoos of my own family as far as I shall find them docible [10] animals, to behold my figure often in a glass, and thus if possible habituate myself by time to tolerate the sight of a human creature; to lament the brutality of Houyhnhnms in my own country, but always treat their persons with respect, for the sake of my noble master, his family, his friends, and the whole Houyhnhnm race, whom these of ours have the honour to resemble in all their lineaments, however their intellectuals came to degenerate.

I began last week to permit my wife to sit at dinner with me, at the farthest end of a long table, and to answer (but with the utmost brevity) the few questions I asked her. Yet the smell of a Yahoo continuing very offensive, I always keep my nose well stopped with rue, lavender, or tobacco leaves. And although it be hard for a man late in life to remove old habits, I am not altogether out of hopes in some time to suffer a neighbour Yahoo in my company without the apprehensions I am yet under of his teeth or his claws.

My reconcilement to the Yahoo-kind in general might not be so difficult if they would be content with those vices and follies only which Nature hath entitled them to. I am not in the least provoked at the sight of a lawyer, a pickpocket, a colonel, a fool, a lord, a gamester, a politician, a whoremonger, a physician, an evidence,[11] a suborner, an attorney, a traitor, or the like; this is all according to the due course of things: but when I behold a lump of deformity and diseases both in body and mind, smitten with *pride*, it immediately breaks all the measures of my patience; neither shall I be ever able to

[10] Teachable.
[11] Paid informer.

comprehend how such an animal and such a vice could tally together. The wise and virtuous Houyhnhnms, who abound in all excellencies that can adorn a rational creature, have no name for this vice in their language, which hath no terms to express anything that is evil, except those whereby they describe the detestable qualities of their Yahoos, among which they were not able to distinguish this of pride, for want of thoroughly understanding human nature as it showeth itself in other countries where that animal presides. But I, who had more experience, could plainly observe some rudiments of it among the wild Yahoos.

But the Houyhnhnms, who live under the government of reason, are no more proud of the good qualities they possess than I should be for not wanting a leg or an arm, which no man in his wits would boast of, although he must be miserable without them. I dwell the longer upon this subject from the desire I have to make the society of an English Yahoo by any means not insupportable, and therefore I here entreat those who have any tincture of this absurd vice, that they will not presume to appear in my sight.

FINIS

Both the First Voyage and the Third contain a large number of political allusions. Many have found these sufficiently consistent and sustained to constitute a political allegory. Successive interpretations, each of the later ones correcting earlier versions, are to be found in Sir Charles Firth, "The Political Significance of *Gulliver's Travels*," reprinted in *Essays, Historical and Literary* (Oxford, 1938); Arthur E. Case, *Four Essays on Gulliver's Travels* (Princeton, 1945), pp. 69–96; and Irvin Ehrenpreis, *The Personality of Jonathan Swift* (London, 1958), pp. 85–91.

At one time, the allegory was seen as an oblique account of Swift's own public career. The most obvious instance of this would be the Lilliputian Empress' indignation at Gulliver's method of putting out the fire in her palace. This was taken to refer to Queen Anne's refusal to give Swift high church office because of his offensive book, *A Tale of a Tub*, which, ironically enough, Swift wrote in defense of the Church of England.

Recent critics have found greater consistency in an allegorical account of the Oxford-Bolingbroke ministry. Only a few instances will be given here. Much of the tone of the First Voyage is set by the personal and partisan suspicions that met the efforts of Oxford and Bolingbroke to negotiate a peace with France in order to end the War of the Spanish Succession (1701–1713). The Earl of Nottingham, for example, led Parliament in imposing the condition that no peace could be made that left Spain and the Indies in the possession of the Bourbons. One can see a reflection of this in the humiliating conditions imposed upon Gulliver's freedom (Part One, Chapter Three). The quenching of the fire in the royal palace may be seen as the Tories' illegal negotiation of the peace, and the Empress' outrage may be taken as the fusion of this event with Queen Anne's personal distrust of Oxford (Case); or her outrage may represent the charges of treason which kept Bolingbroke (as chief negotiator of the peace) in exile for almost ten years (Ehrenpreis). The accusations against Gulliver, at any rate, resemble the charges made against both Oxford and Bolingbroke after the fall of their ministry, and the proposed blinding of Gulliver may be taken as the barring of these ministers from future political power (although Oxford later resumed his place in the House of Lords).

It should be said that even unconvincing arguments for sustained political allegory often turn up interesting counterparts for Swift's fictional incidents. There is great difficulty, however, in drawing a clear distinction between what may have stimulated the author's imagination and what he means to be an allusion or an allegorical reference. Irvin Ehrenpreis, in the book cited above, explores the way in which Swift's conception of the King of Brobdingnag was influenced by his memories of Sir William Temple and his treatment of the Houyhnhnms by his attitudes toward Bolingbroke's views.

APPENDIX II

There have been attempts to decipher and to decode the names and the languages in *Gulliver's Travels*. The first procedure seeks a consistent translation of letters or syllables; the second seeks, through etymological study or tracing of literary echoes, to translate full names. The "little language" that Swift used in his *Journal to Stella* has provided the basis for some rather elaborate deciphering by Paul Odell Clark in "A Gulliver Dictionary," *Studies in Philology*, L (1953), 591–624. Other methods have been used by Harold D. Kelling in "Some Significant Names in *Gulliver's Travels*," *Studies in Philology*, XLVIII (1951), 761–778. The fragmentariness of the results and the arbitrary variations in method have cast some doubt on the procedures so far employed, if not on the quest itself. Among the oldest and best known of suggestions are: for Lilliput, little "putt" or boy, or corrupted child; for Laputa, by way of the Spanish "la puta," prostitute.

It is generally agreed that the name of the Houyhnhnms is to be pronounced "Whinnems," in imitation of a horse's whinny; however, an alternate pronunciation is sometimes suggested—"hōo - ĭn-ŭmz."

The Library of Literature

· ·

CRANE, STEPHEN, *The Red Badge of Courage,* ed. Frederick C. Crews, 6

DICKENS, CHARLES, *Great Expectations,* ed. Louis Crompton, 2

HAWTHORNE, NATHANIEL, *The Scarlet Letter,* ed. Larzer Ziff, 1

MELVILLE, HERMAN, *Moby Dick,* ed. Charles Feidelson, 5

One Hundred Middle English Lyrics, ed. Robert D. Stevick, 7

SWIFT, JONATHAN, *Gulliver's Travels,* ed. Martin Price, 3

TWAIN, MARK, *The Adventures of Huckleberry Finn,* ed. Leo Marx, 4

The Library of Liberal Arts